A Forbidden Love Novella Series

Also By Bree

Historical Romance:

Love's Second Chance Series
#1 Forgotten & Remembered - The Duke's Late Wife
#2 Cursed & Cherished - The Duke's Wilful Wife
#3 Despised & Desired - The Marquess' Passionate Wife
#4 Abandoned & Protected - The Marquis' Tenacious Wife
#5 Ruined & Redeemed – The Earl's Fallen Wife
#6 Betrayed & Blessed – The Viscount's Shrewd Wife
#7 Deceived & Honoured – The Baron's Vexing Wife
#8 Sacrificed & Reclaimed – The Soldier's Daring Widow
#9 Condemned & Admired – The Earl's Cunning Wife
#10 Trapped & Liberated – The Privateer's Bold Beloved
#11 Oppressed & Empowered – The Viscount's Capable Wife
#12 Destroyed & Restored – The Baron's Courageous Wife (soon)

A Forbidden Love Novella Series
#1 The Wrong Brother
#2 A Brilliant Rose
#3 The Forgotten Wife
#4 An Unwelcome Proposal
#5 Rules to Be Broken
#6 Hearts to Be Broken
#7 Winning her Hand
#8 Conquering her Heart

A Forbidden Love Novella Series

(Box Set Two: Novellas 5 - 8)

by
Bree Wolf

A Forbidden Love Novella Series

Box Set Two

By

Bree Wolf

This is a work of fiction. Names, characters, businesses, places, brands, media, events and incidents are either the products of the author's imagination or used in a fictitious manner.

Any resemblance to actual persons, living or dead, or actual events is purely coincidental.

Cover Art by Victoria Cooper

www.breewolf.com

ISBN-13: 978-3-96482-045-7

To the dedicated english teachers of my past
I was fortunate to have you teach me

ACKNOWLEDGEMENTS

A great big thank-you to all those who inspire me daily, those who tell me to keep writing, and those who laugh and cry with my characters and me. I love being a writer, and I could never sit down every day to do what I love without all of you. Thank you.

Table of Contents

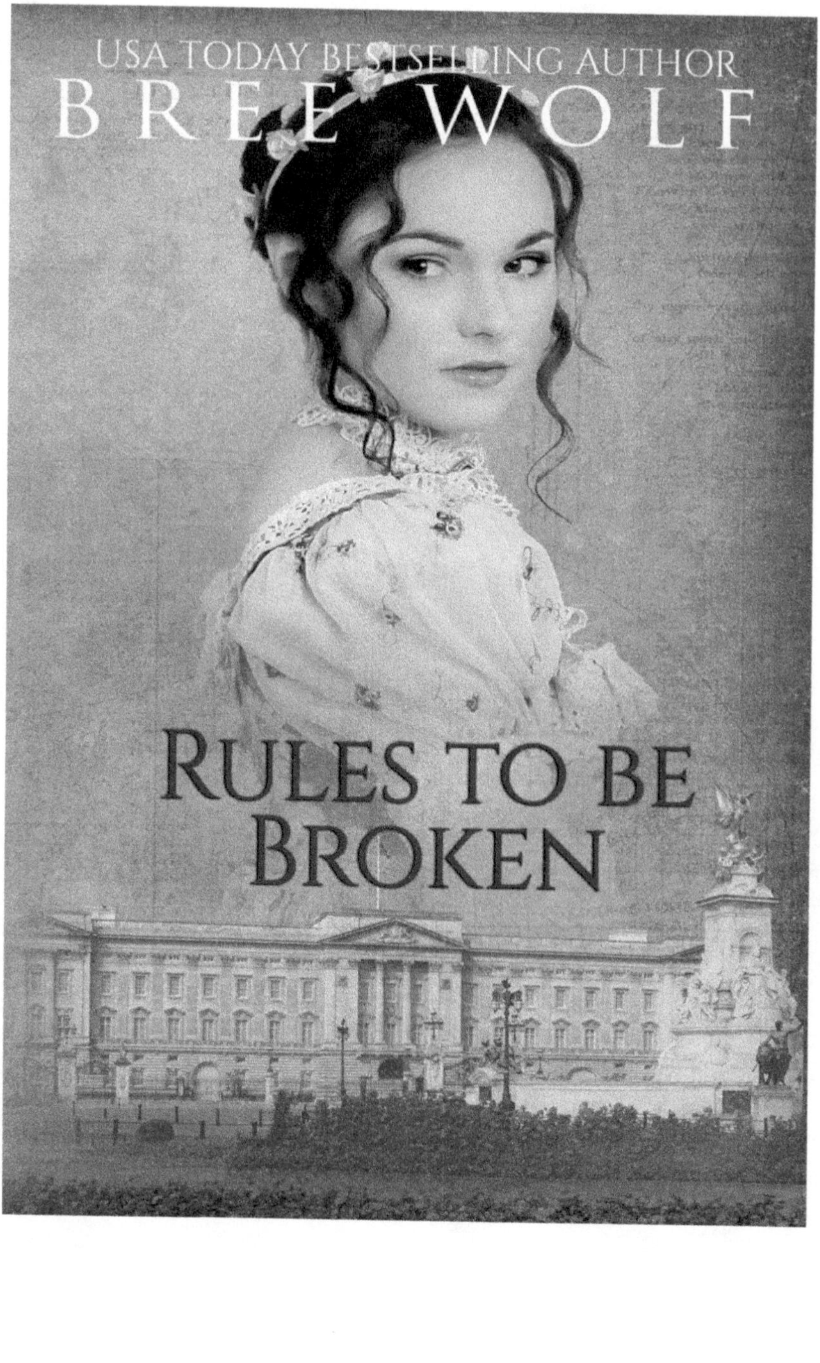
USA TODAY BESTSELLING AUTHOR
BREE WOLF
RULES TO BE BROKEN

PROLOGUE

London, Summer 1815
Four Years Ago

Her heart thudding in her chest, Diana tiptoed down the small cobblestone path as her dainty steps echoed through the night air. The moon shone overhead, casting its silvery light into the shadowy dark of the gardens, and from the terrace, the sounds of music and laughter reached her ears. The earl's ball was still in full swing, and to Diana's delight, it had been rather easy to escape her parents' watchful eyes and sneak out into the night.

A part of Diana's mind warned her, cautioned her that such a behaviour could have disastrous consequences. Her heart, however, was focused on one thing alone: the man she loved.

If she could only speak to him for a few moments and assure him that his pursuit was indeed most welcomed, he would surely speak to her father that very night and ask for her hand in marriage.

At the thought, the breath caught in her throat, and she stopped in her tracks. Drawing the fresh night air into her lungs, Diana sought to steady her nerves. When the slight dizziness that had seized her so unexpectedly finally subsided, she swallowed and then proceeded down the path.

In the dark, the tall-growing hedges and bushes looked ominous, and more than once, Diana drew back with a startled gasp because she feared she had stumbled upon someone lurking in the shadows, intent on doing her harm.

"Where is he?" she mumbled under her breath craning her neck, hoping to catch a glimpse of his tall, striking figure.

After he had asked her to follow him into the night—the gaze in his smoldering eyes saying more than a thousand words ever could—Diana had not hesitated. Ensuring that her parents were otherwise occupied, she had slipped out the terrace doors, following his silhouette until it had disappeared among the shadows.

As the chilled night air brushed over her heated cheeks, Diana's feet carried her onward until at last she found the small pavilion standing like an island in the midst of a green ocean, its tall, white-washed pillars reaching into the sky.

His back to her, he stood motionless on the other side of the small space, sheltered under a canopy roof, his strong arms resting on the small rail, and stared out into the night.

At the very sight of him, Diana's heart soared and a rush of emotions swept through her body. Her lips began to tingle at the mere thought of his mouth pressed to hers, and her palms grew moist with nervous anticipation.

Taking another deep breath, she stepped forward, her dainty steps all but silent as she approached him. His intoxicating scent mingled with the soft night smells as the jasmines began to bloom, and

Diana thought for a moment she would faint on the spot as her heart raced in her chest.

Coming to stand behind him, she lifted her hands, desperate to be in his arms, and softly placed them on the top of his back, gently letting them slide down over his strong muscles.

The moment Diana touched him, he froze before drawing in a deep breath. "I've been waiting for you," he whispered in that deep, raspy voice that made her breath catch in her throat every time it reached her ears.

A smile spread over her face, and joy filled her heart.

Like a feline, he suddenly spun around and pulled her into his arms, his hungry mouth seeking hers.

Locked in his tight embrace, Diana abandoned all thought as her body responded to his touch as though it recognized him from a previous life. Deep down, Diana had always known that he was her soul mate.

As his lips roamed hers, she held on to him, feeling her knees grow weak. A soft gasp escaped her as his hands travelled upward, and he suddenly drew back.

In the dim light of the moon, he gazed into her eyes, a slight frown curling his brows before he stepped back. "I apologise, Miss–"

"Diana!"

At the sound of her father's enraged voice, Diana's head spun around. Finding her parents standing by the tall-growing hedge that shielded the pavilion from passersby, she swallowed as their disbelieving eyes stared at them, shifting from her to the man by her side.

Turning to face her parents as they hurried toward them, their faces pale in the moonlight, Diana smiled, "Father, Mother, I can explain."

"I most certainly hope so," her father snapped, his sharp eyes travelling from her to her future husband. "Norwood, what is the meaning of this?"

Clearing his throat, Robert Dashwood stepped forward. "I apologise, Sir. There has been some misunderstanding. I–"

"Whatever misunderstanding you thought has occurred, I expect the next words I hear to include a proposal considering the liberties you've just now taken with my daughter!"

With love in her heart and a smile on her face, Diana turned to the man by her side. Butterflies fluttered in her belly as she took a deep breath. *This was it! The moment she had been waiting for her entire life.*

"A proposal?" Laughing, her soul mate shook his head. "I'm afraid I have to disappoint you."

Staring at him, Diana felt the blood rush from her cheeks as the world grew dim around her. "What?" she gasped, her knees suddenly weak as pudding as the butterflies in her belly died a slow death.

"I apologise," he said, his eyes shifting from her father to her. "As I said, this was a misunderstanding."

"A misunderstanding?" her father boomed as heart-wrenching sobs tore from Diana's throat, and she sank into her mother's arms. "You take advantage of a young girl, and then you refuse to do the only decent thing left. What kind of a gentleman are you?"

Chuckling, Robert Dashwood leaned against the rail. "The worst kind, I assure you."

"Social etiquette dictates that–"

"I don't care about social etiquette–"

"You will be ruined. Your reputation–"

"My reputation will not suffer for all of London already knows the kind of man I am." Standing up straight, the notorious viscount stepped forward, fixing her father with serious eyes. "Your daughter, on the other hand, has everything to lose. Therefore, I suggest you be reasonable."

"You downright refuse to marry her?" her father huffed.

"Yes, sir," he confirmed. "You will be well-advised to return to the festivities before we are discovered. No harm has been done so far."

Shaking his head, her father coughed, "No harm? You've compromised her."

"Upon my honour–or what is left of it–it was only a kiss."

Only a kiss? Diana's head spun as she clung to her mother, her hopes crashing into a black abyss that was threatening to swallow her whole. What was happening? Did he not love her? Had he not told her so a million times? Had his loving gaze not spoken the words that his lips had confirmed a mere few minutes ago?

Glaring at the man she loved, her father returned to her side. "You are without honour, Norwood. I sincerely hope that one day you will reap what you sow."

An amused smile on his face, Lord Norwood nodded to her father before his eyes dropped to hers. "All my best to you, Miss…Lawson, is it?" Then he turned and walked away, the shadows swallowing him whole as though he had never been there.

Supported by a parent on either side, Diana placed one step before the other, her mind tormented by the incomprehensibility of what had just happened and her heart aching with the love so unexpectedly ripped from her life.

"I can only hope that Norwood keeps quiet," her father mumbled under his breath, anger still ringing in his sharp voice. "If anyone finds out what happened here tonight, your chances for a favourable match will be ruined."

In that moment, Diana could not bring herself to care. After all, what value could her reputation possibly have when her heart had just been ripped into pieces?

1

CAUSE & CONSEQUENCE

London, Spring 1819
Four Years Later

"You have truly outdone yourself with the refurnishing, Diana," her cousin Rose praised her green eyes gliding over the drawing room, taking in the exquisite curtains, the newly acquired antiques as well as the polished pianoforte that stood under the tall, arched window. "It is as though it shines."

Diana nodded as was expected of her, then mumbled, "You're too kind." Glancing at her husband, his haggard face in an ever-present frown, he nodded his approval, then turned to Rose's husband, Viscount Norwood, as well as her father, Mr. Lawson, offering both gentlemen a drink.

Glancing at her own father, his eyes blank as he stared into nothing, Diana sighed. Ever since her mother's death not two years ago, the lively man her father used to have been had vanished. These days he spent his time seated in a comfortable chair, mourning the loss of his wife without an outward sign. Occasionally, Diana's efforts would coax a monosyllabic answer out of him, but his eyes barely saw her, and she believed that most days he was not even aware of his surroundings.

"You have a fine collection here, Mr. Reignold," Mr. Lawson mused as his eyes slid over the bookshelf, his gaze occasionally narrowing as he read the titles on the spines. "Who is your book dealer?"

Unable to look at her husband's self-satisfied face any longer, Diana drew in a slow breath as her eyes came to linger on her cousin's husband, Viscount Norwood.

A shiver went down her spine, and she jerked her head away, knowing that prolonged exposure to his charms would only reopen old wounds.

Almost four years had passed since that fateful night that had shattered not only her reputation as well as her heart, but also her belief in the goodness of this world.

Now, she lived in a nightmare, married to a man who reminded her at every opportunity that he had saved her from certain ruination.

Although Lord Norwood had promised to keep that night in the gardens to himself, the whispers had started nonetheless. Soon, Diana had been the centre of gossip, her reputation damaged beyond repair. Her only option had been to marry her father's old friend. A man who had lost his first wife as well as his son in childbirth and never remarried until Diana's father had begged him to save his daughter.

As he considered her own judgement to be impaired, her husband had set strict rules for her. He determined how she dressed, who she could call on, where she could go, what pastimes she could indulge. Nothing was left for Diana to decide on her own.

Even her son's name had been chosen without her being consulted.

Benedict. What an ugly name! Diana thought.

"Are you all right?" Rose asked, leaning closer as her watchful eyes slid over Diana's face. "You seem out of sorts."

Diana forced a smile on her face, only too aware of her husband's presence. "I'm perfectly fine, dear cousin. Thank you."

Rose's brows furrowed as though she meant to argue. Then, however, she took a deep breath and a gentle smile came to her face. "How is Benedict? Does he already sleep through the night?"

Taken aback, Diana shrugged, "How would I know?" she snapped before she could stop herself. Glancing at her husband to see if he had noticed her slip-up, Diana felt a cold shiver run down her spine when she found his shoulders tensing. Although he stood with his back to her, by then, Diana had learnt to interpret his signs of displeasure and disapproval that told her she had once more acted in an unsuitable way.

As certain as the sun rises in the east, another lecture would await her that night.

"I cannot say," Diana replied, her voice once more soft and melodious. "However, his nurse says that his development is age-appropriate."

A soft frown came to Rose's face as her mouth opened and then closed it. Clearly, she did not know how to respond!

"He is a delightful boy," Diana's husband chimed in, making her flinch as he turned from the bookshelf and approached them. "Strong and healthy with a sunny disposition."

Following her husband, the other two men joined their little circle as well, and to Diana's great dismay, she was unable to overlook the gentle smile that came to Lord Norwood's face as he met Rose's eyes. His arm brushed against hers as though by accident, and he almost imperceptibly leaned toward her, his eyes tracing the curve of his wife's mouth.

Almost shunned by society at large, Diana mostly spent her time in her cousin's company and had had ample opportunity to observe the delicate signs of the deep love that existed between Rose and her husband.

To this day, every little sign of affection felt like a stab to her heart. Did she still love him? Diana wondered. She couldn't be certain, for the past few years had dulled her emotions in such a way that now—with the exception of the occasional meltdown—she barely felt anything at all.

Nothing but regret.

As though on cue, her son's agonising wails drifted down from the upper floor, slowly growing in intensity.

"Oh, the poor baby," Rose murmured, her gaze shifting to the hall where a large staircase led to the upper floor and the nursery. "Should we not see to him?" she asked, her eyes almost pleading as she turned back to Diana.

"His nurse will—"

"That is a marvellous idea," Diana's husband interrupted, his narrowed gaze fixed on her face, ordering her to comply. Then he turned to the other two gentlemen, drawing them into yet another conversation about dusty, old books and the utterly boring topics they discussed.

"Come," Rose whispered, drawing Diana forward toward the staircase. As they ascended the stairs, she turned to look at Diana. "Has he said *Mama* yet?"

Diana shrugged, "Not that I know of."

Again, Rose looked at her with that slight frown, her eyes filled with incredulity as though nothing Diana said or did made any sense.

Diana could not blame her. Ever since that night four years ago, nothing had made sense anymore.

When they entered the nursery, they found Benedict's nurse, holding him in her arms, slightly bouncing in her step as she tried to soothe the wailing one-year-old.

"Hello, Miss Sharp," Rose greeted the woman, "what seems to be the matter? Did something frighten him?"

"I cannot say, my lady," Miss Sharp replied, her eyes shifting to Diana, a touch of unease resting in them. "I apologise, Mrs. Reignold. I hope he did not disturb your dinner party."

Gritting her teeth against the agonising cries, Diana kept her eyes fixed on her son's nurse. "Of course, he did. Can you not keep him quiet?"

"I've changed him. I've fed him," the nurse began to stammer, rocking the child with more speed as though hoping that sheer willpower would calm him.

"May I?" Rose asked, stepping toward Miss Sharp, her arms held forward to receive the child.

With a glance at Diana, Miss Sharp relinquished the boy.

"Hush, hush, little darling," Rose whispered, her voice soft and gentle. Then she began to hum as her arms shifted Benedict into a more comfortable position, rocking him slightly as she began to walk around the room.

"You may leave us," Diana said to Miss Sharp, who almost fled the room. Taking a deep breath, Diana watched her cousin as she continued to rock the small child. A deep smile shone on Rose's lips as she gazed down at his tiny face.

Slowly, his wails grew quieter and his eyelids began to droop. A large yawn opened his mouth before he snuggled into the crook of Rose's arm, his little hands curled into the fabric of her dress as though afraid she would leave him.

Swallowing, Diana tore her gaze away and stepped up to the window, allowing her eyes to drift over the dark street below. Breath by breath, her heart calmed down until she heard a soft rustling behind her.

Glancing over her shoulder, she found Rose gently laying Benedict down in his crib. "He is such a sweet little boy," she beamed, then stepped up to the window the moment Diana returned her gaze to the street. "You must be very proud."

Diana remained quiet. Was she proud? She couldn't say that she was. Why would she be?

Beside her, Rose drew in a deep breath, then she whispered into the dark. "I'm with child."

As though a fist had struck her in the stomach, Diana groaned, pain shooting up and down her body as she almost fell forward, catching herself against the cool window pane.

"Are you all right?" Rose asked, her voice full of concern, as she placed a gentle hand on Diana's shoulder. "Do you need to lie down?"

Diana couldn't answer. Didn't know how to. How could she explain that Rose was living the life Diana had always dreamed of? With the man she loved? The man she had loved since she'd first laid eyes on him?

And now, Rose would have a child. His child! A child she could love!

Closing her eyes, Diana shook her head.

There were no words.

After a hearty breakfast, eggs with bacon and a slice of toast as was his routine, Arthur Abbott, Earl of Stanhope, retreated to his study as he was accustomed to do that time in the morning. There, he spent an hour on his correspondence before his steward Mr. Hill arrived to discuss matters of Stanhope Grove as he always did on the first Monday of each month during the Season.

"Splendid," Arthur replied after listening to Mr. Hill's account of the latest developments. "I do believe my mother wishes to make certain improvements with regard to the lower floor as she has her heart set on holding a New Year's Ball at Stanhope Grove this year."

"I understand," Mr. Hill said, nodding his head. "I shall await your orders."

Although New Year's was still months away, Arthur knew that once his mother had set her mind to something, she would not rest until it was accomplished. He might as well warn his steward and hope that his mother's ideas for a most *legendary* ball would not be too extravagant.

Even though his mother had a tendency to display their wealth and remind society in general of their impeccable reputation and considerable influence, Arthur had to admit that he was surprised she held on to the idea of such a ball after what had happened at Lord Hampton's Christmas Ball this past year.

Despite their mother's objections, Arthur's younger sister Eleanor had kissed a man of doubtful repute under the mistletoe, sending their mother into a hysterical fit. Arthur would remember that night for as long as he lived.

A knock on his door drew his thoughts back to the here and now. "Enter."

"Arthur, we need to talk," his mother stated as she rushed into the room, startling Mr. Hill, who quickly jumped to his feet, then bowed.

"We shall continue this later," Arthur told his steward, who immediately left the room. Rising from the leather chair behind his desk, Arthur turned to his mother, wondering what was amiss now. "How can I help you?"

"It is that man!" His mother snarled, her nostrils flaring as though she smelled something rotten. "He had the audacity to send a letter to her." Lifting the item in question, she waved it in front of Arthur's face. "You must speak to him and put an end to this."

"I assume you're speaking of Henry Waltham."

"Of course, I am," his mother hissed, a frown coming to her face as she shook her head at him. "Did you not see the way he almost…compromised poor Eleanor at the Christmas Ball? Have you not seen him around wherever we go? And now, this letter!"

Arthur drew in a deep breath, knowing that indulging his mother was the best way to avoid the hysterical fit that always seemed to lurk on the horizon whenever she was displeased with something. Unfortunately, she was displeased quite frequently.

"Do you truly believe his attention is unwelcome?" he asked, carefully broaching the subject. After all, from what he had observed the night of the Christmas Ball, it seemed that his attentions were indeed *most* welcome.

At least to Eleanor.

"Of course, it is," his mother insisted. "More than once I instructed Eleanor to keep her distance, and because she knows her place, she has done so without fail. Naturally, she cannot be rude. After all, he is still the son of a peer. However, enough is enough. This has gone much too far. I want this man removed from our circle. If he comes near her one more time, I do not know what I might do."

Arthur sighed, "What do you want me to do, Mother?"

Gesticulating wildly, his mother shook her head, red blotches creeping up her neck and into her cheeks as she failed to remain calm. "I do not care what you do, but I want that man to stay away from my daughter. Call him out if you must!"

Arthur's brows rose in surprise. "Do you truly wish for me to do that?"

His mother sighed, then drew in a deep breath, meeting his gaze for a moment before shaking her head. "I simply want Eleanor to be safe from that man."

"May I enquire," Arthur began, his voice placating as he sought to avoid yet another hysterical fit, "what exactly has given you such a bad impression of young Henry Waltham? As far as I know his father, Baron Caulfield, is well respected."

"Well-respected?" his mother snorted, her eyes narrowing into slits as she fixed him with a calm stare. "That was long ago." Again, she shook her head, her gaze now calculating as she observed him. "Maybe you were too young to remember when it changed."

"I am four-and-thirty, Mother," Arthur reminded her, feeling slightly annoyed that whenever she could not support her claims with reasonable arguments she would insinuate that he was simply not yet seasoned enough to comprehend the ramifications of the issue in question. Deep down, Arthur had to admit that it riled him.

"Then why do you ask?" his mother snapped, the calm that had so suddenly befallen her gone as though it had never been. "Despite their parents' reputation, that family is not of our standing, and Henry Waltham is not a suitable match for your sister." Her eyes narrowed as she stepped forward, her hands on her hips. "Do you not agree?"

Arthur took a deep breath, bracing himself for what was to come. And yet, he felt compelled to speak honestly as he always did. "Neither do I agree or disagree for I have barely spoken a word to that young man. Have you?"

"There's no need," his mother hissed, waving his concerns away. "The misdeeds of his elder brothers speak for themselves."

"Has he committed any misdeeds himself?" Arthur tried, wondering why he was suddenly defending a man he barely knew.

For a moment, his mother's lips thinned into a grotesque sneer as her gaze hardened, determination and an unwillingness to yield plainly visible in her grey eyes. "It is only a matter of time until he finds a victim." Her voice trembled with the effort to contain her emotions. "As his brothers before him, he will gain the trust of an innocent young girl and ruin her in the worst possible way." Her shoulders drew back, and she raised her chin. "I will not allow that to happen to Eleanor."

Arthur frowned, wondering at his mother's reaction. "Neither do I, Mother, I assure you. I never meant to suggest we allow anything untoward to happen to Eleanor. I merely sought to question whether young Henry Waltham truly deserves our distrust." Taking a step closer, he met his mother's gaze. "He is not his brothers. It would not be fair to condemn him for something he didn't do, something he had no control over."

The muscles in his mother's jaw clenched. "I'd rather condemn him unjustly than see Eleanor come to harm." Turning on her heel, she strode toward the door, but then stopped in the doorway and looked back, meeting his eyes. "Take care of this," she ordered, then left, the sound of her angry footsteps echoing down the hall.

Arthur sighed, wondering what had given his mother such an atrocious impression of that young man.

2

A CHANCE ENCOUNTER

Praying that the mild pain that began to throb under his temples would subside, Arthur took a deep breath, trying to concentrate on the harmonious melody of the orchestra in the corner of the ballroom. Maybe the gentle notes could soothe his frayed nerves.

"There!" His mother snapped, leaning closer to catch his attention. "Do you see him? He is looking at her."

Taking another deep breath, Arthur turned in the direction his mother indicated. "He is merely glancing in her direction." From what Arthur could see, young Henry Waltham stood almost all the way across the room from Eleanor, his eyes watching her as a shy smile played on his features. Eleanor, too, seemed rather bashful as she glanced at the man she had kissed under the mistletoe not three months ago, biting her lower lip before averting her gaze.

Never had Arthur seen a more innocent love then theirs. If only he could understand his mother's objections!

"You must go and stop him!" His mother insisted, her voice slightly hysterical as she attempted to push him in the general direction of Henry Waltham. "Go at once!"

Planting his feet firmly on the ground, Arthur turned and met his mother's gaze. "He is merely looking at her, Mother," he said, trying to reason with a woman who barely knew such a sentiment existed, "the same way she is looking at him. There is nothing untoward going on here."

Pressing her lips into a thin line, his mother glared at him as though he had just refused to protect his sister from a highwayman lying in wait. "She is your sister and—"

"—and she is perfectly safe," Arthur interrupted, immediately annoyed with himself for stooping so low as to break decorum. It was inexcusable! Gritting his teeth, he forced air into his lungs, ignoring the growing pain behind his template. "I apologise, Mother. It was wrong of me to interrupt you."

Her features relaxed, and she nodded her head, accepting his apology.

Relieved, Arthur stepped back, his gaze once more turned to the dance floor, hoping that this would be the end of it.

However, luck was not on his side.

"That is Mrs. Reignold," his mother observed, and her eyes narrowed as she watched her daughter speak to a young woman, whose expression was a far cry from the warm glow on Eleanor's face.

"I've never met her," Arthur replied, slightly concerned at the new pitch that had come to his mother's voice. "Are you acquainted with her?"

At his words, his mother's head snapped around and she stared at him with wide eyes. "Good God, of course not. Why would you assume such a thing?"

As his headache pounded against the insides of his skull, Arthur resigned himself to losing the war. "I meant no offence, Mother. I have never met the woman, and I am not familiar with her name."

"That is almost unfathomable!" his mother exclaimed, eyeing him with suspicion. "After all, her fall from grace has been on everyone's lips. How can you not know?"

"I do not care for gossip," Arthur said. "Often it distorts the truth into a grotesque mask that has no resemblance to reality. I am certain that at least half of what you have heard of this woman—or anyone else for that matter—is pure fiction."

"How can it be fiction if there were witnesses?" his mother objected, her eyes fixed on the young woman, who in that moment received a glass of—presumably—lemonade from Eleanor.

Although he knew his mother was anxiously waiting for him to ask for details, Arthur remained quiet, equally well-aware that his failure to enquire for more information would not stop his mother from sharing it with him.

"It was maybe four years ago when she chased after a known rake, making a fool of herself," she continued as expected. "Unfortunately, everyone was aware of what was on her mind but her own parents. Otherwise, I would have thought they would have prevented any untoward behaviour on her part." A disapproving frown came to her face. "Nonetheless, Mrs. Reignold—or Miss Lawson as she was still called then—left Lord Barrett's ballroom to follow Lord Norwood out into the gardens where she allowed him to compromise her."

"Allowed him?" Arthur asked, remembering the many atrocious tales he had heard about that man before he reminded himself not to lend an ear to gossip. Most of those were probably false or at least wildly exaggerated. After all, had he not been married a year ago? Was the eternal bachelor not off the market now?

"When he refused to marry her—as was to be expected considering his reputation," his mother continued, her voice eager as she related the information she had obtained, "her father arranged for her to marry Mr. Reignold. However, Miss Lawson seemed rather dissatisfied with the arrangement. I suppose she had her sights set on marrying a viscount and finds that she is displeased with being the wife of the younger son of a baron." His mother snorted in disgust. "After risking his own reputation and standing in society, Mr. Reignold truly deserves better than an ungrateful wife. After all, no one thought she would ever be married after the way she allowed herself to be ruined. It is quite a shame."

"Even if what you say is true," Arthur interjected, unable to overlook the deep sadness that seemed to radiate from the young Mrs. Reignold, "it has been four years. Should we not allow her to move past her earlier mistakes? I am certain she has learnt her lesson." The miserable look on her face suggested that her lessons were still ongoing.

His mother chuckled as though he had been jesting. "A reputation once ruined is lost forever—I expected that you of all people knew that—which is why it is of the utmost importance that we keep Eleanor away from Henry Waltham. Who knows what might happen? She might end up like Mrs. Reignold." A shudder shook his mother's frame.

Arthur could not help but think that no one deserved to end up like Mrs. Reignold.

Not even Mrs. Reignold herself.

Long ago, the idea of a ball had filled Diana's heart with excitement. Now, all she did was cringe under the hostile stares of society. And yet, she noticed that those stares were only meant for her alone. Her husband, however, was received with politeness and respect as they made their rounds, greeting friends and acquaintances—her husband's friends and acquaintances. For apart from her immediate family, Diana had lost all favour in society the moment she had been considered ruined. Now, only very few people remained who would speak to her directly.

One such person was her cousin Rose.

As soon as she caught sight of Diana, her cousin leaned closer to her husband and whispered something in his ear. He looked up then, and the moment, his eyes caught Diana's—be it only for a split second—her heartbeat sped up and her palms became moist. How was he still doing this after all those years? Diana marvelled, wondering what pained her more: society's unwillingness to forget her one mistake in judgement or the sight of undying love between Rose and her husband.

"Oh, I'm so glad you could come," Rose beamed after walking over on her husband's arm and greeting them warmly. "It is truly a marvellous night."

"It is indeed," Lord Norwood agreed, nodding his head in greeting, his eyes aglow with love as he gazed down at his wife. "I believe we shall spend the entire night on the dance floor."

Rose laughed, then leaned over to Diana and whispered conspiratorially, "Although I wish I could, at present I do not believe that I have the strength to do so...considering my condition."

At her cousin's words, Diana cringed inwardly, but managed to maintain a polite smile. Caught up in the excitement of the night—as well as her life in general—Rose did not see the wistful expression that came to Diana's eyes as she carefully glanced at Lord Norwood, a new ache coming to her heart as he continued to act as though they barely knew each other.

Whenever Diana looked at him these days and their eyes happened to meet, she never saw a spark of recognition, of remembrance of the night that had so shaped her life. It was as though he had forgotten her.

Soon, Rose and her husband rejoined the many couples occupying the dance floor while Diana's husband excused himself and ventured toward the gambling room.

Left alone, Diana once again wondered how to fill her evening. Years ago, she would have danced the night away. Now, that was not an option. No one ever asked her to dance any longer. Not even her husband.

As she walked around the room, doing her best to ignore the hushed whispers that followed her, Diana came to stand in front of the garden doors. Beyond them, a green oasis lay in darkness, calling her forth, promising peace and tranquillity.

However, the moment her hand came to rest on the door handle, Diana shrank back as though it had been seared by fire. Again, the night four years ago flashed before her eyes, and she knew she would only be fuelling gossip if she ventured out into the night alone. Who knew what would happen? Her husband would be most displeased.

And yet, for a split second, Diana was tempted to go nonetheless. Could her life truly become any worse? Didn't people already gossip, already shun her, already ignore her? What else could they do to her that they hadn't already?

Resisting the lure of the gardens, Diana stepped away from the doors and instead headed in a safer direction toward the refreshment table. With her heart still hammering in her chest, she felt parched as though it was sheer exercise to merely be in the same room with London Society. As she reached for a glass of refreshing lemonade, her hand collided with someone else's and she shrank back. Her head snapped up, and she stared wide-eyed at the young woman before her. How come she had not noticed her before?

"I'm sorry," the young woman assured her, a large smile on her face as she gestured for Diana to take the glass. "I guess I was lost in thought."

"As was I," Diana mumbled, wondering why this woman would address her so kindly. Did she not know who she was? Had she not heard the whispers? Had no one warned her not to socialise with Diana?

An expectant look in her eyes, the young woman then reached for the glass and handed it to Diana. "Here, you seem in need of a refreshment." As though in a trance, Diana accepted the drink. "Have you been dancing a lot? I suppose it must be wonderful to…" Her voice trailed off as her eyes drifted to the side, looking at something or someone beyond the twirling couples.

Unable to ignore the sadness that had suddenly come to the young woman's eyes, Diana sighed. She, too, had been young once.

And although only a few years had passed since her first Season, Diana felt as though she had lived a lifetime in those years. In fact, she felt like an old woman who looked back upon her youth with wistful melancholy, regretting the turn her life had taken.

"Are you all right?" Diana asked, wondering if she had sunken too deep into her own misery to not have noticed the pain others suffered.

The young woman turned back to face her, a reluctant smile drawing up the corners of her mouth. "Yes, I'm fine. Thank you." Then she drew in a deep breath, and a touch of determination came to her features. "My name is Eleanor Abbott. I'm Lord Stanhope's sister."

Diana drew in a sharp breath. Clearly, Lady Eleanor did not know who she was, and once she did, her kind smile would surely die faster than Diana could mumble an apology. "I'm Mrs. Reignold, Diana Reignold," she finally said, watching Lady Eleanor's face with rapt attention.

Strangely enough, the smile on the young woman's face stayed where it was. "It's a pleasure to meet you, Mrs. Reignold. Is your husband here with you?"

"He is," Diana answered still as though in trance. "However, he prefers the gambling table to the dance floor."

"But surely, he has danced with you at least once, has he not?" Lady Eleanor asked, a jesting tone to her voice as she reached for another glass of lemonade and took a sip.

"He has not," Diana admitted, feeling a sudden but desperate desire to keep their conversation going…by any means necessary if need be. "To be frank, I do not mind. He is an awful dancer."

Lady Eleanor laughed, and once more her eyes shifted to the other side of the room.

"Is there someone special you wished would dance with you?" Diana asked, wondering if everybody was in love but her…or at least happily in love.

Lady Eleanor sighed, and a slight blush came to her cheeks. "Is it that obvious?"

Diana nodded, feeling her heart go out to the young woman who seemed saddened despite the obvious fact that her heart almost overflowed with love. "Does he not return your feelings?"

Again, Lady Eleanor's mouth curved upward and the blush on her cheeks deepened. "I do believe he does." Then she nodded her head as though needing to convince herself. "No, I *know* he does."

Diana frowned. "If that is indeed the case, I am surprised to see you so miserable."

Lady Eleanor sighed, and for a moment, her eyes came to rest on Diana's face, studying her, determining how much to say. "My mother does not approve," she finally explained, her shoulders suddenly slumped in resignation.

"Is he not of your station?" Diana asked, feeling a touch of guilt for the delight their conversation brought her. Despite Lady Eleanor's misery, Diana could not help but savour the rare moment that someone addressed her as though she were worthy of their attention. Years had passed since that had last happened.

"He is the fifth son of a baron," Lady Eleanor explained. However, her eyes had become distant as she spoke. "Still, I do not believe that to be enough of a reason for my mother's vehement objections. I do feel as though she knows something I do not." Then Lady Eleanor blinked, and her gaze returned to meet Diana's. Instantly, a bashful smile came to her features. "I apologise for ruining your night with my worries. Surely, there are friends and acquaintances you wish to attend." Nodding her head in appreciation, Lady Eleanor stepped back. "Thank you for listening though."

Before Diana could object, urge her to stay, assure her that her worries were not a burden but a blessing instead, Lady Eleanor walked away, and Diana was alone again.

Once more, her heart plummeted into the black void that usually engulfed her upon leaving her home and subjecting herself to the judgement of others. At least for the duration of their conversation, Diana had been able to ignore the occasional stare or frown cast in her direction. Would it ever end? She wondered. Could one error in judgement truly live on forever?

In the beginning, Diana had been certain that she only needed to be patient until another piece of gossip would arise, overshadowing her own mistake and allowing people to forget a little more every day. However, although other rumours and whispers now sounded louder than those directed at her, Diana now knew that society never truly forgot, and she had come to realise that her parents had been right: a reputation once lost was gone forever.

The rest of the evening progressed as expected—as it always did. Keeping to herself, Diana observed the happy lives of those around her while desperately trying to shield her heart from the torturous sights before her eyes: Her cousin in love with the man Diana had once thought her soul mate.

And although she knew that Rose meant well by including her, by seeking her out and asking if she needed anything, for Diana it only increased the sense of loneliness she had felt these past years.

On their carriage ride home, Diana kept her eyes out the window, unable to look at her husband as he sat slumped in his seat, reeking of liquor. As impeccable as he liked to appear to the ton, Diana knew by now that her husband merely wore a well-crafted mask, and she had to admit that he deserved credit for hiding his own sins from the world at large with such skill. If only she had had the foresight to do so as well.

A moment after the carriage drew to a halt in front of their townhouse, the door was opened and the steps lowered. However, her husband remained in his seat, merely nodding his head at her, bidding her a good night.

Taking a deep breath, Diana allowed the coachman to help her out of the carriage before he once more closed the door and climbed back up onto the box. As Diana ascended the few steps to their front door, the carriage drew away from the kerb and was soon lost in the dark.

Shaking her head at the unfairness of life, Diana retired to her chamber, wondering why it was merely frowned upon if a man had a mistress, but if a woman spent even one moment in the company of an unrelated gentleman, she was ruined? Irredeemable. Forever.

Who had made these rules?

Diana scoffed. Men, of course! Those who benefit from rules were usually the ones who had set them.

Blowing out the candle, Diana slipped into bed, pulling the soft blanket tightly around herself and decided to count her blessings. If her husband was with his mistress, then at least tonight, he would not bother her.

3

LIFE & DEATH

Looking at herself in the mirror, Diana stared at the pale creature she saw there. Dressed in black from head to toe, her white skin in stark contrast to the gloom of her gown, her gloves, her scarf, her hat, she felt as though dead.

Had she died, and no one had told her?

For a moment, her lids closed and then opened, and her gaze focused on the pale blue colour of her eyes, the only colour in an otherwise colourless apparition.

No, it was her husband who had died, and yet, she could not say she *knew* how. No one had told her. After all, she was a woman, and women were shielded from the ugliness of the world. They were not strong. They could not bear the weight of knowing the truth.

At least that is what she *had* been told.

Not in such direct terms, of course, but Diana had understood nonetheless. What she also understood was that it was a lie.

A lie that was not meant to protect her, to shield her, but instead to protect her late husband's reputation, for although no one had breathed a word of the circumstances of his demise in her presence, Diana knew very well why that was the case.

Her husband had died in the arms of his mistress.

And although rumours probably already ran rampant, Diana knew that once the initial shock had died down, it would not be her husband who would be held accountable. If the past few years had taught Diana anything, it was that blame was rarely bestowed where it was deserved.

Even today, the day of her husband's funeral, Diana knew beyond the shadow of a doubt that she, his widow, would not receive sympathy for losing him, for the circumstances of his death. She would not be pitied. She would not be comforted and consoled.

No, eventually she would be blamed. Maybe not for causing his death outright, but for driving him into the arms of a mistress, for not being the kind of wife whom her husband would have deserved, for failing him.

Diana's heart sank at the thought of what awaited her.

Would it never end?

Or would only death set her free?

Not her husband's.

But her own.

Returning home from the funeral, Diana realised she had barely heard a word that had been spoken, barely remembered a face she had seen. It was as though she saw everything through a black veil. Faces looked distorted and indistinct. Voices sounded muffled and dulled in comparison to the constant thoughts coursing through her head.

All she could focus on was: what now?

"Are you all right?"

Lifting her head, Diana blinked, turning toward the familiar voice. A moment later, Rose's face came into focus, her brows drawn down in concern. "Do you need to lie down?"

Diana took a deep breath. "I'm fine," she whispered, wondering what that meant.

Glancing at the other mourners, Rose drew her aside and led her into the library where they were out of earshot. "Please, Diana, tell me what I can do to help you."

Forcing her thoughts to focus, Diana looked at her cousin, noting the signs of honest distress and concern, and a slow smile came to Diana's face. "Thank you, dear Rose." Then she shook her head. "But, there is nothing you can do. My fate is sealed. It has been these past four years. Nothing will ever change."

Rose swallowed, her eyes slightly narrowing, and Diana could see that her cousin had meant something else. "You were referring to my husband's death?"

Rose nodded. "How do you feel?"

"You know better than anyone that I did not love him," Diana said, her voice slowly growing stronger as a sense of impatience washed over her. For the past four years, she had done her best to appear the devoted wife, and yet, it had done her no good. Would she now have to continue as the devoted widow for the rest of her life?

Rose sighed, "I do know, yes. But lately, you seemed less…displeased with him," she stated carefully, her bright green eyes searching Diana's face. "At first, you were so forceful in your rejection of him, that I had hoped you would have come to care for–"

"I gave up!" Diana interrupted, surprised by her sudden outburst and the one lonely tear that spilled over and slowly ran down her cheek. Swallowing, she held her cousin's pitying gaze. *Maybe pity was worse than blame after all!* "I gave up," she repeated quietly, stepping back as Rose reached out a comforting hand toward her. "I do not know how to live this life as I am forced to pretend from sunup to sundown." She shook her head in resignation. "I didn't have the strength to hold on to the woman I once was and still attempt to please my husband. At some point, I suppose I stopped caring. Or at least, I tried to."

"Oh, Diana, I'm so sorry," Rose exclaimed, her arms once more rising with the intention to comfort. However, when she saw Diana's rigid posture, she let them drop once more. "I had no idea you felt that way. How could I not have seen it?"

A wistful smile came to Diana's face. "Because you're happy," she said, remembering the blissful ignorance of those early days when she had believed herself in love. "You married the man I wanted. He refused me, but he chose you."

"I'm so sorry," Rose whispered once again, tears brimming in her eyes as she wrung her hands, desperate for something to do, to help, and still knowing that there was no such thing.

"It was not your fault," Diana said, wondering when she had come to that conclusion.

In the first year after Rose had married Lord Norwood, Diana had despised her with all her heart for her betrayal. However, slowly over time, Rose's gentle insistence to remain in Diana's life had worn her down, had breached her defences…and today Diana was glad for it, for Rose was the only one she dared to speak to and hold nothing back.

"It was not your fault," she repeated. "It was mine. I know now that I acted wrongly, and yet, I still feel that the punishment I suffered was too severe. It still is." Diana drew in a deep breath. "You know how he die, do you not?" she asked, noting the slight paleness that came to Rose's cheeks as she averted her eyes.

"What he did was far worse, and yet, it doesn't matter. Soon, it'll be forgotten. Maybe referred to here and there as a hushed whisper, but people will not think less of him. Not truly. Not the way they think less of me." Shaking her head, Diana fought down the urge to grab a book off the shelf beside her and hurl it at the wall with all her might. "Tell me that's fair! Tell me that I deserve this! Because the more I learn about the life I am forced to live, the less I understand it. And I don't know what to do next. I simply don't know. Tell me, Rose, what am I to do?"

4

WIDOWS & BRIDES

After a fortnight of sitting at home and mourning a husband she never wanted to marry in the first place, Diana was no closer to an answer than on the day of the funeral. What was she to do?

The mere thought of continuing her life in the same manner turned her stomach upside down, and yet, she could not see an alternative.

Possibly after the end of her mourning period—which was a year away—she could return to society and look for another husband. But would anyone even want her? Would she want to subject herself to the same degrading treatment she had suffered at her late husband's hands?

Maybe she simply ought to remain a widow. It certainly was the easier, the safer option, and yet, Diana knew that she wanted more.

A part of her felt as though it had been awakened from a long slumber as though prince charming had ridden up on his white steed and broken the spell with his kiss. Only there had been no prince and no kiss.

Her husband had died…and set her free…if only in the sense that her desire to taste life beyond the dullness of her home had re-awakened.

In a word, what Diana wanted was to feel. Something. Anything.

"Maybe we should take a stroll through the park," Rose suggested, setting down her teacup as her eyes shifted over Diana with the same concerned expression that had been there constantly in the past fortnight. "The sun is shining, and there is a gentle breeze."

Sighing, Diana nodded. "Maybe you're right."

Encouraged, Rose almost jumped to her feet and immediately drew Diana to the foyer lest she change her mind. There, they reached for their jackets and hats held at the ready by attentive footmen and turned to the door without delay.

However, the moment Diana stepped forward to follow her cousin, she caught the soft shimmer of light blue out of the corner of her eye. Turning back, her gaze narrowed as it slid over the armchair in the corner all the way down to its leg. There, she saw one of her scarfs, half-hidden in the shadows, its radiant blue shining even more brightly after a fortnight of gloomy black.

Diana drew in a deep breath, and an involuntary smile curled up her lips.

Without thinking, she stepped forward and pulled it out from behind the chair's leg. Running it through her fingers, Diana did not see the occasional speck of dust that had settled onto the fabric here and there. All she saw was the shimmering colour, and in that moment, Diana could not have parted with it for anything.

"Is something wrong?" Rose said as she walked up and came to stand beside Diana. "Did you change your mind?" Then her eyes shifted down to the blue scarf clutched tightly in Diana's hands as though it was a priceless treasure before they returned to her cousin's face, a hint of suspicion in Rose's emerald eyes. "You're not…?"

The corners of Diana's mouth rose into a wide smile that she simply could not suppress even if she had wanted to. And she didn't. "Yes, I am," she declared triumphantly, winding the scarf around her arms so that the ends hung down in the front, gently swaying as she walked.

"But you're in mourning!" Rose objected as she followed Diana toward the mirror. "You simply cannot! Your husband's funeral was barely a fortnight ago. Diana, be reasonable!"

Taking a deep breath, Diana stared at her reflection in the mirror, delighted with the way the brilliant blue seemed to sparkle in contrast to the black of her dress, like stars shining in the night sky.

"Diana, please!"

Turning to face her cousin, Diana met her eyes. "No," she simply said, the expression on her face calm, her eyes steady as they held Rose's gaze. "I need this. These past few years, I've barely been myself, always worried about what people would think, and no matter what I did, no matter how hard I tried, they always thought the worst of me." Suddenly feeling liberated, Diana drew in a deep breath, and an honest smile came to her lips. "Now, I'm done living by everybody's rules. Now, I shall only live by my own."

Staring at her dumbfounded, Rose swallowed. "Are you certain you wish to do this? Think about the consequences."

At her cousin's words, an old fear slowly crept up Diana's spine, sending chills up and down her body. "No!" she said vehemently, her eyes hardening. "The last few years have knocked out my legs from under me, if I don't stand up now, I know I shall never rise again."

Holding her gaze for a moment, her emerald eyes searching Diana's, Rose nodded. "All right. Then let's go." A soft smile, encouraging and devoted, came to her face. "Before the sun changes its mind."

"Thank you," Diana whispered, her heart hammering in her chest as she followed her cousin outside, leaving behind the safety of her home and facing the world.

"Lord Grafton's daughter would be suitable," Lady Stanhope stated, her sharp eyes shifting over the list of potential brides in her hand. "This is her second season. She is from a well-respected family and behaves with all the graces and manners befitting a young lady."

"I agree," Arthur mumbled, slightly annoyed with his mother's insistence to ignore anything he had said about his sister's potential spouses. "However, as I informed you before, I am determined to see Eleanor married first. Despite the age difference between us, she seems already far more suited to marriage than I shall ever be."

Inhaling deeply, his mother slowly lifted her eyes off the sheet of paper in her hands. "But not to Henry Waltham," she hissed, her pale eyes drilling into his as though her stare had the power to force him to submit to her wishes.

"Why are you so insistent?" Arthur enquired, remembering the way his sister and Henry Waltham had looked at one another from across the dance floor. "Eleanor seems fairly taken with him."

"Nonsense!" Lady Stanhope snapped, the list of potential brides crushed into a little ball when anger seized her, painting her face a darker shade of red. "It's merely an infatuation. It'll pass." She shook her head vehemently, tossing the crumpled list onto the floor. "And besides, there are far more important aspects to a marriage than love, believe me." Gritting her teeth, she inhaled deeply. "He is not worthy of her, and it is our duty to prevent Eleanor from doing something rash. I want her married to a suitable gentleman before the end of the Season."

Arthur's eyes widened. "Something rash?" he asked, stepping closer, his eyes trained on his mother. "What on earth do you speak of? Do you truly believe she would run off to Gretna Green if we do not give our consent?"

Holding his gaze, his mother shrugged. "I do not know, and that frightens me."

"Eleanor is far too reasonable to agree to such a shameful wedding," Arthur objected, unable to imagine that his little sister would ever go against the sense of decency that had been instilled in her from the moment she had been born. "No, she would never do that."

"I certainly hope not," his mother said, a touch of fear in her voice as she spoke. "However, we cannot be certain. Even morally impeccable women have succumbed to bad influences before. It is not unheard of."

"Bad influences?" Arthur asked, wondering about the slightly distant look that had come to his mother's face. "Who do you speak of? Henry Waltham?"

"Among others."

"Among others? Who else?"

Blinking, his mother swallowed, then met his eyes once more, her own once sharper and more determined. "Mrs. Reignold."

Arthur frowned. "Mrs. Reignold? Who…? What? You're speaking of that woman Eleanor spoke to at the ball a month ago?"

"Have you already forgotten what I told you about her?" his mother chided, clearly displeased that he was not taking this issue as seriously as she did herself. "She is of questionable character and not a good influence on my daughter." His mother drew in a deep breath, and her eyes shifted from side to side as though ensuring that no one was within earshot. Then she leaned closer, and Arthur knew that another titbit of gossip was imminent. "From what I've heard, she's been seen walking around in public," here, she paused for dramatic effect, and Arthur could barely keep himself from rolling his eyes, "wearing a blue scarf." His mother's eyes widened, looking at him expectantly, as she drew back and shook her head. "Outrageous!"

Arthur frowned, honestly confused. "Was she not recently widowed?"

Now, it was his mother who rolled her eyes. "Of course, she was. Otherwise, what I just told you would be of no importance! Do you never listen?"

Arthur drew in a deep breath, fighting down the urge to lash out at his mother. "I apologise," he forced himself to say, annoyed with himself for allowing his mother to influence his own sense of proper attitude to such a degree. Maybe she was right after all to worry about Eleanor. "Do you truly believe Mrs. Reignold would urge Eleanor to run off to Gretna Green? Have they even see each other since that ball a month ago?"

"Not as far as I know," his mother admitted, her voice a little feeble. "However, we cannot be certain. Eleanor might simply meet her in secret."

Why would she? Arthur wondered, but refrained from expressing his sentiments out loud. "If it makes you feel any better, I shall keep an eye on Eleanor."

"Thank you," his mother breathed, relief palpable on her face. "However, I fear I shall not find a moment of peace until my daughter is suitably married."

Arthur sighed, hoping that such an event would take place sooner rather than later for he was not certain how many more of these conversations he could have with his mother before he would be unable to hold himself in check.

All his life, he had hated it that his mother knew very well how to enrage him. It was a side of himself that he disliked, feared even, for it was far from reasonable.

As long as it merely resulted in a conversational outburst, which he could easily enough apologise for, it was barely noteworthy. However, Arthur wondered if one day he might break a far more important rule, one that was by far more difficult to apologise for, and that thought frightened him even more.

5

A FATEFUL NIGHT

"I must take my leave," Rose stated, rising to her feet, an apologetic smile on her face.

Confused and–admittedly–a bit saddened, Diana asked, "Why so soon?" Ever since her husband had died and Diana had begun to gradually accessorise her black wardrobe with more cheerful colours, Rose had been her tower of strength. Although it was still far from easy to see her cousin in the arms of her husband, Lord Norwood, Diana had come to cherish Rose's friendship and support.

Now, more than ever, society looked down on Diana, crinkling their noses at her audacity to treat her husband's memory with such disregard, but despite all reasonable objections, Rose remained by her side, remained loyal and kind.

And for the first time in her life, Diana realised how precious Rose was to her and how lonely she would be without her.

"I'm afraid I must," Rose insisted, her voice apologetic. "We are going to the theatre tonight, and I do not wish to be late."

Diana smiled wistfully. "That sounds wonderful," she mumbled, a touch of disappointment tainting an otherwise delightful day.

"Do not worry," Rose counselled, looping her arm through Diana's as they walked toward the foyer. "Before long you'll be out of mourning, and then I shall invite you to the theatre. Promise."

"Thank you," Diana said, bidding her cousin a good night. As the door closed behind Rose, Diana wished she could go as well instead of once more being left alone in a house that still did not feel like her home.

Would she ever find a place where she could be happy?

Sighing, Diana wandered from room to room, picturing her cousin getting ready for the theatre, her walking down the large staircase and taking her husband's arm. In her mind's eye, Diana could see the glowing smiles on their faces, and her own heart yearned to leave her prison and trade it for the entertainment of a night at the theatre.

If only.

Diana's head snapped up, and her feet stilled.

But why ever not? She wondered, and a wickedly cheerful smile came to her face as she pictured the shocked expressions of society's matrons if she were to attend the performance tonight.

The first afternoon she had gone out for a walk with Rose, wearing her blue scarf with her black dress, the stares and whispers had reminded Diana of all those years of trying to be accepted, but ultimately of being deemed unworthy.

In answer, she had lowered her head, unable to meet the stares that followed her. She had almost given in and allowed Rose to persuade her to return home.

However, in the last moment, Diana had realised her mistake. It did not matter any longer what people thought of her…simply because it *should not.* It only mattered how Diana saw herself, and whenever she pictured herself cowering under society's hateful eyes, Diana was disgusted with herself.

This was not the woman she wanted to be.

The woman she had dreamed of becoming once.

The woman she had never had the chance of becoming.

But now, here, this was her chance.

And she would be damned if she let it slip through her fingers.

"We are late," Lady Stanhope mumbled, the edge in her voice unmistakable as they ascended the stairs to Covent Garden.

Offering Eleanor his arm, Arthur did his utmost to ignore his mother's reproachful tone since their being late had in fact been her doing. Once again, she had lectured her daughter on her behaviour toward Henry Waltham, accusing her of encouraging his attentions.

Although Arthur had to admit that his mother did have a point that Eleanor did in fact welcome the young man's affections, he had recently come to realise that nothing he or his mother could say would have any effect on Eleanor's heart.

His sister's mind might be persuaded to ignore the young gentleman; however, her heart would be a different matter. Arthur could see it in her eyes.

The conflict.

The dilemma.

The torturous agony.

His own heart twisted in his chest at the sight of her misery; yet, he did not know what to do. Naturally, as head of the family, it was within his power to grant Eleanor her happily-ever-after. However, he knew the young woman Eleanor had become, and he was certain beyond the shadow of a doubt that no matter what consequences she herself would have to suffer, she would never go against her mother's wishes.

Why? Arthur could not be certain. Although the relationship between mother and daughter appeared rather strained and void of deep emotions, there was something in the way they sometimes looked at each other that had Arthur convinced that there was something he did not know.

Something that stood between them, and yet, connected them beyond reproach.

As they crossed the large foyer heading toward the grand staircase, Lady Stanhope drew in a sharp breath. A second later, Arthur felt his sister's arm tense as she stopped in her tracks. Following their line of vision, Arthur stiffened.

There, at the top of the staircase, dressed in simple elegance, his dark hair neatly brushed back, stood Henry Waltham. Although he seemed tense, his eyes never swayed from Eleanor, and Arthur could see the slight blush that came to his sister's cheeks.

"What is he doing here?" his mother hissed under her breath, her eyes shooting daggers at the young man before turning on her daughter. "Did you send him word to meet you here? This is truly unbelievable! I never would have thought you would act in such a selfish way!"

"Mother, but I didn't–"

"At this point, I cannot believe a word you say." Crossing her arms over her chest, Lady Stanhope drew in a deep breath, her eyes narrowing even farther as they slid over Henry Waltham's face.

Clearing his throat, Arthur stepped in his mother's line of vision. "Escort Eleanor to our box," he said, his voice calm as he knew that any sign of emotion would only send his mother into another fit. "I shall deal with Mr. Waltham."

His mother blinked, and then her eyes met his. "Yes, that is a splendid idea," she agreed, nodding her head vigorously. Then she looped her arm through Eleanor's, and together, they followed Arthur up the stairs.

While Arthur stopped in front of the young gentleman, his mother dragged Eleanor onward. However, Mr. Waltham stepped forward, his eyes fixed on the woman he loved, and whispered, "Good evening, Lady Eleanor."

Arthur sighed as he saw how much these few simple words affected his sister. Craning her neck to look at Mr. Waltham, she reluctantly followed their mother down the corridor toward their box.

Once they were lost from sight, Mr. Waltham swallowed, and his gaze turned to Arthur. "I apologise for showing up here tonight," he said, his shoulders squared and his chin raised. "I assure you I had no intention of causing a problem."

Arthur snorted, "I'm afraid, Mr. Waltham, you *are* the problem."

Instead of being offended, the young man nodded. "I am aware of Lady Stanhope's dislike of me and my family, and at least, partially, I cannot fault her. My elder brothers have acted against the generally accepted code of conduct more than once, which undoubtedly gives Lady Stanhope good reason to distrust me."

Surprised at the young man's view on the situation, Arthur decided to speak openly. "What are your intentions towards my sister, Mr. Waltham?"

Despite the tension that seized his shoulders, a warm smile came to his face. "I intend to marry her."

"I appreciate your honesty," Arthur said, his eyes slightly narrowed as he watched the young man, looking for a sign of dishonesty, duplicity, falsity, anything that might prove his mother's opinion of him justified. "Then tell me equally honestly, if need be, would you run off with my sister to marry her without the consent of her family?"

Mr. Waltham stiffened, and the smile slid off his face. Holding Arthur's gaze unflinchingly, he stepped forward. "I would. Yes. However, Eleanor would never agree. She would never go against her family, and I would never put her in the position to choose."

Arthur nodded, his face solemn as he considered what he had just heard. Despite Mr. Waltham's admission, he could not fault the young man. For deep in his heart, Arthur knew that Henry Waltham was a good man, one who did not deserve to be judged for the mistakes of others, one who had a conscience and placed Eleanor's well-being above his own.

"Once again, I appreciate your honesty, Mr. Waltham," Arthur said. "Although I doubt that it shall do you any good, I shall speak to my mother on your behalf."

A sudden smile drew up the corners of Mr. Waltham's mouth, and he seemed to sag into himself as relief flooded his being. "I thank you, Lord Stanhope," he stammered, almost breathless. "I truly appreciate your support."

Arthur nodded, cursing himself for stirring up the young man's hopes. It had been a moment of weakness, knowing the misery these two-young people found themselves in through no fault of their own. If only there was something he truly *could* do.

After all, changing his mother's mind was an Herculean task indeed.

Almost impossible.

"I bid you a good night," Mr. Waltham said, slightly bowing his head, before he descended the stairs, his arms hanging by his sides, his hands opening and closing as though they had gone numb.

Arthur sighed. What was he to do?

Rubbing his hand over his brows, Arthur turned toward the corridor that led to his family's box when he caught movement out of the corner of his eye. A moment later, the sound of footsteps echoed to his ears as a young, unchaperoned lady hastily crossed the foyer.

With a frown drawing down his brows, Arthur watched her, then squinted his eyes. Who was she? She did look familiar. If only he could remember where–

The ball!

His mother's latest gossip.

If Arthur was not completely mistaken, then this woman was Mrs. Reignold, the young widow who in the past month had been spotted all over town, her black mourning wardrobe adorned with colourful accessories.

Arthur swallowed for the woman who now hurried up the staircase in his direction wore not only colourful accessories, but a stunning gown in the deepest violet he had ever seen. Her light blue eyes sparkled with a mixture of mischief and excitement as she brushed a stray curl of her hazel tresses behind her ear.

Stepping back from the landing, Arthur withdrew until he stood slightly hidden behind a large column. What was he to do?

His knowledge of proper etiquette told him that they must not be seen alone together. Not only would it cause disastrous rumours, but it would also ruin every chance she might have of reacquiring society's favour—although her mere presence at tonight's performance might be enough to accomplish that on its own.

However, there was something in her eyes, in the way she moved that spoke of a hidden motivation as though she was driven by an unseen force, as though she could not be held accountable for what she was doing, and Arthur felt it to be his duty to warn her of the disastrous consequences of her actions.

For he believed deep in his heart, that she could not possibly be aware of them. If she was, she would most certainly act differently. After all, no one in her right mind would willingly ruin herself in such an irredeemable way.

Still torn about what to do, Arthur froze when her head suddenly turned in his direction and their eyes met.

6

AN UNUSUAL WOMAN

During the whole of the carriage ride to the theatre, Diana's heart had thumped in her chest as her mind had screamed at her to return home. And yet, she couldn't.

Even though her muscles were tense, her palms moist and her legs trembled, she could not turn back now. For the first time in years, she felt…alive.

Although her stomach twisted and turned, her heart was beating excitedly in her chest; her pulse was dancing under her skin.

This was life!

If there was no way for her to follow society's rules and feel alive at the same time—experience had taught her that there truly was not—then Diana decided she'd rather break them than spend the rest of her days with that dull ache in her heart.

The moment she stepped into the foyer of the theatre, her heart stopped as she expected the full force of society's disapproval to fall on her like a pack of wolves. However, a moment later she shook her head, laughing, as she remembered that the performance had already begun.

There was simply no one about.

Here she was, a young widow, dressed in a scandalous dress, and there was no one to see it. What a shame!

Hastening up the stairs, Diana could not help but wonder what would happen once she appeared in Lord Norwoord's box. Would everyone stare? Would they whisper? Would the performance stop?

Excited, and yet, terrified to her core, Diana rushed on, taking one step at a time, until her gaze fell on a dark-haired man, half-hidden behind one of the large stone columns that supported the massive roof.

Although he did look surprised to see her, the expression in his eyes spoke neither of disapproval nor outrage. Rather it was a mixture of confusion and curiosity.

Intrigued, Diana held his questioning gaze before her feet—as though following their own path—turned away from the corridor that led to Lord Norwood's box and toward the half-hidden gentleman. As he saw her approach, his eyes widened and he took a step back, his gaze quickly surveying their surroundings as though looking for a way to escape.

Had he recognised her? Diana wondered. Did he know that rumour, gossip and scandal followed in her wake? Did he now fear for his own reputation?

With a wicked gleam in her eyes and a touch of devilish delight in her heart, Diana ignored the small voice of reason somewhere in the back of her head yelling at her to be careful.

Not today.

Today, she wanted to enjoy herself.

"Good evening, my lord," she greeted him, delighted with the way his sharp, grey eyes narrowed as they seemed to search her face. For what she did not know. "Would you be so kind as to escort me to Lord Norwood's box?"

He swallowed, and his gaze abandoned their search and focused on hers. "To be frank, I am confused."

"Confused?" Diana echoed, feeling that very feeling spread through her being. Indeed, she had expected him to comply without argument, hoping to rid himself of her as quickly as possible, or to refuse outright, informing her in harsh words of the despicable behaviour she portrayed. However, the man before her looked neither embarrassed nor outraged, which indeed was confusing. For even if he had not recognised her, her behaviour alone should speak volumes. After all, she was alone at the theatre, unchaperoned, speaking to a man she had never met before.

Or had she?

Squinting her eyes, Diana tried to recall where she had seen his face before when suddenly Lady Eleanor's voice echoed in her mind, *My name is Eleanor Abbott. I'm Lord Stanhope's sister.*

Indeed, they had the same watchfulness to their eyes.

"Although your behaviour is ill-advised," Lord Stanhope began, a clear reproach in his voice now, "you do appear in possession of your faculties."

Annoyed with his tone, Diana glared at him. "Well, thank you for such a heart-felt compliment, my lord."

For a short moment, he seemed taken aback with her retort as though he had never exchanged harsh words with a woman. "I apologise for upsetting your sensibilities. However—"

"My sensibilities?" Diana laughed. It had been a long time since anyone had been concerned about her like this. This man was truly entertaining!

Again, his brows drew down into a speculative frown. "What I meant to say was that I cannot fathom why you would act the way you do." He shook his head as though the thought of something not following the path of logic had never occurred to him. "I cannot think of a single reasonable explanation for your presence here," his gaze dropped from hers and took in the deep violet of her dress, "and in such a gown no less."

"Quite frankly, my lord, I'm not certain if I should take this as a compliment or an insult," Diana replied, surprised how much she enjoyed their conversation. After all, it had been years since she had exchanged even a single word with a man whom she would not consider family. It was exciting, and she noticed the trail of goose bumps running up and down her arms.

"It was meant as neither," he assured her. "I simply find myself wondering about your motivation. You are aware of the repercussions should anyone see you here like this, are you not?"

Diana drew in a deep breath, slightly annoyed with the turn their conversation had taken. "Yes, my lord, I assure you I know very well what people will think. After all, I've spent the past four years paying for a minor indiscretion."

At the defeated tone in her voice, Lord Stanhope's eyes narrowed and he inhaled deeply, his gaze still trained on her, still watchful, enquiring. "I am aware of that."

Although he spoke calmly, Diana could detect a touch of compassion in his voice. Holding his gaze, she wondered why he would speak to her like this. "I admit I am surprised that you would speak to me so directly, my lord. Few people would."

"I suppose that's true. However, I've always despised gossip. It serves no purpose other than distorting the truth." He nodded at her encouragingly. "Do not worry. I shall not breathe of word of this to anyone."

For a second, Diana felt as though she would break out into hysterical laughter.

After everything she had done tonight to shock and appall—coming to the theatre unchaperoned, dressed in a scandalous dress, speaking to a man to whom she had never been properly introduced—it appeared all her efforts had been for nothing. For despite her intentions, she had apparently found the only gentleman in all of England who despised gossip!

Watching Mrs. Reignold intently, Arthur frowned as he saw her eyes close for a moment and a disbelieving smile come to her face as though she was displeased with his reaction. There was something truly strange about this woman, that he could not make sense of.

And it bothered him.

"Your reaction leads me to believe," he began, trying to sort through the chaos in his head, "that you were never concerned about the possibility that I spread word of our encounter," he chuckled, "and not because you deem me trustworthy, but because…you wouldn't mind. Was it your intention in coming here tonight to cause yet another scandal?"

Mrs. Reignold shrugged, then sighed as her shoulders slumped. "I admit I would have enjoyed seeing shocked faces all around me. Yes. However, initially, I only…," she drew in a deep breath, her eyes having lost their sparkle, "…I only meant to enjoy myself."

"Then I suggest you find less harmful ways to do so," Arthur advised, wondering why he even bothered as she seemed well aware of the potential consequences of her actions. If indeed it was her intention of ruining herself further, then there was nothing he could do to prevent it. And yet, there was something in her eyes that stopped him from simply walking away for it reminded him of his sister.

A deep-seated sadness and the almost firm belief that all hope was lost.

Did she truly see her life like this?

Shaking her head, Mrs. Reignold took a step toward him, her eyes suddenly ablaze with barely contained fury. "I appreciate your concern, my lord," she snarled into his face, "however, it is much too late for such advice."

Surprised at her outburst, Arthur felt his muscles tense.

"My reputation will not suffer," she continued, her hands on her hips, "for it is already lying dead at my feet."

"What about your son?" Arthur asked, trying to remember the many details his mother had recently shared with him. At that point, however, he had done his utmost not to commit such gossip to memory.

Again, Mrs. Reignold laughed, a touch of hysteria to her voice. "He will not suffer. After all, he is a man. Men can do whatever they want and not suffer the repercussions. The best example is my husband." Her eyes flashed with anger as she fixed him with a daring glare. "You know how he died, do you not? You've heard the rumours, isn't that true?"

With a sense of guilt in his heart, Arthur nodded. "I'm afraid I have." He scoffed, shaking his head. "Unfortunately, it is fairly impossible to go through life and not have other people's business carried to your ears."

"Then you know that despite the occasional whisper here and there, my late husband's reputation has not suffered. In fact, ever since his passing, people look at *me* as though I've committed yet another faux pas. Somehow it is all my fault." Shrugging her shoulders, she shook her head, her eyes clouded with injustice and resignation. "My son will undoubtedly follow in his father's footsteps. He will learn that men can do no wrong and that women are always to blame."

Where before she had seemed like a raging fury, now all strength seemed to have left her, and for a moment, Arthur feared she would faint. However, then her chin rose a notch, and she met his gaze.

"I'm sorry to hear about the course your life has taken," Arthur began gently. However, he hastened on when her mouth opened in protest and her eyes began to flash with anger once more. "Still, what becomes of your son is mostly dependent on you."

As though taken aback, she blinked.

"You're his mother," Arthur reminded her. "You're the one who will shape who he is and who he will become. Raise him into a man you can be truly proud of, and the past will not repeat itself." Holding her gaze, Arthur waited, and from the look in her eyes, he thought that that possibility had never occurred to her. Did she truly only see her husband's misdeeds when she looked into the face of her little boy?

A moment later, Arthur's thoughts were interrupted when footsteps echoed to his ears from the opposite side of the large staircase. Instantly, panic seized him—a rather unfamiliar feeling—and he acted without thought—a rather untypical event.

Reaching for Mrs. Reignold, he pulled her behind the large stone column, hoping that it would shield them both, praying that whoever was approaching would turn down the stairs and not come in their direction.

"What are you doing?" Mrs. Reignold demanded, confusion on her face as she stared up at him. Then her gaze shifted to his hand where it rested on her arm.

Instantly, Arthur dropped his hand. However, he could not step back or he would reveal himself. "Someone is coming," he whispered, hoping she would remain still and not force him to play a part in her next scandalous deed.

At his words, however, she froze, her gaze fixed on his face as she listened intently to the approaching footsteps.

Forcing himself to ignore the rapid beating of his heart, Arthur could make out the couple's voices as they—to his utmost relief—turned toward the staircase.

"Do not worry, my dear," the woman said. "I'm perfectly fine. Simply a bit exhausted."

"Rose," Mrs. Reignold whispered before she clamped a hand over her mouth.

"Nevertheless, we should return home so you can lie down," the gentleman replied, his voice slowly fading away as they reached the ground floor.

Releasing the breath he had been holding, Arthur closed his eyes. "They're gone," he whispered then, surprised to find Mrs. Reignold gazing up at him, a tentative smile giving her lips a slight curl. "Is something wrong?" he asked, uncertain what to make of her reaction.

Her smile grew wider. "Why are you trying to protect me?"

Arthur swallowed as her clear blue eyes held his, shining with such delight that he could not bring himself to look away. "I don't know." Again, he swallowed. "You should return home. Next time, we might not be so fortunate as to remain undiscovered."

"Next time?" she asked, a teasing gleam in her eyes.

Clearing his throat, Arthur finally realised that Mrs. Reignold was still trapped between the stone column and himself and hastily took a step backward. "I apologise," he mumbled, wondering when right and wrong had become such ill-defined concepts. After all, his world had been quite balanced a mere few minutes ago. However, now, it appeared to be more unhinged than he had ever known it to be.

"There is no need to apologise," Mrs. Reignold assured him as she took a step forward, once more closing the distance between them. "After all, your only intention was to protect me, was it not?"

"Certainly," Arthur assured her, feeling rather flustered suddenly. "However, my intention did interfere with yours."

"It did," she confirmed as her eyes met his once more, and what he saw there made the breath catch in his throat. "Are you willing to make amends?"

"Amends?" Arthur croaked for although he could not say why, a cold shiver suddenly ran down his back.

A slow smile curled up the corners of her mouth, and before Arthur knew what was happening, she stepped toward him. Her hand brushed over the side of his face, pulling him down to her, before her lips claimed his in a gentle kiss.

It only lasted a moment, and yet, Arthur could have sworn that the world had been set ablaze.

Pulling back, Mrs. Reignold smiled at him. "Thank you," she whispered, her soft breath caressing his skin, before she turned around and hurried down the stairs. At the doors, she looked over her shoulder for one short moment and a deep smile curled up her lips.

Then she was gone, swallowed up by the dark night, and Arthur could not help but wonder if he had merely imagined her.

After all, women like her did not truly exist, did they?

At least, he had never met one.

Not until today.

7

A HEART'S DESIRE

The whole carriage ride home, Diana marvelled at the smile that seemed to be stuck on her face. As much as she tried, she could not convince the corners of her mouth to abandon their post. They were set firmly in place, causing her heart to skip a beat every now and then as she remembered how differently the evening had gone from how she had hoped it would.

And yet, she had no regrets.

Diana had wanted to enjoy herself, to feel something, to feel alive.

And she had.

The moment Lord Stanhope had pulled her behind the column, his grey eyes dark with concern as he had shielded her from the threat of discovery, her heart had leapt into her throat. She had seen the rapid beating of his pulse right above his collar. She had felt the warmth of his body as he had towered above her. And from one moment to the next, she had felt like the young, innocent girl she had once been.

Not since that night when she had followed Lord Norwood into the garden had she felt like this.

Her heart seemed to dance in her chest. Her breath could barely draw enough oxygen from the air around her. And her skin tingled with the memory of their kiss.

Had she truly kissed him? Diana marvelled once again, shocked to have acted in such a brazen way.

After spending the past four years living a life dictated by countless rules and restrictions, tonight had Diana feeling beyond daring and bold. Tonight had been an adventure, and she could only hope that the next one would find her sooner rather than later.

Almost dancing up the steps to the upper floor of her townhouse, Diana stopped just outside her door when a soft wail reached her ears.

At first, she was confused. What could possibly make such a pitiful sound?

Then, however, the wailing increased, and Diana froze when she realised that it was her son.

Instantly, Lord Stanhope's voice echoed in her mind. *Raise him into a man you can be truly proud of, and the past will not repeat itself.*

As her heart thudded in her chest and her breath came in laboured gasps, Diana slowly made her way down the hall toward her son's nursery. Never had she felt a desire to see him, to hold him, and always had she wondered what that said about her as a woman, a mother.

However, such thoughts had always been more disturbing than beneficial, and so Diana had refrained from entertaining them too often. After all, they had served no purpose.

Tonight, however, everything seemed different.

For a reason she could not name, her son's wails drew her near. Opening the door, a distant part of her mind wondered where his nurse was, but it was quickly silenced by a new sense of awe as she spotted her little son, standing in his crib, his cheeks stained with tears and his tiny hands reaching for her.

Swallowing to dislodge the lump in her throat, Diana stared at the small child. What was she to do?

Usually when he started fussing, the nurse would take care of him. But how? What did one do to soothe a crying child? With no younger siblings or cousins, Diana was at a loss. Never had she considered herself a maternal person, and considering the circumstances under which her son had been born, she never thought that that would ever change.

Then why did his tear-streaked face as it glistened in the soft light of the moon cause her such discomfort?

Taking a step into the dark room, Diana drew in a deep breath, her mind racing, still unclear as to what to do.

Sobs escaped her son's lips, but the wails had stopped as he watched her, his little fingers stretched as he stood on his tiptoes, reaching for her.

Why did he want her? Diana wondered. Never had she been a mother to him. Why would her presence comfort him?

You are his mother.

Again, Lord Stanhope's voice echoed in her ears, and for a reason Diana could not name, she believed him, believed that—despite all the evidence to the contrary—there might still be a connection between her and her son. If only she could find a way to…

Coming to stand in front of the crib, Diana lifted her arm and carefully—and a bit awkwardly—patted her son's head. "Hush, hush," she whispered. "Go back to sleep."

However, her son had another plan.

The moment her hand came within reach, his own reached up and closed around it, holding on tight as though for dear life.

Stunned, Diana tried to pull back, but her son held on, pulling himself toward her, his left foot already lifted off the mattress.

Afraid he might fall, Diana suddenly acted on instinct.

Stepping forward, she bent down and scooped him into her arms, feeling his little hands curl into the fabric of her sleeves as his tiny head came to rest on her shoulder. Then a loud yawn reached her ear, and she could feel his soft breath against her neck before he snuggled closer.

As her son fell back asleep, feeling safe and content, Diana stood stock-still in the middle of the room, staring at the far wall, overwhelmed and unable to process the myriad of emotions that suddenly flooded her heart.

How had this happened? How had she gotten here? And what was she to do now?

Feeling his tiny weight resting in her arms, Diana noticed the gentle sway that had come to her movements as she carefully walked around the room. He was soft and warm in her arms, and a sudden desire to protect him washed over her. How could she ever have seen him as an extension of her husband?

Coming to stand in front of the small mirror on the side wall, Diana glanced down at his sleeping face and delighted at the gentle smile that came to him as he dreamed. In answer, the corners of her own mouth strode upward, and Diana's gaze shifted from her son to the image of the two of them together.

In that moment, she noticed that she was crying.

Large tears ran down her cheeks and dropped onto her dress as well as her son's nightshirt. And yet, the image she saw was incredibly peaceful, and Diana wondered how she could have ignored him for that long. Had she truly never longed for him? Or had she never allowed herself to feel that longing out of fear?

What if she had tried to love her son only to discover that she couldn't? That thought had always been in the back of her head, urging her to stay away, whispering that it would be better for her not to know.

Only now he was here sleeping peacefully in her arms, and although her hands were trembling and her legs felt as though they were made of pudding, Diana felt something stir deep inside her that was nott fear.

It felt warm and comfortable, and yet, she was afraid to trust it for love which was inevitably lost, was it not?

Could she risk her heart yet again? What if she simply could not be the mother her son needed and he would come to resent her? Would she be able to survive being rejected by her own child? Would it not be better for them to maintain a safe distance?

As though in answer, her son's little hands curled more tightly into the fabric of her sleeves as he snuggled closer, his little nose resting against the side of her neck.

At that moment the door opened and the nurse walked in, her eyes widening as she saw Diana. "Mrs. Reignold," she exclaimed a bit too loudly.

Instantly, Benedict stirred, a small noise of complaint leaving his lips.

"Hush, hush, little man," Diana whispered in his ear, gently rubbing one hand over his back. "Sleep."

When he had quieted down again, the nurse stepped forward. "Do you want me to take him?"

As though in reflex, Diana's hands tightened on her child. However, her mind reasoned that she did not even know how to take care of him. After all, she could not spend the whole night in the nursery holding him in her arms, could she? No, of course not. What a ridiculous thought!

"Yes," Diana finally said, feeling her muscles tense in objection when she handed her son to his nurse. Her arms felt suddenly empty, and a shiver ran over her at the absence of his warm, little body. Somehow, it was as though he belonged in her arms.

"Good night, Mrs. Reignold," the nurse whispered, and reluctantly, Diana turned to the door, wondering about the strange events of that night. Nothing had gone as planned, and yet, Diana had no regrets.

On the contrary, new possibilities seemed to be waiting for her around each corner.

Sitting down for breakfast with his mother and sister by his side, Arthur was still contemplating the events of the previous night. As promised, he had not breathed a word of Mrs. Reignold's appearance at the theatre to anyone, especially not to his mother, who would likely have spread it to the rest of the ton in less than a day.

And yet, Arthur felt the inexplicable desire to know more about the contradictory woman he had met the night before. Although he had spent all night convincing himself that her well-being did not concern him, the early morning sun had found him still remembering her soft kiss. Despite her frank speech and scandalous behaviour she openly portrayed, Arthur did not believe that she was the kind of woman who went around, kissing strangers.

Then why had she kissed him?

"Arthur!"

His mother's sharp voice cut into his thoughts, and his head snapped up. "I apologise," he stammered, clearing his throat. "What did you say?"

A frown on her face, his mother looked at him, her eyes watchful. "You seem distracted today, my son. Is something on your mind?"

"Nothing important," Arthur lied, almost cringing at the breach of his own principles. After all, he could count on two hands how often he had been dishonest with his family. "I'm merely thinking about Mr. Hill's last visit."

"The steward?" his mother asked. "Is something the matter?"

"Nothing that would concern you, Mother."

"Very well." Taking a sip from her teacup, his mother turned her attention back to the breakfast on her plate. However, Arthur could tell from the slight tension in her shoulders that she was not convinced.

Apparently, he was not a good liar.

Arthur chuckled silently, wondering if he ought to consider that a compliment or not.

"Lady Oxbridge told me last night," his mother began, dropping another lump into her tea, "that she saw Mrs. Reignold in Hyde Park that very morning."

Arthur's head snapped up once more, his ears eagerly awaiting the next bit of information.

"Once again, she was in Lady Norwood's company," his mother continued, glancing at her daughter as though trying to determine if Eleanor possessed a deeper knowledge of the woman's whereabouts, "and once again, she had accentuated her gown with…accessories." Her nose crinkled at the last word as though she smelled something rotten. "Unbelievable! Apparently, she is determined to continue her outrageous behaviour. Poor Mr. Reignold. After he saved her from ruination, she treats his memory with such disrespect."

Arthur gritted his teeth, feeling the sudden and rather inexplicable need to defend Mrs. Reignold. However, that would only draw his mother's suspicion, and so he held his tongue on the matter.

"Eleanor," his mother said, turning sharp eyes on her daughter, "I want to take this opportunity to remind you to keep your distance from that woman."

"I barely know her, Mother," Eleanor objected. Her voice, however, held no strength. "I only spoke to her once, but I have to say she was very kind." Her eyes dropped to her plate, and Arthur thought to see a similar sadness to the one he had seen in Mrs. Reignold's eyes. Had his sister noticed a certain kinship to her as well?

"That is of no importance, Eleanor," Lady Stanhope protested. "I insist that you keep your distance lest an association to that woman ruin your marriage prospects."

An even darker cloud descended upon Eleanor's face. "Yes, Mother."

After breakfast, Lady Stanhope strode from the room, calling for her carriage. However, Eleanor stayed behind, waiting until her mother was lost from sight before she approached her brother. Wringing her hands, she looked up at him, the expression on her face strained.

"Is something wrong?" Arthur asked, finding himself concerned for his sister's well-being. "Are you unwell?"

A sarcastic snort escaped his sister before she nodded her head. "I'm fine," she insisted; however, the look on her face spoke to the contrary. "I only meant to ask you…"

"Yes?" Arthur prompted, wondering why his sister would barely meet his eyes. "Why are you so nervous?"

Closing her eyes, Eleanor took a deep breath, then met his gaze. "I meant to ask you about Mr. Waltham."

"I see," Arthur mumbled, finally understanding and wondering why he had not seen this sooner. "And what would you like to know?"

Eleanor swallowed, "What did you talk about at the theatre? Did he say anything?"

"About what?" Arthur teased, carefully trying to gauge how deep his sister's feelings were for the man their mother spoke about so harshly.

As her eyes narrowed, Eleanor fixed him with an impatient stare, her hands coming to rest on her sides. "Me, of course." She took a deep breath. "I would ask you not to tease me so. Believe me, it is most hurtful."

Placing a gentle hand on his sister's shoulder, Arthur said, "I'm sorry. I didn't mean to hurt you. I merely wanted to see how much he means to you."

Dropping her gaze, Eleanor sighed. "He's my other half," she whispered much to Arthur's surprise. Because of their age difference, Arthur still saw her as the little sister he had doted upon. It was difficult for him to see her as a grown woman.

"He said that it was his intention to marry you," Arthur said, finding the breath catch in his throat at the sight of his sister's happiness. A deep smile came to her face and her cheeks flushed red as she stared at him with huge eyes. Strangely enough, in that moment, she seemed more like the little sister he had known than ever before.

"Truly?" she asked almost breathless.

Arthur frowned. "Has he never said anything like that to you?"

Eleanor shook her head, a hint of doubt coming to her eyes. "I sometimes wondered why, but I was afraid he didn't…"

"Care about you the way you care about him?" Arthur prompted, feeling slightly uncomfortable about the emotional depth of their conversation. Matters of love were not his strong suit as he usually found them confusing and far from rational.

Eleanor nodded, a question burning in her eyes.

Arthur sighed, yielding at the sight of her unease, "He said he would even marry you without your family's consent." Eleanor sucked in a sharp breath, and Arthur wondered if it was truly wise telling her this. "However, he knows that you would never agree, and he did not want to put you in a position where you would have to choose between him and your family."

A large tear rolled down Eleanor's cheek before she turned away, trying to hide the evidence of her emotional upheaval. "Thank you," she whispered after a while, silent sobs echoing to Arthur's ears. "Thank you for telling me. I've always wondered. Now, I know." She nodded and strode for the door. "At least, I know."

Then Arthur was alone, and the many emotions that suddenly assaulted his heart felt like a burden he had never known before. Life had been far easier without this marriage business!

8

A DESPERATE ATTEMPT AT HAPPINESS

About a fortnight after Diana had returned from the theatre and gone into the nursery to comfort her son, she still did not know what to do. More than once—actually whenever she laid eyes on her little boy these days—she felt a strange yearning to wrap her arms around him and feel the warmth of his little body hugging hers. And yet, something stopped her.

Standing in the downstairs parlour, Diana spent many hours staring out the window at the busy street below, wondering what she ought to do. Torn between Lord Stanhope's advice as well as her own desire to change her life, Diana knew very well that she had not the slightest idea what it was she truly wanted.

Yes, she wanted to be happy, to feel something, to feel alive, and here and there, she had experienced moments that had made her skin tingle and placed a deep, heart-felt smile on her face.

And yet, these moments had been fleeting. They had vanished as quickly as they had seized her, and she did not know how to bring them about…even though she wished for nothing else more desperately.

Despite Lord Stanhope's counsel, Diana still went out wearing colourful accessories. However, she refrained from exchanging her black gown for a more scandalous variation. Strangely enough, there was a part of her that could not bear the thought of disappointing him.

Except for Rose, he had been the only one in a long time who had spoken to her without distaste, without condescension. He had seemed truly concerned for her, trying to understand why she would desire to provoke a scandal.

If only Diana could explain it beyond the almost desperate urge to rebel against those who had never even given her a chance when she had tried her best to act as expected. Deep down, Diana knew that she was acting out of spite. She wanted to show the whole world that no matter what, she would not bow her head and simply accept their rejection.

No, she did not need their approval. She would find her place without it.

And still, Diana did not feel better. Her life did not truly change. She was still trapped in the same old life she had hated from the first day.

"Maybe I need to try harder," she mumbled to herself, wondering what would have happened if she had not run into Lord Stanhope that night at the theatre. What if she had made it to her cousin's box? What if the ton had seen her out of mourning barely two months after her husband's passing?

Would something have changed? Would she have felt liberated somehow?

Diana sighed, remembering the night at the theatre. At first, she had not seen the concern in Lord Stanhope's eyes. All she had been aware of had been his censure of her behaviour. However, then he had risked his own reputation to protect hers.

The day after the performance Rose had called on her, and Diana had taken that opportunity to enquire after Lord Stanhope, mentioning that she had met the man's sister at a ball not too long ago.

And although Rose did not know Lord Stanhope personally, she had shared what little she did know about him.

Now, Diana knew that the man who had acted so gallantly had in fact been London's most notorious stickler for etiquette. Still she could not believe it! In retrospect, she would have expected him to leave the moment she had shown up unchaperoned. She would have expected him to be appalled by her lack of decorum.

Only he had not been.

Instead, he had been kind.

And in return, she had kissed him!

A deep smile came to Diana's face. Yes, he had made her feel. The moment he had pulled her behind the column, her heart had thudded in her chest in a way she had not expected it ever would again. If she were to meet him again, would his presence have the same effect on her?

For two days, Diana mulled over what to do. Yes, she wanted to feel, and although she did not dare risk opening her heart to her son, she could not help but yearn for the feeling Lord Stanhope had evoked in her. After all, it was a mere flirtation. Nothing to endanger her heart, for it had already learnt its lesson long ago.

And so, with her mind firmly made up, Diana awaited her cousin's carriage two nights later, after having spent the entire afternoon persuading her to be allowed to attend Lord Timbell's ball alongside Rose and her husband.

Strangely enough, the presence of Lord Norwood did not affect her as it usually did when she climbed into their carriage that night, her thoughts focused on the ball and the question whether Lord Stanhope would attend.

"Are you certain this is a good idea?" Rose asked, her forehead in a frown as her gaze swept over Diana's midnight blue gown.

"I cannot attend a ball wearing black, now can I?" Diana retorted, still exhausted from their disagreement that afternoon. "What choice did I have?"

Apparently, Rose knew when a battle was lost, and so she leaned back in her seat, exchanged a knowing look with her husband and said not another word on the matter.

When they finally reached Lord Timbell's townhouse, Diana had to admit that she felt sick to the stomach. Following her cousin out of the carriage, Diana took a deep breath, steeling herself for the hateful stares and appalled whispers that awaited her inside, and for a moment, she could not recall why she was even here.

Surely, she was mad to subject herself to such censure!

Upon entering, Diana forced a sweet smile on her face, which barely faltered as Lord and Lady Tinwell's jaws dropped open when they saw her. "You have a lovely home," she said in greeting, pushing her shoulders back and raising her chin to meet their eyes unflinchingly.

In that moment, Diana could not help but be proud of herself.

The rest of the night continued as expected. Wherever Diana went, whispers and stares followed her. While some guests at least attempted to hide their interest in London's latest scandal, others made no effort to appear unobtrusive.

However, Diana could not have cared less. With each moment that her eyes failed to detect Lord Stanhope's presence, her heart sank.

"Where is he?" she mumbled venturing through the many rooms, eyeing her cousin with a familiar touch of envy as her husband twirled her across the dance floor.

"Mrs. Reignold?"

Turning around, Diana felt her heart thudding in her chest as her eyes fell on Lady Eleanor. Hearing her name called, Diana thought she had strayed into a dream as the consensus of the assembled guests was to not interact with her at all.

Whisper behind her back: yes.

Speak to her directly: no.

"Lady Eleanor," Diana beamed, trying to glance behind the young woman in the hopes of spotting her brother. "How lovely to see you."

"Are you enjoying yourself?" Lady Eleanor asked, a twinkle in her eyes as they shifted down and came to rest on Diana's midnight blue dress.

For a moment, Diana tensed, but then she noticed the touch of envy in Lady Eleanor's eyes, and her heart warmed to the young woman. From what she knew, Lady Eleanor had every reason to feel disappointed with her lot in life as well.

Diana drew in a deep breath and met Lady Eleanor's gaze openly. "I came here in the hopes of enjoying myself, yes," she spoke freely, sensing that the young woman did not and would not fault her for it. Why was it that only the two Stanhope siblings seemed to have any compassion these days?

"I admit I am awed by your courage," the young woman said unexpectedly as she glanced at the many intruding glances around them. "I often wish I were more daring."

Diana smiled. "But you are. After all, you're speaking to me." Eleanor chuckled. "Apparently, people are of one mind not to address me tonight. I am glad you have a mind of your own and are not afraid to use it."

"Thank you." Sighing, Lady Eleanor held her gaze, and Diana wondered if there was any chance of befriending the young woman. After all, it would be wonderful to have someone like Lady Eleanor with whom she could spend her time.

However, the moment that thought entered Diana's mind, an elderly matron appeared behind Lady Eleanor's shoulder, her eyes narrowed and a rather familiar frown of disapproval on her face. "My dear," the woman stated in a cold voice, her gaze settling on Lady Eleanor, who seemed to deflate at her mere presence, "Lord Ebbington is asking for you."

With a last apologetic look, Lady Eleanor followed the older woman—whom Diana presumed to be her mother, Lady Stanhope—to the other side of the ballroom. From what Diana could see there was no Lord Ebbington there, eagerly awaiting the pleasure of Lady Eleanor's company.

The only one who stood there waiting for them was Lord Stanhope.

At the sight of him, Diana's heart leapt into her throat, and for a moment, she thought she would faint as her pulse began to hammer in her veins. Smiling at him, she tried to catch his gaze, but although he occasionally looked in her direction, his eyes never locked with hers.

Was he avoiding her?

Instantly, Diana's spirits crashed to the ground, the excited tingle that had danced over her skin all night turning into cold shivers that raised goose bumps up and down her arms. Swallowing, she stepped back until her back came to rest against a wall, her legs barely able to support herself.

How foolish she had been! Diana cursed herself. Thinking him different from everyone else! Apparently, her heart had not learnt its lesson after all, for she had once more rushed after a man who did not care about her, making a fool of herself.

Maybe she was destined not to be loved, Diana thought. Maybe it was her punishment for her reckless behaviour. Could she truly not redeem herself? Was one error of judgement enough to ruin an entire life? Was there no way back?

Diana sighed, the muscles in her jaw tightening as determination once more settled over her. Well, if that was indeed the case, then nothing she did truly mattered. Her life, her reputation was forfeit. All she could do now was make the best of an awful situation.

If not Lord Stanhope, then maybe she could find someone else who would make her forget the life she so desperately tried to escape…at least for a few moments.

Glancing around the ballroom, Diana smiled as her eyes came to rest on Lord Oakridge, a known rake without morals or conscience.

Perfect!

The moment he caught sight of her, Arthur froze. What was she doing here? And in that dress? Had she not heard a word he had said to her the other night at the theatre?

Dragging his gaze away before his mother would notice, Arthur did his utmost to ignore her until it was in fact Lady Stanhope who became aware of her daughter's intimate conversation with a woman she deemed undeserving of their mere presence.

"Unbelievable!" she huffed and immediately set off to save her daughter—or rather her reputation—from Mrs. Reignold's toxic influence.

Arthur sighed as he saw his sister's smile vanish the moment their mother interrupted them, and he felt guilty for not interfering on Eleanor's behalf…if only he knew how. Short of defying her mother and marrying Mr. Waltham without familial consent, there was no possible way for Eleanor to be with the man she considered her other half. Had Mrs. Reignold's company truly presented a temporary distraction? Was she a potential friend Eleanor would be able to confide in?

As his mother and sister returned to his side, Arthur once more averted his gaze, pretending he had not even noticed Mrs. Reignold's presence…and it made him feel cowardly as he never had before.

Out of the corner of his eye, he noticed her beautiful face light up as she caught sight of him, and he drew in a sharp breath, feeling the sudden urge to approach her, to gaze into her eyes and ask why she had come tonight. Had it been for him? Had she truly desired to see him? That could not possibly be.

Reminding himself that any connection between them was impossible, Arthur forced himself not to acknowledge her, but instead stared right through her as though she was not even there.

Instantly, he felt even smaller.

Turning back to his family, Arthur stepped forward as his mother lectured Eleanor on her misstep. "I do believe Eleanor was merely being kind to her," he interfered. "After all, all people do is whisper behind her back. She must feel rather lonely."

Lifting her head to stare at him, his mother shook her head, her eyes narrowed in confusion. "Are you suggesting that society ought to welcome a woman who displays not even the smallest bit of decency and manners?"

Arthur drew in a careful breath as his muscles tensed. "I merely meant to point out that everyone condemns her without knowing her reasons."

"It does not matter what her reasons are," his mother huffed. "There is no excuse for such an open portrayal of impropriety."

Arthur swallowed, and his heart sank as he realised he could not rationally refute his mother's argument. Stepping back, he looked at his sister apologetically, for the first time in his life feeling utterly incapable of resolving a situation to his liking.

The remainder of the night, Arthur spent almost rooted to the spot, only moving to keep his eyes firmly fixed on Mrs. Reignold. Every once in a while, he would curse himself, berate himself for his inability to simply enjoy the evening and ignore her latest escapade.

But he could not.

As though they were two magnets drawn to one another, he followed her, watched her, and the pulse in his neck became more erratic with each minute that passed.

At first, she appeared somewhat dejected, and Arthur wondered if it had something to do with the way he had looked through her, not seen her. However, she had quickly recovered—too quickly for Arthur's liking—and had soon—to his great dismay—asked Lord Oakridge to dance. Although the man had seemed somewhat surprised, he had accepted and led Mrs. Reignold onto the dance floor.

After spending some time chatting after procuring themselves a drink from the refreshment table, they had once again stood up together. This time for a waltz!

Gritting his teeth, Arthur watched as she smiled up at Lord Oakridge, wondering why she would insist on ruining her reputation further. After all, there was no rational reason for her actions, and yet, a part of him thought she might be acting out of spite. Was that it?

Arthur shook his head. No matter what had happened, he could not help but believe that her motivations spoke of a deeper emotion than mere spitefulness. That night at the theatre, she had seemed truly disheartened, disappointed by the world and on the brink of abandoning hope. He had feared for her then.

He feared for her now.

When the dance ended, Mrs. Reignold and Lord Oakridge slipped through the crowd toward the back of the townhouse, just when Lord Timbell stood up to address his guests, drawing their attention.

Retreating to the back, Arthur weaved his way past the throng of guests as they listened with almost rapt attention. Lord Timbell truly did his reputation justice as the most entertaining man in London!

Spotting Mrs. Reignold and Lord Oakridge by the terrace doors, Arthur quickened his steps, his heart pounding in his chest as he saw the doors close behind them. What was she doing? Was she intent on having an affair? And with Lord Oakridge no less? Or was she not aware of his reputation? If not, then she would be soon…unless Arthur could reach her in time! After all, was it not the responsibility of the strong to protect the weak? Was it not his duty to ensure her safety?

Although his firm belief in right and wrong told him that his argument was sound, he still knew that Mrs. Reignold's affairs were none of his business. After all, she was a grown woman, capable of making her own decisions. Had she not already ignored his advice? Did that not mean that she had made her choice?

Nevertheless, Arthur found himself crossing the terrace and hastening down the few steps into the gardens as they lay before him, dark and threatening. Hesitating, he waited until his eyes had grown accustomed to the lack of light before he strode down the path. Mumbled voices drifted to his ears then, and he took a sharp turn to the right, like a bloodhound following a scent.

The moment he saw them, standing under the large maple tree, Lord Oakridge's hand cupping Mrs. Reignold's cheek, Arthur almost toppled over. It felt like a blow to his stomach, knocking the air from his lungs.

Fighting to stay upright, he strode toward them, a part of him wondering what on earth he was doing! For quite obviously, both parties wanted to be there, had chosen to be there freely. Who was he to interrupt?

And yet, he did. Rational reasons be damned!

"Get your hands off her, Oakridge," he growled, now only a few steps away. "This is not how you treat a young widow."

At the sound of his voice, their heads snapped sideways, eyes wide, startled. However, neither showed the proper amount of shock he would have expected considering the nature of their meeting and the severity of the consequences should it become public knowledge. What was the world coming to? He could not help but wonder.

"Stanhope?" Lord Oakridge asked, his brows rising in question as he looked from Arthur back to Mrs. Reignold.

"What are you doing here?" the lady in question asked, the look in her eyes strangely contradicting. For although she appeared to be annoyed with his appearance, there was something in the way she looked at him, the way the corners of her mouth twitched as though wishing to be allowed to smile, that made him think—hope—that she was glad to see him.

Arthur drew in a deep breath as he came to stand before them, relieved to see that Lord Oakridge had already taken a step back, his hands no longer touching Mrs. Reignold. "I came because it is quite obvious that you are in no state of mind to make decisions tonight that affect the rest of your life."

At the harsh tone in his voice, her eyes narrowed and her lips pressed into a thin line. Then her mouth opened in protest.

However, before she could speak, Lord Oakridge interfered. "Since it is obvious that I'm not needed here," he said, a touch of humour and calculation in his voice as he glanced from Mrs. Reignold to Arthur, "I shall take my leave."

Arthur merely nodded, his eyes fixed on the woman before him, who seemed to be ready to tear his head off. Had he truly expected her to be grateful? After all, she quite obviously did not care for her reputation; why would she appreciate that he was trying to save what was left of it?

With a last chuckle, Lord Oakridge left, walking back the path they had come, whistling a merry tune as though it had been a truly entertaining spectacle.

Holding out his hand, Arthur glanced around, aware of the precariousness of their situation. How was he going to return her to the ballroom without anyone noticing?

"How dare you?" Mrs. Reignold snarled, disgust on her face as she glared at him, ignoring the hand he offered her. "How dare you interfere? This is none of your concern!"

Inhaling deeply, Arthur dropped his hand.

9

A TEMPTING DARE

Forcing her hands to stop trembling, Diana placed them on her hips, her eyes narrowed as she stared at the man who had ignored her all evening, only to interfere in the very moment she thought she might feel something again.

Well, now she did.

Only it was not excitement and passion.

No, right then in that moment, Diana was furious.

"How dare you ruin everything?" she demanded, the muscles in her jaw clenching as she did her best to hold her emotions at bay.

At her words, Lord Stanhope's jaw dropped open and his eyes narrowed. "I ruined everything?" he spoke, his voice dangerously calm. "Do you even hear yourself? What were you doing out here? And with him? You have no idea what a precarious situation you've put yourself in. Lord Oakridge is…of questionable character. You were fortunate I came by or he might have—"

"Kissed me?" Diana snapped, shaking her head at him. "Has it ever occurred to you that that was my intention in bringing him out here?"

"You?" Lord Stanhope gawked at her as though she had sprouted another head, his voice sounding strangled. "Why on earth would you do such a thing? Have you no regard for your reputation?"

Diana snorted, her head suddenly feeling heavy as she looked at the uncomprehending expression on his face. "You truly don't understand," she mumbled, her hands sliding off her hips as the weariness of life—of her life—returned, weakening her limbs. "My reputation is already lost no matter what I do or how I act. It will not suffer from an association with Lord Oakridge."

"That is not true. You—"

"Why do you even care, my lord?" Diana interrupted as he stepped toward her, the tone in his voice appeasing. "I am nothing to you."

Staring at her, he swallowed, clearly at odds about what to do, about what to say or whether to leave. His gaze, however, remained kind as he studied her face, took in the sorrow that rested in her eyes as well as the tension that held her body rigid.

Watching him watch her, Diana drew in a deep breath, and her eyes narrowed. Had she been wrong? Quite obviously, he *had* noticed her. "You acted as though you didn't see me," she accused, and the pain she had felt earlier that evening claimed her heart anew. "You wouldn't even meet my eyes."

Drawing in a deep breath, he swallowed as his jaw clenched. For a moment, he closed his eyes before they once more sought hers. "I apologise," he said, his voice quiet and serious. "I acted wrongly. I had my reasons. I—"

"You sought to protect your reputation," Diana finished for him, nodding her head in understanding. How could she fault him for that? After all, he still had a reputation that was worth protecting! "Your mother even considered it necessary to interrupt her daughter and me to save her from my harmful influence." Diana's heart sank. Never had she felt so insignificant, so alone and worthless.

"She was wrong to do so."

Lifting her head, Diana watched him. More than once, his words and actions stood at odds with one another. Why was he even here if he was so afraid to harm his reputation? After all, they were still alone in the gardens. If someone were to happen upon them…

"You ought to return inside, my lord."

Again, he stepped forward and offered her his arm.

Diana shook her head. "No, it would be harmful to you and your family if we were seen together."

His eyes narrowed, and a determined set came to his jaw. "I am not leaving you out here by yourself."

Diana scoffed. "Why did you even come? You've already counselled me, and I've disregarded your advice." She held his gaze as he looked at her, her question reflected in his eyes. "Why did you come?"

"I do not know," he whispered, a touch of unease in his eyes as he looked at her. Then he swallowed, and his shoulders drew back, new determination coming to his gaze. "I consider it my duty to look after…"

Enthralled by the way his grey eyes considered hers, Diana felt her heart quicken. "Me?" she asked, and almost imperceptibly, his head bobbed up and down. "And you consider it your duty?" she pressed, her heart now dancing in her chest, sending shivers of excitement through her body. "Or is it rather a desire?"

His eyes narrowed, and the muscles in his jaw clenched.

"My dear Lord Stanhope," Diana exclaimed, a deep smile claiming her features as she stepped toward him, "if I didn't believe it to be impossible, I would think that you were jealous."

At her words, all colour drained from his face. "That is ludicrous," he croaked, his voice far from steady.

"I should think so," Diana agreed, delighting in his telling reaction. Could this be true? Had he followed her because he was jealous? "And yet, all evidence points to the contrary. Do you deny it?"

He drew in a deep breath and for a moment averted his eyes as though unable to bear her inquisitive gaze. "Why did you come out here?" he asked then, his eyes studying her face once more. "Did you truly wish to have an…affair with Lord Oakridge? Would you rather I had not followed you?"

Diana sighed. "Do you not remember what I told you that night at the theatre? I told you that I wanted to enjoy myself, did I not?" He nodded. "And I did enjoy myself that night." Holding his gaze, Diana took another step toward him, noting the slight tension that came to his posture. "I enjoyed our encounter. I enjoyed it very much, more than I ever would have expected. You made me feel," she whispered, reaching out a hand, and gently placed it on his arm.

The muscles in his arm jerked at her touch, and yet, he remained perfectly still.

"I came here tonight," she whispered, looking up into his eyes, "because ever since that night, I've found myself yearning for that feeling." She sighed, revelling in the closeness that echoed between them. "Only then you ignored me, and it…it hurt."

Guilt came to his eyes as his gaze continued to hold hers. "I never meant to hurt you," he whispered as his hand closed over hers, still resting on his arm.

Diana nodded. "I know." She drew in a deep breath, pushing away the sadness that had washed over her at his rejection. "And so, I sought out Lord Oakridge because I thought he would have no scruples–"

"Taking advantage of you?" Lord Stanhope growled, anger and jealously clear in his voice.

Diana smiled, surprised how much his reaction pleased her. "Making me feel," she corrected him. "Something. Anything." Holding his gaze, Diana decided to test how much he truly cared for her. "And I shall continue to do so until I succeed."

Instantly, his eyes narrowed. "What are you saying?"

"You know very well what I'm saying."

"Is this a threat?" he growled, his hand tightening on hers possessively. "Either him or…?"

"You," Diana confirmed, her insides dancing with joy as honest temptation came to his eyes. "It's your choice."

Feeling the warmth of her hand under his own, Arthur could no longer tell up from down or right from wrong. In a few short moments, all he thought he knew to be true and right had lost its meaning. Dimly, he was aware that they stood outside in the gardens at night…without a chaperone, without anything to protect their reputations.

He should never have followed her. He should have alerted someone of her family to the precarious situation she had put herself in. And yet, that had never even occurred to him. Not for a moment had he hesitated to follow her, his rational thought overruled by a deep desire to…

To what? Protect her? Her reputation?

Or was that a lie?

"What do you want?" he asked, the look in her eyes telling him more than words ever could.

"Kiss me," she whispered, biting her lower lip as a deep smile came to her face. "I dare you. Make me feel, and I promise I shall never seek out Lord Oakridge again."

With his lips pressed into a thin line, he stared at her as his hand closed over hers more tightly, unwilling to ever let her go as the mere thought of her and Oakridge turned his stomach upside down. And yet, he couldn't…he couldn't kiss her. It would not be right. After all, she was a widow. A widow technically still in mourning.

"I've heard you're very fond of rules, Lord Stanhope," Mrs. Reignold whispered, her watchful eyes noting every little change in his reaction. "Is that true?"

"Why do you ask?"

"Because I would propose a game," she said, a sense of mischief in her voice that sent a cold shiver down his back. "I admit I have broken many rules in the past weeks whereas I assume that you, my lord, have broken…"

"None," he supplied. "Until now."

A smirk came to her face as delight danced in her eyes. "Then you've already had some practise."

He frowned. "Doing what?"

"Breaking rules." Licking her lips, she leaned closer, and Arthur almost took a step back. Laughing, she shook her head. "Do not worry. I have no intention of ruining your reputation, my lord. I merely propose the following: For every rule you want me to uphold, I want you to break one of my choosing...only in secret, of course."

Frowning, Arthur could not deny that a sense of excitement coursed through his body at her suggestion, and his eyes unwittingly travelled down to her lips. "Why should I agree to this?"

A soft chuckle escaped her. "Because you want to," she whispered, leaning closer. "Have you never been tempted to break a rule?" Pushing herself up onto the tips of her toes, she inched closer, her gaze drifting lower. "Not ever?"

As desire and duty battled within him, Arthur only stood there, unable to move. What ought he to do? If he allowed her to walk away, she would undoubtedly ruin herself. And for a reason he did not dare admit to himself, he could not allow that to happen. However, if he were to kiss her…

"Well, I suppose I should go then," she said rather abruptly, stepping back, and her hand began to slip out of his grasp. "If I hurry, I might still catch up with Lord Oakridge before he–"

Without thought, his hand closed around hers, not allowing her to slip away, and he pulled her into his arms. As he lowered his head to hers, Arthur noticed the delighted smile that played on her face before his lips closed over hers.

After that all rational thought was lost.

10

DIFFERENT PERSPECTIVES

"Lord Stanhope and Lady Eleanor."

The moment the butler announced their arrival, Diana's heart began to dance wildly in her chest and she tried to inhale deeply, hoping to banish the telling signs of her excitement before her guests would enter.

Rising to her feet, Diana smiled. Of course, he had not come alone. After all, he was Lord Stanhope, champion of London's code of conduct.

And yet, the night in the gardens, he had broken a rule. He had broken more than one, and it had been the best night of Diana's life.

"Mrs. Reignold," Lady Eleanor exclaimed, greeting her kindly, her big eyes slightly narrowed as she glanced at her brother. "How kind of you to invite *us*."

"It is my pleasure," Diana assured her, wondering if Lady Eleanor suspected anything or even if her brother had confided in her. However, one glance at the man who had so passionately kissed her only a few nights before told her that he was not the kind of man to profess his feelings openly. "Please do sit. Would you like some tea?"

As her guests sat down on the settee opposite her, Diana rang for tea, all the while watching Lord Stanhope out of the corner of her eye. He sat rather solemnly beside his sister, his gaze only occasionally meeting hers. However, when their eyes did meet, Diana thought to see a touch of embarrassment come to his face as the night in the gardens resurfaced in his memory.

Never had Diana felt this alive, her skin humming with delight and excitement. Not even when she had thought herself in love with Lord Norwood had her heart and soul felt this content. Strange, how quickly things could change, Diana mused.

Forcing herself to focus, Diana exchanged a few pleasantries with Lady Eleanor—about the weather as well as Lord Tinwell's ball—when all she wanted to do was speak to the young woman's brother. He, however, remained uncharacteristically silent, his usually strong opinions silenced by the witness in the room.

As much as Diana enjoyed Lady Eleanor's company, she could not help but wish the young woman were not here. Then at least, she could speak plainly.

"I hear you have a son," Lady Eleanor said, her eyes shifting back and forth between her brother and their hostess after a prolonged stretch of silence. "How old is he?"

Ignoring the slight stab to her heart at the mention of her son, Diana worked to keep the pleasant smile firmly placed on her face. "He's one-year old."

"I do love children," Lady Eleanor exclaimed, her eyes suddenly aglow in such a way that Diana had to smile. "Please tell me if I'm being too forthright, but I would love to meet him." A shy smile on her face, she glanced at her brother before returning her gaze to Diana. "There are no children in our family yet, and so, I've rarely had the opportunity to enjoy their delightful company."

Although the thought of seeing her son made her fidget in her seat, Diana could see how much it meant to Lady Eleanor. "I do not mind at all," she said, once again hoping that the smile still resting on her face did not seem insincere. However, as her gaze shifted to Lord Stanhope, she could see the slight narrowing of his eyes as he watched her intently.

When the nurse brought Benedict down into the drawing room, he tried to hide behind her skirts, glancing cautiously at the strangers present in his home. While Diana drew in a shaky breath at the sight of her son's apprehension, feeling strangely contrite for not being able to put him at ease, Lady Eleanor's face overflowed with joy.

Rising to her feet, she gently approached the boy, speaking to him in soft tones, her voice slightly melodious as she pointed at the little wooden horse he dragged behind him on a string. At first, he looked at her suspiciously, holding his precious toy clutched in his arms. However, before long, he allowed Lady Eleanor to take the horse for a turn about the room, smiling as they walked.

Staring at her son, Diana rose to her feet, turning as they walked, her eyes fixed on his little face. A heavy lump rested in her stomach, and yet, her heart seemed to bounce around her chest with joy. Blinking her eyes, Diana noticed tears clinging to her eyelashes, but she could not say if they were tears of joy or sadness.

"He is a wonderful child." Coming to stand next to her, Lord Stanhope watched his sister for a long moment as she played with Diana's son on the other side of the room. Then he inhaled deeply, and Diana could feel his gaze shifting to her, her own still fixed on the little boy by the far wall. "I cannot say that I see a strong resemblance to his father."

Diana drew in a deep breath before she closed her eyes for a moment and then turned to the man beside her. "Neither do I," she whispered, her gaze shifting back and forth between her son and Lord Stanhope. "However, when I look at him, all I can think of is that he wouldn't be here if I hadn't made that…one mistake." She swallowed, fresh tears welling up in her eyes. "I would never have married his father, and he would never have been born." Turning to Lord Stanhope, she met his eyes, relief washing over her as she read neither judgement nor disapproval in them. "I cannot bring myself not to regret that night, and yet, if it had never happened, he wouldn't be here." Shaking her head, Diana tried to put the chaos that lived in her heart and mind into words. "How can I open my heart to him when at the same time I cannot help but wish he had never been?"

With arms crossed before her chest, her fingernails digging into her arms, Diana looked at Lord Stanhope, wishing with all her heart that he would know what to do, that he knew what to say to set everything right.

Deep down, Diana knew that such a thing did not exist. Nothing could reconcile these two contradicting emotions.

And yet, he gave her hope.

"We all have regrets," he finally said, glancing over her shoulder at his sister and her son. "However, regrets serve no one. They only help us understand what it is we truly want." Stepping into her line of vision, he held her gaze. "You may regret your marriage to Mr. Reignold; yet, I do not believe that you regret the birth of your son. Would you not have wished for a little boy like him?"

Diana drew in a shaky breath, "Yes, but he's also my late husband's son, and–"

"He is *your* son," Lord Stanhope insisted, his eyes determined as they held hers. "He is here now as are you. Nothing will change the past. Only the future is affected by our actions." As though they were alone in the room, he gently placed his hand on her rigid arm, and Diana felt her muscles relax. "Allow yourself to love him. He is a wonderful boy, and if you let yourself, I have no doubt that you will be a wonderful mother for him."

Staring into his eyes, Diana felt an all-consuming warmth engulf her. "Do you truly believe so?" Swallowing, she shook her head. "How would you know? You do not have children, do you?"

For a moment, she held her breath.

"No, I do not," he said, putting her mind at ease. "However, having a sister almost fifteen years my junior has taught me a little about children and the way they conquer your heart no matter how many barriers you put up." A knowing smile played on his lips as he glanced at his sister. "Believe me, you will come to love him. I only hope you will not spend too much time fighting the inevitable before you can be truly happy." A calculating expression came to his eyes as he looked at her. Then a mischievous smile spread over his face. "Now, it is your turn to break a rule," he whispered, and Diana's heart skipped a beat.

"What rule?" she asked almost breathless.

Arthur could feel heat rushing to his cheeks as he held her gaze and saw the memory of the night in the gardens resurface. Even when he and Eleanor had entered and he had met Mrs. Reignold's eyes had he been reminded of their kiss.

"A rule of your own making," he finally said, attempting to push the night in the gardens from his mind…and failing to do so. "As a rule, you spend as little time as possible with your son, am I right?" Mrs. Reignold nodded, and her eyes narrowed in concern. "Then I dare you," he said, speaking the same words she had used that night, "to spend the whole day tomorrow with your son." Her eyes went wide with shock. "Play with him, share your meals, take him outside into the park for a picnic, put him to bed at night."

Arthur held his breath, watching her as a myriad of emotions played over her face. He could see that she was terrified, and yet, almost unbearable temptation rested in her eyes as she glanced over her shoulder and looked at her son. "The whole day?" she whispered, turning back to him. "Why would you ask that of me?"

"Because I believe it would do you good," Arthur replied. "Both of you."

A soft smile came to her lips. "You always seek to protect me, Lord Stanhope. Why is that?"

Arthur swallowed, uncertain how to reply, for although he could not escape the memory of their kiss, he had so far managed to avoid analysing its meaning to a further degree, afraid of what he might find.

Although Arthur found himself at odds, a knowing smile came to her face. "And what do I get in return?"

"In return?"

She chuckled. "If you demand I break a rule, then you need to break one yourself."

Inhaling deeply, Arthur felt his muscles tense. Would she ask for another kiss? He wondered, and his gaze involuntarily drifted lower. Noticing, he quickly snapped his eyes back up, finding a dazzling smile on her face as she looked at him, a touch of mischief in her eyes. "Only when we're alone," she began, and he held his breath, "call me Diana."

Taken aback, Arthur frowned. "But that–"

"I know," she interrupted. "However, I'm afraid I must insist on it."

Seeing the teasing smile on her lips, Arthur could not help but return it. After all, what harm could come from calling her by her first name? "As you wish," he said, then leant forward and whispered, "Diana."

Later that day after he and Eleanor had taken their leave, Arthur found himself seated in the carriage on their way home, his sister's watchful eyes on him. At first, he tried to ignore her, however, with each passing minute, that proved less and less bearable. "Is there something on your mind?" he finally asked, his tone harsher than intended.

In answer, Eleanor laughed, a delighted twinkle in her eyes. "I do believe you lied to me, dear Brother."

"I beg your pardon?"

"As far as I recall," Eleanor began, that teasing smile still clinging to her lips, "you offered to escort me to Mrs. Reignold's because you thought it wrong that mother had forbidden me from seeing her." She shook her head, laughing. "Even then I should have seen it coming. You, who never acts against the rules of propriety, would never have gone against mother's wishes." Smiling, she held his gaze. "We did not call on Mrs. Reignold so that I could visit with her, did we? *You* wanted to see her."

Arthur swallowed, uncertain how to react to his sister's accusation. After all, he had barely admitted to himself why he had felt compelled to see Mrs. Reignold—Diana—that day.

"What are you afraid of?" Eleanor asked unexpectedly.

"I beg your pardon?"

Shaking her head, Eleanor watched him. "You care for her, do you not?"

Arthur swallowed, uncomfortably fidgeting in his seat.

"I do believe she is a wonderful woman," Eleanor said when he remained quiet, "and that you would suit each other."

"You do?" Arthur asked rather surprised. So far, he had done his utmost to ignore the nagging feeling that they in fact did not suit each other. "We are nothing alike."

A big grin came to Eleanor's face. "Exactly."

Arthur frowned. "I'm afraid I don't understand."

"Where you are rational, she is emotional," Eleanor explained. "Where she is impulsive, you are cautious. You complement each other, and together, you can help each other see the world from a different perspective."

Staring at his little sister, Arthur felt awed. "I had no idea you were so wise."

A slight chuckle escaped her before her eyes grew serious. "We have not spoken much in the past few years, have we?" she asked, regret clear in her voice. "Somehow, you've become less of a brother and more of a father, who seeks to protect me. When I was little, you were the one I told all my secrets to, but now…" She shook her head. "Something has changed."

Arthur nodded, knowing it was true. "You're right," he mumbled, "and I, too, regret that we've drifted apart." Then he leant forward and grasped her hand. "But that changes now. I do want to be the one you share your secrets with, and I shall try and share mine with you."

Eleanor smiled, gently squeezing his hand. "I would like that very much, big brother." Then she leant toward him and whispered conspiratorially, "Just a little sisterly advice: admit to yourself how you truly feel about Mrs. Reignold before Mother has you engaged to a suitable bride and there is no turning back."

Reminded of his mother's list of potential brides, Arthur stared at his sister, knowing only too well that although she had already honoured her own advice, her own future would likely see her married to a suitable husband and not the man she loved.

Gritting his teeth, Arthur vowed that he would do everything in his power to change his mother's mind and allow his sister her happily-ever-after.

After all, stranger things had already happened.

And to him no less.

11

IN HYDE PARK

Standing in front of the mirror, Diana looked at her own pale face, her eyes slightly widened and her pulse hammering in her neck. "You can do this," she whispered to herself, and yet, a lump of panic settled in her stomach, making her hands tremble. "You can do this!"

Taking a deep breath, Diana turned and left her room, not allowing herself another moment of hesitation, afraid that she would change her mind. Walking down the corridor to the nursery, she concentrated on setting one foot in front of the other, willing them to continue whenever they seemed to be slowing as though of their own accord.

Coming to stand in front of the door, Diana took another deep breath, then strode inside, barely noticing the surprised look on the face of her son's nursemaid. "Mrs. Reignold, is there anything I can do for you?" the woman asked, rising to her feet.

Diana drew in a deep breath, her eyes focused on her son as he sat on the floor, his favourite toy clutched in his tiny hands. The moment he saw her, a dream–like smile lit up his chubby little face, and he reached out a hand to her. "Mama!"

Diana's breath caught in her throat, and she swayed on her feet as that one little word echoed in her mind and heart.

Smiling through a curtain of tears that suddenly streamed down her face, Diana approached her son, gently sinking down onto the floor beside him, her gaze fixed on the delighted smile on his little face. "I'm here," she whispered, reaching out a trembling hand and brushing a blond curl from his forehead. "I'm here."

Releasing his toy horse, Benedict pushed himself onto his feet, gently swaying until Diana reached out a hand to steady him. Instantly, his fingers closed around one of hers, and he set one foot in front of the other, his pale blue eyes fixed on her face as he stumbled toward her.

As he stood before her, his little eyes holding a touch of curiosity, he reached out his other hand, touching it to her cheek, his finger brushing over the wetness her tears had left behind. A hint of a question lay in his eyes, and Diana smiled at him. "I'm happy to be here," she told him, stunned beyond belief when she realised that she spoke the truth.

After dismissing Benedict's nursemaid, Diana spent the morning in the nursery with her son, playing with his little toy horse, building a tower out of wooden blocks and delighting in its destruction or simply crawling around the room in search of things unknown.

His delightful giggles soon echoed in her heart, and although Diana had felt somewhat self-conscious at first, she quickly forgot her concerns at the sight of his joy.

Until he stumbled over his little feet and fell, hitting his nose on the floor.

Painful wails rose from his throat, and Diana froze, her gaze instantly rising to beckon Benedict's nursemaid forward, forgetting for a moment, that she had dismissed the woman for the day.

With her hands shaking, Diana rushed to her son's side and picked him up. His little face was contorted as he screamed in pain, his hands curling into the fabric of her dress as he buried his head in the crook of her arm.

For a moment, panic welled up in Diana's heart, and she cursed herself for sending away the nursemaid. What did one do with a child screaming in pain?

Sitting on the floor, Diana began to rock him in her arms as she thought about who might be able to help her. She did not know much about her staff. Was there anyone who had a child? Anyone who might be able to help her?

"Hush, hush, little Ben," she whispered, holding him closer as she continued to rock him. Looking down at his face, she saw his cheeks were bright red with a few loose strands of his golden hair stuck to them as they were wet from the tears that ran down his face.

With both arms wrapped around her son, Diana leant down toward him and gently blew on his face, hoping to dislodge the stray hairs. One by one they came loose before she even noticed that his cries had ceased and he now rested calmly in her arms, his eyes closed as he inhaled deeply, the ghost of a smile playing on his face.

"Are you all right, little Ben?" she asked, suddenly wondering at the name that had so easily left her lips. Always had she hated the name Benedict, possibly because it had been her husband's middle name, and by giving it to their son, it had always been as though he had claimed the child as his.

Diana shook her head. "You're mine now, little Ben," she whispered, once more looking down at his face as he opened his eyes and peered up at her.

"Mama."

Again, a jolt went through Diana, and for a moment, she closed her eyes, holding her son tightly in her arms and wondering how she ever could have thought that she could not love him.

"Did she say she would be here?" Eleanor asked as they walked through Hyde Park.

With his eyes sweeping his surroundings, Arthur frowned. "Who?"

Eleanor laughed. "I thought you were going to share your secrets with me?" Stopping in her tracks, she turned to him, her gaze holding his as she looked at him with that knowing sparkle in her eyes. "You're looking for her, aren't you?"

Arthur drew in a deep breath, feeling the muscles in his jaw tighten. He knew what he had promised, and yet, it wasn't easy. "She did not," he finally admitted. "However, I suggested that she take her son out for a picnic."

A deep smile came to Eleanor's face as she continued to search his. "And you believe she would take your advice?"

Arthur sighed, knowing that if he judged from experience, Mrs. R…Diana would not be here. However, deep down, he thought that something had changed that day. "I do not know."

"But you are hoping?"

Arthur nodded, his gaze once more searching his surroundings.

"Then let's keep an eye out for them." Striding onward, Eleanor looked back over her shoulder, motioning for him to keep up.

After another hour walking around the green oasis in the middle of London, Arthur felt defeated as though he had tried hard for something and failed. Ready to head home, he was about to turn around when he caught sight of them.

"There they are!" Eleanor exclaimed in that very moment, grabbing his arm and almost dragging him toward the shaded spot near a grove of pine trees a little off the path.

Seated on a blanket, a picnic basket in one corner, its contents strewn about, Diana sat with her son, his head resting in her lap, his little eyes closed as his chest rose and fell with the sweet oblivion of sleep.

As they drew nearer, Diana noticed their approach and lifted her head. The moment she saw them coming, a deep smile came to her face that had Arthur's heart thudding in his chest as though he had just run a marathon.

"Good day, Mrs. Reignold," Eleanor greeted her, and Arthur felt a strange sense of relief at his sister's presence. For a reason, he could not name, the growing intimacy between him and Mrs. R…Diana terrified him.

A calculated gleam came to Diana's eyes as she gazed at them with a mixture of humour and curiosity. "Have you come to see if I would keep my word?" she asked, her gaze holding his in such an intimate way as though they were once more alone together.

Barely noticing his sister take one step backwards and then another, Arthur felt a touch of embarrassment heat up his face as he looked at Diana. "I never meant to suggest that you would not keep your word."

"Is that so?" Diana asked, a hint of mischief in her eyes. "Then what brings you here?"

What indeed? Arthur wondered. After all, today was the first Monday of June, and he was supposed to meet with Mr. Hill, Stanhope Grove's steward, as he did every first Monday of every month. And yet, he had cancelled his meeting to stroll through Hyde Park, searching for…

"I wanted to see you," he finally said, surprised at his bold statement.

In answer, her eyes widened, and for a moment, she simply stared at him before the corners of her mouth curled upward. However, this time the smile that played on her lips held no mischief or humour. It spoke of simple joy, and it drew Arthur in as though he had spent his whole life searching for it.

"Would you like to join us?" she asked, her voice gentle, as she pointed to the blanket.

Nodding, Arthur sat down across from her, his gaze shifting to the sleeping child in her arms before he met her eyes once more, a question resting in them.

Diana sighed. "It does feel strange," she admitted, a touch of red coming to her cheeks.

"But you're enjoying it, are you not?"

Her smile grew deeper, and she gently brushed a stray lock from the boy's face. "I am," she said, awe ringing in her voice. "I never thought I could, but I am. I don't understand how this happened."

"You never allowed yourself to be a mother," he said, wondering how he knew, and yet, merely looking at her made him feel as though he knew who she was deep down. "It no longer matters who Benedict's father was. He—"

"Ben," she interrupted, a look of joy and peace coming to her eyes as she glanced down at her sleeping child. "I like Ben."

Arthur nodded. "It is a beautiful name."

"I think so, too."

As though the peace and joy he could read on her face were contagious, Arthur felt his own heart grow lighter. "He will grow up to be a good man," he said, conviction strong in his voice. "He will not look at you as your late husband did. He will respect and honour you, and he will love you."

"I hope so," Diana whispered, tears clinging to her eyelashes as she held his gaze. "With all my heart."

"I am certain of it, Diana."

At the sound of her given name, she drew in a deep breath as though a shiver had just then seized her.

Knowing it to be wrong, and yet, being unable to help himself, Arthur smiled, saying, "Call me Arthur, will you?"

"When we're alone?" she whispered, delight brightening her face until he felt as though the sun were shining through her eyes.

Arthur nodded. "When we're alo—" As the thought registered, his head snapped up and he glanced around. "Where is Eleanor?"

Searching her surroundings, Diana looked up as he jumped to his feet. "Are you worried?"

"I'm not certain," he replied. "It is not like her to leave without saying a word." Then he turned back to Diana, and for a moment, he held her gaze, the reluctance and regret to leave plainly visible in his own. "If you'll excuse me?"

"Certainly."

With one last look back, Arthur turned around and strode toward the path that led around the small grove of pine trees. With each step he took, he wondered what had motivated Eleanor to leave. Had she thought to force him into a position where he had no choice but to propose to Diana?

As that thought struck, Arthur felt his insides warm, and yet, he forced his attention on the more pressing matter at hand. Later, he could contemplate how today had changed things.

Unable to believe that his sister had simply left, Arthur strode deeper into the grove, his eyes trying to see through the dense growing trees, until a spark of light blue caught his attention.

Pushing onward, he soon could make out his sister's sky-blue dress as she stood under the canopy of trees, her face turned away from him as she looked at…Henry Waltham, their hands linked, their heads bent toward one another.

The moment they noticed him coming, they dropped their hands, reluctantly releasing their hold on each other. However, they stood their ground, and after exchanging a whispered word with Eleanor, Mr. Waltham stepped forward. "Lord Stanhope."

"Mr. Waltham," Arthur returned the greeting, his voice holding a note of displeasure as he turned questioning eyes on his sister. "If you would be so kind as to leave us alone."

"Certainly," the man said, however, his eyes held deep sorrow as he glanced at Eleanor one last time, a soft smile playing over his lips. Then he turned and walked away.

"Do not even pretend that this was a chance encounter?" Arthur demanded, trying his best to calm down his rattled nerves. "You sent word to him, didn't you?"

Forcing her gaze from Mr. Waltham's receding back, Eleanor turned sad eyes to her brother. "I would have told you," she whispered. "Nothing happened. We simply…" Shaking her head, she shrugged her shoulders, clearly at a loss for words that would do justice to the longing that lived in her heart.

And yet, Arthur could understand as his own heart urged him to return to the small picnic space on the other side of the grove.

"What if you had been seen?" he asked, unable to ignore the notion of right and wrong that he had lived by not too long ago. "You could have been compromised. We both could have…because you walked away."

Eleanor sighed before a soft smile came to her face. "I don't think I would have minded." Then her gaze met his. "Would you?"

"That is not the point," Arthur rushed to say, clearing his throat as he felt his own heart dance in answer. "I thought you said that you would not marry him against our wishes. Did you change your mind? If so, you need to tell me."

For a moment, Eleanor closed her eyes, her shoulders slumped as though the weight resting on them had become too much to bear. "It was a moment of weakness," she mumbled and once more met his gaze. "I do not wish to hurt you or Mother, but…" She sighed. "I do not know what to do." Then her hands grabbed a hold of his, squeezing them desperately, as he found pleading eyes looking into his. "Please, Brother, tell me what to do."

Exhaling slowly, Arthur shook his head. "I wish I could."

12

TO RISK IT ALL

"Do not run, Ben," Diana called after her son as he stumbled around the nursery on fast, but still shaky legs. "You'll fall and hurt yourself."

As though she had not spoken, her son continued onward, pulling his little horse after him, its wooden wheels spinning faster and faster. "Neigh! Neigh!" he sang, a large smile on his little face as his eyes glowed with excitement.

Watching him, Diana smiled, her heart dancing with joy, and still, a part of her was convinced that she had strayed into a dream. After all the sadness and regret that had dominated her life for so long, she could hardly believe that such happiness could be real, could be true and lasting, and she feared that she would wake up and realise that it had never been.

A knock sounded on the door, and Diana turned to see her late husband's butler standing in its frame. "Lady Norwood is downstairs."

"Thank you, Denton," Diana said, then turned back to her son, calling him over. "Ben, you go ahead and play with your horse. I'll be downstairs, talking to Aunt Rose."

Nodding his little head vigorously, he immediately set off on yet another race around the room, his nursemaid watching him carefully as Diana stepped into the hall and proceeded downstairs.

"How are you?" she asked her cousin, beckoning her to take a seat. "Would you care for some tea?"

"Certainly," Rose replied, her large emerald eyes watching Diana with a sense of surprise.

"Is something wrong?" Diana asked, wondering what had inspired the rather unusual expression on her cousin's face.

Smiling, Rose shook her head. "You seem different," she mumbled as though trying to make sense of something. "Happy."

Diana smiled, then sighed as she realised that—as unlikely as it was—it was true.

"What happened?" Rose shook her head once again, her eyes still as round as plates. "What brought on this change?"

Diana's head swam at the question. "I do not know where to begin," she mumbled and then simply started at the very beginning, the night at the theatre.

With each word she spoke, her cousin's stare grew wider and occasionally even her mouth dropped open in amazement. And yet, honest delight danced in her eyes, and she clasped her hands together happily when Diana spoke of how she had spent the morning playing with her son. "Oh, Diana, I've always wished you would find such happiness."

"I never thought it was possible," Diana admitted, still stunned by the abrupt changes that had come to her life. "I suppose at some point, I simply accepted that my life would never be any different. But then…"

"Then you met Lord Stanhope," Rose finished, shaking her head laughing. "I never would have suspected anything like this when you asked me about him a few weeks ago. Maybe I should have; after all, you've never shown any interest in a man since—"

Clasping a hand over her mouth, Rose stopped, her eyes wide…and apologetic.

"Since your husband?" Diana finished this time. Drawing in a deep breath, she tried to remember how she had felt four years ago before the night that had ruined her life. However, try as she might, everything seemed dull and detached as though it had not been *her* emotions, *her* feelings. "A lot has happened since then," she finally said. "I do believe I have changed." She smiled as another thought occurred to her. "Maybe everything that happened—all the regret and heartache of the past few years—helped me become the person I needed to be to…" Diana sighed, not knowing how to finish the sentence she had started. A part of her was still afraid to voice the hope that lived in her heart, lest it be shattered as it had been before.

"Has he given any indication of his intentions?" Rose asked, seeing the hesitation on Diana's face.

Diana shook her head. "I do believe he feels something for me. However, you yourself know better than anyone that our two lives do not suit."

Leaning forward, Rose grasped her hand. "If he truly cares for you, then circumstances do not matter. It might be difficult, but not impossible."

"Not impossible," Diana mumbled, and a slow smile came to her face. Meeting her cousin's encouraging gaze, Diana nodded. "Tomorrow is Lord Barrett's ball. Would you assist me in attending?"

A frown drew down Rose's brows. "Are you certain that is a good idea? After what happened there four years ago, I would have thought you wouldn't want to—"

"Me, too," Diana whispered, remembering that it had been four years—almost to the day—when her life had taken a turn for the worse at Lord Barrett's ball. "Maybe it is the perfect place to begin again," she finally said, nodding her head vigorously as excitement began to dance through her body. "Will you help me?"

Annoyed with his mother's insistence that they attend Lord Barrett's ball, Arthur found himself standing by his sister's side, discouraging potential suitors as best as he could. While his behaviour earned him a grateful smile from Eleanor, his mother's eyes seemed to be shooting daggers in his direction.

"Pray tell what is it you hope to accomplish tonight?" she hissed after drawing him to the side. "Why would you want to ruin your sister's chances?"

Arthur drew in a deep breath, wondering at what point exactly he had decided to oppose his mother and further his sister's hopes to be united with Henry Waltham. "I do believe this topic needs to be discussed further," he finally said, knowing that Lord Barrett's ball was neither the time nor the place. "I suggest we talk about this later."

Clamping her mouth shut, his mother glared at him through narrowed eyes, a sense of shock resting in them at his sudden and rather strange behaviour. Never had he spoken out against his mother's wishes, but now Arthur realised that that might have been a mistake.

After all, right and wrong could not be separated from one another as easily as black and white. Was it truly wrong of Eleanor to have fallen in love with Henry Waltham? Was it right of his mother to forbid the relationship?

Everyone involved had their own motivations, their own intentions, which—based on his own experience—were rarely meant to inflict harm. However, right and wrong always rested in the eye of the observer.

"If you insist on thwarting Eleanor's prospects," his mother finally said, a calculated gleam in her eyes, "would you at least further your own?" Nodding her head in the direction of the refreshment table, Arthur caught sight of Lady Abigail, Lord Hunston's daughter, who—according to his mother—was currently the most eligible lady in London and, therefore, at the very top of the list of suitable brides she had presented to him.

Arthur sighed, "I have no intention of proposing to Lady Abigail," he stated, surprised by the vehemence in his voice.

His mother's eyes narrowed. "Be that as it may," she grumbled. "The lady still expects you to ask her to dance."

Arthur's gaze narrowed, matching his mother's. "And why would she think so?" he asked, wondering what else his mother had orchestrated behind his back.

"Do not speak to me so disrespectfully," his mother chided, shaking her head as though she did not recognise the son she had reared. "How was I to know that you would change your mind?"

"Change my mind?" Arthur demanded. "At what point exactly did I agree to this?"

"I presented you with your options, and you did not refuse," his mother stated, the look in her eyes daring him to contradict her.

Arthur sighed as a cold shiver went down his spine. "Mother, what did you do?"

Rolling her eyes at him, his mother turned to look at Lady Abigail. "Nothing worth mentioning."

"Mother!"

She sighed as though he were a headstrong child, demanding more biscuits. "I merely indicated to Lord Hunston that you seek to get better acquainted with his daughter tonight. Therefore, she has already saved you a dance."

"My name is on her dance card?" Arthur asked, staring at his mother.

Lady Stanhope nodded. "I suggest you follow through, or our reputation will suffer. It is not the way of a gentleman to thwart a lady."

Gritting his teeth, Arthur found Lady Abigail had turned her gaze in his direction, and a gentle smile came to her face as their eyes met. She was indeed beautiful and had all the graces and good breeding of an earl's daughter. However, as their eyes met, his heart beat on in a steady, rather unaffected rhythm that made him realise that not a single name on his mother's list of suitable brides would be suitable for *him*.

"Fine," Arthur gritted out through clenched teeth. "I will ask her to dance, but that is the extent of it. I ask you to refrain from interfering in my affairs in the future." Striding toward Lady Abigail, Arthur barely noticed the open-mouthed shock on his mother's face as she stared after him.

Taking a deep breath, Diana followed her cousin, who walked on her husband's arm, into the foyer of Lord Barrett's townhouse. Instantly, memories from four years ago rushed to the forefront of her mind, and Diana cringed under the pain that so abruptly assaulted her heart.

Inhaling deeply yet again, she forced a polite smile on her face, greeting their hosts with as much sincerity in her voice as she could manage while they stared at her as though she were risen from her grave only to torment them.

"Are you all right?" Rose whispered to her as they proceeded into the ballroom. "Or would you rather return home?"

A part of Diana wholeheartedly agreed that attending Lord Barrett's ball had been a mistake after all. However, a spark of hope still burnt in her chest, forbidding her from giving into her fears. After all, had she not already lived through her darkest nightmare? Could tonight truly be any worse?

"No," she croaked out, then cleared her throat. "I am fine, and I wish to stay." Smoothing down her dress, Diana glanced down at the midnight blue ball gown she had chosen for tonight's occasion. While she could not—and would not—wear black to a ball, Diana had decided to take a step back from her little rebellion against society, for deep down, she knew that she wanted to live among them as one of them and not as a curiosity to be stared at. And besides, it had been Lord Stanhope's—Arthur's—advice, had it not?

Even though her heart still cringed at the thought of being hurt yet again, Diana could admit to herself that his opinion mattered to her…even more than society's. If she were truly honest, she had chosen the midnight blue ball gown as a compromise to him, hoping that he would understand it as her attempt to be the woman he thought she was.

As they stopped beside the dance floor, Lord Norwood turned to his wife, his eyes glowing with love. "May I ask for this dance, my lady?"

A deep smile came to Rose's features, and Diana could see her desire to accept. However, she turned back and looked at Diana, a question in her eyes…as well as concern.

However, before Rose could open her mouth to speak, Diana shook her head. "Do not worry about me, dear cousin. Go and dance with your husband," she commanded, surprised how unaffected her heart was at the prospect of seeing her cousin in her husband's arms. "Believe me, before long you won't feel like dancing." A teasing smile came to her face as she glanced at Rose's slightly thickened midsection.

"Thank you," Rose whispered, then took her husband's hand and allowed him to lead her onto the dance floor.

For a moment, Diana watched them, and her heart ached. Not because she was jealous and wished herself in her cousin's place, but because she yearned to be looked at with such devotion. Only now the man she wanted to look at her like that was no longer Lord Norwood.

Craning her neck, Diana prayed that he had come tonight. Apart from the symbolic significance of Lord Barrett's ball regarding time and place, Diana simply felt as though she could not wait any longer to learn how he felt about her. Was he merely trying to protect her out of a sense of duty? Or did he truly care for her?

Diana nodded her head. Of course, he cared for her. There had been evidence more than once. And yet, she could not help but wonder if it would be enough. Could a man like him ever truly love a woman like her? Whenever Diana thought about all their many differences, she felt despair encroaching on her heart.

However, she would be forever left wondering if she did not seek him out to receive the answer she needed. Whatever tonight would bring, it would be another turning point in her life.

Only a moment later, Diana realised how right she was as her mouth dropped open and tears filled her eyes, for right there on the dance floor holding a stunningly beautiful lady in his arms was Lord Stanhope.

Blinking her eyes, Diana could not believe what she was seeing. Never had she seen him dance. He was not the type to dance…at least not much. Rose had said so as well. If he danced now, it had to mean something. Perhaps he…

Unable to watch them any longer, Diana pushed through the crowd, stumbling almost blindly toward the terrace doors.

As though she had travelled back in time, she rushed outside, her feet carrying her down the path and into the green labyrinth of Lord Barrett's garden. On and on, she walked as tears streamed down her face until she came upon the small pavilion that had been the sight of her greatest misery.

Stopping in her tracks, Diana moaned as she realised how wrong she had been. This was far worse than it had been four years ago. Then, she had been a young girl, who had fancied herself in love. Now, she was a grown woman, who…

Diana shook her head, then slowly began to climb the few steps into the pavilion, inhaling the night scents around her. Instantly, her heart clenched in her chest, she almost sank down, resting her hands on the rail before her. "I'm such a fool," she whispered into the dark as the tear in her heart slowly opened again. "How could he love me?"

Although Lady Abigail was perfectly polite—her conversational skills impeccable—Arthur found himself yearning for the end of the dance. Somehow it felt wrong to hold her in his arms.

Swallowing, he turned his head, unable to look at her, when something caught his attention.

For a bare second, he thought to have seen a set of familiar blue eyes looking back at him before they had widened in shock and filled with tears.

Had he imagined it?

Craning his neck as he twirled Lady Abigail around the dance floor, Arthur felt his heart begin to race, and fear sent his pulse into a rapid spin.

Then he caught sight of her as she spun around and pushed her way through the crowd, displeased murmurs following her as she rushed for the terrace doors.

"What is she doing?" Arthur mumbled under his breath, trying to see if anyone was following her. Was she meeting someone out in the gardens? Had she still not learnt her lesson?

"Pardon me?" Lady Abigail asked, a puzzled frown on her face as she looked at him, trying to understand his distraction. "Is something wrong?"

Very wrong indeed, Arthur thought. "Not at all, my lady," he replied, sighing in relief when the music finally came to an end. Without another thought, he bowed to her and immediately took his leave, his feet carrying him in the direction of the terrace.

As his pulse thudded in his veins, Arthur hurried down the dark path, his gaze sweeping his surroundings, ears alert. Had someone followed her? He wondered yet again, aware that in the moment when he had turned away to respond to Lady Abigail's question, someone could have slipped out unnoticed by him.

Was it Oakridge? Arthur wondered, his hands clenching at his sides as he strode down the path toward the centre of the green labyrinth.

When the pavilion came into view, Arthur stopped short as his eyes immediately found Diana standing with her back to him, her hands resting on the rail, her head sunken forward as though she could no longer hold herself upright.

Although Arthur's heart softened at the sight of her, he could not soothe the burning anger that had sent him out into the night after her. "What are you doing out here?" he demanded as he climbed the few steps of the pavilion. "Alone and unchaperoned? Have you still not learnt your lesson?"

At the sound of his voice, she flinched, then turned to face him, and he was shocked speechless as he saw her tear-stained face and the misery clouding her lovely eyes.

Holding his gaze, she swallowed and her hands came up to brush the wetness of her cheeks. "I am not yours to teach," she spat, her lips pressed into a hard line as she regarded him with such disappointment that Arthur felt himself cringe.

And yet, he had to know. "Who are you meeting here?"

A slight frown came to her face before she shook her head. "I'm not meeting anyone," she whispered as though the question alone was ludicrous, "and even if I were, it would be none of your concern." Then she turned her back on him. "Leave me alone."

Standing stock-still, Arthur stared at her, feeling the fear that had held his heart in its clutches slowly subside. As it left, he could sense his rational mind reawaken, and he realised that he had overreacted.

There was no one here. Only her, and from the looks of it, she had not come out here to meet anyone. Then why? He wondered.

"I asked you to leave me alone," she spoke into the dark, keeping her back turned on him.

As though by reflex, Arthur took a step backward before he stopped once more, his resolve strengthening. If he left now…

Squaring his shoulders, he raised his chin, determined not to yield. "No."

At his response, she spun around, anger edged into her eyes.

13

A LIFE'S REWARD

"Go!" Diana snapped, her voice harsh as she glared at him. How dare he torture her so?

His gaze remained fixed on hers as the muscles in his jaw clenched. "No," he repeated, determination clearly visible on his face as he took a step toward her.

Diana's eyes narrowed. "Why are you doing this to me?" she asked, feeling the protective wall she had once more begun to erect around her heart begin to crumble. "Why can you not simply leave me alone? Go and dance with…" She shrugged, her lips pressed into a tight line.

For a long moment, he stared back at her, his eyes travelling over her face as though he had suddenly realised something that had eluded him before. Then he drew in a deep breath and took another step toward her. "I was worried about you."

Diana scoffed, "You were worried about me?" she challenged. "Rather about my reputation, is that not true? You can simply not abide that there are people in this world who would risk it all for–" She clamped her mouth shut before she could say anything unwise. "Go!"

Again, his jaw clenched as his eyes hardened with determination. "I will not leave," he finally said, and the indecision she had seen on his face before vanished. Instead, she watched in terror as he came toward her with measured strides, undeterred and unwavering. "Why did you come out here?" he demanded, his eyes holding hers as he came to stand in front of her, a mere arm's length away.

Diana swallowed, wishing he would simply leave her alone. At least, Lord Norwood had been honest about his disregard for her. He had not pretended and then…

Drawing in a shaky breath, she met his gaze. "I came out here to be alone," she said pointedly.

"Why?"

Diana felt her muscles tense as she instinctively retreated from the looming threat before her. If he did not leave soon, her heart would shatter all over again, and she did not think she was strong enough to survive that.

Shaking her head, Diana took a step back, feeling the rail cut into her lower back.

"You saw me dancing with Lady Abigail," he finally said as though his sharp eyes could read her mind.

Instantly, Diana's head snapped up as though he had struck her.

For a long moment, he held her gaze, gauging her reaction, waiting.

After their silence became too painful to bear, she nodded, "I did." Perhaps now that he had his answer, he would leave her alone.

However, he did not.

Instead, his eyes seemed to sharpen as though he was getting closer and closer to unearthing a secret. "It bothered you."

As it was not a question, Diana remained silent, wishing she could simply walk away, but knew that he would never allow her to step past him. What did he want?

A touch of impatience came to his eyes as she failed to answer, and he took a sudden step toward her. "Did it bother you?" he demanded, and Diana shrank back. Never had she seen him so fervent, his gaze so intense as it seemed to burn into hers.

Leaning back, the rail cutting into her lower back painfully, she looked at him defiantly. "It did!" she snapped. "Is that what you wished to hear? Yes, it bothered me. Now, will you please leave me alone?"

A grim smile came to his face. "Why?"

As her head began to spin and her emotions ran rampant, Diana felt as though she was losing her mind. She could no longer tell up from down or right from wrong. All she knew was that she needed him to leave or she would crumble onto the ground and never be able to rise again.

"Why?" he demanded once more as though his life depended on her answer.

Flinching at the snap of his voice, Diana lost her footing as her whole body strove to get away from him.

In the last moment before she would have tumbled over the rail, he shot forward, his hands coming around her waist lightning-quick, pulling her back against him.

Breathing heavily, Diana looked up into his eyes, surprised to see a flicker of fear there as he gazed down at her, his own breathing elevated as well. And yet, his hands still rested on her waist, their warmth in stark contrast to the chill that coursed through Diana's body. "Why?" he whispered once again, only this time his voice was gentle, and his warm breath sent a tantalising shiver down Diana's back as it brushed over her lips.

Swallowing, Diana knew the danger she found herself in as her heart urged her to confide her feelings. However, no sound came out, and she continued to stare at him, trying to read on his face what lived in his heart.

Finally, he sighed. "It bothered me when I saw you with Oakridge," he admitted, his jaw clenched and his voice harsh as he spoke.

"It bothered me to think that you were meeting him again…here…tonight."

Despite her best efforts, joy began to blossom in her heart; Diana felt a careful smile tug at the corners of her mouth. "Why?" she asked, returning his question to him, seeing the same hesitation on his face that she herself had felt only a moment before.

He inhaled deeply through his nose, and the muscles in his body tensed as though he was preparing himself for an attack. His mouth opened…but then closed again, and Diana's hopes sank.

Dropping her gaze, she lifted her arms and urged him to release her.

For a moment, he seemed to comply before he suddenly drew her to him with even greater force than when she had almost gone over the rail. His fiery eyes met hers, held hers, as he opened his mouth and said what she had longed to hear. "Because I love you."

Before Diana could even comprehend what he had just said, before she could revel in the soft feeling that slowly built within her, his lips claimed hers in a passionate kiss.

Holding her in his arms, Arthur wondered how he could ever have lived a day without her and fancied himself a content man. Now, however, he was more than simply content. He felt deliriously happy.

As she returned his kiss, he wrapped his arms more tightly around her, determined to never let her go again.

In answer, her arms snaked up and came around his neck, pulling her closer against him. Her fingers brushed over his neck, sending tingles all over his skin. However, then she suddenly stepped back, pushing him off her, and his heart stopped, dread filling his being.

Smiling up at him, she held his gaze, and his heart slowly calmed. Then she whispered, "I love you, too," and for a moment, he closed his eyes, suddenly aware how desperately he had needed to hear that, "I thought you might want to know."

Delighted with the teasing tone in her voice, Arthur rested his forehead against hers, feeling the strain of the past minutes leave his body.

"What do we do now?" she whispered, a touch of uncertainty and apprehension in her voice.

Lifting his head, Arthur frowned, praying that she would not refuse him. Not when he had finally realised what he wanted and on top of that had found the courage to admit to it. "We get married," he stated simply, unaware that he was holding his breath.

In answer, her eyes bulged and the air rushed from her lungs as though her head had just broken the surface after diving into the ocean. Then she closed her eyes, drawing new air into her body, and a soft smile lifted the corners of her mouth. "Are you serious?" she whispered, searching his face.

He chuckled, unable to help himself. "Have you ever known me not to be?" Her face aglow with happiness, Arthur felt his own heart sing with joy. "Are you truly surprised that I wish to marry you?"

Diana swallowed, and a dark shadow crossed her eyes.

"What is it?" he asked as tension once more gripped his body. "Do you not wish to marry me?"

Instantly, she shook her head. "No, that's not it. I do. Believe me, I do." She drew in a deep breath, needing to fortify herself for expressing what was on her mind. "It's simply that I've been here before." Shaking her head, she snorted as her eyes drifted over their surroundings. "In this very spot four years ago, I had my heart ripped from my chest because a man I thought I loved refused me, and it changed everything. It changed me."

Inhaling deeply, Arthur pulled her closer with one arm as his other hand cupped her face, making her look up at him. "I'm sorry for the pain you had to go through;" he whispered, "however, I am glad that you did."

A frown came to her face.

"For if he had wanted to marry you then, I would have lost my chance," Arthur said, terror filling his heart at the mere thought of it.

"Never in my life have I been more grateful that there are dishonourable men in this world, for if he had done his duty, I could not marry you now…not out of duty, but for love."

"Truly?" Diana whispered, her face flushed, her eyes filled with awe as though he had just descended from the heavens.

Arthur nodded, a large smile on his face. He could not remember ever having smiled as much as he had this night. "The world—my world—would be empty without you." Clearing his throat, he held her gaze, needing her to understand. "Emotions have never come easy to me—I cannot say why—but loving you simply happened." He shrugged, still at a loss, unable to explain even to himself how this had come to pass. "I cannot even remember how or when, but it did." Gently, he brushed his lips over hers, then met her eyes again. "I do love you."

A teasing smile lit up her face. "Does that mean you were jealous?"

"Of course, I was," he growled before his voice softened once more. "As were you."

Taking a deep breath, Diana nodded. "I was." Then she swallowed, and tears formed in the corner of her eyes. "I thought I'd lost you or rather that I'd once again imagined your affection…as I had before." Sniffling, she brushed a tear from her cheek. "Once again, I thought that no one could love me. It has always felt like a cruel joke. As much as I always dreamed of it, it appeared that it would never happen. Not for me."

"I know what you mean." Seeing incomprehension on her face, Arthur sighed. "I've never been in love myself. I've never even felt the slightest inclination to be closer to someone." He shrugged. "I don't know why, but it always made me wonder." A deep smile tugged at the corners of his mouth and he allowed it to spring free. "But not anymore. Now, I know why."

"Why?" Diana asked, hope shining in her beautiful eyes.

"Because I was waiting for you," he whispered.

A moment later, she flung herself into his arms, her blissful sighs music to his ears.

"Will you marry me then?" he asked, realising that she had not yet given him an answer.

Pulling back, she met his eyes and her lips parted. However, then she hesitated, and for a moment, his heart stopped, only to pick up where it left off when he saw a teasing curl come to her lips.

"What is going on in that devilish mind of yours?" he asked, his eyes searching her face.

Biting her lower lip, she grinned, a mischievous sparkle in her gaze. "Oh, I will marry you. However, it just occurred to me that…I am technically still in mourning."

"Technically?" he asked, raising an eyebrow at her.

"Well, you know what I mean," she replied mockingly before her gaze grew serious. "Can you wait a year?"

Arthur swallowed as he realised that the circumstances of their situation had never even occurred to him. Of course, she was still in mourning. If they married now, people would talk. Their reputations would suffer. It would be a scandal.

Everything he had tried his utmost to avoid would come to pass if he were to break this particular rule. And yet, Arthur could not help but smile as he realised that he did not care.

Seeing his reaction, Diana's face broke into a deep smile as well. "Neither can I," she declared. "However, I feel compelled to warn you that…if I were with child, it would be considered yours, your rightful heir."

For a moment ,his eyes narrowed. "Are you?" he asked earnestly.

Holding his gaze, she shook her head. "I simply meant to say that society might believe any child born to us within the first year to be my late husband's. Could you live with the whispers?"

Arthur frowned as his eyes searched her face. "Are you trying to convince me *not* to marry you?"

Diana laughed, "I simply mean to warn you," she said, and the expression on her face grew serious again. "The life I've lived these past few years was far from easy. I don't want you to wake up one day and regret the path you've taken."

Shaking his head, he pulled her closer. "The only regret I'm afraid of ever waking up to is not having married you." Holding her gaze, he nodded, needing her to believe him. "Any child of yours is mine as well. Including Ben. If you're willing to share him."

For a second, she closed her eyes, seemingly savouring the moment before her eyes were on him once more. "What about your mother?" she asked teasingly.

"To hell with my mother," Arthur declared laughing, knowing only too well that she would be yet another obstacle they would have to overcome. However, with Diana by his side, he did not care. "So, will you finally answer me?"

"I thought I already had."

"That was not an answer," he insisted. "That was a warning. I want a clear answer. Yes or no?" Holding his breath, he waited, a part of him still thinking that this could not be true.

Only when she pushed herself up on the tips of her toes, her arms wrapped around his neck, her fingers once more trailing over his skin, sending shivers through his body, and kissed him with all the passion he felt in his own heart did he dare believe that miracles did happen after all.

"Yes!" she declared in a steady voice when she pulled back, looking up at him with eyes that held nothing but promise and hope. "My answer is yes." Then a flash of mischief returned to her gaze. "How soon do you think we could dare to get married?"

Pulling her back into his arms, Arthur kissed her breathless, congratulating himself on finding the one thing he had never known he had wanted, wondering if tomorrow might be too soon.

EPILOGUE

Summer 1820
One Year Later

"Hush, hush, hush," Diana cooed as she gently rocked her newborn daughter in her arms. Bouncing in her step, she slowly moved around the nursery, humming under her breath as her eyes occasionally shifted to her son and her husband.

At almost two-and-a-half, Ben had grown tall, and his face had lost most of the adoring chubbiness that had given his face such a sweet roundness as a baby. Sitting on the floor in the middle of the large room, he slowly lifted his hand, picked up one of the many wooden blocks strewn about the room and carefully moved it to the top of the tall tower in front of him.

"Slowly now," Arthur cautioned, his gaze narrowed as he held his breath watching their son as he worked, his little forehead scrunched up in concentration. "Yes, that's it. Hold it steady."

Smiling, Diana watched them as they sat together on the floor, heads bent toward each other as though they shared secrets with one another she was not privy to.

A lot had happened in the past year, and in rare quiet moments, Diana could still not believe the change her life had taken. Ever since that night at Lord Barrett's ball, regret and misery had been emotions of the past, their absence allowing for the excitement and happiness she now felt whenever she awoke in the morning, remembering the many joys her new family brought her.

Yes, it had not been easy. Arthur's mother had been beside herself with shocked rejection as she had not seen it coming. Never would she have imagined that her virtuous son would propose to a woman who had been at the centre of society's gossip for the past years.

However, Arthur had been adamant in defending their relationship, making Diana's dreams come true. Finally, she had found a man who truly loved her, who not only said so with his eyes when he caught sight of her across the room, but who also would wake up every morning pulling her into his arms and whispering those very words into her ear.

And still, sometimes Diana wondered if she was only imagining her happiness as the past had clearly left its mark on her. Would her heart ever completely recover? Would she always feel this insecure when it came to believing that someone truly loved her?

Gazing down at her sleeping daughter, her little face completely at peace, Diana sighed, sinking into the upholstered armchair in the corner of the room.

Perhaps the remnants of insecurity she felt were not a curse after all, she realised as she once more lifted her gaze and felt her heart dance in her chest at the sight of her family. Perhaps it was the very means that helped her cherish her life and the happiness it brought, that helped her see that she never ought to take it for granted.

After all, she knew only too well that it could be different.

As her daughter continued to sleep peacefully in the crook of her right arm, Diana once more turned to the short list she had laid down on the small table beside her when her daughter had started crying. Reading through the names listed there, Diana opened her mouth to address her husband, but then hesitated as she lifted her gaze and found him beaming at her son.

"Well done, Ben," he exclaimed, patting their son on the shoulder before brushing a hand through his wild curls. "I'm proud of you."

His face aglow with accomplishment, Ben stared at the tall tower in front of him. For although the top block stood a little crookedly on the one below and the tower had swayed slightly when he had removed his steadying hand, it still stood, tall and proud.

"Wonderful, Darling," Diana praised her son before her eyes shifted to her husband.

Meeting her gaze, Arthur smiled, a sense of blissful joy in his eyes as he smiled at her and their daughter. "Is she asleep?"

Diana nodded, then once more looked at their guest list for the dinner party a fortnight from today. "Lord Harrington and his wife will attend," she mumbled, her eyes shifting over the names. "As well as Mr. and Mrs. Everett."

Her husband nodded. "Yes, I received their confirmation this morning."

"Good. Rose and her husband shall attend as well, now that their daughter finally sleeps through the night. However, she wasn't certain yet if her brother-in-law and his wife would be back from Italy in time. We shall wait and see." Lifting her gaze, Diana looked at her husband, a bit of apprehension in her eyes. "What about your mother?"

A touch of an apologetic smile on his face, Arthur nodded. "She confirmed."

"Willingly?" Diana enquired, a smirk on her face.

Arthur laughed. "A lot has happened since last year," he reminded her with a twinkle in his eyes. "For her as well. We've all changed."

Diana nodded, remembering the previous summer and its rather tumultuous developments. "What about Eleanor and her husband?"

Again, her husband laughed. "You know that she would never miss an opportunity to see the children, especially now that she is expecting as well."

Diana smiled. "She will be a wonderful mother."

"Yes, she will," her husband agreed as he rose from the floor and strode over. Stroking a gentle hand over his daughter's head, he met Diana's eyes and her heart skipped a beat at the unconditional devotion she could see there. "As are you." Leaning down, he placed a gentle kiss on her lips, a promise of more passionate ones to come later that night.

Diana sighed happily, barely remembering that at one time in her life she had believed that she had wasted her heart on the wrong man, convinced that love would never find her again.

But it had.

And she would never take it for granted.

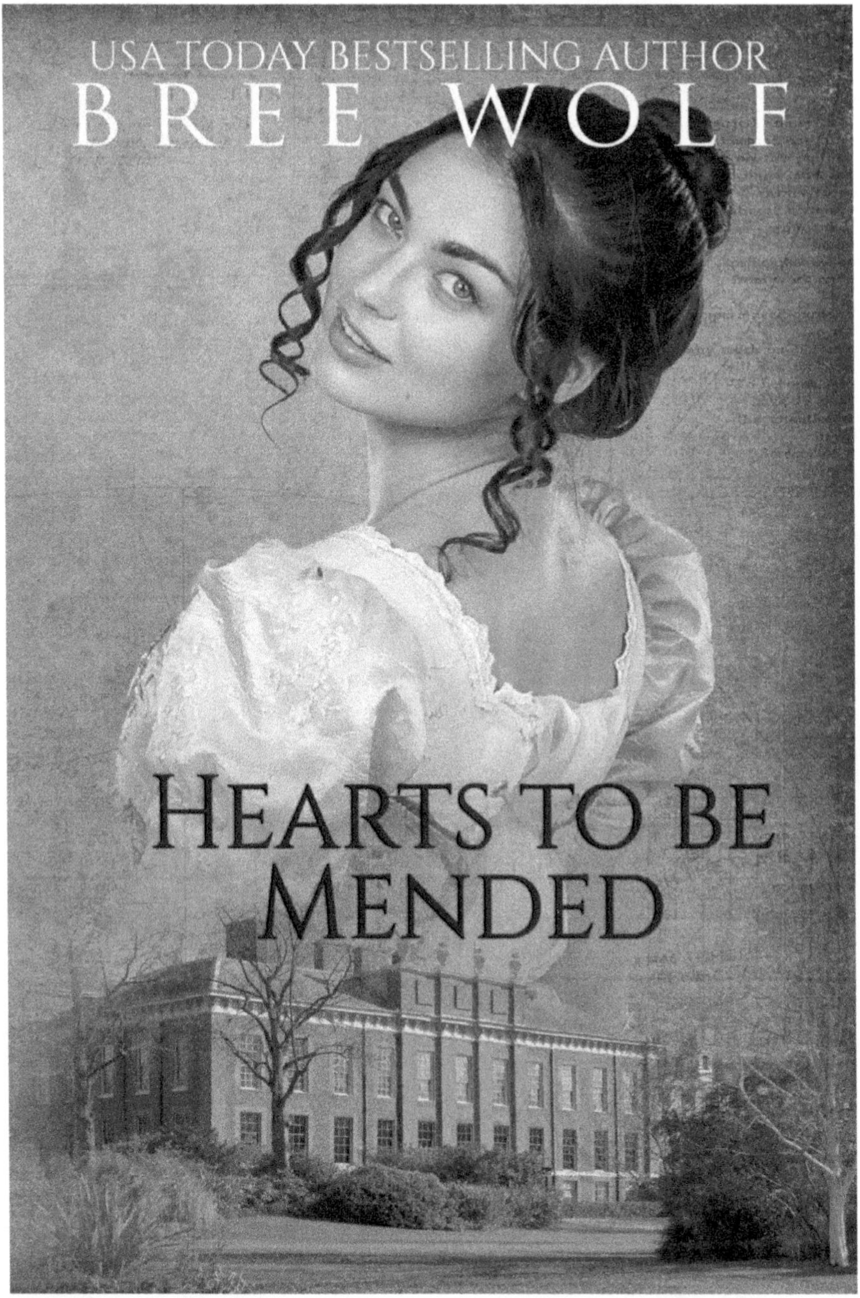
USA TODAY BESTSELLING AUTHOR
BREE WOLF
HEARTS TO BE MENDED

PROLOGUE

London, November 1818

Eight Months Ago

Inhaling deeply, Eleanor felt her mind slowly return from the depths of slumber. Her limbs were heavy as she lay under the warm blanket, the softness of her pillow gently cradling her cheek. Although her eyes had not yet opened, she knew that it was dark around her. Not a single ray of light touched her being, and she vaguely found herself wondering what was happening.

Was she still dreaming? Her languid mind marvelled before the howling wind echoed to her ears and she heard the faint, yet, distinct sounds of a storm not too far off.

Step by step, her senses returned and she regained control over her body. Sighing, Eleanor brushed a hand over her face, seeking to chase away the last remnants of sleep that made her mind heavy.

Then she stopped, wide eyes staring into the darkness above her, and listened.

Someone was breathing nearby.

She was not alone.

Who had come to her room at night? Eleanor wondered as goose bumps rose on her skin and a cold chill crawled down her spine. And without announcing themselves? Was there some kind of emergency?

No, that couldn't be it. Surely, if there was, someone would have woken her.

Taking a deep breath, Eleanor allowed her hand to slide from her face, her eyes immediately falling on the shadowed figure sitting on the side of her bed.

A gasp tore from Eleanor's throat as adrenaline shot through her, and she immediately tried to scoot away.

"Hush, Darling," her mother's voice whispered. "Everything's all right. Go back to sleep."

Blinking, Eleanor stared into the dark. "Mother?" she whispered, shaken to her core, unable to make sense of this new development.

Never had her mother come to her room. Never had her voice sounded so…

Eleanor blinked, trying to see through the dark. Squinting her eyes, she could make out her mother's face, her head almost slumped forward as she sat with her hands folded in her lap.

As the wind pushed the clouds onward, the moon's silvery rays momentarily touched her mother's face, and Eleanor could see that she had been crying as the faint light seemed to set her face aglow, the path her tears had taken glistening in the dark.

Swallowing, Eleanor sat up, uncertain as to what to do.

While Eleanor had always felt closest to her late father, who had been a caring and compassionate man, an easy smile on his face and kindness in his voice, she knew very well that her mother's as well as her brother's cold and distant demeanour did not speak of an unkind soul. They, too, felt emotions deeply, but did not possess the ability to share them with the people around them.

As a young girl, unhindered by society's restrictions, Eleanor had managed to coax her brother, who was almost fifteen years her senior, into showing his affection for her more openly. He had smiled at her, pulled her into his arms and hugged her tightly, his eyes lighting up with delight. Over the years, as they had both grown older, he had come to show more restraint with regard to portraying his emotions. And yet, Eleanor did not doubt that he loved her.

However, their mother was different. Why? Eleanor did not know. While she was not unkind, she seemed cold and distant. Never had Eleanor seen her laugh, truly laugh because her heart had been touched. Neither had she ever seen her cry, not even when her husband had died.

Although her mother had never given any indication, Eleanor knew from her father's open portrayal of affection that theirs had not been a marriage of convenience. And yet, despite the love and loss her mother had to have felt, she had not shed a single tear upon his death, never revealing what lived in her heart.

Eleanor did not know why, but it had made her fearful for her mother.

Seeing her now sitting at her bedside in the middle of the night with tears streaming down her face terrified Eleanor to her core, more so than discovering an intruder in her room would have.

"Mother?" she whispered, slowly reaching out a hand. "Are you all right?"

Clearing her throat, her mother drew in a shaky breath. Then she lifted her head. "Everything is fine." Nodding her head, she hesitantly reached out her own hand and gently grasped Eleanor's. "Go back to sleep."

"What's wrong?" Eleanor asked, torn between fear of what had happened and the desperate desire to see her mother show emotion…any emotion…if they were real…and true…and honest.

"Do not worry yourself," her mother replied, her hand squeezing Eleanor's, as a hard determination came to her voice. "No matter what happens, I shall protect you. You have my word."

Staring at her mother, Eleanor found herself unable to react as Lady Stanhope rose to her feet, then gently brushed a hand over her daughter's cheek and left without another look back.

As her hands began to tremble, Eleanor sank back into her pillows, her wide eyes staring into the distance as her mind tried to make sense of what had happened.

But what *had* in fact happened?

Once again, her mother had not dared to reveal anything at all, leaving everyone around her in the dark. What had brought on this emotional reaction? There had to have been a reason. Could it have had anything to do with Corinne's departure?

After her cousin's parents had been killed in a robbery ten years ago, Corinne had come to live with them and easily found her way into their family, for all intents and purposes a new sister. And yet, Eleanor's mother had shown her the same cold detachment that she showed everyone else. Could Corinne's departure truly have affected her so? Or was there another reason?

Closing her eyes, Eleanor sighed, knowing that her mother would never share with her what had truly happened that night, what had brought on the first tears she had ever shed since Eleanor could remember.

No, her mother would handle this alone as she handled everything else.

1

HOPE

London, July 1819

Eight Months Later

Her brother's wedding was a rather intimate affair as it broke one of society's utmost rules and neither he nor his bride wished to see disapproving faces on their wedding day. The only exception was their mother, Lady Stanhope, whom her brother could hardly have not invited.

However, even alone, their mother's scowl managed to dampen the joyous atmosphere that such an occasion usually conjured. With her arms crossed and her lips pressed into a thin line, she glared at the happy couple exchanging their vows, mumbling under her breath and shaking her head in disapproval. "Unbelievable! The nerve of that woman."

Eleanor sighed. "They seem happy," she whispered, dreading the war that would soon be waged within her brother's household.

"She is a widow!" her mother hissed, turning cold eyes on Eleanor. "Her late husband has been dead not even half a year. Do not tell me you approve of this! Can you not see the scandal they are bringing on themselves? What if she is with child?" Closing her eyes at such a horrendous possibility, Lady Stanhope shook her head. "I never thought he would allow a woman to make such a fool of him. I always thought he had more sense."

Inhaling deeply, Eleanor said, "Love doesn't make sense. It simply is, no matter the circumstances."

Feeling her mother tense beside her, Eleanor kept her gaze fixed on the happy couple, hoping with all her heart that one day she would be equally blessed…and yet, her mother's unyielding gaze instantly crushed the small spark of hope that had still managed to survive despite everything that had happened.

If only, Eleanor thought, knowing her wish to be futile.

After the ceremony, they all returned to the townhouse for the wedding breakfast where they were met by a rather small number of close friends. While most had been taken aback when her brother, the new Earl of Stanhope, had declared his intentions to marry Diana Reignold less than half a year after her late husband's demise, some had been able to see past societal restrictions and focus on the glowing faces of the newly-weds.

"They do look happy, do they not?"

At the sound of his voice, Eleanor spun around, her heart hammering in her chest as though it was about to burst. "Henry?" she gasped, feeling the familiar weakening of her knees and the excited flutter in her stomach at the mere sight of him. "What are you doing here?" Glancing around, she found her mother's gaze fixed on them, deep-seated anger burning in her eyes.

"Your brother invited me."

Jerking her head back to the man she loved, Eleanor stared at him. "He did what? Truly?" Instantly, her heart warmed, and she could not keep the smile off her face.

"Are you glad to see me?" Henry asked, his warm brown eyes holding hers as he stepped closer, his hand reaching for hers.

Eleanor swallowed as his fingers brushed over her skin. "I am," she whispered, and her breath caught in her throat. As always, she marvelled at the effect his mere presence had on her and knew in that moment that she could never bring herself to marry another man. "However, I'm afraid my mother is not."

Instantly, his face sobered as he glanced over her shoulder. "I suppose it is safe to say that she despises me even more now." Gritting his teeth, he shook his head, then once more met Eleanor's eyes. "I'm sorry. I wish there was something I could do to convince her that my intentions are honourable." He inhaled deeply. "I am not my brothers."

"I know," Eleanor whispered, torn between utter joy at seeing Henry so unexpectedly and the hopelessness of their situation.

"Your brother promised to speak to her on our behalf," Henry replied, a touch of hope in his voice. "Do you suppose he can be successful where we were not?"

Eleanor sighed, "I wish I could believe so," she admitted, the deflated expression on his face breaking her heart, "but I fear that no one and nothing on the face of the earth will be able to change her mind." A lump settled in her throat, choking her words, as tears came to her eyes. "I fear this is hopeless." Shaking her head, she met his eyes. "Maybe we should simply accept that we shall never marry. Maybe you should try and find someone el–"

"There is no one else!" he all but snarled, his eyes determined as they held hers. "There's only you. Don't ever doubt that. If I cannot marry you, I shall remain a bachelor until the end of my days."

A deep smile came to Eleanor's face at his vehement declaration, and yet, her heart filled with sorrow for if he did not let her go, he would forever remain trapped in this place where happiness was just around the corner, but always out of reach.

Swallowing, Henry took a deep breath before his hands closed more tightly around hers. "Your brother has given his consent," he whispered, and she could read the question in his eyes.

"I cannot," Eleanor replied, her voice low as though ashamed of what she had to say, and again, the look on his face broke her heart. "I'm so sorry, but I cannot go against my mother's wishes."

"Why?" he demanded, a hint of exasperation in his voice.

Eleanor shrugged, unable to explain that quiet fear that had lived in her heart ever since that night her mother had come to sit at her bed. Glancing over her shoulder, she met her mother's gaze, her own searching, and despite the anger and disapproval Eleanor saw there, she also detected a touch of fear.

Fear of what? She wondered, knowing even if she asked, her mother would not explain. Was she wrong to seek to protect a woman who so vehemently and without giving an explanation denied Eleanor her own happiness?

She's your mother, a quiet voice whispered. *No matter what has happened, she loves you and only seeks to protect you.*

But from what? Eleanor wondered yet again.

"Has not your brother done exactly what you will not?" Henry asked, his gaze shifting to the newly-weds. "He's married a woman your mother disapproves of. Is this not the same?"

Taking a deep breath, Eleanor shook her head. "I'm sorry. I cannot explain. There's something…I…." Swallowing, she closed her eyes, wishing that there was a way for her to explain.

She does not look at him the way she looks at me, Eleanor thought. *There is no fear there, only disapproval and anger over his choice, but not...*

"We shall not give up," Henry vowed, his thumb gently brushing over the back of her hand as his gaze held hers. "We shall never give up."

Eleanor nodded as his open love made her heart soar. "If you insist."

A small smile touched his lips. "I'm afraid I must, my lady, for my life would be empty without you."

Returning home, Henry exhaled loudly as he found his brothers lounging in the drawing room. While the three eldest, Stephen, Andrew and Owen, appeared to have only just returned from yet another night about town, Nick once more sat in the armchair by the window, a drink in his hand, his eyes focused outside, and yet unseeing, a dark cloud hanging over his head.

"Where have you been so early, little Brother?" Stephen demanded, a slight sway in his step as he came walking over. "Or are you only getting home now?" An insinuating gleam came to his eyes as Andrew and Owen hooted in delight.

Squaring his shoulders, Henry met his eldest brother's gaze. "I was at Lord Stanhope's wedding," he replied, open disapproval in his voice. "Not everyone begins their day at noon."

Stephen chortled, "While that may be true, I assure you our way is much more fun."

While Andrew and Owen openly expressed their support for Stephen's statement, Nick remained quiet, his face pale, his clothes dishevelled as he had probably been sleeping in them yet again. What had happened to his brother?

"Nevertheless," Henry began, fixing his three elder brothers with a stern gaze, "I would appreciate it if you could refrain from making your escapades public knowledge…at least for the moment."

"Why?" Stephen asked, his eyes narrowing as he glanced at Nick before returning his gaze to Henry. "What is it to you?"

"If you must know," Henry said, hating the role this situation forced him into, "it is your reputations which have led Lady Stanhope to believe that my intentions toward her daughter are less than honourable."

The humour that had been on Stephen's face a moment before vanished as he seemed to sober. Maybe all hope was not lost, Henry thought.

"And what *are* your intentions?" his eldest brother asked, a touch of suspicion in his tone.

"I wish to marry her," Henry said without preamble, hoping that his brothers would support him if they knew about the depth of his feelings for Eleanor. "I'm in love with her, and I wish to make her my wife."

"Are you mad?" Owen demanded, his eyes unbelieving as he shook his head. "It's our reputations that keep us safe, that keep us from being forced into marriage. After all, no woman in her right mind would assume that any of us have honourable intentions."

Henry gritted his teeth. "That is precisely the problem, for Lady Stanhope believes me to be just like you and, therefore, withholds her blessing."

"You're welcome," Stephen said, a disgusted snarl on his face. "You are much too young to be thinking about marriage, dear Brother. You have too much living to do, and right now, you're wasting your time mooning over that girl." He shook his head. "I'd thought it only a temporary infatuation, but—"

"I assure you it is not," Henry stated, shocked by his brothers' outlook at marriage. He had deemed them immature and carefree, not dead-set against marriage. "I am determined to marry her, and I shall do whatever it takes to achieve that goal." He inhaled deeply, meeting his brothers' eyes one by one. "I had hoped to have your support in this matter."

"Sorry, little Brother," Owen said, shaking his head, "women are nothing but trouble. I'd advise you to keep a safe distance."

After gulping down his drink, Nick sat his glass down on the side table with a loud *clank*. "I agree," he slurred, his eyes solemn as he once more stared into nothing.

Shaking his head, Henry stared at his brothers in disbelief. Although he had often thought of himself as a bit of an outsider, they had always been a close-knit family. Even today, he remembered his childhood fondly and could not believe that the very same brothers who had always had his back on every adventure they had embarked upon as children would now abandon him when he needed them most.

"Whether you help me or not," he forced out through gritted teeth, "I shall find a way, and despite everything, I can only hope that when the day comes that you lose your heart, you will not have it ripped out of your chest." Then he turned on his heel and walked out the door, unable to bear the disapproving frowns on his brothers' faces any longer.

2

A NEW PLAN

Resting on the settee in the drawing room, Eleanor absentmindedly watched her new sister-in-law Diana as she sat on the floor, building yet another slightly swaying tower with her one-and-a-half-year-old son Ben.

Smiling, Diana watched her son as he carefully tried to set yet another block on top. Again, the tower began to sway slightly, and both their eyes widened, their breaths stuck in their throat.

For a moment, it appears the construction would stabilise, but then Little Ben jumped up and down in excitement, clapping his hands, and before his mother could warn him, the blocks came crashing down.

Eleanor flinched as the commotion drew her attention back to the people in the room. Her eyes focused on Little Ben and the slight tremble in his lower lip as he surveyed the collapsed tower. "It's all right, Ben," she tried to comfort him, exchanging a careful smile with

Diana. "It was a truly wonderful accomplishment, but sometimes towers have to fall. How else are we ever going to build a new one?"

For a moment, her new nephew looked at her as though she had lost her mind. Then his eyes narrowed in concentration before he plopped down on the ground and began collecting the remnants of his masterpiece, once more setting to work.

Smiling, Diana rose from the floor and came over to sit next to Eleanor. "I love how excited he gets," she beamed, her eyes aglow as she looked at her son.

Eleanor wondered if she would ever be fortunate enough to call a child her own. Considering her mother's refusal, she doubted it very much. Any child of hers would most likely not be Henry's. The thought pained her greatly.

"Are you all right?" Diana asked, a slight frown drawing down her brows as she looked at Eleanor. "Is it about Henry?"

Eleanor sighed, "I don't know what to do. The thought of him makes me so happy, but then it also reminds me of the impossibility of our situation." Looking at Diana and seeing the compassion in her eyes, Eleanor knew how fortunate she was that her brother had found a wife who already felt like a sister to her. She had felt a certain kinship to Diana from the first moment they had met at a ball—even before Diana's first husband had died—and to this day, there was a lightness between them that allowed Eleanor to share her deepest secrets.

"Please, my apologies for being so blunt," Diana said, her sharp eyes resting on Eleanor's, "but why do you not simply marry him?"

Eleanor frowned. "Because Mother objects."

"Yes, I know," Diana confirmed, a slightly indulgent smile playing on her lips. "But your brother gave his blessing. There is nothing but your mother's opinion standing in the way of your happiness. Will you truly allow her to keep the two of you apart forever?" Shaking her head, Diana frowned. "I'm afraid I don't understand."

Again, Eleanor sighed. "To tell you the truth, neither do I." How was she supposed to explain that feeling of dread, of impending doom that had settled in her stomach the night her mother had come to sit at her bed, that night she had cried…probably for the first time in her life? "I'm sorry. I'm afraid I cannot explain this in any way for you to understand. There is something in the way she looks at me that…" She shook her head.

Reaching out, Diana patted Eleanor's hand. "There is no need. I loved my mother, too, even more when she died and I lost her." A lone tear clung to her eyelashes. "That's when I realised how precious she had been to me." Diana sighed, then brushed the wetness from her eyes. "I remember how hurt she was the night she and Father found me with Lord Norwood in the gardens, and it wasn't only the scandal or the way society treated me after that that broke her heart. There was something in the way she looked at me that told me that my pain was also hers, and she could not bear it."

Eleanor nodded, relieved that Diana understood. "I could not find the words to explain this to Henry, and I could see the confusion and the disappointment in his face."

"He would marry you on the spot if you only said yes," Diana chuckled. "He's in love with you."

"He is, isn't he?" Eleanor whispered, remembering the intensity in Henry's eyes as he had held her hand as though unwilling to ever let her go again. And yet, they had never openly spoken of love. Yes, Eleanor knew she loved him and she was certain that he loved her, too, and yet, they had never spoken those words. "I just wish I could see him again."

Diana frowned before her eyes cleared and she nodded in understanding. "Now, that the season is over, your paths will not cross as easily, you mean?"

Eleanor nodded. "We will depart for Stanhope Grove in a few days, and then…" She shook her head, biting her lip to hold back the tears that threatened. "But maybe it will be for the best," she tried to convince herself, once more torn between hope and resignation. "Maybe this will allow us to move on."

"Nonsense!" Diana exclaimed. "Not seeing your brother again after that night at Lord Barrett's ball would not have helped me move on. Nothing would have." Drawing in a deep breath, her sister-in-law watched her carefully for a long moment. "There must be something we can do," she finally concluded. "I shall speak to Arthur. I'm certain we will find a way for you to see Henry. Who knows? Maybe if we force Lady Stanhope to see the two of you together, she will eventually see that he truly loves you."

The ghost of a smile tugged on Eleanor's lips at the image of a possible future Diana's words painted. However, deep down she did not believe it to be true. "Do you think my brother would know what to do?"

Diana smiled. "He doesn't need to," she whispered conspiratorially. "He only needs to agree to my idea."

Eleanor laughed. "Arthur is so fortunate to have found you."

Diana snorted, "Tell that to your mother."

Once more reading through the few short lines of the message he had just received from Lord Stanhope, Eleanor's brother, Henry felt his heart quicken. "Parton, have my bags packed," he called to the butler. As he strode across the foyer, he noted a slight bounce in his step and smiled. "I'll be travelling to the country on the morrow. By the way, have you seen my brother Nick?"

The thin, balding man glanced at the closed drawing room doors and a touch of disapproval came to his pale eyes. "I believe he wished to escape the teasing and has retreated to the library."

"Thank you, Parton," Henry replied just as another burst of laughter echoed to his ears from the drawing room. "I believe I shall do the same," he muttered under his breath, feeling in no mood to meet his older brothers.

Opening the door to the library, Henry spotted his brother seated under the tall arched window, another glass in his left hand while the other skimmed through a book lying open on his lap. His appearance was dishevelled as it always was these days, and his eyes appeared glassy and unfocused…and burdened with sadness.

As his brother continued to turn page after page, Henry slowly approached, wondering what had happened to have changed him so. Not too long ago, his brother had been a lively, carefree man who–according to his own words–knew how to enjoy life. Now, he seemed a mere shadow of himself.

Glancing over his brother's shoulder, Henry was surprised to find his fingers trailing over the lines of a love poem. However, before he could enquire further, Nick flinched, and the drink in his hand spilled over, half its contents splashing onto the floor.

"Good gracious, Henry, why would you sneak up on me?" Nick huffed, trying to calm his nerves as he discreetly slid the book closed, moving it out of Henry's line of vision. "What are you doing here?"

"I could ask you the same thing," Henry replied, his eyes holding his brother's before Nick blinked and turned his gaze out the window, clearly unwilling to talk. "What happened to you?" Henry asked nonetheless. "You've not been yourself lately."

"That is none of your concern," Nick grumbled, then took another gulp from his drink.

Henry sighed, wishing his brother would confide in him. Was he in love? He wondered, remembering the book Nick had been reading. If so, then it appeared to be a one-sided love. Had someone broken his heart? Henry could not recall that his brother had shown a certain partiality to any one lady during the last season…or before.

Whatever the reason, Henry could not help but worry about his brother. Left to fend for himself, Nick would surely spend the next months sitting in a chair, drowning his sorrows. Who knew if this downward spiral would ever end?

Drawing in a deep breath, Henry cleared his throat. "I'm leaving for the country tomorrow."

"Safe travel," his brother muttered, not even lifting his eyes to look at him.

"You're coming with me," Henry stated, his tone unwavering as he fixed his brother with a determined stare.

Although Lord Stanhope's invitation to stay at a neighbouring estate to Stanhope Grove did not expressly extend beyond Henry himself, he doubted that the man would object to his brother's presence. After all, had he not granted his permission to assist his own sister?

"The hell I am," Nick growled, his eyes narrowing as he turned them on his brother. "You have no say in where I go."

Henry gritted his teeth, his heart aching as he saw his brother's misery. "Let me put it this way: you're coming and that is final." Again, Nick's mouth opened to object, but Henry cut him off. "I swear I shall tie you to my horse if need be." For a long moment, their eyes remained locked, and Henry could see his brother's indecision in the way his lips thinned and his nose crinkled.

Then Nick turned his gaze away, shrugging his shoulders. "Fine. After all, it doesn't truly matter where I drink." And with that, he downed the remaining contents of his glass.

Henry sighed. What had he gotten himself into?

3

KNOW THY ENEMY

Returning from a stroll in the gardens, Eleanor laughed as Diana whispered to her, "The first time I kissed your brother, he stared at me as though I had suddenly sprouted another head." A deep smile came to Diana's face as she sighed. "It was the night my life began."

Delighted to share her days with her new sister-in-law, Eleanor hugged her on impulse, feeling her own spirits lifted now that not only Diana but also her little son had come to live with them. Their mere presence made the house seem brighter, more cheerful, full of hope and possibilities.

However, when Eleanor stepped back, she caught her mother's eye, and a lump of guilt settled in her stomach before she could fend it off.

Standing in the doorway to the drawing room, Lady Stanhope watched them through narrowed eyes, her lips pressed into a thin line and her jaw set in anger. And yet, her gaze spoke of sadness, of disappointment.

"Hello, Mother," Eleanor addressed her, forcing a smile on her face while her pulse hammered in her veins. "Would you like to join us for tea?"

Lady Stanhope's gaze momentarily shifted to Diana before she met Eleanor's eyes. "I'd rather not," she said as she strode past them, then added, "The company in this house isn't what it used to be."

Eleanor's eyes widened at such an open insult to Diana; however, her sister-in-law merely shook her head, a rather exhausted sigh escaping her lips. "I'm so sorry," Eleanor offered the moment her mother had disappeared through the door to the back parlour. "She shouldn't have–"

"I know," Diana interrupted, her kind eyes holding no grudge. "I'm used to such treatment."

"But it isn't fair," Eleanor objected, wondering how Diana could bear not only society's resentment but also her own family's.

"It is not," her sister-in-law agreed as she lifted her chin a notch. "However, I've made up my mind not to let it sadden me. I have a lot in my life to be grateful for. Not long ago, I believed I should never be happy again, never know love, and now…" A deep smile came to her face. "Nothing can spoil this. I have Ben, I have Arthur, and I have you."

Squeezing Diana's hands, Eleanor nodded. "I'm proud to call you my sister."

"As am I." Looping her arm through Eleanor's, Diana pulled her toward the drawing room. "Come. There is much to think about."

After settling onto the settee and calling for tea, the two women found their conversation once more turning to the man who had stolen Eleanor's heart. "Arthur told me he had the message delivered this morning," Diana said, a conspiratorial gleam in her eyes. "Apparently, Lord Harrington is a friend of his and–"

"Harrington?" Eleanor exclaimed, surprised she had not thought of it herself. "Oh, yes, I remember him. He had an accident last year and forgot all about his wife and their marriage. How sad!"

Diana nodded. "Truly. How unfortunate to find true love only to lose it to such a tragic event. I cannot imagine what it would feel like if Arthur woke up one morning and did not recognise me." She shuddered at the thought.

Eleanor nodded her agreement before a soft smile lifted the corners of her mouth. "However, I hear he is slowly remembering his wife. At his brother's wedding, they seemed as much in love as ever before." Eleanor sighed, "Sometimes it is good to remember that others suffer as well. It helps not to feel too alone in one's own misery."

"Love is rarely easy," Diana agreed, "but worth fighting for." Then she sat up and grasped Eleanor's hands. "So? What's the plan?"

"What do you mean?"

"I mean, we've managed to settle Henry at Sanford Manor—thanks to Lord Harrington's gracious offer—which will put him in the vicinity of Stanhope Grove. However, how do we ensure that your paths cross…frequently?" Diana wiggled her eyebrows, and Eleanor laughed, relief filling her heart at the knowledge that she was not alone in fighting for her love.

"Oh, I know!" Diana suddenly exclaimed. "A house party! We'll invite a few friends—Henry among them—and this way he will be simply *one* of the guests. Maybe that will placate your mother and keep her from strangling him the moment he crosses the threshold. At the very least, it will give the two of you time to be together and your mother the opportunity to see how much he cares for you."

"That is a marvellous idea!" Eleanor beamed, her heart thudding in her chest with excitement. "Who shall we invite?"

"How about Lord and Lady Harrington," Diana suggested, walking over to the small desk in the corner to retrieve a pen and paper, "as well as his brother and his new wife, Mr. and Mrs. Everett."

"How about Lord Amberly and his sister," Eleanor added. "We've known each other since we were children, and it has been a while since we've last had the chance to meet."

Adding two more names to the list, Diana looked up. "I would also like to invite my cousin Rose, if you don't mind."

"Not at all," Eleanor agreed. "What about Lord Norwood's brother and his wife? Are they back in the country?"

Diana shrugged. "I'm not certain, but I'll ask. Anyone else?"

"I wish we could invite my cousin Corinne. However, when my great-aunt died recently, she received a nice inheritance and is now travelling Europe as she's always dreamed to do." Eleanor shook her head, realising how much she missed her cousin. "Let's not make this too big an affair."

"You're right."

Eleanor's hands tensed. "I can only hope most will accept our invitation. What if they already have plans?"

"We shall see," Diana mumbled, then rose to her feet. "Come, we shall write the invitations immediately and have them sent out today."

As they stepped up to the desk in the corner, the drawing room door swung open and Eleanor's brother walked in, a large smile coming to his face as his eyes fell on his sister. "I have just received word from Mr. Waltham," he said, his grey eyes dancing with merriment. "He has gratefully accepted our invitation to stay at Sanford Manor."

"Oh, Arthur, thank you!" Eleanor exclaimed, throwing herself into her brother's arms and hugging him tightly.

"You're very welcome," he whispered, brushing his hands up and down her back, the same way he had when she had been little. "Anything to see you smile."

"We have decided to hold a house party," Diana remarked, her head already bent over the first invitation as her nimble fingers guided the quill across the sheet of paper. Then she looked up and met her husband's gaze, a mischievous gleam in her eyes. "I hope you don't mind."

Arthur laughed, "Would you change your plans if I did?"

Rising from the chair, Diana smiled. "Definitely not; after all, you couldn't possibly have a reasonable argument for your hypothetical objection."

A smile on her face, Eleanor stepped back as Diana approached her husband and their eyes locked, the usual teasing banter flying from their lips. As she sat down at the desk Diana had just vacated, Eleanor hoped with all her heart that one day she and Henry would have an equally happy marriage.

"So, you do not object?"

"Not at all," Arthur assured his wife as his arms came around her, pulling her closer. "However, I'd advise you to tread carefully regarding Mother. She may refrain from causing a scene in public, but that does not mean she will not retaliate in secret."

"Retaliate?" Diana asked with a frown. "You make it sound like war."

Arthur laughed, "I've come to think of it as a suitable comparison."

Eleanor sighed, knowing her brother was not wrong. However, if her mother could indeed be considered *the enemy*, then she truly needed to learn all she could about her reasons for her refusal. Why indeed did her mother object to Eleanor marrying Henry? Could it truly only be because of his brothers' reputations? Or that he was merely the fifth son of a baron? Or was there another reason?

In any case, since Lady Stanhope had so far refused to name it, it was highly unlikely that she would do so if asked.

There had to be another way.

Despite the relatively short distance from London as well as his eagerness to reach their destination, Henry abandoned his idea to ride ahead to Sanford Manor on horseback as Nick was in no shape to keep himself securely in the saddle…and despite his original threat, Henry had no intention of tying his brother to his horse.

Sitting in the carriage as it rumbled along country lanes, Henry watched his brother as he sat slumped in his seat, his eyes glassy and unfocused, a flask in his hands that he refused to relinquish. "Do you plan on drinking like this for the foreseeable future?"

At the sound of Henry's voice, Nick's head snapped up, his clouded gaze barely focusing on his brother's face. "I told you I would be poor company," he slurred, running a hand through his unkempt hair, "but you insisted."

Henry sighed, "Yes, I'm beginning to doubt the wisdom of that decision." Once they reached Sanford Manor, he would make certain to hide every bottle of liquor in the house as well as instruct the servants not to provide his brother with anything in that regard.

Nick would be furious, but it could not be helped. After all, was it not Henry's responsibility as Nick's brother to protect him? Even from himself?

"I'd appreciate it," he began after a while, "if you would remain sober when in company."

"Company?" Nick snorted. "Is that how you refer to yourself these days?"

"I'm not talking about myself," Henry snapped, watching his brother through narrowed eyes, "although I admit I would appreciate your restraint. However, I was referring to Eleanor as well as her family. As I've mentioned before, I wish to make a good impression." On second thought, inviting his brother might have been a monumental mistake.

At Henry's words, Nick's features darkened, and he grumbled something under his breath.

"What was that?" Henry enquired.

As his brother's red-rimmed eyes met his, Henry could not help but shudder at the pain resting in them. Once again, he wondered what had happened to put it there? "Women are nothing but trouble," Nick forced out through gritted teeth. "You'd do well to forget about Eleanor before she forgets about you."

Henry drew in a deep breath, watching his brother intently. "You sound as though you speak from experience."

At his observation, Nick dropped his gaze and his hands clenched into fists. Then he glanced at the door, a desperate need in his eyes, and Henry knew that he wanted nothing more than to run away from the pain that haunted him.

"Who was she?" Henry asked, knowing very well that his brother would not answer him.

Nick refused to look up and once more turned to the numbing drink in his hands. "It does not matter," he growled after taking a long swig. "They're all the same."

"Not Eleanor," Henry stated, remembering the deep glow in her eyes whenever they met as though his mere presence lit up her world…as hers did for him. "She is one of a kind."

Nick snorted, shaking his head. "Believe what you wish, but don't pretend I did not warn you." For a long moment, his brother looked out the window at the passing landscape. At first, his eyes seemed unfocused, unseeing. However, as time passed, they seemed to take in the wide expanse of forest in the distance as well as the small stream trickling through the meadow framing the road on one side. Ever so slowly, his gaze began to narrow, and his hands gripped the flask more tightly.

Dragging his eyes from the passing landscape, Nick swallowed and met his brother's confused gaze, his cheeks pale as though he was about to be ill. "Where are we going?" he asked, his voice hoarse, sounding almost strangled.

Stunned by his brother's unusual reaction, Henry frowned. "Sanford Manor. It's a neighbouring estate to Stanhope Grove," he said, and the remaining colour drained from his brother's face. "Are you all right? Is something wrong?"

Nick swallowed. "We need to turn around."

"What? Why?"

"I changed my mind," he huffed, a slight tremble shaking his shoulders. "I'd rather stay in London."

"Tell me what's going on," Henry insisted, annoyed with his brother's secrecy.

"Nothing!" Nick snapped, a touch of panic in his eyes. "Turn the carriage around! Now!"

"I will not," Henry insisted, realising now more than ever that his brother needed help. "Whatever happened to put you in such a state, it's been going on for too long. You've been alone with this for too long." Leaning forward, he met his brother's eyes. "I will not stand idly by and watch you destroy yourself. You're coming, and that is final."

Defeated, Nick slumped down in his seat, the expression in his eyes one of unimaginable pain and terror as though he had been placed in the cart that would take him to the gallows and his own execution.

Shaking his head, Henry wondered once again what had happened to his brother and who had broken his heart.

4

HONOURABLE INTENTIONS

The moment Eleanor stepped over the threshold at Stanhope Grove, a sense of nervous expectation seized her. Her skin hummed with what lay ahead, and she constantly felt as though her breath caught in her throat. Her thoughts were focused on the house party to take place within a fortnight, and she prayed that her friends would accept and help her ease the tension that was surely to arise with Henry's arrival.

"You need a change of scenery," Diana declared that morning and then sent Eleanor upstairs to change into her riding habit.

With the wind whipping through her hair and brushing over her face, Eleanor followed her brother and his wife across the meadow to the south of Stanhope Grove. Her gaze glided over the different shades of green dotting the countryside, and her ears rejoiced in the soft birdsong echoing across the expanse. The smell of wildflowers reached her senses, and she felt herself relax with the rhythmic sway of her horse's gait.

As they neared the forest, a lone rider approached from the other side, and Eleanor's heart stopped as she took note of his dark-brown hair and bronze skin. A delighted smile rested on his lips that reached his eyes, which seemed to see only her.

Forcing air into her lungs, Eleanor halted her mount next to her brother's. "Henry," she whispered, barely noticing the indulgent smile on her brother's face.

"Good day, Mr. Waltham," her brother greeted him, a rather unfamiliar touch of humour in his voice. Marriage truly had changed him! "What a surprise to run into you here. Quite unexpected I must say."

Forcing his gaze from her, Henry met her brother's eyes, an answering smile playing on his lips. "Quite unexpected indeed," he replied, a hint of laughter in his voice.

"I do not find it unusual at all," Diana interspersed, her eyes twinkling with delight as she glanced at Eleanor. "After all, it is such a beautiful day. My lord," she turned to her husband, a rather imploring look in her eyes, "I think I saw a lovely patch of bluebells not too far from here. Would you escort me so that I may collect some?"

Understanding her intention, Arthur drew in a slow breath. Then he glanced at Eleanor, a hint of indecision in his eyes.

Smiling, Eleanor nodded almost imperceptibly.

For a moment, her brother gritted his teeth before his gaze turned to Henry. "We shall return momentarily," he said, emphasising each word carefully.

"I assure you, my lord," Henry said earnestly, "your sister will be quite safe with me."

Arthur nodded. "I would not leave if I did not believe so." Then he kicked his horse's flanks and followed his wife down a small slope toward the field of bluebells she had indicated. However, the tension in his shoulders told Eleanor that he only did so reluctantly.

After urging his horse closer to hers, Henry dismounted and came toward her. "May I help you down?" he asked, unadulterated hope shining in his dark eyes.

"You may," Eleanor replied, her voice a mere whisper as her heart hammered in her chest. Swinging her right leg over the pommel, she turned to him as he came to stand before her, his hands lifted to her waist.

Swallowing, Eleanor held his gaze as she allowed herself to slide off the saddle and into his waiting arms. The moment his hands touched her waist, she drew in a sharp breath, and her heart felt as though it was about to jump from her chest.

Except for a rather chaste kiss under the mistletoe last Christmas, Henry had never touched her beyond acceptable courtesy. Admittedly, every now and then, he had taken her hand when it had not been necessary. However, Eleanor could count on one hand how often that had happened.

Resting her hands on his upper arms, Eleanor found her breath once more caught in her throat when Henry did not merely lift her down and set her on her feet, but allowed her body to slide down his, his arms holding her tightly, not releasing her once her feet touched the ground.

Gazing up into his eyes, Eleanor felt her body tremble with what she saw there.

Gritting his teeth, he swallowed as though fighting for control as his gaze dipped lower and touched her lips. While one arm was still wrapped around her middle, holding her firmly against his body, his other hand rose to touch her face, gently tucking a strand of her chestnut tresses behind her ear. The tips of his fingers touched her earlobe, grazing her skin, before they travelled down the side of her neck, his thumb gently skimming over the line of her jaw. Like never before, Eleanor felt her knees grow weak.

"I've missed you," he whispered, his warm breath tickling her skin. "These last few days have been too long."

A deep smile came to her face as his words warmed her heart. "I've missed you as well," she returned his gift, wanting him to know that she felt the same way.

As his gaze continued to burn into hers, Eleanor felt a touch of panic well up in her chest. Never had they been alone like this before, and suddenly the weight of their endeavour was too much. Swallowing, she searched for something to say, anything, to escape the weight of his stare. "We decided to hold a house party," she blurted out the moment his head lowered toward hers.

Taken aback, he blinked, then cleared his throat, the ghost of a smile playing on his features. "Yes, I received your invitation. That was a good idea."

"Thank you," Eleanor replied, feeling rather silly at her own nervousness. "We thought if we invited you as a guest among many, Mother would not see you as such a threat to…"

"Her daughter?" he asked teasingly, his hands tightening on her back as he drew in a deep breath.

Feeling her cheeks grow hot, Eleanor averted her gaze. "I am merely hoping that this will be an opportunity for her to see that you are a decent man."

Henry drew in a deep breath, and his chest rose and fell under her fingertips. "Do you truly believe that your mother might change her mind?" he asked, trying to look into her eyes.

Unable to meet his gaze, Eleanor kept her eyes downcast, knowing in her heart how little hope she had. Had anyone ever been able to change her mother's mind?

Looking down at her bent head, Henry swallowed. "Eleanor, look at me." When she did not comply, he gently took hold of her chin, feeling a slight tremble go through her body at his touch, and tilted up her head. "Look at me, Eleanor."

Swallowing, she took a deep breath before raising her eyes to his, and in that moment, he knew that despite her plans and encouraging attitude, she had very little hope that they would ever be allowed to marry.

His heart sank, and despair began to rush through his body like a poison. She would never be his. Although he held her in his arms in this precious moment, she would not be allowed to stay. Her mother's opinion could not be changed, and Eleanor would have to marry a man her mother deemed worthy of all she had to offer.

In answer to these dark thoughts, Henry felt his arm tighten around her possessively. If only he could hold on to her. If only he did not have to let her go. "Why is your brother's consent not enough for you?" he asked in a moment of weakness, instantly regretting the harsh tone in his voice as well as the dilemma his question forced on her.

Holding his gaze, she drew in a deep breath. "Even if I could explain, I doubt you would understand," she whispered, deep sadness clouding her beautiful eyes. "It is something between a mother and daughter that…" She swallowed. "You must understand that she is not withholding her consent out of spite. She is only doing so because she seeks to protect me."

"Protect you?" Henry ground out as his blood ran cold. "From me?" He drew in a deep breath at the hidden insult. "Do you believe that my intentions toward you are anything but honourable?" His voice rose with every clipped word leaving his mouth, and his muscles tensed reflexively, yanking her against him.

Eleanor gasped, and her eyes widened in surprise.

Instantly, regret filled his body, and he forced his arms to loosen their hold on her. "I'm sorry," he mumbled, barely able to meet her eyes. "I didn't mean to frighten you." How could he have lost his temper? Had her mother seen something in him that he himself was not even aware? Did he pose a threat to Eleanor?

"I'm sorry, too," she whispered, placing a gentle hand on his cheek, her eyes seeking his. "I never meant to imply that your intentions were not honourable. I know they are, but my mother does not know you the way I do." Licking her lips, she swallowed. "I do not know the reason for her objection. However, I do believe she has one."

"My low rank?" Henry ground out, unable to check the anger that coursed through his veins. "My brothers' reputations? I'm not good enough for you?"

For a moment, Eleanor remained quiet, a distant look in her eyes. Then she shook her head. "I know she has said so, but I doubt that these reasons would bring such anger, such pain to her eyes." Again, she shook her head. "No, there must be something else. Something we are not aware of."

Hope began to blossom in Henry's heart as he looked at the determination that came to her face. "Do you truly believe so? Do you truly believe that there is…hope?"

Smiling up at him, Eleanor nodded. "I want to with all my heart," she said, biting her lip as she inhaled deeply. "I will speak to her again." Taking a step back, she glanced over her shoulder at the patch of bluebells in the distance where her brother and his wife stood by their horses, picking flowers. "I suppose we should return," she said, once more meeting his eyes. "I shall see you at the house party. You will come, will you not?"

The hopeful tone in her voice brought a smile to his face. "Not even your mother could keep me away."

Laughing, Eleanor patted her horse's neck.

"Do you mind if I invite my brother along?" Henry asked, knowing only too well that it would probably not help his intentions. However, over the last few days, Nick had grown more and more erratic, and Henry felt as though he were standing up on a ledge about to fall at any moment.

"Your brother?" Eleanor asked, surprise on her face.

"Yes, my brother Nick. He's been out of sorts lately, and I fear for him. Maybe all he needs is a distraction." Henry doubted that it would be enough, but at least, it might be a start.

"Not at all. I'd love to meet him," Eleanor said, a deep smile on her face, before a touch of red rose to her cheeks that made him frown. "After all, he will be my brother soon, too." Biting her lower lip, she beamed at him before turning toward her horse. "I shall ride out again tomorrow. Maybe—"

Unable to let her leave, Henry strode over and reached around her, placing her hands on hers before she could mount her horse and vanish from his life. Who knew when he would see her again? Who knew what could go wrong?

Surprised, she turned to face him, the pulse in her slim neck hammering as fast as his own. "Will I see you tomorrow?"

Sliding his hands down her arms and back around her waist, pulling her closer, Henry inhaled deeply, his eyes fixed on her full lips. "May I kiss you?" he forced himself to ask despite the waning control he had on his desire. However, he did not wish to frighten her. After all, the only kiss they had ever shared had been a soft peck on the lips amidst a sea of onlookers.

Her body trembled in his arms as she looked at him with wide eyes. For a moment, she seemed to hesitate and his hopes sank, but then she nodded her head shyly and leaned closer.

Slipping a hand to the back of her neck to hold her against him, Henry captured her lips with his own, unable to wait a moment longer. Her mouth felt soft and yielding under his, and shots of desire coursed through his body that urged him on. Her arms came around his neck, her fingers tangling in his hair, as she parted her lips.

Feeling his desire for her rise beyond his control, Henry forced himself to take a step back. Still, his arms remained wrapped around her, unwilling to release her just yet. Meeting her eyes, intense and, yet, shy as they looked into his, he inhaled deeply. "You're mine," he whispered hoarsely. "Mine alone. I shall never let you go."

5

DOUBTS

With relief Eleanor received letter after letter of acceptance from her friends regarding her impromptu house party, and thus her days were spent readying Stanhope Grove for the event that would hopefully lead to an engagement celebration some time later. If only her mother could see what she saw, Eleanor thought with a sigh.

Whenever she and Henry's paths crossed these days, he acted the perfect gentleman, kind and respectful and always considerate of her feelings. Although she had to admit that—to her utter delight—his gaze often strayed to her lips, a deep desire to draw her into his arms only too visible in his eyes, Eleanor marvelled at the power of his restraint. Was it not the true definition of a gentleman to have these emotions course through him but not allow them to cloud his judgement? His notion of right and wrong? His decency?

Admittedly, Eleanor could have done with a little less restraint on his part; however, as they were rarely alone, mostly in the company of her brother and sister-in-law, she understood his need for discretion. After all, once they were married—if that day should ever come—there would be more than enough time for…intimacies.

"Are you ready to leave?" Diana asked from behind her as Eleanor fastened her new bonnet on her head.

"I am," she breathed, casting a last glance in the mirror, her heart still thudding in her chest as it constantly did these days when her thoughts strayed to Henry.

A knowing smile touched Diana's face as she stepped closer, leaning in conspiratorially. "Being in love truly becomes you, dear sister."

Unable to suppress a pleased grin, Eleanor averted her gaze, then closed her eyes for a short moment, savouring the precious feeling in her chest, hoping that it would last a lifetime.

As they rode south toward Sanford Manor, Eleanor could barely contain the expectant joy that danced through her body. The closer they drew to the small manor house situated in a cluster of trees, the more she feared she would not be able to keep herself in the saddle.

The moment Henry stepped out of the door, his eyes fixed on her as they approached, she felt herself sway slightly. Gripping the mane of her mare, she felt the muscles in her thighs tense, working to keep her from falling off as her head spun with the usual light-headedness that always seemed to engulf her whenever he drew near.

In answer to her slight sway, his shoulders seemed to tense and he stepped forward, completely oblivious to the other two riders.

Drawing up the reins as her mare stepped through the small gate and toward the house, Eleanor breathed a sigh of relief.

Instantly, Henry appeared beside her. "Are you all right?" he asked, concern clouding his eyes as he took her mare's reins. Without lifting his eyes off her, he led her horse toward the side of the house where her brother and Diana were just dismounting, stable hands seeing to their mounts.

"I'm fine," Eleanor breathed, slightly annoyed with her loss of control over her own emotions. Avoiding his enquiring gaze, Eleanor felt her cheeks flush with heat as embarrassment settled in her chest. Was she the only one who had her emotions so clearly written all over her face?

Beside her, Henry chuckled, and her head jerked toward him, her gaze meeting his. "I feel the same way," he whispered, reaching out to assist her down.

"You do?" Eleanor replied before her eyes travelled to just above his collar where his pulse beat frantically, matching her own. A soft smile came to her lips, and she leaned forward, allowing herself to slide into Henry's open arms.

Holding her gaze, Henry pulled her tight against him as her feet touched the ground. "Sometimes I feel as though my heart will jump out of my chest at the mere sight of you," he whispered, his dark eyes aglow as they looked into hers as though they were the only two people in the world.

As though on cue, her brother cleared his throat rather loudly.

A jolt went through them, and Henry immediately stepped back, his hands slowly—and to her delight, rather reluctantly—sliding off her waist. Swallowing, he turned to her brother. "Welcome to Sanford Manor," he greeted Lord Stanhope and his wife. "Once again, I wish to express my gratitude for allowing us to stay here."

Her brother nodded, his shoulders slightly tense as his gaze travelled back and forth between his sister and the man she wished to marry. "My pleasure," he mumbled before his wife rather openly elbowed him in the side. "I…I hope you've found it to your convenience."

"Indeed, we have," Henry replied as he stepped forward, gesturing to the entrance while holding out his hand to Eleanor. "Shall we?"

As he escorted her inside, her brother and Diana following on their heels, Eleanor felt a new excitement grow in her chest. Although she had occasionally seen his brothers at social events, she had never exchanged a word with any of them. From the way Henry had spoken of Nick, Eleanor knew that he was deeply concerned about his brother, and she hoped with all her heart that their house party would do him good. After all, if it were her own brother, she would wish for nothing less.

Since it was not yet time for dinner to be served, Henry showed them to the drawing room, ringing for tea and asking the butler to inform his brother that their guests had arrived. "It is truly beautiful out here," Henry observed, his voice a bit strained, and Eleanor could see that he almost desperately searched for something to say while his eyes strayed to her again and again.

"It is indeed," her brother agreed. "It is in stark contrast to the noise of the city. I admit I do prefer the quiet solitude of the country."

Diana chuckled, her face the only one free of nervous tension. "Solitude is all good and well. However, if I were stuck out here without another soul to speak to, I know I should go raging mad." She smiled at Eleanor. "Hence, the house party."

Smiling, Eleanor nodded. "Indeed, good friends are necessary for one's happiness. I am delighted that they have all agreed to join us out here on such short notice."

"Mr. Waltham," Diana addressed Henry, "from my cousin I've heard that you are acquainted with her husband, Lord Norwood."

Before Henry could answer, a snort escaped Arthur, and all eyes turned to him. Swallowing, he cleared his throat, then reached for his tea. "I apologise," he mumbled, taking a sip before making a show of clearing his throat again and again as though something had lodged there.

Eleanor sighed, casting a disapproving glance at her brother. Yes, Henry was acquainted with Lord Norwood, and yes, before his marriage to Diana's cousin Rose, Lord Norwood had been the most notorious rake in all of London. However, there was no reason to hold such an acquaintance against Henry. After all, many people had made Lord Norwood's acquaintance at some point or another, and had he not changed his ways since meeting his young wife? From what Diana had told her, Eleanor knew that more than a year after their wedding, the young couple was still madly in love.

"Yes," Henry finally replied, a slight tension coming to his shoulders as he, too, understood only too well the implications of such an acquaintance. "He and my eldest brother, Stephen, went to Eton together. I myself haven't seen him in a few years. However, I am delighted that he will be at the house party as I haven't yet had the opportunity to congratulated him on his nuptials."

"Well spoken," Diana commented, her eyes aglow with delight as they glanced at Eleanor. "Friends of my husband's will also be in attendance. I do not know if you're acquainted with them: Lord Harrington as well as his younger brother, Mr. Wesley Everett."

Eleanor could hardly suppress a grin as her brother rolled his eyes. Like Lord Norwood, Wesley Everett had been a rake in his day as well…until he had met his wife and fallen head over heels in love with her.

"I haven't had the pleasure," Henry replied, his shoulders relaxing as he saw the large smile on Eleanor's face, and the tension in the room dissipated. "However, I am looking forward to making their acquaintance."

Shaking his head, Eleanor's brother sighed, a soft smile tugging at the corners of his mouth. "I'm certain we shall have a marvellous time." He turned his gaze to his wife, and a deep smile lit up his face. "A house party was a wonderful idea."

As Diana returned his smile, footsteps echoed from down the hall.

"This will be my brother Nick," Henry said, rising to his feet a moment before the door opened, and the man in question stepped over the threshold.

Watching him with curious eyes, Eleanor immediately noticed a certain resemblance between Nick and Henry. Nick shared his brother's dark hair and watchful gaze as he took in the room and those seated in it. However, while Henry always appeared amiable, his eyes kind as he met friends and strangers alike, his brother's gaze was dark, troubled, almost tortured.

Eleanor drew in a steadying breath, understanding Henry's concern for his brother.

"Nick," Henry began, gesturing to their guests, "may I introduce you to—"

"I'm afraid I cannot stay," Nick interrupted, his voice almost a growl as he took a step back. Tension held his body rigid, and his lips were pressed into a thin line as though to hold back words he knew he ought not to speak. Shaking his head, he retreated farther until he suddenly spun around and stormed from the room.

Taken aback, Henry stared after him, then cleared his throat, a touch of embarrassment colouring his cheeks. "I do apologise for my brother's behaviour," he said, his voice holding displeasure as well as concern. "If you'll excuse me."

Hastening after his brother, he gently closed the door behind him, casting Eleanor an apologetic glance.

"That was odd," Diana observed, turning enquiring eyes on Eleanor. "Do you have any idea what upset him so?"

Eleanor shook her head, deeply troubled by the thought that yet another member of their two families seemed to disapprove of her and Henry's union.

In the distance, they could hear mumbled voices arguing, their tones harsh and unyielding.

Arthur sighed, "Apparently, Mother is not the only one opposing your match," he said, regretful eyes meeting Eleanor's as though he had read her thoughts.

Drawing in a deep breath, Eleanor closed her eyes, wondering if it would always be like this. Whenever she felt as though they were one step closer toward their happily-ever-after, something happened that would force them two steps back.

Outrage giving his legs speed, Henry rushed from the room, humiliation and a sense of terror heating his face. As much as he had expected his brother's presence to complicate things, he had never anticipated that his brother's behaviour would present such a problem. How could he have done this? Did Nick not know how important it was to make a good impression? What if Lord Stanhope changed his mind and decided to side with his mother's opinion after all?

All would be lost. Henry was certain of it.

In the hall, he finally caught up with Nick, grabbed him by the arm without a word and dragged him into the library. Only when he had shut the door firmly behind them did he spin around, fixing his brother with an icy stare. "Why?" he growled, words eluding him. Shaking his head, he stared at Nick, barely noting the trembling fury that seemed to hold him in his grip as his hands clenched and unclenched as though he had no control over them. "Do you have any idea what you've done?"

Gritting his teeth, Nick met his angry gaze, his lips pressed into a tight line, the muscles in his jaw tense to the point of breaking. "I told you I shouldn't have come," he forced out, his voice hoarse, "but you wouldn't listen."

Swallowing, Henry inhaled deeply, hoping to calm the anger that coursed through his veins. "So, you acted out of spite? Is that it? I forced you to accompany me, and this is your revenge?"

Nick's nostrils flared at the accusation, and he raised his chin. "Do you truly believe I would intentionally hurt you, Brother?"

Henry shook his head, not knowing what to believe. "How would I know? These past few months you have been so different that I hardly recognise you. All you do is drown your sorrows—whatever they are—in one drink after another. What happened to you?"

Again, Nick clamped his mouth shut, his eyes closing for the barest of moments as though he could not bear to look at the world any longer.

Torn between compassion and anger, Henry took a step toward his brother. "I love her," he said, allowing all the emotions that thudded in his chest to show in his voice. "She is my other half, and the thought of losing her is the worst torture."

Blinking his eyes rapidly, Nick turned his head toward the floor, and for a split second, Henry thought to see the hint of tears in his eyes. What had happened to his brother?

"This is my chance," Henry went on, hoping that Nick would listen—truly listen—and understand what was at stake. "Lady Stanhope is dead-set against the match, and Eleanor cannot bring herself to go against her mother. At least we have her brother's support—or we did until you acted the way you did—but it will not be enough. We already need a miracle to occur," placing a hand on his brother's shoulder, Henry waited until Nick met his eyes, "please do not make this anymore impossible than it already is."

Feeling his brother's shoulder tremble under his grasp, Henry found his anger waning. He took note of the pain clearly visible in his brother's eyes as well, his face alternately flashing hot and then paling again as though he, too, felt torn. "I would never seek to ruin your chances," Nick finally said, meeting his brother's gaze, his own eyes shining with tortured determination. "However, I must implore you to forget Eleanor and return to London before this ends badly."

Henry swallowed, his heart frozen as though dipped into ice at the mere thought of losing her. "I cannot do that," he breathed, his voice barely audible, shrouded in shock. "How can you ask that of me? I thought you understood. I thought despite everything you knew how much I love her."

Nick's face contorted into a grimace. "You love her, yes, I am aware. But does she love you as well?"

Stunned beyond comprehension, Henry stumbled backwards, his eyes focused on his brother's face, and yet, he could not help but feel as though he was talking to a stranger.

Nick swallowed, regret and resolve waging a war within him. "I'm not saying this to hurt you. Quite the contrary, I seek to put you on your guard." Again, he swallowed, and deep pain came to his face. "The regard of a woman can be as fleeting as that of a man."

Still stunned into speechlessness, Henry forced himself to look at his brother. He forced himself to see the tension that held him rigid, the heavy weight resting on his shoulders that threatened to crush him at any moment as well as the anguish that echoed in his voice whenever he spoke. Taking a deep breath, Henry held the need to lash out at Nick at bay. "I've asked you this before," he began, his gaze trained on his brother, "do you speak from experience?"

Instantly, Nick averted his gaze, his hands once more clenching into fists.

"I cannot believe that you would speak the way you do without cause, without an emotional involvement," Henry continued, watching his brother's face carefully. After a long moment of heavy silence, he finally asked the question he should have asked months ago…only he had been too occupied with his own misery to notice his brother's. "Who broke your heart? Who was she?"

Nick's head snapped up like an arrow released from a bow, his eyes ablaze as he stared at Henry. His lips quivered, and for a moment, Henry thought he would finally receive an answer. However, a second later, Nick once more turned away and stormed off, slamming the door shut behind him.

Hanging his head, Henry drew in a deep breath, wondering who the woman was who had stolen his brother's heart and then ripped it to pieces. He remembered Nick's shocked reaction when he had told him that they were to spend the summer in the country at Sanford Manor…near Stanhope Grove.

Henry swallowed, then closed his eyes as some of the pieces fell into place. Could it be that the woman in question had a connection to Eleanor's family? To Eleanor herself?

From a dark place inside him, ruled by fear alone, a quiet voice whispered: *Could it be Eleanor?*

6

OLD FRIENDS

As the day of their guests' arrival to their house party finally came, Eleanor was beside herself with fluttering nerves. Her stomach turned every which way, threatening to expel its contents, and her heart raced in her chest in such a painful way that she feared she would faint on the spot.

Despite her careful planning and Diana's encouraging words, Eleanor could not help but feel as though the day had finally come that she would have to give up her hopes for the future.

Although her mother still did not know that Henry and his brother had taken up residence at Sanford Manor, Eleanor could tell from the way her mother watched her that she knew something was going on. Whenever they spoke, her mother's eyes would narrow in speculation, and Eleanor felt guilty for keeping this secret from her and in fact plotting to change her mind.

Every fibre of her being spoke out against such a heinous idea of intentionally deceiving her mother, and she feared that that alone would be reason enough for her mother to refuse Henry. After all, would her mother not see it as his negative influence on her?

Eleanor shook her head, feeling suddenly exhausted. Had life always been this complicated? More than anything, she wished she could return to her room, curl up beneath the covers of her bed and let the world move on without her.

When the first carriage drew up to the house, Diana came rushing over. "They're here!" she exclaimed, her voice betraying her excitement. After all, for years, Diana had been treated as an outcast in society, which had not improved much when she had married Eleanor's brother only a few months after her first husband's death. However, today, only friends would be in attendance, giving Diana the rare opportunity to enjoy social life outside her immediate family.

As they came to stand by the door beside Arthur and Lady Stanhope, Eleanor smiled, delighted to see Diana so happy. Squeezing her sister-in-law's hand, she turned toward the carriage, feeling herself relax as William and Catherine Everett, Lord and Lady Harrington, emerged, greeting them warmly.

Maybe this was not such a bad idea after all.

"They look happy, do they not?" Diana whispered to Eleanor as they observed the intimate way the earl and his wife interacted. "The way he looks at her says more than a thousand words."

Eleanor nodded, hoping that if the earl could find his way back to his wife after losing his memory, there was still a chance for Henry and herself.

Shortly after, more guests arrived. First, Lord Norwood and his wife Rose, and then Mr. and Mrs. Everett. While Diana was still greeting her cousin, Eleanor rushed to welcome Mrs. Everett. "Christine, it is so good to see you," she exclaimed, delighted to see the happiness shining in the woman's eyes. After meeting her last Christmas, she had hoped that Wesley Everett would find a way to persuade her into marriage. It had been a rocky journey, and yet, they had found happiness in the end.

Another inspiring tale that gave Eleanor hope.

"I was delighted to receive your invitation," Christine beamed, her quick eyes gliding over Eleanor before the corner of her mouth quirked and she leaned closer. "And I am glad you have not yet bowed your head and chosen one of your mother's *suitable* suitors," she whispered, drawing Eleanor aside. "In fact, you look more determined than ever to marry for love. Tell me, what's your plan? Maybe I can help."

Staring at Christine, Eleanor shook her head, a soft smile on her face as she marvelled about the other woman's impeccable perception. In a few quick words, she shared all that had transpired since they had last seen each other, and before long, Christine's eyes were aglow with excitement.

"Marvellous!" she exclaimed, squeezing Eleanor's hands. "It has been too long since I've had the opportunity to...," she wiggled her eyebrows as a mischievous gleam came to her eyes, "interfere in someone else's life. I promise I shall do what I can to aid you."

Eleanor sighed with relief, "Thank you for your kindness."

Laughing, Christine shook her head, "Oh, it has nothing to do with kindness, dear Eleanor. I'm doing this strictly for selfish reasons."

Eleanor's brows drew down in confusion. "How do you mean?"

Christine sighed a bit theatrically before a large smile came to her face. "You see, the great pity with happiness is that there is rarely an opportunity to meddle." She laughed, "And I do love to meddle as you might recall."

Delighted, Eleanor nodded. After all, it had been Christine who had aided her at Lord Hampton's Christmas ball. Enlisting her future husband's help, she had distracted Lady Stanhope long enough to give Henry the opportunity to lead Eleanor onto the dance floor and kiss her under the mistletoe. It had been a wonderful night...thanks to Christine.

"I'm glad to have you by my side," Eleanor assured her in a whisper before Lady Stanhope walked over and drew Christine into a conversation about the New Year's Ball she was already planning for the end of the year.

With all their guests already deep in conversation, Eleanor turned to look out the front door and spotted yet another carriage rumbling up the gravel path. It bore the crest of the Earl of Amberly, and Eleanor felt her heart rejoice. How long had to been since she had seen Griffin and Winifred?

After their parents' death, not yet five years ago, the siblings had retreated from the world and taken to travelling. As Griffin had already been of age, he had ascended to his father's title, taken over guardianship of his sister, and then within a few weeks' time, they had quit England.

As they stepped from the carriage, Eleanor stared at the two adults before her, their rich auburn hair glowing in the sun as their chocolate brown eyes came to rest on her. For a moment, she barely recognised them, their features matured, the look in their eyes speaking of new experiences and wisdom gained. However, the moment Winifred saw her, a deep smile came to her old friend's face, and before long, they were hugging each other fiercely.

"It has been too long," Winifred exclaimed, suddenly stepping back, her gaze gliding over Eleanor's face. "You look different...somehow."

Eleanor nodded. "As do you." She turned her head to look at Griffin, then frowned. "Have you always been this tall?"

A rumbling laugh echoed from his throat as his warm eyes settled on hers, "Not at all. In fact, I've grown significantly since I was an infant."

Rolling her eyes, Winifred grinned. "I hope you remember never to take him seriously."

Eleanor laughed, then escorted the siblings inside and introduced them to the rest of their guests. However, before long, she found herself strolling through the gardens with Winifred and Griffin beside her as the assembly of guests had almost naturally separated into those who had already tied the knot and those who were still looking for their perfect match.

"I was rather surprised to receive an invitation to a house party," Winifred stated, her eyes slightly narrowed as she glanced at Eleanor. "In fact, from your last letter, I expected a wedding invitation. Or did your mother change her mind?"

Eleanor sighed, not knowing where to begin.

"All right, that's my cue to leave," Griffin interrupted, then inclined his head in farewell. "I'll leave you two lovely ladies to discuss your…secrets in private." He grinned as Winifred rolled her eyes, then he turned to look at Eleanor. "Remember that her opinions," with a nod of his head, he indicated his sister, "are a bit odd at times…to say the least. Don't take her too seriously." And with another laugh bubbling out of his throat, he walked away.

Eleanor smiled, realising how much she had missed the siblings. Only three years apart, they had a different relationship than Eleanor and Arthur did considering that more than a decade separated them.

"He can be so obnoxious," Winifred muttered, glaring after her brother.

"But you love him."

"Fiercely," Winifred stated without hesitation. Then she shrugged. "What can I say? Despite his wayward ways, he's my best friend." Drawing in a deep breath, Winifred shook her head as though to clear it. "Well, then about your wedding. Am I mistaken or did you not write to me in your last letter about your mother's ultimatum? Did she not expect you to find a match before the end of the season?" Looking around at the gardens in full bloom, Winifred cocked her head. "Am I wrong, or is it the end of the season? Are you betrothed?"

"I am not," Eleanor replied, equally saddened and relieved by that fact. "Although I have found a man I wish to marry, my mother opposes the match."

Winifred drew in a sharp breath. "I see," she mumbled, her sharp eyes slightly narrowed as her mind worked. "What objections does she have?"

"I'm not certain."

Winifred's eyes narrowed further.

Eleanor sighed, "She says it is because of his low rank and reputation…or rather his brothers' reputations; however, I cannot help but feel as though she is not being completely honest with me."

"Who is he?"

"His name is Henry Waltham. He is the youngest of Lord Caulfield's sons."

"Youngest?" Winifred enquired.

"The fifth."

"I see," her friend replied. "And I assume his…or rather his brothers' reputations are those of common rakes?"

Eleanor nodded, remembering the rationality with which Winifred approached every issue. "You would assume right."

Sighing, Winifred drew Eleanor down next to her onto the stone bench by the small fountain gurgling happily in the bright afternoon sun. "Do you truly believe such a man would be a good match for you?" she asked, her eyes not judging but merely interested.

Eleanor frowned, for a moment not knowing how to answer or what exactly her friend was asking. However, before she could attempt an explanation, Winifred continued. "I'll be frank. Now, that my parents are dead, I am quite at a loss about how best to choose a suitable match. Preferably I would defer to Griffin in this matter. However, I cannot help but wonder if he would treat the matter with the necessary importance."

"You would allow your brother to choose your husband?" Eleanor asked, mouth slightly agape. Despite Winifred's rational tendencies, she would never have expected that.

Looking at Eleanor with a hint of incredulity in her eyes, Winifred nodded. "Naturally. After all, he knows me best and is in the perfect position to judge my character with the necessary objectivity." She snorted, "Or he would be if he weren't so immature."

"But how would he know what lived in your heart?" Eleanor asked. "Is it not difficult enough to judge your own heart's desire for yourself? How is someone else to know?"

"That is precisely why it is wise to allow someone who knows you well to make the choice," Winifred insisted. "After all, what lives in your heart is not a constant. It changes with the seasons; therefore, it would be most unwise to choose a spouse based on a momentary infatuation."

Stunned, Eleanor shook her head. A lot had changed since she had last seen her friend. "Then you are a supporter of arranged marriages?"

Winifred opened her mouth, then hesitated as her eyes narrowed. "If by *arranged marriage* you mean a union based on fortune and title, then no." She took a deep breath, and Eleanor could see how she sought to find the right words to explain herself. "Choosing a spouse based on material gain is similarly unwise—possibly even more so—than choosing one for *love*." As she said the last word, a touch of annoyance came to her voice. "I believe it would be beneficial to all if unions were formed based on the potential spouses' character traits, their interests and expectations of life. While our heart changes with the wind, at our core we are who we are. That never changes. At least, not to a degree where it would matter." A soft smile came to her face as she took Eleanor's hand and squeezed it lightly. "You, my dear friend, are kind to a fault. Always do you strive to see others happy, willingly surrendering your own happiness if it meant to spare someone else pain. However, you also have a strong, rather determined and unyielding side, which allows you to make your way without suffering too much from the disregard of others. What you need to ask yourself is, does Mr. Waltham's character match yours? Are you compatible in that regard? Or does your mother object because her objectivity allows her to see what you cannot, that he is not right for you?"

Eleanor sighed, unwilling to allow Winifred's words to sway her. And yet, had she not been wondering why her mother would so steadfastly refuse her consent? Why her eyes burned with determination whenever Eleanor dared approach the subject of Henry? Could it be possible that her mother was merely trying to spare her the pain of discovering that once their love would vanish that they would not in the least be compatible?

"I strongly urge you to reconsider," Winifred whispered, gently squeezing Eleanor's hand, her kind eyes holding concern as well as sympathy, "or you may regret it for the rest of your life."

"Why?" Nick demanded, his eyes wide with incredulity as he stared at Henry. "Have you lost your mind? I thought you were trying to win Lady Eleanor's hand, not be thrown off the premises."

Henry sighed, a slight headache beginning to form under his left temple. "I assure you my intentions have not changed, nor will they ever. However, since you won't allow me to assist you in dealing with the pain you clearly suffer," Nick swallowed, and his gaze momentarily dropped to the floor, "then I would appreciate it if you would assist me in winning the woman I love."

Staring at his brother, Henry waited. For two days, he had waged a battle within himself, ever since the day the Stanhope party had been invited to dine with them at Sanford Manor. That day, doubts had invaded Henry's mind, and no matter what he did, he could not seem to shake them. Nick's reaction upon seeing Eleanor and her brother had been too telling. He had been greatly agitated, and yet, Henry had clearly seen the torment and pain in his brother's eyes. Had Eleanor been the one to break his heart? Had she refused him?

Unable to believe what his observations suggested, Henry could not help but feel the need to discover the truth. Had Eleanor kept this from him? How well did he truly know her? And yet, after everything they had been through, he felt like the worst scoundrel to doubt her.

"You're serious?" Nick asked for the hundredth time. "You want me to accompany you to the house party? Why?" Again, he shook his head. "Be assured that my presence will not serve you. Quite the contrary."

Henry inhaled a deep breath, then took a step toward his brother, his gaze holding Nick's. "As far as we know, Lady Stanhope refuses her consent due to my brothers' reputations." Nick almost cringed at his words, and once again, Henry wondered what had happened to change his brother so. "Since there is no way to alter the past, the only option we have is to show Lady Stanhope that *now* we are different men, that not all of my brothers still behave the way they used to." Clapping a hand on Nick's shoulder, he nodded encouragingly. "You are a good man, and I believe that if she sees that we both treat her daughter with the necessary respect, that that will change how she sees us."

Nick sighed, "Do you truly believe so? Or is it simply your last resort?"

Henry shrugged, no longer certain how to answer that question. "I cannot give up without trying everything within my power. I well know that it might not change anything, but I know that I won't be able to live with myself if I lose her and know that I did not fight hard enough. Will you help me, Brother?"

For a long moment, Nick held his gaze, his own distant as though his mind was far away. Then he blinked, and a tormented sigh escaped his lips. "I shall do what I can," he vowed, a touch of reverence in his tone, "for I do not wish for you to know what it feels like to have your heart ripped from your chest."

Henry sucked in a sharp breath at his brother's words. It was the first time he had admitted to having had his heart broken. "Thank you, Brother." Holding Nick's gaze, he asked, "Will you tell me about her?"

Nick swallowed. "There is nothing to say." Then he turned and walked away, his shoulders slumped as though the weight of the world rested on them and he was no longer strong enough to bear it.

Seeing his brother's misery, Henry once more felt a wave of guilt wash over him for deep down he knew that one of the reasons he wished for his brother to attend the house party was to see him and

Eleanor interact. How would they behave? Would their behaviour reveal a previous attachment? Or was he insane for suspecting as he did?

Brushing his hands over his face, Henry shook his head, praying that his suspicions were unfounded.

If they were not, he was not certain he would survive.

7

A HOUSE PARTY

After breakfast, everyone headed outdoors into the gardens, the clear morning air beckoning them forward as the sun's warm rays bathed everything in a beautiful light. Walking down the small gravel path, arm in arm with Winifred, Eleanor smiled as little Ben came running down the small slope leading down into the gardens, dragging his small wooden horse behind him on a string.

"He is a sweet child," Winifred observed, her eyes shining as she watched him. "Such a lovely disposition."

Eleanor nodded. "Yes, I'm very fond of him, and I cannot wait to have a child of my own."

Watching her friend carefully, Winifred stopped. "First, you need to choose the child's father," she observed. "Have you thought about what I told you?"

"I have," Eleanor said, remembering the sleepless night that had brought nothing put torment.

"And?"

Eleanor sighed, "I admit what you said has merit. However, I cannot discount love as easily as you do."

A touch of disappointment came to Winifred's eyes as she sighed. "It was never my intention to discount it; however, I do believe that affection should only be based on compatibility. Does affection not naturally develop when two people share interests and find themselves at ease in each other's company? Is that not the kind of affection that will last a lifetime because it has a strong foundation?"

Now, it was Eleanor's time to sigh for she could not refute that Winifred's argument was sound, very convincing indeed. And yet, her heart refused to acknowledge any warning that would stand in her and Henry's way to a happily-ever-after.

Still, doubt remained.

"I'm not saying you are wrong," Eleanor finally said. "However, you only speak from a strictly theoretical perspective because in this very moment you are not in love, are you?"

"That is true."

"Have you ever been?"

Winifred shrugged. "Not that I know of. From what I've heard others say, it seems to be a rather powerful emotion unable to be ignored. Therefore, I conclude that I have never felt anything beyond a certain affection."

For a long moment, Eleanor closed her eyes, allowing the love that lived in her heart to wash over her, feeling it in every fibre of her being.

"Are you all right?" Winifred asked after a while, concern ringing in her voice. "You seem…"

Eleanor smiled, her eyes returning to her friend. "I'm in love with Henry. I cannot help it, but I am. I think about him in every waking minute, and I dream about him at night. My heart aches because I haven't seen him in two days, and the thought of not spending the rest of my life with him makes me physically ill." Shrugging her shoulders, Eleanor shook her head, trying to ignore the dumbfounded and rather concerned look on Winifred's face. "I'm sorry, but whether we are compatible or not, I need him like the air I breathe."

Watching her friend closely, Winifred finally said, "While I do respect your decision, I must say that the depth of your dependence on him is rather alarming."

Eleanor swallowed and was just about to enquire what her friend meant by that when her mother, accompanied by Winifred's brother Griffin, approached.

"Isn't it a beautiful day?" Lady Stanhope beamed, her eyes shining in a way Eleanor had not seen in days. "It was indeed a marvellous idea to hold a house party."

Winifred nodded. "I'm indeed grateful for the opportunity to see Eleanor again, Lady Stanhope. It has been too long."

"It has indeed," Lady Stanhope agreed, her gaze drifting to Griffin. "My dear Lord Amberly, why don't you share some of your marvellous travel stories with my daughter. I'm certain she would love to learn of the many wonders the world holds."

"It would be my pleasure," Griffin said, holding out his arm to Eleanor. There was a mischievous twinkle in his eyes that gave Eleanor pause. What was he up to?

In the meantime, her mother turned to Winifred. "Would you be so kind as to accompany me into the parlour? I simply must hear your opinion on a painting I recently acquired. From what I remember your artistic qualifications are not to be ignored. I cannot wait to hear what you think."

Accepting Griffin's arm, Eleanor watched over her shoulder as her mother and Winifred headed back up to the house and then disappeared inside. "That was odd," she finally mumbled, confused by her mother's behaviour. "Never has she shown particular interest in art. I wonder what happened."

Next to her, Griffin chuckled, and Eleanor turned to see what had amused him so.

"I hear you have a most unsuitable suitor," he said with a wide grin on his face.

Eleanor's gaze narrowed.

Laughing, Griffin lifted his hand in a placating way. "I only repeat what I hear. However, from what I can gather, your mother is intent on seeing you marry another."

Eleanor frowned. "But who?"

Winking at her, Griffin leaned closer. "Me."

As the breath rushed from her lungs, Eleanor raised her eyes to his, and a deep blush spread to her cheeks.

As their luggage was brought upstairs, Henry and Nick proceeded toward the terrace of Stanhope Grove, joyous voices drifting to their ears, their cheerfulness in stark contrast to the tortured look on Nick's face. With his hands clenching and unclenching, a haunted expression in his eyes, Nick looked the picture of uncomfortable.

"Have you ever been here before?" Henry asked, holding his breath as he waited for his brother's answer.

Nick's eyes narrowed. "What makes you say that?"

"I admit your reaction to meeting Eleanor and Lord Stanhope the other day made me wonder. Why is it that you resent them so?"

"I do not resent them," Nick forced out through clenched teeth, then stepped around Henry and out onto the terrace.

Following his brother, Henry was about to enquire further when his gaze fell on Eleanor and his heart beat a little faster.

Standing below in the gardens, she was in conversation with an unknown young woman when her mother came walking over with an equally unknown young man by her side. Words were exchanged as Henry strained to listen. However, from the terrace he could not make out what was said.

Then his heart stopped when he saw Lady Stanhope draw the young woman away, leaving Eleanor in the company of the rather handsome young man, who seemed overly familiar with Henry's future bride. The way he watched her before leaning in and whispering something to her ear made Henry's stomach turn. However, it was the way Eleanor suddenly blushed that almost brought him to his knees.

Red, hot jealousy burnt in his heart, and he could not help but wonder if his brother had been right. Did Eleanor love him as much as he loved her? Or was her regard as fleeting as that of his eldest brother Stephen, in this moment moving on to the young man escorting her deeper into the gardens?

"I want you to know that I take no pleasure from this," Nick spoke beside him; "however, I am glad that you saw this. Maybe now you can understand your love is not meant to be. Maybe Stephen is right, and our reputation is what keeps us safe from falling into love's trap."

Gritting his teeth, Henry hurried down the steps, barely aware that his brother was following on his heel, his eyes fixed on the young couple until they walked around a tall hedge and were lost from sight.

Quickening his steps, Henry felt his heart hammering in his chest, ready to burst.

"Mr. Waltham."

Head snapping up at the sound of his name, Henry blinked, his vision momentarily unfocused.

"Welcome to Stanhope Grove," Lord Stanhope addressed him, a small assembly of guests watching the two latest arrivals with curiosity.

"How wonderful that you could join us," his wife added, her face aglow as she smiled at him. "I know Eleanor will be very pleased to see you."

Forcing himself to remain where he was, Henry greeted his host and endured the seemingly endless introductions. However, the moment Lord Stanhope addressed Nick, he mumbled an excuse and hurried away, unable to care about the rudeness of his behaviour. All he could think about was Eleanor in the arms of another man.

Coming around another hedge, he spotted them up ahead, and once more, his legs were almost knocked out from under him.

Biting her lower lip, Eleanor shyly averted her gaze, her cheeks flushed, a moment before the young man took her hand in his, his eyes focused on her, a deep smile on his face.

Storming toward them, Henry hoped he would be able to restrain himself and not challenge the stranger to a duel over Eleanor's hand.

Never would he have seen this coming!

8

JEALOUSY

"Is it true that someone stole your heart?" Griffin asked without preamble, his dark brown eyes intent on her face.

Drawing in a sharp breath, Eleanor almost flinched as she stared at him.

A soft chuckle rose from his throat. "Winifred told me," he explained, his gaze openly searching hers as though seeking to uncover her secrets. Eleanor had all but forgotten Griffin's annoying ability to read those around him like open books. "We have no secrets," he added, a slightly apologetic expression in his eyes. "Please do not hold it against her. She would never betray your trust."

Eleanor sighed, feeling her muscles relax. Although she had not seen Griffin in a long time, he, too, was an old friend, and she realised that she felt comfortable in his presence. Smiling, she shook her head. "I know that she wouldn't. Believe me I'm not angry. I was simply…surprised." As the tension that had held her body rigid in the last few weeks slowly dissipated further, Eleanor sighed. "To tell you the truth, it is quite a relief to be able to speak of Henry openly."

"Ahh," Griffin replied, another mischievous twinkle in his eyes, "he has a name. Henry it is then."

"Henry Waltham," Eleanor added.

For a moment, Griffin frowned before he shrugged. "I can't say I've heard the name before."

Eleanor inhaled deeply, the words about to leave her tongue twisting her insides painfully. "I suppose my mother would not be surprised. After all, she considers him a no one, someone not worthy of our lineage and position." Closing her eyes, Eleanor exhaled slowly.

"Obviously, you disagree," Griffin observed, his kind eyes watching her carefully as she struggled to find words to explain the turmoil that had lived in her heart for so long.

"He is a good man," Eleanor finally said as she believed with every fibre of her being that that was what was truly important. "He is kind and caring. He puts my well-being before his own. He respects my wishes even if doing so is a torment to him." Eleanor sighed, wondering if she was being fair to Henry. "He is the one who deserves better."

"Better than your mother?" Griffin said, a touch of humour in his voice. "Possibly. Better than you?" He lowered his head slightly and held her gaze, his eyes so insistent as though he could will his words into existence. "Not possible."

A soft smile came to Eleanor's face, and she felt herself relax as relief flooded her heart to have found an ally. After the way Winifred had reacted—although she had only meant to be helpful—it was incredibly liberating to speak to Griffin so openly and have him understand. "It feels wonderful to be able to speak about Henry so freely," she told him honestly. "From the moment we met, the moment we fell in love, my mother made it clear that our hopes were not to be. I don't even remember a time when we were carefree in our joy to have found each other. It feels like one endless struggle, and with each day that passes, my fear grows that we will not succeed in changing her mind."

"There is always a solution," Griffin whispered, his eyes steady as though he had already found it. "If you truly love him, you must not give up."

"I won't," Eleanor assured him, his words giving her strength. "Thank you, Griffin. I have truly missed you."

Griffin laughed, his eyes twinkling with mischief. "And I have missed you, dear Eleanor. Let us agree not to be strangers again."

Nodding vigorously, Eleanor smiled.

Again, a grin tugged at the corner of Griffin's mouth. "Your Henry truly must be an exceptional man if he managed to win your heart." Awe shining in his eyes, he shook his head as though in disbelief. "I've never seen your eyes shine like that. If that isn't proof enough, I don't know what is."

Speechless, Eleanor smiled as a slight blush crept up her cheeks, and she stared at Griffin in amazement. Had he always been this intuitive? This sensitive?

Gently, he took her hand in his, giving it a tender squeeze and said, "I wish you two all the best. Should you need my help, you need only ask."

"Thank you, Griffin," Eleanor whispered, lowering her head as she wondered if there was anything he could do. "I shall not forget this."

In that moment, angry footsteps echoed to her ears, and she turned her head as Griffin looked up and over her shoulder. Instantly, her eyes widened and worry crept into her heart as she saw Henry striding toward them, his face in an angry scowl. Never had she seen him like this. Something awful must have happened.

"Henry!" Eleanor exclaimed, turning to the man she loved without hesitation. "What's happened? Did my mother—?"

"What's going on here?" Henry snarled, his hands clenched at his sides as though he could barely keep his anger under control. With gritted teeth, he stared at her before his gaze shifted to Griffin, glaring at her friend with unconcealed hatred.

"What do you mean?" Eleanor asked, confusion drawing down her brows. "May I introduce you to—"

Griffin chuckled beside her, "He's jealous, dear Eleanor." He turned a questioning gaze on Henry. "Is that not true?"

Instantly, Henry's shoulders tensed and his hands balled into fists, his eyes shooting daggers at Griffin, who apparently found this whole situation terribly amusing as another round of chuckles echoed to Eleanor's ears.

"I shall take my leave then," Griffin stated, slightly bowing his head to Eleanor before he stopped in front of Henry. "You have nothing to fear," he said, his voice serious without its usual touch of humour. "Her heart is yours. Never doubt that."

Then Griffin turned and walked away, leaving them behind in a cloud of awkward silence.

For a long moment, they remained quiet as they each were lost in their own thoughts. Feeling his anger dissipate, Henry glanced at Eleanor, hoping she would not be offended by his lack of decorum, his lack of restraint. Had he just now almost attacked a guest at Eleanor's party? A man who was obviously a friend?

Instantly, a new wave of jealousy rushed to his chest, and Henry forced a deep breath down his lungs, seeking to control it.

"Is it true?" Eleanor demanded, her blue eyes watchful as they roamed his face. "Are you jealous?"

Gritting his teeth, Henry nodded. He would not make it worse by lying to her. How could he ever have thought that she had broken his brother's heart? He must have been insane to think so even for a moment. There had to be another explanation for Nick's odd behaviour.

A soft smile came to Eleanor's face, and the air rushed from Henry's lungs in a wave of relief as he realised that she was not angry with him. "He is only a friend," she said confirming his thoughts, her clear blue eyes holding his without wavering. "We've known each other for years, and I've never looked at him the way I look at you. Can you not see that?"

Joy soared through him, and yet, a touch of doubt remained. Stepping closer, Henry tentatively reached for her hands. "Is it true?" he whispered, his eyes searching hers. "Does your heart truly belong to me?"

Again, Eleanor blushed, and she momentarily averted her gaze before meeting his eyes once more, her cheeks aglow. Then she inhaled deeply and nodded her head in affirmation. "It is."

Henry swallowed, and all his doubts vanished. Wrapping his hands more tightly around hers, he pulled her closer. "I apologise for the way I acted, for jumping to such a conclusion." He inhaled deeply, realising that baring one's heart to someone was not as easy as he had thought, even if that someone was Eleanor. After all, today had taught him how vulnerable she made him and how much his happiness depended on her. "Despite everything we've been through," he whispered, "we've never told each other how we truly feel, have we?"

Swallowing, Eleanor shook her head, her gaze holding his as she waited for him to continue.

Again, Henry drew in a deep breath, a shy smile tugging at the corner of his mouth. "I want you to know how I feel, to truly know and not just suspect." He nodded his head in emphasis. "I love you, Eleanor. I have since the moment I first saw you. You're everything to me, and I cannot imagine my life without you. I *refuse* to imagine it without you, for I know beyond the shadow of a doubt that I shall never be happy without you by my side." He gripped her hands more tightly, his head lowering as he gazed into her eyes, now slightly moist with tears. "I love you."

Sniffling, Eleanor blinked, and a single tear ran down her cheek as a delighted smile—heart-breaking in its intensity—lit up her beautiful face. "I feel the same way," she breathed, pushing herself against him in an almost desperate need to be closer. "I love you as well."

As utter joy invaded his being, Henry yanked Eleanor into his arms and claimed her mouth in a desperate kiss.

At first, she tensed, startled at the ferocity of his feelings. However, only a split second later, she leaned into him, her arms snaking up and coming around his neck, pulling herself closer, as she returned his kiss with the same passion that lived in his heart.

Henry could have stayed in this moment forever if only Lady Stanhope's enraged voice had not drifted to their ears in precisely that moment, cutting through their joy like a sharp knife.

Jerking their heads apart, they stared at each other.

"Mother?" Eleanor exclaimed as she gathered her skirts and ran back to the house.

9

THE TRUTH OF THE MATTER

As her heart thudded in her chest, partly from Henry's kiss and partly from the tone of outrage in her mother's voice, Eleanor willed her legs to move faster. Never had the path up from the gardens stretched before her so endlessly.

Before long, Henry was by her side again, offering her his arm as he pulled her forward and around the last hedge separating them from the terrace.

As before, their guests stood in small clusters. However, where moments ago they had conversed amiably with one another, they now stood staring at Lady Stanhope.

With arms akimbo, she had stopped only a few steps onto the terrace, her eyes wide with shock and her face pale as a sheet.

Terror seized Eleanor's heart at the sight, and she released Henry's arm and rushed forward. "Mother? Are you all right?" Reaching her just as her brother stepped forward as well, his gaze narrowed in concern, Eleanor grasped her mother's hands.

Blinking, Lady Stanhope swallowed, and her gaze drifted to Eleanor. "What is *he* doing here?" she snarled, a mixture of outrage and pain tainting her voice.

Casting a glance over her shoulder, Eleanor frowned as her gaze fell on Henry's brother, Nick. Rooted to the spot, he, too, seemed shaken to his core. However, while her mother seemed near fainting, Nick appeared ready to burst, hatred burning in his eyes as he glared at his hostess.

Eleanor swallowed, wishing she could understand what had happened. "I invited him," she whispered, guilt rushing to her heart even without knowing why.

Turning her head, her mother stared at her in disbelief and would have stumbled backwards if Eleanor had not held her hands tightly in her own. Then her gaze drifted upward and angled slightly to the side, and even without looking, Eleanor knew that her mother had just now taken note of Henry's presence.

Instantly, the muscles in her jaw tensed even further.

With deadly calm, her mother drew back her shoulders and raised her chin, the look in her eyes drilling into Eleanor's soul. "Never have I been this disappointed with you as I am now," she stated, her words like knives to Eleanor's heart. Then she yanked her hands out of Eleanor's and turned to glare at the two brothers. "I demand that you leave my house this instant." Her eyes narrowed as she looked at Henry as though he were a bug she wished to squash. "I will not stand idly by and watch Eleanor be ruined as well." Then she spun on her heel and returned to the house, her breath coming in fast gasps as though her control on her emotions was slipping and she was near fainting.

Never had Eleanor seen her mother so emotional, so vulnerable, and it terrified her to her very core. Something was very wrong, and now the time had finally come to learn what.

Shaking her head at her brother as he stepped forward, Eleanor turned to Henry. "Please stay," she said, nodding her head for emphasis.

"Are you certain?" he asked, doubt in his voice as he glanced at the drawing room doors through which her mother had left.

"I am," Eleanor said with determination. "I need to speak to her and find out what happened. We need to put this to rest once and for all."

Henry nodded. "I'll be here if you need me."

"Thank you."

Turning toward the house, Eleanor wasted no time and hurried after her mother, finding her in the drawing room, pacing the length of the Persian rug frantically, her arms gesturing wildly as she mumbled under her breath.

As Eleanor closed the doors behind her, her mother finally noticed her presence, turning angry eyes on her daughter. "Mother, what happened? Please tell me what is going on."

Her mother's lips contorted into a snarl, "Get out!"

Shaken by the rude tone in her mother's voice, Eleanor swallowed as every fibre in her body told her to comply. And still, she stood her ground, knowing that if she left now, she might as well set Henry free and accept that their love would never lead to a happy future.

That thought terrified her more than anything else.

"I will not," she stated in a calm voice, stepping toward her mother, her gaze unwavering as she gathered her strength for this battle of wills.

A hint of surprise came to her mother's eyes. "I do not wish to speak to you. Now, go!"

"But *I* wish to speak with *you*," Eleanor retorted. "I should have demanded an explanation weeks ago, no, months ago, but I hoped that if I gave you time, you would tell me willingly." Shaking her head, Eleanor snorted. "But I was wrong. No matter the consequences, you intend to take this to your grave, do you not?"

Her mother swallowed, and the anger in her gaze slowly melted away, replaced by deep sorrow. "It was never meant for your ears."

"Whether it was or not does not matter," Eleanor insisted, hope surging to the surface as she realised that her mother was at the end of her rope. "I need to know for it affects my life in the worst way. I can no longer live with the secrets around me. You want me to send away the man I love, but you won't even tell me why."

Her mother gritted her teeth. "He is not a good match for you. He is not worthy of–"

"You're wrong!" Eleanor shouted, shaking her head in anger at her mother's insistence to hold on to her secret. "And you would see that if you weren't so terrified to learn the truth."

"Terrified?" her mother gasped, staring at her with wide eyes. "I'm outraged. I'm–"

"Why?" Eleanor snapped. "Because I went against your wishes and invited him? No, that's not the reason, and you know it." Pointing through the doors at the terrace, Eleanor stepped toward her mother. "I saw your face out there. You were not outraged. You were frightened. I saw it in your eyes. There was pain and anguish and terror." Eleanor swallowed as tears gathered in her mother's eyes, and her voice softened, "I need to know why." Grasping her mother's hands, Eleanor looked into her eyes pleadingly. "Please, Mother. If you love me, you need to be honest with me. You are not protecting me by keeping this secret." As her mother's gaze focused on hers, Eleanor shook her head. "You're not. You're breaking my heart."

A sorrowful gasp escaped her mother's lips, and she closed her eyes, tears running freely down her cheeks as her hands tightened on Eleanor's. Instantly, the memory of that night months ago as her mother had sat by her bed at night surged to the surface of Eleanor's mind. "I had hoped you would never have to find out," her mother whispered before her eyes opened, and she looked at her daughter. "I had hoped your regard for him would dissipate over time so that you would never have to learn the truth. I'm sorry, dear child. I never meant to break your heart. All I've done, I did to protect it."

"I know," Eleanor assured her, praying that her mother would not refuse to share her secret now. "I never believed that you withheld your consent out of spite or disregard for my feelings. I always knew you had a reason. But I'm not a child any more. You need to trust me enough to share it with me. I deserve to know. This is my life, my happiness, and I have a right to know. Please, Mother."

Exhausted, her mother stumbled to the settee, seating herself before she might faint after all. Coming to sit next to her, Eleanor met her gaze expectantly. "What happened?"

"It's about Corinne," her mother finally said, barely able to meet her daughter's eyes. "I failed her." Anger returned to her voice. "I failed my sister. I promised her to look after her daughter, and when she needed me, I wasn't there."

Confused, Eleanor stared at her mother. "What are you talking about? What happened to Corinne? She is travelling on the continent…is she not?" Fear seized her heart, squeezing it until Eleanor felt as though she could not breathe.

Placing a gentle hand on her daughter's, Lady Stanhope met her eyes. "She's with child," she whispered, her words knocking the air from Eleanor's lungs.

"What?" she gasped, not having expected anything remotely like this.

Her mother nodded, guilt and pain darkening her eyes before the muscles in her jaw tensed in anger. "Nicholas Waltham is the father."

Staring at her mother, Eleanor could not form a coherent thought. It could not possibly be true? Did Henry know? How? Why? Her mind ran rampant.

Her mother's lips pressed into a thin line, disgust clearly written all over her face. "That *man* ruined Corinne and then refused to marry her. He is without honour, without decency. He didn't even have the courage to tell her himself. All he did was sent a note." Shaking her head, her mother closed her eyes. "It broke her heart. I've never seen her like this. The picture of misery, all her hopes crushed with a few simple words."

Waiting for the rest of the tale, Eleanor held her mother's hand as tears of her own streamed down her face.

For Corinne.

For her mother.

For her own love.

"I sent Corinne to Halford House to have the baby," her mother continued. "I pray that no one will learn of this and that she'll be able to return to us some day and not be subjected to the evil gossip of the ton." A snort escaped her. "And I should know for I am usually at its core. I pretended that nothing had changed, that the world was still the way it was supposed to be." Again, tears came to her eyes. "I treated poor Diana horribly. She, too, suffered the dishonesty of a so-called *gentleman*. She didn't deserve my derision. I wronged her."

Eleanor swallowed. All these months her cousin, her friend had been so close–only a few days' ride away–and Eleanor had not known. All alone, Corinne had to face the horror of losing the man she loved and realising that her future lay shattered before her. And now, there would be a baby.

"Is that why you came to my room that night?" Eleanor asked, remembering her mother's tears as well as her promise to protect her.

Lady Stanhope nodded. "I had just seen her to Halford House. I wished I could have stayed, but how should I have explained my absence?" She shook her head. "I didn't want to burden you."

Eleanor nodded. "I will send Nick away." She drew in a deep breath and met her mother's eyes. "But Henry is not his brother. He has done nothing to deserve your hatred for him."

For a long moment, her mother looked at her. "Have you been intimate with him?"

Taken aback, Eleanor shook her head, a touch of red coming to her cheeks. "I have not. He has never treated me with anything but respect."

Her mother nodded, and a glimmer of hope began to blossom in Eleanor's heart. "I shall send Nick away, and then I need to see Corinne."

"I'll take you to her," her mother agreed, a soft smile coming to her face. "She'll be happy to see you."

10

A LOVE ONCE LOST

"What on earth was that about?" Henry mumbled to himself as he paced the length of the front hall, every now and then casting an expectant glance at the closed doors to the drawing room. After a while, everything had gone quiet, and Henry did not know if that was a good sign or not. Had Eleanor been able to reach her mother? Was Lady Stanhope at this moment explaining herself to her daughter?

Stopping in his tracks, Henry blinked as his mind drew him back to the moment they had come upon Lady Stanhope on the terrace, her eyes burning with hatred as she had stared at…

"You," Henry mumbled, then slowly turned on his heel until he faced his brother, who sat hunched over on one of the bottom steps of the large staircase. "She looked at you."

Lifting his head, Nick met Henry's gaze for the barest of moments before his eyes dropped to the ground once more, a new tension coming to this shoulders.

"She was displeased to see *me*," Henry continued, his mind recalling all the details of that one fateful moment, "but beyond herself with anger when she saw *you*." Swallowing, Henry stared at his brother, the question that once again formed in his mind stuck in his throat. What if he had been right before? What if there had been something between Eleanor and his brother? What if it had ended…? Henry shook his head, forcing the possibility from his mind. And yet, he could feel it lingering at the edges of his consciousness.

As he was about to open his mouth and address his brother, footsteps neared, and Henry flinched, turning his head from his brother with a mixture of relief and regret.

Lord Stanhope approached, his gaze narrowed as he glanced back and forth between the two brothers. "They're still in there?" he asked, and yet, his voice did not rise to ask it a question. Then he nodded. "Good. It is about time they spoke to each other." Again, he glanced at Henry before his gaze travelled to his brother still seated on the stairs, head hanging between slumped shoulders. "Is everything all right?"

Henry drew in a deep breath. "I suppose we shall know soon."

Lord Stanhope nodded. "Send for me when the doors open." Then he took a step toward the terrace. "I shall see to our guests."

As the doors closed behind him, Henry once more turned his attention to his brother. Although every fibre of his being urged him to ignore the question burning in his heart, trying to convince him that ignorance could indeed be bliss, a small but rather insistent part of him could not pretend all was well…or would be well.

"Again, I ask you," Henry spoke into the silence hanging like a shroud over them, "are you acquainted with the family?"

At his words, his brother's frame tensed and he inhaled deeply, sending Henry's heart into a tailspin.

Gritting his teeth, Henry balled his hands into fists to keep himself in check. "Tell me what you know," he demanded, his voice harsh and abrupt. "Are you acquainted with the family? With…Eleanor? And don't you dare lie to me. What I saw out there on the terrace speaks for itself. Clearly, Lady Stanhope despises you." He shook his head, a tortured snort escaping his lips. "And here I thought it was our brothers' reputations that stood in the way of my happiness with Eleanor, but it is you, isn't it?"

Drawing in a deep breath, Nick lifted his head and met Henry's gaze.

To his surprise, he saw neither guilt nor regret in his brother's eyes, but only pain and sorrow. Had he been wrong? Had he judged too quickly? Could there be another explanation?

Swallowing, Nick pushed himself to his feet and came to stand before Henry. "I assure you," he began, his voice calm as he held Henry's gaze, "I have no prior connection to Lady Eleanor. You have nothing to fear from me, Brother."

Henry exhaled loudly, "Then, why…?"

"I knew her cousin," Nick replied, the muscles in his jaw tensing. "Corinne."

"Her cousin?" Henry asked, relieved at his brother's answer, and yet, confused by it all the same. Indeed, as far as he could recall Eleanor had mentioned a cousin at one point or another, but was she not travelling on the continent? "I don't understand."

As Nick opened his mouth to reply, the doors to the drawing room flew open and Eleanor rushed out.

Turning to her, Henry was taken aback by the hostility in her eyes as she glared at his brother, her usual calm demeanour gone. Whatever had happened between his brother and her cousin, it had to have ended badly.

"You!" she snarled, pointing an accusing finger at Nick's chest. "Get out!"

With wide eyes, Nick stared at her, momentarily frozen to the spot.

"What's going on?" Henry interjected, placing a gentle hand on Eleanor's arm. "What happened? What did your mother say?"

Turning her gaze to him, Eleanor swallowed, and he could see raw pain lurking out from beneath the anger that held her rigid. "Ask your brother. He's the one who ruined everything."

Glancing back and forth between Nick and Eleanor, Henry felt ready to explode as they both kept their silence. "Will one of you please tell me what is going on?" he snapped, glaring at both.

While Nick remained immobile, his face inexpressive like a mask, Eleanor inhaled deeply, then turned her gaze to Henry. "He...," she began, then swallowed, needing to gather all her courage to continue. "He ruined my cousin, and then he refused to marry her."

As though he had been slapped in the face, Henry's head whipped around, his gaze seeking his brother's. However, what he saw there made his head spin. Once again, instead of guilt and remorse, he saw only stunned disbelief. "Is this true?" he asked, placing a hand on his brother's arm.

Nick blinked. "What?" he breathed, then swallowed as though something had lodged in his throat that he could not seem to rid himself of. "I...She...What?"

"Is this true?" Henry asked again, slightly shaking his brother as his mind still seemed somewhat far away. "You just told me that you knew Corinne. Did you...?"

Holding his breath, Henry waited, Eleanor standing beside him, her gaze hard as she glared at his brother. If this was indeed true, then their happily-ever-after would never be. How could they overcome such a betrayal? The simple answer was: they could not. Eleanor would never marry him out of respect for her cousin, and he would never be able to forgive his brother for coming between him and the woman he loved.

"It's not true," Nick finally said, and for a moment, Henry felt as though he would faint with relief. "That is not what happened." Shaking his head, he looked at Eleanor, his eyes now clear and the tone in his voice steady. "I loved her. I *wanted* to marry her," his jaw clenched, "but then she changed her mind, saying she had received a better offer than the fourth son of a baron." Anger gripped his voice, and he swallowed, his teeth clenched.

"You're lying!" Eleanor snapped, shaking her head in disbelief. "How can you say that? How can you pretend that you acted honourably? She trusted you, and you betrayed her. And now–" Mid-sentence she stopped herself, her eyes glancing around the empty front hall, before her voice dropped to a whisper. "And now she is with child, hiding out in the country to avoid a scandal. Her life, however, will be ruined no matter what happens."

The news that Corinne was with child hit Henry square in the chest. However, his own surprise was nothing in comparison to his brother's. Even if he had not been certain before, now Henry had no doubt that there had been a terrible misunderstanding and that nothing was as it seemed.

"What?" Nick stammered, his eyes bulging as he stared at Eleanor. "She's with…She's having…I…We…" Then he swallowed, and the light that had come to his gaze darkened. "Is it mine?"

A deep frown came to Eleanor's face, and for a second, Henry thought she would lash out at his brother in anger. Then, however, it was as though she had suddenly seen something that had escaped her notice before and she looked at him for a long moment before finally nodding her head. "My mother assures me that it is, yes."

A large smile came to Nick's face at her answer, and all the sorrow and misery of the last few months seemed to be lifted off his shoulders. "I'm going to be a father," he stammered, eyes glowing with disbelief and joy. "I'm going to be a father." Stumbling backwards, he once more sank onto the bottom steps of the large staircase, for a moment resting his head in his hands as he drew one deep breath after another into his lungs.

"Are you all right?" Henry asked, casting a careful glance at Eleanor, who looked similarly concerned…if a little puzzled as well. Maybe all hope was not lost after all!

Abruptly, Nick rose to his feet, a sense of urgency in his gaze. "Where is she? I need to see her." With his eyes fixed on Eleanor, he stepped forward. "Tell me where she is. You said she's hiding out in the country. Where?"

Her gaze narrowing, Eleanor shook her head. "I don't think she wishes to see you. Mother said she was very shaken when you refused to mar–"

Frowning, Nick interrupted her. "But I didn't. I had every intention of marrying her until she sent me a letter informing me that she'd changed her mind. I tried to speak to her after that but she was suddenly gone. All this time I thought she had married another." Shaking his head, he stepped forward, eyes intent on Eleanor. "But she's not married, is she?"

"She's not," Eleanor replied, and Nick's shoulders slumped in relief. "That's the problem."

Drawing in a deep breath, Nick closed his eyes for a moment before seeking Eleanor's gaze once again. "I don't know what happened or how this misunderstanding came to be, but I can assure you that it is nothing more than a misunderstanding. I never would have left her. I loved her. I still love her." Shaking his head, Nick sighed, and Henry could see Eleanor's resolve wavering. "To this day, I haven't been able to forget about her, and if she'll have me, I'll marry her on the spot."

A gentle smile drew up Eleanor's lips, and Henry took her hand in his urging her to look at him. "He's telling the truth," Henry said with a glance at his brother. "These past few months he has been a mere shadow of himself. He's been mourning her loss." Looking at his brother, Henry shook his head. "And I never knew. I'm deeply sorry, Brother, that I didn't see your pain, didn't recognise it for what it was."

Nick shrugged. "That is all in the past now. Lady Eleanor, please," he begged, "will you tell me where she is?"

Taking a deep breath, Eleanor nodded, hope lighting up her eyes as she turned to look at Henry. "I shall speak to my brother without delay," she said before whispering in his ear, "Maybe we shall all find our happily-ever-after."

Squeezing her hand before she hastened away, Henry then turned to his brother, a relieved smile on his face. "Tell me about Corinne."

A deep smile came to Nick's face, the likes of which Henry had not seen in months.

11

NOT GONE FOREVER

Despite feeling guilty for abandoning their guests, Eleanor could not wait to set out for Halford House and see Corinne and Nick reunited.

Since her mother insisted on accompanying them, two carriages were readied, and within the hour, they were on the road. At first, Nick had demanded to be told where Corinne was so that he could ride ahead on horseback and reach the estate faster. However, still not convinced of his intentions, Lady Stanhope had refused to name their destination and glared at Eleanor until she had promised not to breathe a word of it either.

"I'm responsible for her," her mother huffed as they began their journey south. "I've already failed her once. I shall not allow her to be confronted by a man whose intentions are still not clear."

"Not clear?" Nick demanded, a touch of outrage in his voice. "My intentions have always been clear. I never once—"

"Calm down, Brother," Henry interrupted, placing a soothing hand on his arm. "It is admirable that she is protecting her niece so diligently. After all, she barely knows us, and our brothers' reputations would worry any decent parent."

"There you have it," Lady Stanhope huffed, still unable not to glare at Nick.

Seeing her mother's narrowed gaze as it swept Henry's face in puzzlement, Eleanor had to suppress a smile. "Mother, can you once more tell us what happened?" she asked, seeking to uncover the origin of this rather unfortunate misunderstanding concerning her cousin and Henry's brother. "Why did Corinne believe that he no longer wished to marry her?"

Her mother drew in a deep breath, her gaze shooting daggers in Nick's direction. "As far as she told me, they were bound for Gretna Green—not the most civilised way to get married, I might add—when she received a letter from him, saying that he had changed his mind. He wrote that he must have been mad to consider matrimony and was now more convinced than ever that he would never relinquish the carefree life of a bachelor that he'd always loved." A growl rose from her mother's throat. "What a scoundrel! I cannot believe I'm allowing him to see Corinne. I must be mad!"

Frowning, Eleanor looked at Nick just as he opened his mouth. "I never sent such a letter," he defended himself, outrage burning in his eyes. "Why would I? I admit I might have acted wrongly on occasion, but that was of in the past moment I met Corinne. In fact, it was I who received a letter."

"That is very strange," Eleanor mumbled glancing from Nick to Henry, "that you both received letters that the other never sent. Who on earth sent these letters? And why?"

Glancing at her mother, Eleanor waited, hoping that this was not yet another way her mother had meddled in affairs that were not her own…at the time tragically unaware that Corinne had already been with child.

"Don't look at me like that," Lady Stanhope snapped at her before she could open her mouth. "Had I known about their relationship, considering his reputation, I surely would have told her not to see him again. However, I would never hide behind forged letters. That is beneath me!"

Turning her gaze to Henry, Eleanor froze when she suddenly realised that something seemed to bother him as his body had gone rigid and his eyes were open wide. The moment their gazes locked, he swallowed and his hands clenched into fists as he tried to remain outwardly calm.

Drawing in a deep breath, Eleanor could barely keep herself from asking him what he had just realised. However, there was something in his gaze that urged her to keep quiet.

Fidgeting in her seat, Eleanor prayed that the three days to Halford House would pass quickly. However, with each day, Nick grew more restless. Every night when they stopped at an inn, he urged them to continue through the night and growled at them whenever Lady Stanhope refused. By the third day when Halford House finally came in sight, Nick was beside himself with anxiety, his face haggard from lack of sleep and his eyes blood-shot as he had spent most of the journey staring out the window, barely saying a word.

As the two carriages drew up in front of the small estate, Nick jumped out before the wheels had even stopped turning. Lady Stanhope shrieked in outrage and made to follow him until Eleanor grabbed her arm and held her back. When the carriage had finally drawn to a halt, Henry stepped out, helped them both down before they immediately rushed toward the open front door without another glance at her brother's family in the second carriage.

The moment they stepped into the front hall, Corinne's startled shriek reached their ears, rushing them onward to the drawing room.

Cursing under his breath, Henry hastened down the corridor, following in his brother's footsteps, praying that he had not done something unwise in his desire to see Corinne. However, when Henry burst into the drawing room and found the woman he presumed to be Corinne standing at the far wall, a hand clutched to her chest as she stared at his brother wide-eyed, open terror in her gaze, he realised that his brother's mere presence was enough to scare her out of her wits.

"This is unacceptable behaviour!" Lady Stanhope panted as she rushed through the doors, Eleanor on her heels. Her eyes darted back and forth between Corinne and Nick, and she immediately strode forward, positioning herself in-between them, her eyes fixed on Henry's brother. "I must insist that you leave at once!"

Nick drew in a slow breath, and Henry could see the deep emotions that pulsed under his seemingly calm demeanour. His gaze was fixed on Corinne, barely acknowledging Lady Stanhope's presence. Almost lovingly, he looked at her, a soft smile tugging at the corners of his mouth.

After her initial shock, Corinne, too, seemed to have slipped into some sort of trance as her light green eyes swept over Nick's face. Swallowing, she took a step back until her back came to rest against the wall, and she took a deep breath, brushing a trembling hand over her face as though she feared she had strayed into a dream. Her auburn hair ran over her shaking shoulders, and her other hand rested gently on her protruding belly. Although Henry had very little experience with pregnant women, he thought that the birth of his niece or nephew was not far off.

"What are you doing here?" Corinne asked as her eyes filled with tear, and she shook her head as though the movement could banish Nick from the room.

Swallowing, Nick took a step toward her.

Instantly, Corinne sucked in a sharp breath, and the tears in her eyes spilled over. "Please, go," she begged, hugging her arms around her body. "I can't," she stammered, still shaking her head. "I can't. Not after everything you did to me. I can't. You can't be here. I'm not strong enough to mourn you again."

Silently, Eleanor stepped forward and drew her mother aside, who—to Henry's great surprise—allowed her daughter to lead her to the other side of the room. However, no matter what Eleanor said they could not persuade her to leave. "I need to be certain that he does not hurt her," Lady Stanhope insisted, and for the first time, Henry felt a touch of understanding as he knew the desire to protect someone only too well.

On the other side of the small drawing room, Nick ran his hand through his hair, his eyes tortured as he saw Corinne's fear. After a couple of deep breaths, he finally said, "I received a letter from you."

Watching him, Corinne frowned, the pain in her gaze shifting to confusion. "What letter?"

"A letter saying that you no longer wished to marry me," Nick explained, carefully taking a step toward her, "that you had received an offer from a titled gentleman, and that you wished to marry him instead."

With each word he spoke, Corinne's eyes grew wider.

"It broke my heart," Nick said, his voice thick with emotions as open tears streamed down his face. "These past few months have been torture, imagining you in the arms of another man. It nearly killed me."

Corinne swallowed. "I never sent such a letter." The muscles in her jaw tensed. "I received one from you. You wrote that…" Again, she swallowed back tears. "You wrote that you didn't love me anymore. You wrote that you didn't want to marry me after all." With wide eyes, she stared at Nick, and Henry could read the longing to have her assumptions refuted on her face. And yet, she remained tense, afraid to allow herself to hope.

"I didn't," Nick finally said, his gaze holding hers, willing her to believe him. "I never wrote such a letter as it is not true." He swallowed. "I still love you."

At his words, Corinne's knees almost buckled and a heavy sob escaped her. Crying openly, she shook her head as Nick stepped toward her. "Don't. Please, don't. I beg you don't play with me."

Slowly, Nick approached her. "I'm not. I would never. It's not only your heart that is in danger here; it is mine as well." Looking deep into her eyes, he held out his hand to her. "I don't know who sent these letters…or why. All I know is that I never wanted to be without you, and the past few months did nothing to change that. I still want you."

A soft smile came to Corinne's face as she looked up into Nick's eyes, her own shining with careful hope. "Is that true?" she asked, her voice trembling as she carefully slipped her hand into Nick's. "Can I trust you? I did before and then…"

"I would never have left you, had I known," Nick vowed as his fingers closed around hers more tightly. "Had I known you never wanted me to leave, nothing could have persuaded me from your side." Nick took a deep breath. "I love you, Corinne, and I have from the moment I first laid eyes on you."

A nervous chuckle escaped Corinne as she allowed Nick to pull her into his arms. "I love you, too," she whispered, awe shining in her eyes as she looked up at him. "I thought I'd never see you again."

Swallowing, Nick nodded. "I thought so, too." Lowering his head to hers, he placed a gentle kiss on her lips that had Lady Stanhope huff in indignation. Eleanor, however, glanced up at Henry, and a large smile came to her lips as tears glistened in her eyes.

"Marry me," Nick said suddenly.

Pulling back, Corinne looked at him, a puzzled frown on her face. "What?"

"We were supposed to be married for months," he said, the frown lines on his face slowly dissipating as a smile claimed his mouth, "and this is my child, is it not?" Despite the question, his voice held no doubt, and he gently placed a hand on Corinne's swollen belly.

"Do you truly want this?" Corinne asked, hesitation still giving her voice a slight tremble.

"I've always wanted this," Nick assured her, his face suddenly at ease as though the past few months had only been a bad dream. "Marry me."

For another moment, Corinne hesitated, too overcome by these sudden events. However, before Nick had time to doubt her feelings for him, she nodded her head yes, flinging her arms around his neck. "Yes, I'll marry you."

Hugging her tightly, Nick closed his eyes and inhaled deeply, savouring the moment he had feared would never come.

"We'll better call for a priest then," Henry said, holding out his hand to Eleanor, who smiled at him in a way that made him weak in the knees.

As they were about to step from the room, a low groan slipped from Corinne's lips and she leaned forward, holding her belly. "And the midwife," she panted, her face contorting in pain.

12

LOVE TRUMPS RULES

"The priest alone will do you no good," her brother pointed out as Eleanor and her mother helped Corinne up the stairs and toward her bedroom, Nick by her side, unwilling to part with her for even a moment. "They'll need a special license. We'll have to go to London."

"That's three days!" Henry's voice rang out from the hall.

"In a carriage, yes," Arthur objected. "On horseback, we'll be faster."

"What if that baby is born before they can get married?" Henry asked, deep concern in his voice. "What do we do then?"

"We'll worry about that later," Arthur said. "Let's make haste."

As their voices faded away, Eleanor took a deep breath, praying that all would be well.

Upon reaching Corinne's room, Eleanor's mother took over, bellowing commands and giving orders like a field officer in battle.

Within moments, Corinne was changed and in bed, fresh linens and water on the side table, a stable boy sent to fetch the midwife, and the maids set to the task of boiling water and providing everything else the midwife might need for birthing Corinne's child.

With a touch of awe, Eleanor sat at Corinne's right bedside, Nick on the other, and watched as her mother did what she did best: take control of a situation.

Only this time, Eleanor was beyond grateful to hear her mother's steady voice, giving orders and telling them all what to do.

Never had it felt so reassuring.

"You," Lady Stanhope hissed, a finger pointing at Nick, "out! This is no place for a man!"

With lips pressing into a thin line, Nick shook his head, his arm still wrapped around Corinne's shoulders while she squeezed his other hand every time a contraction shook her body. "I will not leave," he stated in a tone that allowed for no argument. "I left her before, and it was the worst thing I could have ever done. I'm staying."

Annoyed, Lady Stanhope opened her mouth, ready to talk him into submission, when she suddenly stopped. Her eyes narrowed as she regarded him, but Nick did not flinch, his own gaze unwavering. "Fine," Lady Stanhope snapped before spinning on her heel and striding over to the window, throwing it open to allow some fresh air inside.

Eleanor smiled at the subtle sign of approval that she had seen in her mother's eyes at Nick's insistence to remain by Corinne's side.

Less than an hour later, Diana walked into the room, the midwife on her heel. Although a short and slender woman, her greying hair pulled back and tugged into a chignon, she moved with precision and self-assurance, and Eleanor noticed Corinne sigh in relief at the sight of her. "How are you, my dear?" the midwife asked, feeling Corinne's belly. "I'm Mrs. Hamstead. This is your first child?"

Corinne nodded, then gritted her teeth as another contraction held her in its clutches.

Watching Corinne intently, Mrs. Hamstead patted her hand once the contraction had passed. "You're doing fine, my dear. However, it will probably be a while. The first ones always take their time." Then her eyes fell on Nick and immediately narrowed. "I must ask you to leave," she said, her voice as firm as Lady Stanhope's had been. "The birthing room is no place for a man."

Corinne cringed, and her fingers dug deeper into Nick's arm.

Nick, however, remained calm, gently pulling her tighter into his arms. "As I said before I—"

"I recommend you save your breath, Mrs. Hamstead," Lady Stanhope interrupted, a look of amused annoyance in her gaze as she rolled her eyes. "He is fairly stubborn and will not quit the room no matter what you say."

While Mrs. Hamstead looked displeased, a large smile came to Nick's face. "I do believe that is the only nice thing you've ever said about me," he observed, watching in amusement as Lady Stanhope shrugged her shoulders, refusing to look at him.

"If you consider this a compliment, dear boy," she snorted, "you certainly must have been a scoundrel in your day."

"That is in the past," Nick assured her, all humour gone from his gaze. "From now on, I shall only be a husband and father."

Lady Stanhope snorted. However, Eleanor noticed the slight curl that had come to her lips at Nick's words, and she gently squeezed Corinne's hand, whispering, "All shall be well, dear Cousin. With Mother on your side, you have nothing to fear."

Resting her head against Eleanor's shoulder, Corinne sighed, "I never thought this was possible. I dreamt of it, but…" Again, she sighed before her eyes closed and her breathing evened.

All through the afternoon, they took turns sitting with Corinne. Nick, however, could not be persuaded to leave her side even for a moment. In the end, it was only Corinne's gentle insistence that managed to sway him. "You need to eat and freshen up," she said, her eyes holding his imploringly. "Don't worry, I'm not alone, and you'll be back in a moment."

Gritting his teeth, Nick finally forced himself to leave the room, promising to be back within five minutes.

"He truly loves you," Eleanor said smiling as she looked at Corinne. "How come you never mentioned him? I never knew that you…"

With an apologetic look in her pale green eyes, Corinne sighed. "I'm sorry, dear Eleanor. I know I should have. But it all happened so fast. The moment we met, we were in love. I've never experienced anything like it. I was completely overwhelmed and…acted foolishly." Swallowing, she glanced down at her belly before gritting her teeth as another contraction claimed her.

After a moment, she lay back, panting. "Although I hardly knew him, I was certain he was the one." She drew in a deep breath. "And then when everything fell apart, I felt so foolish for believing that he could love me, for not seeing that he only wanted to…"

"But he didn't," Eleanor interjected. "He did love you, and he still does."

Corinne smiled. "A part of me has trouble believing that. After all, I did before and paid for it dearly."

"But now everything is different," Eleanor insisted. "He truly wishes to marry you. You should have seen him before we came here. From what Henry told me, I gathered that he even feared for his life."

Corinne gasped, fear in her eyes.

"He gave up…completely," Eleanor said, hoping her words would put her cousin at ease, assuring her that Nick's intentions had always been honourable. "It was as though without you, life didn't matter to him any longer."

For a long moment, Corinne remained quiet. Then she drew in a slow breath. "I know how that feels," she whispered, the shadow of the past few months hanging over her head.

"Now, you can look toward the future," Eleanor reminded her. "He never stopped loving you, and although you may not know one another that well yet, your love survived the separation forced on you. Believe me, adversity only makes true love stronger."

Corinne smiled before her gaze darkened. "I only wish I knew who sent those letters. Do you think someone intentionally forced us apart?"

Eleanor shrugged, remembering the shocked look in Henry's eyes the day they had set out to Halford House. He knew something, Eleanor was certain of it. Or at least, he suspected something.

Before Eleanor could reply though, the door flew open and a freshly shaved Nick waltzed in, tension resting on his face until his eyes fell on Corinne. Instantly, his features transformed and a deep smile curled up the corners of his mouth. "Are you all right?"

Returning his smile, Corinne nodded. "I'm fine," she said, holding out her hand to him.

As Nick settled back into his spot by Corinne's side, Eleanor took her leave, wanting to give them a moment alone together. After all, before long, there would be three of them.

Feeling exhaustion claw at his body, Henry forced his eyes to remain open as he leaned forward on his gelding, urging the tiring animal on. Beside him, his future brother-in-law looked about ready to drop from the saddle as well, dark circles under his eyes from lack of rest. The only one who appeared refreshed and fully awake was the priest they had dragged from his supper table a mere few minutes ago.

"It won't be long now," Arthur called over the wind as he cast a glance at the setting sun in the distance. "Halford House is only a short distance over that hill."

Henry sighed, his fingers curling into his gelding's mane as he felt his eyelids slide closed once more. Forcing them to open, he rubbed a hand over his face.

When the small manor house finally came in sight, Henry thought he would faint with relief. He could not recall the last time he had slept. Had they only set out for London a mere two days ago? He shook his head as they galloped up to the front door, pulling their horses to a stop at the last moment. It felt like weeks had passed.

Upon reaching London after riding through the night like maniacs and changing horses every few hours, Lord Stanhope had taken care of the special license while Henry had gone to see his brother Stephen.

Seeing the rather bored expression on his brother's face upon hearing what had happened, Henry had not been able to hold himself back. His curled fist had landed squarely on Stephen's jaw, sending him flying through the room. As pain had shot up his arm, Henry had turned and left, disbelief filling his heart and mind as his brother's amused laughter had echoed to his ears from behind him.

However, he had not lingered. After all, time was of the essence, and the moment, Lord Stanhope had returned, they had swung themselves into the saddle again and started on their way back. He could only hope they were not too late.

How long did it take for a baby to be born? Henry wondered as they tossed the reins to the stable boys before rushing up the front steps and into the hall.

"You've returned," Lord Stanhope's wife exclaimed, hurrying toward him and embracing him warmly. "But you look awful," she observed, her nose slightly scrunched in concern as she regarded her husband. "You need rest."

Lord Stanhope nodded as he stepped forward, one arm still slung around his wife's waist. "I couldn't agree with you more, but first–"

The soft wail of a baby pierced the silence that hung over the house, and the three men froze, their eyes widening.

"The baby is born?" Henry stammered, his gaze shifting from Lord Stanhope's equally shocked expression to take in the priest's mild surprise before settling on Lord Stanhope's wife for confirmation.

Nodding her head, she squeezed her husband's hand. "Yes, a few hours ago." A soft smile came to her face. "It's a boy. He is perfect, and his parents are beyond happy."

"You're too late," the dowager Lady Stanhope observed as she strode into the front hall, taking in her son's appearance with one glance, a touch of concern coming to her stern eyes.

"What do we do now?" Henry asked, unable to believe that after everything they'd done to get back in time, all was lost, that his brother's son would be a bastard.

And all because Stephen had—

"It doesn't matter," Lord Stanhope stated, his voice calm and determined as he looked at them. "If they marry today, no one need ever know that the baby was born first." He held their gazes one by one. "Is that clear?"

As they all nodded, Henry exhaled a breath of relief until his gaze fell on the priest's uncomfortable face. However, before he could say anything, Lord Stanhope ordered them upstairs, saying that he needed to speak to the priest alone for a few moments.

Following the two ladies up the stairs, Henry cast a glance over his shoulder and found Lord Stanhope in quiet conversation with the priest. For a moment Henry doubted if he would be able to convince the man, but the determined look in Lord Stanhope's eyes told him everything he needed to know.

Stepping into the bedroom, Henry felt his heart skip a beat as he saw his brother's transformed face, gazing down at Corinne, their little son now resting peacefully in her arms. The change in Nick's appearance was so drastic, that for a moment, Henry merely stood and stared. Gone was the man who had downed his sorrows in alcohol, the man who only looked at the world with misery in his heart, the man who had given up hope.

Now, here before Henry was the brother he remembered. Joy dancing in his eyes, a large smile plastered on his face and an air of blissful happiness engulfing him. Only now, everything seemed magnified a thousand-fold.

"Henry!"

At the sound of Eleanor's voice, Henry dragged his gaze from his brother's happy little family to search for the woman who brought the same joy to his heart that he knew Corinne brought to Nick's. However, before he could savour the sight of her beautiful face, she had already flung herself into his arms, squeezing the air from his lungs as she held him tight.

"I missed you so," she whispered, then pulled back and looked into his eyes, her own narrowing as she took in the exhaustion that he knew must be visible in every fibre of his being. "You need rest."

Henry smiled. "I do," he whispered, then on impulse brushed a gentle kiss on her lips. "However, we must see them married first." In a few quick words, he explained what her brother had said, barely aware of Lady Stanhope's disapproving gaze as it rested on him. Apparently, his quick kiss had not been quick enough!

A moment later, Lord Stanhope and the priest entered. A few quick words were spoken, and Eleanor rushed to Corinne's side, whispering in her ear as the new mother glanced at the priest then up at the father of her child before she nodded, a deep smile on her face.

As the priest took his spot by the foot of the bed, the rest of them gathered around the new parents in a small circle, Henry took a step back and with a subtle nod toward the priest whispered to Lord Stanhope, "How did you convince him?"

Lord Stanhope merely shrugged. "I gave him an incentive."

Henry frowned.

"Everyone has his price."

"You paid him?"

Lord Stanhope shook his head, and Henry realised that the calm authority that radiated off this man was something very few people could ignore.

As Lord Stanhope turned to his wife and their eyes met, Henry held his hand out to Eleanor and pulled her into his arms. Together, they watched as the priest proclaimed Nick and Corinne husband and wife..

13

A BLESSING LONG AWAITED

After offering their congratulations to the newlyweds, Eleanor drew Henry out of the room and down the corridor. Opening the door to her bedroom, she pulled him inside. "You need rest," she said once more, unable to meet his gaze.

Glancing around, he stared at her. "This is your room."

"It is," she confirmed, raising her gaze and meeting his, a shy smile playing on her features. "You've been gone for two days, and after everything that happened, I don't think I can sleep tonight unless I know you're by my side."

He drew in a deep breath before stepping toward her and gently taking her hands in his. Meeting her gaze, his own serious and without humour, he said, "I shall never leave your side. Not ever." Then he blinked, and the tone in his voice changed, became lighter and teasing. "Tomorrow, I shall speak to your mother, and after that, you won't be able to get rid of me no matter how hard you try."

Eleanor laughed, feeling her heart dance with joy. No matter the hardship they had suffered, the future had never seemed more promising. "I'll hold you to that," she finally said. "No matter what."

Henry nodded.

"No matter what?" Eleanor whispered to herself as a frown drew down her brows, and she remembered that there was still a question that needed an answer. Meeting his gaze once more, she swallowed. "Who sent those letters?" she asked, her heart skipping a beat as his gaze momentarily dropped from hers. "I know you know. I could see it in your eyes when we were in the carriage. It was something my mother said, wasn't it? Something about the letter Corinne received?"

"It was," Henry admitted, an apologetic expression in his eyes that for a moment Eleanor feared he would admit to having sent those letters. Then she shook her head though, knowing that Henry did not possess a single malicious bone in his body.

"Will you tell me?" Eleanor asked, seeing his reluctance to speak about it.

Henry took a deep breath, his hands tightening on hers. "It was my eldest brother Stephen."

"What?" Unable to believe her ears, Eleanor stared at him. "But why? Why would he do such a thing? Why would he ruin his brother's life? That is so cruel."

Rolling his eyes, Henry snorted. "That is not how he sees it. In his mind, marriage is the worst fate that can befall a man as it robs him of his freedom. He actually thought he was doing Nick a favour, protecting him from the trap Corinne had set for him."

For a moment, Eleanor closed her eyes, trying to absorb everything his words entailed. "That is truly sad," she whispered, noting the touch of surprise that came to his face. "After all, it means he has never truly loved...or been loved."

Henry sighed, "Or he has, but he lost that love."

"Even then, it's still sad," Eleanor replied. "I do hope that he will one day meet a woman who will make him reconsider. But for now, I'm simply relieved that Corinne and Nick are reunited. Your brother is a completely different man than he was the day I first met him."

Henry nodded, pure joy lighting up his eyes. "He's truly changed. Your cousin made him a better man, a happier man." Pulling her into his arms, he smiled. "As I am because of you."

Wrapping her arms around his neck, Eleanor smiled up at him. "I feel the same way," she whispered. "The world seems brighter, more cheerful when you're around." She drew in a deep breath. "I do love you, Henry, more than I can say."

"I love you just the same," he whispered before he lowered his head and his lips claimed hers, trying to communicate how he felt when words failed him.

Sinking into his embrace, Eleanor enjoyed the feel of his mouth on hers, and a part of her wished the priest had married them as well today. However, then she remembered the exhaustion she had seen in Henry's eyes before and reluctantly pulled back. "You need sleep," she whispered, brushing her fingers down his stubbled cheek. Then she took his hand and pulled him to the bed.

A frown came to his face as he followed her. "Do you think this is a good idea?"

Eleanor took a deep breath, "Can you just hold me? I don't want to be alone tonight."

"Of course," Henry said before a mischievous smile came to his face and he pulled her back into his arms. "Has it never occurred to you that I might be a threat to your virtue?"

Returning his smile, Eleanor shook her head. "Of course not. After all, you're a true gentleman."

Henry laughed, "God, I'm glad I'm too exhausted to prove you wrong."

After having spent the night holding Eleanor in his arms, her soft body moulded to his, Henry felt more than a bit reluctant to leave her bedroom the next morning. However, he reminded himself that he still had not obtained Lady Stanhope's blessing, and until the old crow had given him her word that he could marry her daughter, Henry's heart and mind remained in an uproar, living in fear of the moment when Eleanor would be ripped from his life.

"Mother, please, may we speak to you?" Eleanor asked as they met Lady Stanhope in the parlour that morning.

"Can it not wait until after breakfast?"

"It cannot," Henry said, hoping that the insistent tone in his voice would not irritate Eleanor's mother to the point that she would refuse her consent out of spite. "It is very important to us that we settle this now."

"Most unusual," Lady Stanhope grumbled, seating herself in the armchair by the small fireplace. "Then speak. What is it you wish to discuss?"

Before Eleanor could open her mouth, Henry placed a gentle hand on hers. "Allow me," he said, then turned to look at Lady Stanhope. "I apologise for the circumstances of this conversation. However, we cannot wait any longer. I do believe that you are aware that I am in love with your daughter and that I wish to marry her."

Lady Stanhope inhaled a deep breath, and for a moment, Henry thought to see her eyes softening. Encouraged, he continued, "I apologise for the misery my eldest brother's behaviour brought not only on your niece but also on my brother. It was a tragedy, but one with a happy ending. I can only hope that you will not hold this against us and allow us to find our happily-ever-after as well." He swallowed, his mind grasping for words as he feared nothing he said had truly convinced the lady sitting across from him. "While I cannot offer your daughter a title or a vast fortune, I assure you that I will spend the rest of my life ensuring her happiness. I will treat her with respect and kindness and always consider her my equal in every way."

Glancing at Eleanor, he saw a deep smile on her face and tears glistening in her eyes as she gently squeezed his hand.

"Very well," Lady Stanhope said, and Henry's head snapped around. "You have my consent." Staring at her in disbelief, Henry feared his heart had stopped, and he forced himself to take a deep breath.

"Thank you, Mother," Eleanor beamed, rising to her feet and embracing her mother. Tears clung to her eyelashes as she met her mother's gaze. "You have no idea how much this means to me."

A rather uncharacteristically wistful smile came to Lady Stanhope's face. "I was young once, too," she said, her gaze shifting to Henry. "However, I want you to know that I am not simply giving my consent because you compromised my daughter last night."

Once again, Henry's heart stopped and the blood froze in his veins.

"Don't look so surprised," Lady Stanhope chided, "and don't ever believe I don't know what goes on in my house."

Glancing at Henry, Eleanor smiled. "Nothing happened, Mother. We just…slept."

Lady Stanhope's eyes narrowed as her gaze swept over her daughter's face. "I see." Then she turned her head to look at Henry, and for a moment, he thought to see a touch of approval in her eyes. "I admit that I misjudged you," she finally said, regret in her voice as her gaze shifted back and forth between her daughter and him, "and I'm sorry for the pain I've caused you."

Taking Eleanor's hands into hers, she smiled at her, an apologetic look in her eyes. "I only ever wanted you to be safe…and happy." Lady Stanhope glanced at him. "And apparently, you need *him* to be both."

"I do," Eleanor confirmed, holding out her hand to him.

Coming to stand beside the woman he loved and would marry sooner rather than later, Henry could not believe the joy that suddenly flooded his heart. "Thank you," he said to Lady Stanhope. "This is truly the greatest gift anyone has ever given me."

Inhaling deeply, Lady Stanhope nodded, then without another word strode for the door. However, before she left, she looked back at him and said, "I'm entrusting my daughter's happiness to you. Don't ever be careless with it, or I can promise you will live to regret it."

Without waiting for a reply, Lady Stanhope strode from the room.

Henry chuckled. “I never knew your mother could be so terrifying.” Meeting Eleanor’s gaze, Henry could hardly believe his luck, drawing her into his arms, refusing to ever let her go again. “She will always keep an eye on me, won’t she?”

Eleanor laughed as she snuggled closer. “For the rest of your life.” The gaze in her eyes became serious. “Can you live with that?”

“As long as you’re by my side,” Henry whispered, planting a gentle kiss on her lips, “I suppose I’ll hardly notice.”

EPILOGUE

Stanhope Grove, December 31, 1819

About Four Months Later

"Is it not a marvellous success?" Eleanor's mother beamed beside her, her gaze gliding over Stanhope Grove's first New Year's Ball, as she took in the dancing couples, the beautiful music echoing to the tall ceiling as well as the tastefully lit ballroom.

"It truly is, Mother," Eleanor replied, delighted to see her mother so happy. A lot had changed since their impromptu house party, and despite certain dramatic tendencies, her mother had become rather agreeable in the past few months.

"May I have this dance?"

As always the sound of her husband's voice brought a smile to Eleanor's face, and she turned to him with her heart thudding in her chest as though they had only just met. Would these butterflies leave one day? She wondered, unable to imagine it to ever be so.

"Of course, you may," she replied, delighted when his eyes lit up and he pulled her into his arms.

Before they could escape to the dance floor though, Eleanor heard a barely concealed huff from behind her and turned to look at her mother. "Is something wrong?"

Shaking her head, her mother looked past her and at Henry, a touch of exasperation in her eyes. "Do not monopolise her time, dear boy," she chided as though Henry was about to commit a major faux-pas. "Tonight is an opportunity to mingle and meet new people. Your face she can see every day of the week."

Laughing, Henry stepped forward before respectfully inclining his head to his new mother-in-law. "As always, my dearest Lady Stanhope, I appreciate your advice," he said, fighting hard to suppress a grin.

Her mother rolled her eyes at him.

"I assure you," Henry continued, "I shall do my utmost to keep your daughter entertained."

Her mother snorted, "Of that I'm certain." Then she turned away in search of a more gratifying audience.

As the suppressed grin finally claimed his face, Henry turned to her, shaking his head. "Did she just tell me that I'm boring you with my presence?"

Eleanor laughed, slipping her arm through his, "Don't take it personally. I assure you she didn't mean it as an insult."

Guiding her through the crowd toward the dance floor, Henry glanced down at her. "I'm not boring you, am I?"

The touch of uncertainty in his voice made Eleanor sigh with delight. After all, nothing could be worse than taking each other for granted. Smiling up at him, she shook her head. "My knees still go weak at the mere sight of you."

In answer, a large grin spread over his face. However, it only lasted for a moment before it was chased away by a frown. "Although

I'm delighted to hear you say that, it's not quite what I asked. I suppose a man can do both, weaken your knees and send you off into a deep slumber."

"Enough!" Eleanor exclaimed. "Let us dance, or I shall truly call you boring if you insist on discussing this further."

Bowing deeply, Henry smiled. "As my lady commands."

As they stood up for a cotillion, Eleanor glanced up and down the line and saw many faces very dear to her. Not only had the guests who had attended their house party last August taken the time to witness their wedding ceremony a month later, but most had once more travelled to Stanhope Grove for the New Year's Ball.

Only Diana's cousin Rose and her husband, Lord Norwood, were not in attendance as they had welcomed into their hearts and lives their baby daughter only a few days ago. However, a few steps down, she saw not only Nick and Corinne, but also Winifred and Griffin, each standing up with a partner.

"Who is your friend dancing with?" Henry asked as he followed her gaze around the room. "They seem to know each other although—I have to say—she looks fairly annoyed with him."

Smiling, Eleanor shook her head. "I think that's Griffin's old friend, Lord…Chadwick. I always thought they would be a wonderful match. However, I suppose Winifred disagrees."

A large grin came to Henry's gaze as he observed them.

"Why are you smiling?" Eleanor asked when the steps led them together again.

"Did you see how she rolled her eyes at him?" he whispered to her. "And the way he just leaned in to whisper something in her ear?"

Eleanor nodded, her gaze fixed on the young couple who *seemed* to be bickering at each other. "You're right," she whispered, and a deep smile came to her face at the thought that Winifred might have already found the right man for her without being aware of it. "How can they not see this?"

Henry laughed, then bowed to her as the cotillion ended. Stepping forward, he then led her into a waltz, and Eleanor enjoyed the feeling of his strong arms holding her. "Love is different for different people," he whispered in her ear, his warm breath tickling her skin, sending shivers down her back. "Sometimes it is instant and overpowering," the hand on her waist urged her closer against him, "and sometimes it takes time."

Ignoring the slight tremble that her husband's touch had brought forth, Eleanor leaned into him. "What if they never realise that there is something between them? Wouldn't it be truly sad to see them part ways when they so obviously want to be together?"

Chuckling, Henry twirled her around the ballroom. "I suppose there are always those willing to lend a helping hand. Look over there."

Turning her head, Eleanor found her gaze shifting to Griffin and noticed that he, too, was watching the young couple who had retreated to the refreshment table but was still arguing. A frown drew down his brows, and he looked a bit exasperated as though a well-thought out plan had just gone up in flames.

"There are always those who meddle," Henry whispered in her ear, "in the hopes of seeing their loved ones permanently happy."

Eleanor laughed, her eyes finding his once more. "Maybe I should offer my assistance. After all, without help, who knew what would have become of us? Or my brother and Diana? Don't we all need help sometimes?"

Henry glanced over her shoulder at his brother-in-law. "They do look happy, do they not?" Then his gaze met Eleanor's once more. "Are you?"

"Deliriously so," Eleanor whispered, and her breath caught in her throat as she realised that the moment she had been waiting for for the past week had finally come. "I want us to begin the new year even happier than before," she whispered, fighting the tears of joy that threatened.

"Are you all right?" Henry asked, a touch of concern in his warm eyes as they slid over her face, taking in the small tear in the corner of her right eye.

"Maybe a little light-headed," Eleanor whispered. "However, I suppose that is normal considering my condition." Biting her lower lip, she held his gaze, waiting.

For a moment, he seemed stumped, his brows creasing, before he opened his mouth…and closed it, his eyes going wide. "Are you saying…?" He merely nodded his head, up and down, up and down, unable to finish the question.

Eleanor laughed at the stunned expression on his face. "We're going to be parents…in August. It'll be a while before we get to hold our little bundle of joy, but—"

Almost crushing her in his arms, Henry kissed her deeply, his emotions overwhelming them both. All Eleanor could think of was her own little family, and the sheer happiness that filled her at the thought easily forced the surprised murmurs around her at such a public display of affection into the background.

After all they had been through, all would be well.

Eleanor was certain of it.

Nothing else mattered.

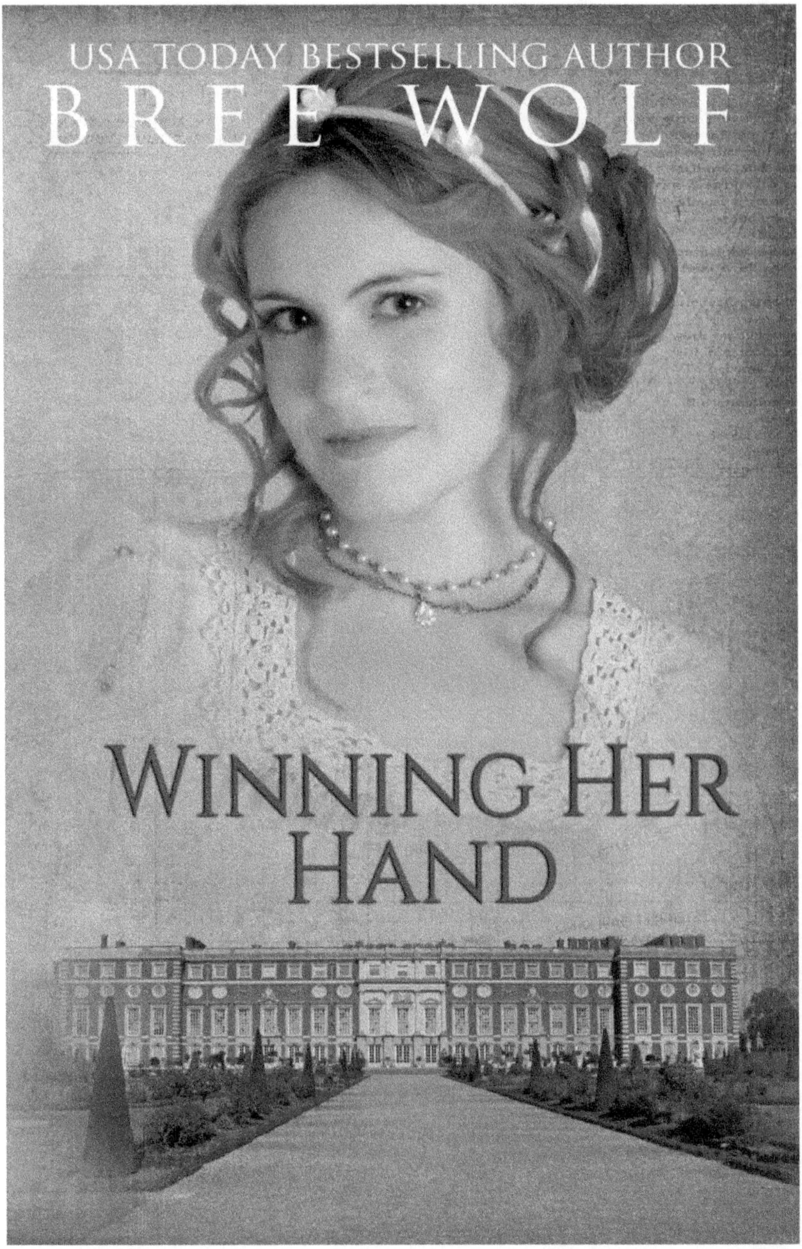
USA TODAY BESTSELLING AUTHOR
BREE WOLF
WINNING HER HAND

PROLOGUE

Stanhope Grove 1819 (or a variation thereof)

Winifred sighed as her eyes beheld the newly-wed couple across the room.

"They look happy, do they not?" her brother Griffin, the Earl of Amberly, observed, his dark brown eyes shifting to her, a touch of confusion resting in them.

"I suppose so."

Griffin frowned. "Then why do you look so glum? Is Eleanor not your friend? Are *you* not happy to see *her* happy?"

Taking a deep breath, Winifred tried to sort through the contrasting emotions coursing through her body. "Of course, I'm happy for her," she defended herself, her voice a tad harsher than intended. "I hope you do not believe me to be someone who wishes others ill?"

"Not at all." Retreating somewhat from the joyous festivities, Griffin urged her to the side and out of earshot of the nearest guests in attendance. "However, you have to admit that your outlook on marriage is rather…what shall we call it?…bleak."

Enraged, Winifred fixed her brother with a stern look, her hands coming to rest on her sides. "How can you say that, Griffin? You know as well as I do that marriage for the right reasons is a most sensible constitution. I've always said so."

A grin came to Griffin's face. *That man had the audacity to grin at her! Oh, if he weren't her brother…!* "Sensible?" he asked, eyebrows raised in question. "I admit you're the only young woman I've ever met—or heard of, for that matter—who does not at least hope for a love match."

Winifred scoffed, "Why is it that you think women ought to hope for a love match while men can consider a sensible marriage?"

Again, a wide grin split his face. "Don't start with me, Winifred. You know as well as I do that your objections have nothing to do with the rights of women." He stood up straight, and his dark brown eyes rested on her face for a long moment. Then he sighed and leaned toward her, all humour gone from his face. "I believe you're simply afraid to have your heart broken."

Winifred's mouth fell open.

"Although I cannot see why," her brother continued. "Growing up the way we did, I always assumed you'd wish for a relationship like our parents'."

Riled from her brother's words, Winifred tried to maintain her composure. After all, a lady did not strike her brother.

An earl.

Well, at least not in public.

Inhaling another deep breath, Winifred waited for her pulse to cease its frantic pace before she met her brother's enquiring gaze. "Whether you know it or not," she began, doing her best to speak slowly, lest her words tumbled about one another as they sometimes did when she was agitated, "but our parents' union is the very reason for my outlook on marriage."

Griffin's forehead creased into a frown. "But they were happy."

"Precisely."

Shaking his head, Griffin lowered his voice as it grew more and more impatient. "You're not making any sense!"

"Our parents did not marry for love," Winifred said, unable to suppress a hint of triumph in her voice. "Theirs was an arranged match. In fact," she dropped her voice to a whisper, "a few years ago, Mother confided in me and told me that before their marriage she had been taken with another man. However, in the end she chose to marry Father because he was the more sensible choice. An infatuation offers a few blissful moments, nothing more. A union based on deeper attributes, however, ensures a lifetime of happiness." With a satisfied smile on her face, she held her brother's eyes, pleased to have made her point.

Unfortunately, Griffin seemed far from impressed. Quite on the contrary, the corners of his mouth drew upward into that annoyingly superior grin of his and his eyes lit up with mischief. "I, too, have heard that story," he laughed. "However, dear Sister, in the version I heard, it was our dear grandfather who persuaded Mother to accept the earl's proposal instead of that of a penniless solicitor." His gaze held hers, a challenging glow in them. "I suppose the deeper attributes you're referring to are fortune and family name. Nothing else. Do you truly believe those will ensure future happiness more reliably than love and affection?"

Feeling the blood drain from her face, Winifred stared at her brother. "How do you know this?"

Griffin shrugged. "Grandfather mentioned it. He seemed rather pleased with himself."

Gritting her teeth, Winifred turned to the window, forcing her gaze to focus on the lush green gardens, currently topped off with a thin layer of ice crystals.

"I apologise for speaking so bluntly," Griffin whispered into her ear. "I never meant to upset you. However, I admit that your outlook on marriage frightens me sometimes." His hand settled on her arm, and he urged her to turn and look at him. "I love you dearly," he said, his voice thick with emotion as he looked into her eyes, "and I wish for nothing more but to see you happy." He drew in a deep breath. "And while I do not wish to undermine your own capabilities, I feel compelled to tell you that your sensible way of thinking of marriage will not accomplish that task."

Winifred swallowed, her limbs suddenly feeling heavy as lead. "But they were a good match, were they not? They were so much alike. They laughed together. Read together. Rode out together. Even if they were not deeply in love, they cared about one another, did they not?" Remembering her parents, Winifred could not believe that the life she had led had been nothing but a lie, a well-hidden secret.

"They did care about each other," Griffin said, nodding his head when she turned doubtful eyes to him. "However, their feelings developed over time. They *came* to care for one another. It was nothing more but…a fortunate coincidence. That's what I'm trying to tell you. Some people are fortunate to find love in an arranged marriage. But most do not." His hands tightened on hers. "I cannot stand the thought that you might end up in a marriage without love." A soft chuckle escaped him. "For despite your insistence to be rational and sensible always, your heart loves with such fierceness and devotion rarely found in people. It deserves its perfect match."

Emotionally exhausted, Winifred did not know what to think. She loved her brother dearly. Always had he been by her side, looking out for her, protecting her, guarding her happiness. Only three years her senior, he had often acted like a man far beyond his years. Especially since the day they had lost their parents in a carriage accident.

At the thought of their parents' loss, old pain flooded Winifred's heart and her eyes misted with tears. Oh, how much she wished to have her mother by her side! She would understand, would she not? At the very least, she would be able to explain the choices she had made in her life. Had she truly chosen to marry their father due to their grandfather's insistence? Or had she simply allowed him to believe so while choosing Father for her own reasons?

More than anything, Winifred remembered her mother's warm eyes, steady and unwavering as though nothing could surprise her, as though she had all the answers. Had she not promised Winifred to aid her when the time came to choose a husband? Had she not told her that impartial eyes might judge more reliably than those blinded by infatuation? Had she not spoken to her of the need for common ground? Shared interests? Expectations? Dispositions?

But now she was gone.

And Winifred was alone in her choice.

Still, walking in her mother's footsteps made her feel connected to the woman who had always known the right course. Somehow, it made her feel closer to her as though her mother was still watching over her, guiding her hand. In any case, Winifred felt less likely to disappoint...after all, was she not heeding her mother's advice?

1

A HARD LOOK IN THE MIRROR

The fortnight after Eleanor's wedding was a blur to Winifred her thoughts were directed inward. Her friend's marriage had dragged something out into the light of day, something that Winifred had ignored for a long time.

For too long.

"I'm two-and-twenty," she mumbled as she stood in the drawing room of Atherton House, her breath misting over the window pane for a moment before it disappeared. "I'm two-and-twenty."

After their parents' death, her brother, who had just been of age at the time, had inherited his father's title and taken over guardianship of his sister. For a few weeks, they had remained at Atherton House, trying to go on with their lives before one day Griffin had come to her with an idea.

"Let's travel the world," he had said, his eyes aglow for the first time since their parents' death. "After all, what is left for us here? Sadness? Grief? Sorrow?"

"Will they not follow us wherever we go?" Winifred had objected, her own heart weighed down heavily by their recent loss. "Do you truly think we can outrun them?"

With determination in his eyes, Griffin had shaken his head. "I'm certain we cannot. However, we need something to balance them. Something good. Something that makes us smile and laugh. We have none of that here."

In a heartbeat, Winifred had agreed, knowing that she would have followed her brother to the end of the world if he had asked. Five years had passed since that day. Five years spent everywhere but here. Five years to come to terms with the loss of their parents.

It still hurt, but they had learnt to live again.

Only now, Winifred was two-and-twenty and still unmarried.

Soon, she would be on the shelf.

Drawing in a deep breath, Winifred remembered the garden party at Stanhope Grove Eleanor had invited them to only a few weeks before her wedding. Her brother and his new wife had been in attendance as well. Diana, the new Lady Stanhope, had a little boy from her first marriage, who had been out in the gardens every day, his explorations leading him through hedges and up trees…with his step-father's assistance, of course, as he was barely three years old.

The memory brought a smile to Winifred's lips, and she remembered that it had been that very moment that she had realised what she wanted.

Marriage. Family. Children.

Although a part of her could see herself travelling the world with her brother forever, she could not deny that another part of her craved something more.

Finally, the time had come.

If she truly wanted to be a mother, she would have to find a husband first.

And now, her own mother was not here to guide her hand.

"There's no putting it off," Winifred mumbled to her own reflection. Then she stepped away from the window and sat down at the small escritoire, pulling out a sheet of paper. Where was she to begin?

If her mother were here, what would she advise her to do?

"I'll make a list," Winifred mumbled. After all, if she was to find a suitable match, she would need to look at herself first and try to judge her character with as much objectivity as she could. Only then could she hope to discover a man among the gentlemen of the ton you would suit her person and share her interests and expectations.

But who was she? What kind of a person?

devoted
loyal
rational
compassionate

Staring at those four attributes, Winifred sighed. Certainly, it was easy to speak well of oneself, was it not? However, everyone–including herself–possessed attributes that others detected with greater ease than one could hope for when looking at oneself, most importantly, because they were far from flattering.

obstinate

Winifred scowled at the word staring back at her from the page. Still, her brother had called her that quite a few times and he knew her well, did he not? Maybe he could help her.

Instantly, Winifred shook her head. No, he would never take this seriously. He would laugh at her, then try to convince her to give up on this endeavour and then he would call her obstinate when she refused.

Despite the rather unflattering word, Winifred felt vindicated. If she only tried, tried to be honest with herself and worked on this as diligently as she could, there was a chance she could accomplish this task on her own.

Good, she thought. What else?

hesitant

As proved by her tendency to ignore even pressing matters, Winifred reluctantly listed yet another unflattering attribute. Still, she had to admit it was fitting. She did take her time making decisions, always worrying that she was about to take a wrong turn, always wanting to be certain that the decision she was about to make was the right one.

Rubbing her temple, Winifred felt the desperate wish to step away from the task at hand. However, if she did so now, she would never finish, never find a suitable match.

What about interests? Her mind suggested, and Winifred welcomed the slight change in direction with open arms. Interests were far less painful, were they not?

Quickly, she jotted down a few things that brought joy to her life.

travelling
painting
dancing

Yes, this was indeed a much safer area. And it would most certainly be much easier to discover whether a gentleman shared any of her interests. Discovering deeper aspects about his personality, however, would prove much more difficult. Who indeed would be a perfect match for her character? Someone like her? Or rather someone who was her opposite? In all ways? Or only in some?

A mild headache began pounding on her left temple, and Winifred leaned back in her chair, stilling her hands for the moment. Unable to keep herself from feeling daunted by this task, she wished her mother were there.

"Ah, there you are."

Startled by her brother's voice, Winifred flinched, and her head throbbed painfully. Glancing over her shoulder, she met his gaze.

"Are you all right?" he asked, looking her up and down, a touch of concern in his dark eyes.

"I'm fine," Winifred lied, carefully placing a hand over the sheet of paper. If her brother were to see it, he would tease her endlessly. "What is that in your hand? An invitation?"

Griffin nodded, his watchful eyes dropping to the envelop in his hand. "It is. To the New Year's Ball at Stanhope Grove." Stepping toward her, he frowned, eyes narrowed. "Am I mistaken? Or is this a new event? I cannot recall any such festivity from before we left England."

Winifred shook her head. "You're not wrong. Eleanor mentioned something at the garden party. She said it was her mother's idea to hold such a ball. Apparently, her mother was a bit miffed that Lord Hampton's Christmas Ball was spoken of as legendary." She smiled. "You know the Dowager Lady Stanhope. She tends to feel the need to surpass everyone."

Griffin laughed. "Very true. Shall we attend?"

"I would like that." It would certainly be a good opportunity to mingle and maybe spot a gentleman or two who would suit her.

"What is this?" Griffin asked, peeking over her shoulder, a touch of incredulity mixed with the usual mockery in his voice.

Flinching, Winifred jerked around in her chair to find a slow grin spread over her brother's face. "Nothing that concerns you!" she snapped, then reached for the sheet of paper.

Griffin, however, snatched it up as quick as a flash and immediately retreated to the other side of the room, his eyes eagerly roaming the page. "What is this? If I didn't know any better, I'd say it was a list of your attributes. However, why would you−?" His eyes went wide before they rose from the paper and met hers. "Tell me this is not your *sensible* way of looking for a husband!"

Gritting her teeth at the sound of the word *sensible*−the way he said it would suggest it was an insult!−Winifred stormed toward him, trying to rip the paper from his hands. Unfortunately, her brother was a good bit taller than she and at present rather disinclined to give up his trophy. "Don't you dare laugh about me! After all, you of all people should be helping me with this."

"Me?" He stared at her dumbfounded. "Why?"

Grabbing him by the sleeve, Winifred yanked his arm down and retrieved her list. "Because you know me better than anyone else," she huffed, cradling the sheet of paper to her chest. "If you weren't so immature, I wouldn't be alone in this." Swallowing, Winifred turned away as she felt the sting of tears. Never had she realised how alone she felt now that her mother was gone.

It was terrifying.

"Why do you wish to marry?" Griffin asked, his voice free of mockery. "I mean, why now? You haven't said anything on the matter since…" He swallowed, no doubt remembering their lives before the shadow of their parents' loss had fallen over them.

"Because I'm running out of time." Dabbing at her eyes, she forced the tears back down, then turned to face her brother.

A frown drew down Griffin's brows as he searched her face. "What do you mean?"

Drawing in an impatient breath, Winifred welcomed the annoyance she often felt toward her brother with open arms. "Men can afford to marry late," she snapped as though the inequality of today's world was somehow his fault. "Women, however, are not so fortunate. I'm already two-and twenty, Griffin, and if I want to have children, there is no time to lose."

For a long time, he simply looked at her, too stunned to say a word. Had it truly never occurred to him that she would get married some day?

Then he swallowed, and she could see his usual self reemerge as a glimmer of mischief came to his eyes. "You want to get married? Fine. I'll help you find your perfect match. But this," he pointed at the list still clutched to her chest, "this is not the way to go about it."

Winifred glared at him. "Do not speak to me as though I am a child. I know very well what I want and how to achieve it."

"Do you?" He laughed. That man had the audacity to laugh! Could he not see how difficult this was for her? "And what good will such a list do?"

Winifred rolled her eyes at him. "It is the only way to ensure compatibility." Swallowing the lump in her throat, she continued, "It is the only way I can think of to achieve what I had hoped Mother and Father would do for me."

Griffin's eyes bulged. "You wanted them to find you a husband?"

Frowning at him, Winifred nodded. "Why would that surprise you? Did you not hope for the same?"

Staring at her, Griffin shook his head. "To tell you the truth, I hadn't yet thought of marriage, but I'm quite certain I do want a say in it. I cannot imagine having that decision taken out of my hands."

A part of Winifred could understand his vehement demand to be included in such a life-altering decision. It echoed within her, and a delicate feeling of warmth and longing rose in her heart. Where had it come from?

"Such a list will do you no good," her brother told her, his gaze soft and yet insistent as it held hers. "Please, Winifred, abandon this nonsense and simply follow your heart." A twinkle came to his eyes. "Is there no one you care for?"

Winifred swallowed as the budding emotion in her chest roared to life, warming her chilled hands, and conjuring an image of dark green eyes, piercing in their intensity and yet kind and gentle as they looked into hers.

"Is there?" Griffin prompted, a hint of suspicion in his dark gaze.

Swallowing, Winifred shook her head, partly to rid herself of the image and partly to shake off the sense of detachment that had come over her. "There's not," she replied, her voice hard as she forced her thoughts back to the task at hand. "Now that Mother and Father are gone, this is my only chance to find a man suited to me." She lifted the sheet of paper, and her eyes travelled over the few simple words that summed up her being. It was a pitiful sight.

For a long moment, silence hung between them before her brother inhaled a strained breath. "Do you want *my* help?" he asked, a touch of incredulity in his voice.

Lifting her gaze to her brother's, Winifred smiled. "It is kind of you to offer, and I know you mean well. However, my marriage is not something to be taken lightly, and we both know that you are not the right person for this task."

All humour left Griffin's face at her words, and the seriousness that came to his eyes was one she had never seen in him before. "I cannot deny that your words ring true," he said, his voice even, and yet, she detected a slight quiver in it as though he felt ashamed to admit the truth. "However, you must know that I would never risk your happiness, dear Sister. As immature as I am," a soft and rather apologetic grin came to his features, "I would not dare gamble with your future." Holding her gaze, he swallowed, waiting for her answer as though he did not already know it, as though he feared what she would say.

Touched by the way he had spoken to her, the way he had revealed a softer side of himself, one that was vulnerable and even afraid, Winifred placed a gentle hand on his arm. "I know you wouldn't," she whispered, noting the sense of relief that chased away the tension on his face. "This is not a question of honour, but of ability. This is something you cannot do for me."

Frowning, he looked at her. "Why not? You must admit that there is no one else in the world who knows you as well as I do. Or do you disagree?"

"I do not, but–"

"Then let me help you. Please! Let me do for you what you'd hoped Mother and Father would."

Staring at Griffin, Winifred could not believe her ears, could not fathom the sudden change she saw in her brother. Always had he been light-hearted and impulsive, smiling his way through life, charming others as easily as drawing breath. Had she misjudged him? How could she not have seen this serious side of him? "Are you saying you want to find me a husband?"

A soft chuckle escaped him, and within an instant, the old Griffin was back. "*Want* may be a bit of a stretch, but yes. I will help you. You're my sister, and I will not leave you alone in this. Please allow me to do so."

Hesitating, Winifred looked at him, saw the earnest concern and devotion in his eyes and noted the touch of humour curling his lips. What was she to do? Certainly, he knew her well. There was no denying that. But given his character, could he take this seriously? Could he see this through? Or would he abandon her once he grew tired of this new game?

No, no matter what he would not abandon her. Still, was it wise to defer to him in this matter? Without hesitation, without a doubt in her mind, Winifred would have allowed her mother to find her a suitable husband, but her brother? Could he do this?

"I promise I will not disappoint you." Grasping her hands, Griffin looked into her eyes, urging her to believe him. "I understand why you would be hesitant." There was that word again! "But you have no reason not to trust me. And to prove it to you, I shall offer you a deal."

"A deal?" Winifred frowned. "What do you mean?"

Her brother took a deep breath as though needing to fortify himself. "Allow me to find you a husband," he said, "and I shall grant you the same permission when it comes to finding my wife."

2

WELCOME HOME

Stepping out of the carriage, Trent Henwood, Earl of Chadwick, allowed his gaze to sweep over Atherton House, an imposing country estate and the place that held his dearest childhood memories. A smile curled up his lips as he remembered the many summers of his youth spent here with Griffin and his sister Winifred.

Winifred. Her name immediately conjured an image of a young lady with rich auburn tresses that framed her kind face, matching those chocolate brown eyes of hers that had the power to upend his world…or set it right.

As he began to climb the steps toward the front door, Trent felt his heart beating in his chest, louder and faster than he had ever been aware of. Always had Winifred managed to keep him on edge with her serious demeanour, always trying to appear older and more mature, often chiding him and her brother for their wild ways. To this day, he remembered how she had stared up at him at age twelve, her hair pulled back in a serious knot, her arms crossed and her right foot tapping with annoyance at the way he and Griffin had come running into the drawing room, knocking the tea tray to the floor with a loud clatter. Oh, even then those eyes of hers had known how to shoot fire!

With a deep breath, Trent stepped over the threshold and greeted the old butler. "Good day, Harmon. How is the knee?"

"Quite all right, my lord." The old man smiled at him. "It's good to see you again."

Nodding, Trent gazed at the familiar hall with the sweeping staircase leading to the upper floor. How often had he and Griffin slid down the banister when no one was looking? How often had they been caught nonetheless?

A smile curled up his lips at the memory.

"Those were good days," the old butler remarked with a wicked gleam in his eyes that Trent remembered only too well.

"They were indeed," he agreed, then glanced toward the old study tucked away in the eastern side of the house. "Is he in?"

Harmon nodded. "His lordship is in the study…and Lady Winifred is painting in the conservatory."

About to take a step, Trent froze, his right foot lifted off the ground, slightly offsetting his balance. Then he cleared his throat and set it down, glancing at Harmon's unreadable face. "Thank you," he stammered as every fibre in his being strained toward the conservatory. "I shall…speak to his lordship first," he said nonetheless, forcing his feet down the eastern corridor.

His footsteps' echo reached his ears, flying ahead as though to announce his arrival. It was a familiar sound, and Trent could not believe that it had been five years since he had last heard it.

When his mother had died giving birth to him, Trent's father had been heart-broken, retreating from the world and his only child, only knowing grief and sorrow, wandering Tredway Manor like a ghost. Thus, the first few years of Trent's life had been marked by loneliness.

Eton had changed that.

On the very first day, he had met Griffin and a lifelong friendship had grown between them. From then on, Trent had spent every free minute at Atherton House, finding a surrogate home with Griffin's family who had welcomed him with open arms. The death of the siblings' parents had affected him as much as his own father's passing a few years past…if not more. After all, they had been the ones to counsel and comfort, chide and praise him.

When Griffin and Winifred had left England, he had been devastated, wishing he could have joined them. However, his late father's affairs had demanded his attention, and he could not in good conscience have left his estate and all those who depended on him to travel the world.

But now they had returned, and the moment he had heard the news, Trent had dropped everything and hastened over.

Home, a quiet voice whispered as he came to stand outside the study, reminding himself that he would not find the old earl on the other side, but his friend instead.

After knocking, he entered upon hearing Griffin's voice and could not help but stare—at least for a moment—at the man he had not seen in five years, the man that had been like a brother to him, the man he had missed dearly for too long.

Stepping around the desk, Griffin strode toward him, a deep smile on his face. "It's been too long, old friend," he announced as though chiding Trent for staying away. Then he pulled him into a fierce embrace. "It is good to see you, Brother."

Inhaling deeply, Trent returned Griffin's hug with the same mixture of longing, regret and joy. "How long have you been back?"

Stepping back, an apologetic grin came to Griffin's face. "A couple of weeks."

"Weeks?" Trent's eyes bulged, and a touch of disappointment washed over him.

"Winifred received an urgent message from a friend," he said by way of explaining.

"A friend?"

"Lady Eleanor," Griffin elaborated. "I mean Mrs. Waltham now."

"I remember her well," Trent said, wondering why *he* had never written, asking them to come home. "I heard that she'd married."

"Yes, a small ceremony a fortnight ago at Stanhope Grove."

Trent frowned. "Knowing the dowager countess, I would have expected a grander event, especially after Lord Stanhope's marriage to the young widow within a few weeks after her husband's passing was an equally private affair."

A wicked grin came to Griffin's face. "Sometimes love cannot wait for a large wedding. However, I have to say the dowager countess seemed quite pleased with the development although I cannot say why." He shrugged. "Something happened during our visit that we weren't all made privy to."

Griffin drew in a deep breath, and the humour left his face.

Then his gaze shifted to Trent's, and yet, he did not speak.

"Is everything all right?" Trent asked, feeling his skin crawl with apprehension. "You seem out of sorts."

With all his heart, Trent wished he had the courage to ask about Winifred. However, he did not dare reveal how he truly felt about her to his friend. Hell, it seemed he had only just realised it himself! After their departure, he had come to realise that his longing for her was different from the way he longed to see his oldest friend again. Always had they been family to him, and he knew he loved them dearly. Still, the way he thought of Winifred did not speak of brotherly affection. How would Griffin react if he found out?

"I'm not certain," Griffin finally said, the expression on his face rather tense while his eyes seemed to search Trent's face. "I've entered into a rather unfortunate pact with my sister."

"Winifred?" Trent all but croaked, revelling in the feeling of her name on his tongue. It had been too long since he had been able to say it! "What do you mean?"

Griffin inhaled a deep breath, his gaze unwavering. "She wants me to find her a husband."

Shock slammed into Trent like a charging bull, and he sucked in a sharp breath, trying to ease the pain radiating through his heart. "A husband? Is she…? I mean does she…already have a certain gentleman in mind?"

Griffin's gaze narrowed before the left corner of his mouth tugged up into a wicked grin. "May I ask you a question?"

Swallowing, Trent nodded.

"Why did you never ask for her hand?"

Trent's eyes bulged as the charging bull hit him square in the chest for the second time that day. "I beg your pardon?" he stammered, suddenly feeling light-headed.

Clasping a hand on his friend's shoulder, Griffin held his gaze. "A blind man could see that you love her, have loved her for a long time." The hint of a frown came to his features. "I understand that she was too young when we left, but to tell you the truth I have been waiting for you to come find us, find her, ever since. Why didn't you?"

Shaking his head as though that could dispel the truth of what he had just heard, Trent tried his best to swallow the lump in his throat. Indeed, why had he not? "Does…does she know?"

Griffin laughed, "Oh, even if she did, she would never admit it to herself. After all, she does not believe you to be a *sensible* choice." He shook his head in annoyance before the humour left his eyes. "However, I do believe she cares for you…if only she were brave enough to admit it."

Did she truly care for him? Could it be possible? Involuntarily, Trent's heart began to dance in his chest before he forced it back into the sad, little room where it had lived these past five years. "I do not believe what you say is true. After all, whenever we lay eyes on one another, all we do is—"

"Bicker?" Griffin cut in. "Yes, I've noticed. Maybe it's time you stop treating her like a little girl. After all, it's been five years."

Disheartened, Trent shook his head. "Quite frankly, I don't know how else to speak to her."

"You've never seemed particularly shy around the fair sex," Griffin observed with a grin. "Why now?"

Trent shrugged. "I wish I knew."

"So, you care for her?"

Trent sighed, forcing himself to meet his friend's gaze. "As you've so shrewdly observed, yes, I do." Again, he tried to swallow the lump in his throat. Again, without success. "Is there a particular gentleman courting her?"

Griffin grinned at him, amusement twinkling in his eyes. "Not at present. After all, we've only been back in England for a few weeks, and the Season has yet to start." For a moment, he looked at Trent, his gaze full of meaning. "However, I doubt that she will be lacking suitors."

Trent nodded, feeling more disheartened by the minute. How was he to go about winning Winifred's heart as well as her hand if he was to compete with the finest gentlemen London had to offer?

After all, in her presence he seemed to lack any kind of finesse. Where otherwise he would be charming and agreeable, striving to be attentive and offering compliments, he knew he was unable to do so when the woman he loved was near. As soon as her gaze fell on him, challenging and daring, he could not help but tease her. In truth, he loved the way she had always rolled her eyes at him, lit up with the fire she all too often kept firmly bottled within.

"There's another matter that complicates things," Griffin added, wringing his hands as though nervous. A rather unusual sight!

"What is it?"

"Since our parents can no longer assist her," he said, his voice grave, "*I*'ve offered to aid her in finding a suitable match. However, she was rather reluctant to allow me to help. In the end, I only gained her acceptance by offering her my trust in exchange for hers."

Trent frowned. "What do you mean?"

Griffin licked his lips, a disbelieving smile tugging on the left corner. "She agreed to let me find her a suitable match—according to her own directives, of course—if I agree to the same, meaning allow her to choose my future wife."

Trent was certain his mouth dropped open for a moment. "You did what?"

"I know. I know. It wasn't my finest moment," Griffin agreed. "However, I could not allow her to choose for herself. As I said she was going about it in her usual *sensible* manner, and believe what you want, but I'm convinced it would only make her miserable. I had to step in."

"So, she wants you to find her a husband?" Trent asked carefully. "She's leaving the choice completely to you? She will marry whomever you choose?"

Griffin frowned. "Within reason, yes, I suppose so." Then his gaze met Trent's, and a large smile curled up his lips. "I can see what you're thinking. However, I will not sacrifice my own happiness because you're afraid to declare your feelings. I know my sister; she would exact revenge in a most *sensible* way." He scoffed, then turned serious eyes on Trent. "I cannot go over her head. I need to take her demands seriously."

"I understand." Trent nodded, knowing that it would be wrong to persuade Winifred into a marriage she did not want to choose freely. Still, for a moment, he had been thoroughly tempted.

"If you want her hand in marriage," Griffin counselled, "you need to win her heart first." He sighed rather theatrically. "And preferably before I'm forced to choose one of those mind-numbingly boring gentlemen Winifred currently has her eye on for my future brother-in-law. Believe me, everyone wins if you can find a way to convince her that she's in love with you and that that is a *sensible* reason for marriage." Shaking his head, Griffin rolled his eyes. "Are we in agreement?"

Staring at his best friend, Trent grasped the offered hand and nodded. "I shall try," he mumbled, feeling his heart ache in his chest as failure and all its consequences loomed on the horizon. Had anyone ever been able to convince Winifred of something she did not want to believe?

"Don't try, my friend," Griffin warned. "Do! Failure is not an option, or all our lives will take a turn for the worst."

3

A GENTLEMAN & A LADY

Stanhope Grove sparkled with lights and laughter that New Year's Eve, and Winifred found herself bewitched by the joyous atmosphere brought on by the promise of a new year and everything it might bring. Music echoed through the vaulted ballroom as couples danced until exhaustion, their cheeks bright red and their eyes aglow, perfectly attuned to the face-splitting smiles that seemed so common that night.

"Is it not wonderful?" the dowager countess beamed, her usually stern expression lost, replaced by one of proud delight. "Is it not the most magnificent ball you've ever attended?"

Noting the way Eleanor rolled her eyes as her mother chased one compliment after the other, Winifred smiled at the dowager countess. "It is indeed. I do believe it shall soon become a legendary event greatly anticipated throughout the entire year."

Instantly, the dowager countess beamed with pleasure, and Winifred looked at her friend, noting the way she shook her head at her, a grateful smile on her kind face.

A moment later, the dowager countess hastened away, no doubt in search of more admirers.

"It was sweet of you to indulge her." Squeezing Winifred's hand, Eleanor smiled at her. "I know she can be quite tiresome in her exuberance."

Winifred chuckled, knowing her friend's words to be an understatement.

"What is so amusing?" Griffin asked as he walked toward them with Eleanor's husband, Henry Waltham, by his side.

"Nothing that would concern you," Winifred said to her brother, unwilling to discuss the dowager's need for compliments any longer than necessary. So, before he could enquire further, she turned to her friend's husband. "It is so good to see you again, Mr. Waltham. I hope marriage is treating you well."

Mr. Waltham smiled, and his gaze momentarily drifted to his wife. As their eyes met, Winifred could have sworn that the lights around them had dimmed—only for a moment as though they knew they could not compete. Then he looked back at her and nodded, gently pulling his wife's hand through the crook of his arm. "Very much so."

Still at odds about her friend's way of procuring a husband—namely falling in love—Winifred watched as Mr. Waltham led Eleanor onto the dance floor.

"They do look happy, do they not?"

Glancing at her brother, Winifred nodded. "They do right now. But how long will it last?"

"No one can know that," Griffin counselled, and she knew from the way he spoke that he was not merely making an observation but meant to prove a point. "While some arranged marriages end in love, some love matches are reduced to a marriage of convenience. These things happen. No one knows the future. We can only ever make the most out of what we do know."

Turning to look at her brother, Winifred narrowed her eyes. "And what is that?"

"How we feel." Holding her gaze, he shrugged. "What we want. What we believe makes us happy."

Getting annoyed with his lectures, Winifred crossed her arms in defiance and fixed him with an icy stare. "I know what you are trying to do, dear Brother, and I am telling you it will not work. I do know what I want as I have told you more than once. You agreed to help me if you haven't forgotten."

With his lips pressed into a thin line, Griffin nodded.

"I'm glad, for your behaviour would suggest otherwise," Winifred chided. "You've done nothing but try to dissuade me from the course I've chosen. So, let me ask you: do you wish to be released from your obligation or will you finally take it seriously?"

Defeat on his face, Griffin held her gaze for a long moment. Still, Winifred could almost see his thoughts racing, trying to think of a way to sway her after all. He was nothing if not relentless!

"Fine," he said, throwing up his hands. "I give up. You win."

Winifred scoffed, "I hardly would call that winning. Did we not agree on this in the first place?"

Grumbling under his breath, Griffin nodded once more.

"Then I would suggest you…" Her voice trailed off as she glanced around the room at the attending gentlemen. Was a suitable man here tonight?

Griffin sighed as though he had been asked to muck out the stables with nothing but a fork. "All right," he grumbled, annoyance clear in his voice. "Then tell me which gentleman strikes your fancy."

Spinning around, Winifred glared at her brother. If she did not know any better, she could swear he did this on purpose simply to aggravate her!

"All right. All right." Throwing up his hands in surrender, he stepped back. "I shall see what I can find out about the eligible bachelors present tonight." He gestured to the dance floor. "You go and enjoy yourself. I suppose someone should." As he walked away, Winifred heard him grumble under his breath, "Now, she's got me hunting down men instead of…" His voice trailed off as his attention was momentarily diverted by a fair-haired beauty in a stunning blue gown.

Winifred sighed in exhaustion. What had she been thinking? Could Griffin be trusted to find her a suitable match? Or was this endeavour doomed from the start?

Oh, how she wished her mother were there!

"Good evening, my lady."

At the sound of his voice, the air rushed from Winifred's lungs, and her heart almost jumped out of her chest. Closing her eyes for but a moment, she felt goose bumps dance up and down her skin.

Then Winifred jerked her eyes back open and, brushing her hands over her arms to chase away the chill, willed her nerves back under control. Turning around to face him, she could only hope that her emotions were not written all over her face.

"Are you cold?" Trent asked, a concerned frown drawing down his brows as his dark green eyes met hers.

Searched hers.

Held hers.

Winifred swallowed, trying to focus on the words he had spoken. "I'm fine," she finally said, her voice barely a whisper. How long had it been since she had last seen him? Had it truly been five years?

A few weeks ago, he had come to Atherton House to visit Griffin. However, he had not come to see her. Only after he had already left, had her brother informed her of Trent's visit, and her heart had ached rather painfully at being overlooked thus. Had they not all been close once? Did he not care for her as he cared for her brother?

A smile curled up Trent's lips as he formally bowed his head to her. "It is good to see you here, Lady Winifred. I hope you enjoyed the continent."

Lady Winifred? Swallowing, Winifred frowned. Never in his life had Trent spoken to her in such a civilised manner. What was he up to? "It was pleasant. Quite diverting."

"I'm glad to hear it."

Moments ticked by as they looked at each other. Would he not say more? She wondered. Would he not tease her as he always had?

When the silence became awkward, Winifred groped for something—anything—to say. "I would ask you not to sneak up on a lady," she chided, her voice harsher than she had intended. "It portrays a severe lack of manners." Shrugging, she sighed, "But then again, you never had any." The moment the words left her lips Winifred realised what she had said, and her teeth clenched in mortification. It was all she could do not to cover her mouth in shock.

Trent, however, seemed neither shocked nor offended. In fact, his sparkling green eyes seemed to light up from inside as though she had just answered his most fervent prayers. His face split into a wicked grin as he stepped forward and leaned in conspiratorially. "You know me too well, Fred."

Fred! There was that name again!

"I'd be much obliged if you would refrain from addressing me thus," she huffed, doing her best to sound outraged and ignore the little somersaults her stomach did as his breath brushed over her cheek.

"It's been five years," he whispered in her ear. "I've missed you."

Winifred swallowed before her eyes sought his. He'd missed

her? Never had he… "You've missed me?" she scoffed, rolling her eyes at him. "Or rather you've missed teasing me? Is that not true? Were you unable to find another woman willing to put up with your manners?"

His smile deepened, and a wicked gleam came to his eyes. "I must admit you never seemed particularly willing, dear Fred. However, I'm glad you've cleared that up. Now, that you're back, I shall not leave your side. After all, we have a lot of time to make up for."

"I'm afraid I must disappoint you." Taking a step back, Winifred squared her shoulders and raised her chin. "At present, I find myself rather," she groped for words yet again, "occupied." Why was it that this man always made her feel like a woman without sense?

"Occupied?" He grinned, once more closing the distance between them. "Doing what?"

"That is none of your concern." She took another step back.

His eyes flashed. "Sounds intriguing. Tell me more."

"I shall not."

"Why?" Again, he took a step closer, unwilling to let her escape.

Rolling her eyes, Winifred felt the familiar feeling of utter annoyance flare to life. "Because it does not concern you!"

At the pitch in her voice, he grinned. "You've already said that."

Crossing her arms over her chest, Winifred glared at him. "Were you born this irritating?"

"What can I say?" He shrugged. "You bring out the best sides of me."

"Hardly." Unbelievable! The nerve that man had!

Unexpectedly, he offered her his arm. "May I have this dance?" he asked, glancing at the dance floor where couples stood up for a cotillion.

Taken aback, Winifred did not know what to say. A part of her almost desperately wanted to know what it would feel like to sweep across the dance floor in Trent's arms. However, at the same time, warning bells went off in her ears! There was something dangerous about him, and if she was not careful, he would upset her carefully thought-out plans.

"I'm afraid I must decline," Winifred said, and for a moment, the touch of honest disappointment that came to his eyes robbed her of all rational thought. "However, I…I've promised this dance to my brother. Therefore, I must take my leave."

As she turned away, her heart pounding in her chest like never before, Trent suddenly stepped into her path, holding out an arm to keep her from stealing past him.

Frowning, she glared at him. "What's the meaning of this?" No manners whatsoever, it would seem!

"I apologise." Still, the look on his face was far from apologetic. In fact, he looked very pleased with himself. Smug even. "However, Griffin asked me to step in for this dance."

Winifred frowned. How could he have? After all, it had been a lie.

"He told me he was rather *occupied* with some sort of *project* you asked him to assist with," Winifred froze, "and knowing how much you love it, he did not wish for you to miss the chance to dance."

Staring at Trent, Winifred felt the blood drain from her face. Did he know? Had Griffin told him? The way he had stressed the words *occupied* and *project* suggested a deeper meaning. Was he teasing her? Did he know and now wanted nothing more but to see her squirm?

Forcing a calming breath into her lungs, Winifred swallowed, willing her muscles to relax. "If that is what he said." Then she lifted her hand and placed it on his, allowing him to lead her onto the dance floor.

The warmth of his hand—even through her glove—sent a jolt through her body, which made her draw in a sharp breath.

"Are you all right?"

Willing a noncommittal smile onto her face, Winifred nodded. "Perfectly fine."

As the music started to play, all the couples began moving up and down the line. Relieved, Winifred concentrated on the steps, the rhythm, anything but the man across from her.

"You seem flustered."

Her eyes snapped up. "I'm not!"

"As you wish," he said with a chuckle.

After that, they managed a few steps in silence. Still, she could feel his eyes on her and wondered what he was up to.

"Your brother seems to be enjoying himself."

Frowning, Winifred looked at Trent, then followed his gaze down the line…where her brother was dancing with the fair-haired beauty in the stunning blue gown, who had caught his attention before.

Heat shot up Winifred's face at having her lie pointed out to her so bluntly.

Still, she refused to submit to defeat. Instead, she turned her glower onto the man who deserved it. "I admit it was an excuse—"

"It was a lie," he corrected smiling as though he was enjoying this…which he probably was. "You lied to me."

Winifred gritted her teeth. "As did you."

A frown drew down his brows. "Care to enlighten me?"

"You said my brother had asked you to step in," she elaborated, wondering how Trent could know about their *project* if he had indeed never spoken to Griffin. "Was that not also a lie, *my lord*?"

"It most certainly was," he admitted freely, drawing her arm through his before he led her off the dance floor and toward the refreshment table.

Frowning, Winifred only now noticed that the music had stopped, and the dance ended.

"You seem parched," Trent observed, handing her a glass of lemonade, his eyes smiling as he stepped closer and his arm brushed hers. "I must say lying becomes you."

Winifred flinched, feeling mortified when he laughed.

"Your cheeks are flushed. Your eyes are glowing." Then he sighed as though he were an art enthusiast gazing at a masterpiece. "Looking like this, you are the image of…"

Unable to stop herself, Winifred prompted, "Of what?"

Instantly, that wicked gleam was back in his eyes. "I fear I must think on that."

Inside, Winifred wilted. Were they truly unable to speak to each other in a civilised manner? What did that say about them? About her? Thinking of her list of attributes, Winifred wondered if she ought to amend it. Was she a petty or even vindictive person? Why could she not let go of the past and meet Trent with a clean slate? After all, it had been five years.

Inhaling a deep breath, Winifred set down her lemonade. "Then I shall leave you to it. Good day, my lord." And without looking over her shoulder, she marched to the other side of the large room, grateful when she spied Eleanor and her husband leaving the dance floor.

"Are you all right?" her friend asked when Winifred drew near. Then she cast a meaningful glance at her husband, who promptly excused himself. "Is something wrong?"

Winifred shook her head, unable to explain the turmoil that had been her constant companion since Trent had materialised behind her. And so, she inhaled another deep breath, forced a delighted smile on her face and said with as much enthusiasm as she could muster, "Not at all. In fact, I'm enjoying myself quite profusely."

Eleanor smiled. "I'm glad to hear it." Still, there was a hint of doubt in her eyes.

Swallowing, Winifred allowed her gaze to sweep across the guests in attendance, only excluding the area around the refreshment table. "Are you well acquainted with most of your guests?" Seeing the slight frown on Eleanor's face, she added, "As I've been out of the country for so long, I fear I hardly know anyone."

Instead of dissipating, the frown on Eleanor's face grew deeper and a hint of suspicion came to her eyes. "Tell me what is going on, Winifred? You seem…not like yourself."

Winifred sighed. Oh, how right her friend was!

"Well, quite frankly, I have decided that it was time I chose a husband."

Eleanor's eyes widened. "You have?"

"Yes, I've already spoken to Griffin, and he's assured me he will do his utmost to find me a suitable match." Her eyes narrowed as she craned her neck but failed to spot her brother. "Although keeping his mind firmly fixed on this task seems to be an act of futility."

"Your brother?" Eleanor asked, her voice momentarily filled with confusion before her eyes opened wide. "You want *him* to choose your future husband?"

Winifred looked at her friend. "Of course. Since my parents are no longer with us, he is the logical choice." A frown drew down her brows at the surprise on her oldest friend's face. "I cannot understand why this would surprise you. Have we not spoken about this subject only recently?"

"We have," Eleanor conceded. "However, I…I cannot believe you would truly do this."

Again, Winifred frowned. "Why wouldn't I?"

"Because…" Shaking her head, Eleanor seemed to be groping for words. Seemingly, it was that kind of evening! "What about love? I know you're rather practical, but is there no one you care for?"

Annoyed at this repeated suggestion from the people who ought to know her best, Winifred tried to contain her anger. "You sound like my brother!" she snapped, instantly regretting the harshness in her tone.

Eleanor, however, did not seem to have noticed as her gaze drifted across the ballroom to the refreshment table. Then she looked at Winifred and taking a step closer whispered, "What about Lord

Chadwick?"

Unprepared for this shock, Winifred momentarily feared she would lose her balance. "Trent?" she all but stammered, trying to keep her wits about her.

In answer to Winifred's reaction, Eleanor's eyes lit up and her lips curled up into a knowing smile. "Trent, is it?"

Winifred huffed, arms akimbo. "We grew up together. He's like a brother to me."

Eleanor scoffed, "He certainly does not look at you as a brother would." Holding Winifred's gaze, she bobbed her head up and down. "You know that as well as I do. Does he make you feel like Griffin does when he's near you?"

Winifred swallowed.

"See?"

"See what?" Remembering Trent's teasing, his obnoxious insistence on calling her Fred, Winifred had trouble holding on to her manners. "If you must know that man is the most annoying, insufferable and completely inappropriate person I've ever met. That is how he makes me feel! So, whatever you hope to accomplish by this line of questioning, I assure you it will not dissuade me. No, we do not suit one another. I wish for a husband who shares my interests, who understands my character because we are alike, because we have the same expectations in life."

"And you think Griffin will find such a man for you?"

Drawing in a deep breath, Winifred mumbled, "He better, or I swear I will make him pay."

4

WHAT TO LOOK FOR IN A HUSBAND

Watching her walk away from him, Trent cursed himself. After all, he had come to Stanhope Grove with every intention of treating her as a gentleman would treat a lady. However, old habits seemed to die particularly hard where Winifred was concerned. The moment she had snapped at him as she had so many times before, he had not been able to resist.

He had even called her *Fred* although he knew perfectly well how much she detested that name. Still, he enjoyed teasing her. The way her eyes lit up with fire, shooting arrows at him, entranced him. He could not say why or how, but on some level, he could swear she enjoyed their bickering as well.

Looking across the ballroom, he saw her speaking to Mrs. Waltham, relieved that at least at present she was not in the arms of another gentleman. The thought alone turned his stomach.

Still, he knew it was inevitable.

After all, she was a rare beauty, was she not? Even if he had not been in love with her, he would have thought her magnificent, the way her dark brown eyes shone in the candle light, the grace with which she had moved when she had followed him during their dance. She had truly grown into a remarkable woman, witty and clever, but also kind and loyal, and with a wicked sense of humour that matched his own.

In that moment as Trent stood on the far side of the ballroom, gazing at the woman he had loved from afar for five years, he finally realised how much he had missed her. How had he survived the past years without seeing her? Without speaking to her?

Glancing at her brother, Trent gritted his teeth as he saw Griffin's gaze drifting over the assembled guests, trying to pick out potential suitors, no doubt. Although his friend seemed annoyed with the task, Trent knew that there was no one in the world whom he loved more dearly than Winifred. She was the one who commanded his loyalty and devotion above everyone else, and he would not fail her.

Again, Griffin's words echoed in his ears. *If you want her hand in marriage, you need to win her heart first. Failure is not an option, or all our lives will take a turn for the worst.*

That day when he had hastened to Atherton House to see his friends after their long absence, Trent had only spoken to Griffin. Although he'd had every intention of seeing Winifred—in fact, it had been the foremost thing on his mind—Griffin's revelations had shaken him to his core and he had needed time to regain his balance, to decide on a course of action to start fresh and prove to Winifred that he could be the man she wanted.

However, so far, he'd only made a mess of things! If the looks she occasionally cast in his direction were any indication, he had managed to anger her quite thoroughly. In fact, she seemed spitting mad!

Throughout the evening, Trent continued to watch the woman he loved dance with one *suitable* gentleman after another while he cursed himself, her and her efficient brother. Did Griffin have to introduce her to all these men? Could he not at least buy Trent a little more time?

Would it matter? A rather annoying voice whispered in his head. *Either she cares for you or she does not.*

Did she?

Seeing the gentle smile on her face as she conversed eagerly with her current dance partner, Trent doubted it very much. For if she liked these *suitable* men, she could never like him, could she? Did that smile on her face truly speak of a certain partiality on her side or was she simply displaying better manners than he had ever possessed?

With each dance, the knot in his stomach twisted and turned, and when the last notes of yet another piece drifted away, Trent strode forward without conscious thought. All he knew was that he would not stand idly by and watch other men sweep Fred off her feet.

So, when she inclined her head to her dance partner and turned to leave, he was there, right in front of her, blocking her path.

Startled, her gaze narrowed, and the soft brown of her eyes ignited instantly. "What are you doing here?" she snapped, casting careful glances around them, trying to keep her voice down despite the anger that made her shoulders tremble. "Let me pass."

Stomping on the fear that had grown in his heart throughout the night, Trent held out his hand to her, doing his best to appear the perfect gentleman. "May I have this dance?"

Instantly, suspicion came to her eyes, and his resolve faltered. How could he ever hope to win her heart if he had to pretend to be someone he was not?

"I'm afraid I've already promised the next dance to Lord Haverton," she told him, satisfaction as well as a hint of a challenge in her voice.

"Lord Haverton?" Trent mumbled as he took a step closer, his gaze fixed on her face. "And does the gentleman know that he has asked you for the next dance?"

Immediately, her lips clamped shut, and steam seemed to be coming out of her ears. "I would appreciate it, my lord, if you would refrain from calling me a liar."

Trent chuckled, "I've good reason to, in case you've forgotten." However, glancing around, he saw a good-looking gentleman heading straight toward them, his gaze fixed on Winifred. "As you wish," Trent said, turning back to her. "However, then I must insist you save me the next dance."

Grinning, she asked, "Why ever would I do that?"

Inhaling a deep breath, he stepped closer and grasped her wrist, surprised to feel her pulse hammering as she tried to tug her hand free. "Believe me, dear Fred," he whispered, and her gaze narrowed, "you would not want to cause a scene. What would all those eligible bachelors think of you?"

At his question, all colour drained from her face and she stared at him, her mouth slightly open. "How do you…? I…"

"Are we in agreement?" he prompted as Lord Haverton drew near.

Winifred swallowed. "Fine."

Reluctantly, Trent released her wrist and nodding to Lord Haverton took his leave. However, from the side of the ballroom, he watched them dance, watched as Lord Haverton tried to make polite conversation, watched as Winifred did her best to answer courteously. Still, her gaze often travelled to him, and Trent could not deny that he felt a deep sense of satisfaction that he had managed to occupy her thoughts so thoroughly.

The moment the dance ended, Trent strode forward and instantly relieved Lord Haverton of his dance partner. Pulling her farther onto the dance floor, Trent rejoiced when the first notes of a waltz began to echo through the large room.

Meeting Winifred's gaze, he reached for her. The moment his hand settled on her waist, she drew in a slow breath. Her gaze, however, remained firmly on his. Only now, her eyes held no anger or annoyance. Now, they held something else entirely.

Encouraged, Trent pulled her closer, as close as he dared, surprised when she did not pull away, did not fight him. Holding her gaze, he kept his hand firmly on her back, the tips of his fingers gently tracing along her spine.

At his touch, she inhaled a sharp breath and sank her teeth into her lower lip as her back seemed to arch of its own volition. "Stop," she whispered almost pleadingly.

Lowering his head, Trent held her gaze. "Why?" When she did not answer, he asked, "What is it you hope for in a husband?"

Instantly, her eyes narrowed, and yet, the anger that flashed in them was only a mild echo of what he had seen before. "He shouldn't have told you," she whispered, for the first time averting her gaze.

"He's my friend," Trent replied, surprised by the seriousness of their conversation. "You're his sister. He wants us to be happy."

A deep frown drew down her brows. "Us?" Before Trent could reply, realisation came to her eyes and she immediately began to struggle in his arms. "I asked him to assist me in finding a husband," she prattled, her gaze fixed on something beyond his shoulder as though she did not dare meet his eyes. "As I cannot turn to my parents for help, I thought he would be the logical choice. He promised to take this seriously, to find me a suitable match, someone to share my interests, my fundamental characteristics, my—"

"What about love?" Trent interrupted, and she immediately stilled in his arms, her gaze flying up to meet his. "And passion?" He inhaled deeply, tightening his hold on her, willing her to see how much she meant to him.

In answer, her muscles tensed, straining to get away. "You ought not speak of such things," she snapped, yet her voice lacked strength. "Release me. This does not concern you."

Belatedly realising that the music had come to an end, Trent refused to let her slip away. Holding on to her, he lowered his head, his gaze trapping hers. "You concern me," he whispered. "You always have…and you always will."

Thunderstruck, she stared up at him until they both sensed someone's approach.

Releasing her from his embrace, Trent looked up and found a rather stocky, young gentleman standing beside them, his pale blue eyes drifting from him to Winifred. "My lady, may I have this dance?"

Winifred swallowed, her lashes fluttering rapidly as she sought to regain her composure. "Certainly, my lord," she croaked and allowed him to pull her arm through his. Then she walked away, not even glancing over her shoulder.

Still, Trent could not help the warmth of hope from spreading into every fibre of his being. If he was not thoroughly mistaken—and he would wager his heart and soul that he was not!—then Winifred did care for him! He almost fainted in relief at the realisation.

However, she seemed afraid—terrified even!—at the thought of venturing away from her path of rational thought and sensible planning. Yes, they were not compatible in the strictest sense. They bickered and snapped at each other, baited the other and found joy in teasing one another beyond compare.

Still, Trent had no doubt that she was his other half, and he would not allow anyone else to claim her.

Sensible suitors be damned!

5
THE WRONG MAN

With the beginning of the new season, Winifred found herself in a carriage traveling toward London. Across from her, Griffin sat slumped in his seat, a stack of papers on his lap, from which he picked up one here and there, held it up to his face, read the notes he had scribbled on it before shifting his attention to the next.

"What are you doing?" Winifred enquired. Never in her life had she seen her brother so devoted to a piece of paper. For all intents and purposes, Griffin was a man of few intellectual interests, at least not those that required him to spend considerable time with pen and paper.

"Excuse me?" A frown on his face, he looked up, saw the confused expression on her face and sat up, straightening his shoulders with a moan. "Hell, my back hurts. Has this carriage always been this uncomfortable?"

"I suggest you change your posture. Now, what is this about?" Gesturing to the stack of papers, she turned questioning eyes to him.

For a moment he frowned, his gaze shifting back and forth between her and the papers on his lap as though the answer should be obvious. "In case you haven't noticed—which I see that you haven't!—I have spent the past fortnight cataloguing potential suitors to the best of my abilities." At her open-mouthed shock, he raised his eyebrows with a touch of haughtiness. "Indeed, after our five-year absence, instead of acquainting myself better with the *ladies* of the ton, I've done nothing but scribble down all those little details I know you think are important about the attending gentlemen at the New Year's ball at Stanhope Grove. There. Happy?"

Unable to form a coherent thought, Winifred stared at her brother. "Thank you," she whispered after a while, feeling tears sting the back of her eyes. "You really do love me, don't you?"

All teasing left Griffin's face as he saw the emotion in her eyes and a large smile claimed his lips. "Most fiercely," he whispered before he swallowed the lump that seemed to have settled in his own throat and held up one of the papers. "Here, I've listed their interests as well as characteristics I've become aware of during the ball. Now that the new season has begun, there will be plenty of opportunity to mingle. Once I narrow down my list, I shall see to it that you can meet the more suitable gentlemen in a more private setting, say a dinner party and the like. Seeing you interact with them will give me a better idea of who would suit you the most. Do you have any objections?"

Winifred shook her head. He had taken her seriously after all! Who would have guessed? After seeing him dancing with that fair-haired beauty, Winifred had assumed he had all but forgotten about his promise. How wrong she had been! "Thank you so much for doing this, Griffin. I know this is not easy for you."

A strained snort escaped him, and for a moment, he rubbed his hands over his face. "That's quite the understatement. To tell you the truth, I've never been more scared in my life."

Winifred frowned. "What do you mean?"

Griffin swallowed, turning serious eyes to her. "You trust me with your life, your future, your happiness. I'm afraid I'll make a mistake. I'm afraid because of me you will end up with the wrong man." He inhaled deeply. "I promise I shall do my utmost to ensure that that doesn't happen." Then with a last smile, he turned his attention back to the notes on the paper before him.

The wrong man? Winifred thought as—unbidden—Trent's dark green eyes flashed before her inner eye. Although she had tried to banish him from her thoughts for the past fortnight, he refused to release her. Remembering the way he had held her during their second dance still sent shivers down her spine, and she found herself closing her eyes, enjoying the memory of his touch.

The way he had held her had made her feel safe as though he would not hesitate to move mountains to protect her. Still, the way his hands had travelled over her back had also sent her heart into an uproar. She could still see the way his gaze had burnt into hers and hear his whispered words in her ear. *You concern me. You always have…and you always will.*

He had seemed so possessive of her during that dance, not at all like the Trent who always teased her, always called her *Fred.* For a moment—a short moment—it had almost seemed as though he had wanted to kiss her.

Winifred's body hummed with the memory of that feeling. *And passion?* He had asked. Was that what she had felt?

Shocked at the boldness of her thoughts, Winifred jerked her eyes open, trying to shake herself out of her daydreaming. Reminding herself that infatuations were always short-lived, she directed her gaze out the window, gazing at the passing landscape.

Infatuation? She frowned, realising the implication of her thoughts. At what point had she become…infatuated with Trent? Or was it not true? Had it only been the heat of the moment? Would she still feel the way she did now the next time she laid eyes on him?

Gritting her teeth, Winifred determinedly pushed that thought away. There was no need for her to see him outside of social events. After all, she had a future husband to find. Someone who suited her beyond the spur of the moment. Someone she could share her life with. Someone who understood her.

And that someone was certainly not Trent Henwood, Earl of Chadwick.

At least, she told herself so.

Sitting in the conservatory Griffin had added to their London townhouse for the sole reason of his sister's desire to paint, Winifred was engrossed in the glowing orchid slowly taking form on the canvas before her.

Her eyes shifted to the side, gazing at the live plant, trying to catch the way the afternoon light streamed in through the glass walls around her and set it aglow, giving it an otherwordly touch. The golden light almost seemed to dance on the snow-white petals, and Winifred sighed at the peaceful scene before her.

After the rather tumultuous beginning of the year, Winifred had spent the past few days locked away in a world of colours and light where the outcome of a painting was controlled by her skill alone. Nothing more. There were no contradicting emotions.

No misunderstood meanings.

No uncertainties.

"Ah, there you are."

Looking over her shoulder, she found her brother standing in the doorway, dressed to go out. "I've been here every day for the past few days," she reminded him, her brows raised in challenge. "If that fact has escaped your attention until now, I feel compelled to question your ability to assist me in choosing a suitable husband for you seem far from observant."

Grinning, Griffin approached. "Are you daring me to quit, dear Sister?"

Winifred swallowed, keeping a careful smile fixed on her face.

"Are you afraid I will choose poorly? Or are you reconsidering the requirements you placed on this endeavour?"

Setting down her paintbrush to have a reason to avert her gaze momentarily, Winifred rose from the stool. Then she took a step toward her brother. "Have you ever known me to change my mind?" she asked, her voice betraying a strength she did not feel.

"Not lightly."

"And I shall not do so now." Turning her gaze back to the window, Winifred felt her hands begin to tremble. Did she have doubts? She did not dare entertain that thought. For if she did and it turned out that it was true, what would she do then? What about her carefully forged plans? What would she do without them?

"I shall be out for the rest of the afternoon," Griffin said, his footsteps retreating toward the door before they stopped, and he took a few steps back. "By the way, your painting is beautiful. However, I must say I've seen similar ones all my life. Why do you never paint people?"

With her gaze fixed on the canvas, Winifred shrugged. "They're too complicated. There is no one way to paint someone. No right way.

I never know what to include and what not, how to…" Again, she shrugged, unable to put into words how people tended to confuse her. "They're not rational."

Griffin grinned. "I know. That's the beauty of it." Then his footsteps retreated once more. "Oh, I almost forgot. Trent will be over shortly; however, I won't be able to receive him."

As her heart hammered in her chest, Winifred turned toward her brother.

"You don't mind entertaining him, do you?"

"Me?" Winifred stammered, her hands gripping the paintbrush a bit too tightly. "Why can't you cancel on him?"

"Because he's already on his way."

"Then cancel your other plans." Her voice sounded almost pleading to her own ears.

Watching her, Griffin took a step closer, his brows drawn down. "If I didn't know any better, I'd think you didn't enjoy his company." A question lit up his eyes.

"How can I?" Winifred huffed, shaking her head at her brother. "He always teases me. He's insufferable."

Griffin chuckled, "I know. I like him, too." Then he turned to leave.

"What is so important that you cannot stay?" Winifred demanded, returning to the actual subject at hand.

"You."

"What?"

Stopping in the door frame, Griffin smiled. "I'm meeting a few *eligible bachelors* at White's."

Winifred's mouth dropped open. "You are? Why?"

Griffin sighed, "How can I judge their character if I don't know them?"

"Oh."

"Exactly." And with that, he turned and walked away, leaving her alone to face the one man who had always managed to turn her world upside down.

Trying to distract herself, Winifred turned her gaze back onto the canvas. However, the orchid failed to capture her attention. Despite Griffin's good intentions, she could not help but curse him for forcing this obligation on her. She could not simply send Trent away, or could she? Would that be in bad manners? After all, it was not she who had made plans with him. It had been her brother.

Feeling anger thudding through her veins, Winifred set down the image of the orchid she had been working on and retrieved a blank canvas. For a long moment, she stared at the white surface as it sat upon the easel, waiting to be filled with colour.

Snatching up her paintbrush, Winifred followed her intuition and quickly sketched her brother's face. Then she began to fill his image with life, giving his eyes a touch of mischief and his lips a curl of amusement. Before long, his portrait—although far from finished—had the same air of high-handedness about it which her brother always showed when doing what he thought right, ignoring others in the process.

It was a true likeness, one that captured his essence, and for the first time, Winifred felt satisfied with a portrait. Maybe once she had completed this one, she ought to try and paint others. Maybe it would help her understand people better.

All their layers.

All their—

"You truly have a talent."

Startled by Trent's voice only a few inches behind her, Winifred spun around, her paintbrush raised as though in defence, and before she knew what was happening the tip of her brush touched his face.

Shrinking back, she stared at the brown smudge on Trent's cheek. "I'm sorry. I didn't mean to…" Then she swallowed, and her gaze met his, taking note of the hint of surprise as well as the tickling amusement that painted a teasing smile on his face. "Have I not told you not to sneak up on a lady?" she snapped. "You're truly impossible!"

Laughing, he retrieved a handkerchief from his pocket and began wiping at the paint. "Oh, I'm impossible? You're the one to disfigure me, and I'm impossible?"

Winifred rolled her eyes, watching him spread the small smudge all over his cheek. "Oh, don't be so dramatic!" Then she stepped forward, "Give me this!" snatching the handkerchief from his hand. "You're making it worse."

He had the audacity to chuckle. "Why do I make you so nervous?"

Forcing her voice not to tremble, Winifred snapped, "You're not. You're mistaking annoyance for nervousness." Then she stepped back, and after dipping an edge of the handkerchief in a little fresh water she had set aside to clean her brushes, Winifred grabbed his chin rather roughly, turning his head sideways. "Now hold still or I swear I shall spread the paint all over your face."

Again, he chuckled as though nothing had ever been more amusing.

6

PASSION

Enthralled, Trent watched her as she began to wipe the paint off his cheek.

Her fingers held his chin tightly, and yet, they seemed to tremble ever so slightly as though the sudden contact had taken her off guard as much as him. Enjoying the feel of her touch as well as the warmth of her skin, Trent noticed her swallow when she caught him watching her, and he could not help but think that she felt something, too.

A woman unaffected did not look as she did, or did she?

Her eyes flicked back and forth between his own and the smudge on his face, and her cheeks seemed to darken with colour as though the emotions coursing through her at that moment ran deep. Still, despite her declaration to the contrary, she seemed nervous as though overwhelmed by their close contact.

"There," she finally said, releasing his chin and stepping back. "Now you look presentable again." Handing him back his handkerchief, she turned back to her painting, her gaze never quite meeting his.

Although Trent could not help but regret that the paint smudge had not been bigger and therefore more difficult to remove, he did not dare act on the impulse that coursed through his veins, urging him to reach for her and pull her into his arms. What would she do? Slap him? Scream?

No, before he did something so bold, he had to be certain of how she felt, of how she would react.

Looking over her shoulder, he tried to find something to say. "Since when do you paint people?"

"Since today."

Surprised, he took a step closer, feeling her stiffen as she straightened her back, the muscles in her jaw tense as she kept her gaze focused on the painting before them. "What brought on this change?" he asked, then chuckled. "Your brother I would presume, judging from the annoyingly superior look in his eyes."

At his words, he felt her relax slightly and a matching smile drew up the corners of her lips.

"What did he do?" Trent asked. "What made you paint him like this?"

The smile vanished from her face; however, she did not say a word.

"Have you ever painted me?" Trent prompted, wondering what her answer would have been if only she had shared it with him. Did it have something to do with him?

Turning her head, she looked at him, a slight frown drawing down her brows and a teasing curl coming to her lips. "Is your memory impaired somehow? Have you recently suffered a blow to the head?" When he frowned, she added, "Can you not recall what I just told you?"

Trent laughed, "I suppose I wasn't paying attention."

Rolling her eyes at him, she turned back to the painting. "To tell you the truth, few things you do surprise me."

He grinned, leaning in closer. "Would you care to elaborate?"

She inhaled a deep breath before stepping away and reaching for her paintbrush. "I'm afraid commenting on that would only make you more insufferable."

Again, he laughed, "Where's your brother?"

She stiffened but kept her gaze on the painting. "Out at White's. He asked me to make his apologies."

Confused for a split second, Trent nodded as he realised the significance of Griffin's absence. Judging from her evasiveness and how uncomfortable she felt in his presence, her brother was most likely working on their little *project* and trying to find her a suitable husband. Was there a deeper reason why she did not want him to know? Or was he simply imagining it?

Unable to help himself, he asked once more, "What do you look for in a husband?"

At his question, her hand tightened on the brush before she turned to look at him, her eyes narrowed, a warning resting in them. "Did I not tell you that this does not concern you?" She swallowed. "I'd much appreciate it if you would take your leave."

Trent swallowed, determined not to allow her to push him away. "Not until you answer me."

"Why?" she demanded, her eyes widening as they searched his face. "Why do you want to know? To tease me some more?"

"Do you not like it?" he asked, grinning, wondering how he had made it through the past five years without teasing her…without…her.

Again, her eyes narrowed. "Why would I? It's highly irritating." She stopped, and her gaze held his for a moment. "Do you?"

Closing the distance between them, Trent held her gaze, noticing the way she forced herself not to take a step back. "Very much so," he whispered, his breath touching her lips, making her shiver. "Now tell me, Fred, what is it you wish for in a husband?"

Swallowing, she held his gaze, determination shining in her eyes. "If you must know, I am hoping for a husband who does not tease me."

"Would that not be a dull life?" he teased as though by reflex, unable not to.

"Not at all." She shook her head. "It would be peaceful."

He frowned. "Peaceful or boring?"

Annoyed, she glared at him. "You're too much like my brother. You cannot take anything seriously." Shaking her head, she shrugged. "Why would you understand? You couldn't. But I…I want my life to be different. I want things to make sense." She inhaled a deep breath. "Griffin should not have told you."

"Why did you ask him for help? Why ask him to find you a husband?" Watching her face, Trent was not certain if he wanted to know. However, if he wanted to win her heart—and her hand—then he needed to know what she hoped for.

Sighing, she raised tired eyes to him. How often had she needed to explain herself? Trent wondered. "Because he knows me best. He knows who I am and what I need to be happy. Now that my parents are…" She swallowed, and he could see that their loss still haunted her. "He is the only one who can find me a suitable husband. Someone who's compatible with me."

Trent drew in a slow breath. "Griffin mentioned something like that."

"Then why did you ask me?" Winifred snapped, her gaze suddenly ablaze with anger. "Is this a new way to tease me? To annoy me?"

Not taking her bait, he held her gaze for a long moment, allowing the ensuing silence to soften her anger. "What about love and passion?"

As she inhaled a sharp breath, her eyelids began to flutter as though trying to hide her, to erase him from her vision. No doubt she remembered their dance at the New Year's ball, the way he had held her, touched her, whispered to her. Had that been her first taste of passion?

"Those…those aspects are of no importance," she stammered before she remembered to raise her chin and face him with those dark brown eyes full of quiet determination. "They are short-lived and no secure foundation for a life-long commitment."

Trent smiled. "Are you certain? Have you ever felt them?" Reaching out a hand, he brushed a stray lock from her face, gently tucking it behind her ear.

At his touch, she flinched. Still, for the barest of seconds, her eyes closed, and he could swear it was only her determination that made her take a step back.

"Why are you retreating from me?" he asked, his voice teasing, the look in his eyes far from it.

"I'm not."

"Then stand still." Holding her gaze, he once more closed the small distance between them. Her pulse in the side of her neck hammered wildly as he reached out to touch her hand. Gently, he brushed the tips of his fingers over her bare skin. At the ball, a layer of fabric had separated them as she had worn gloves. Now, however, the warmth of her skin called to him, and he entwined his fingers through hers, holding her hand in his.

As her chest rose and fell with her rapid breathing, Trent began to feel light-headed. Her gaze held his without wavering, and yet, there was still resistance in the way she stood before him.

"You should leave," she said, her voice almost pleading.

Why could she not simply admit that she felt something for him? "Why?"

"My brother is not here."

A teasing smile curled up the corners of his mouth. "I cannot say I mind for I enjoy spending time with you." His hand tightened on hers, and she drew in a sharp breath. "I've missed you."

Blinking, she stared at him as though she did not believe her ears. "It's been a long time."

He nodded.

"I meant to…I mean." She swallowed. "When my parents died, I was overwhelmed with grief and sorrow. I couldn't…"

Trent frowned. "What are you trying to say?"

She drew in a slow breath. "I never stopped to remember that you lost them, too. And then Griffin and I left and you…" She squeezed his hand. "You remained here all by yourself. I should have thought to…"

"To what?" he prompted, deeply affected by the way she had thought of him. Had he been on her mind every once in a while over the past five years? He could only hope so.

"To ask you to join us." For a moment, her eyes closed before a deep sadness and honest regret showed in them. "Ever since you first came to Atherton House with Griffin, you've been a part of our family. You belong with us…and then we forgot about you." Tears brimmed in the corners of her eyes as she looked at him, her gaze pleading with him to forgive her.

Trying to swallow the lump that had settled in his throat, Trent tried to sort through the renewed feelings of loss that assailed him. "Even if, I couldn't have come. I had responsi–"

"But I should have thought to ask!"

"Griffin did."

Her eyes widened. "He did?"

Trent nodded. "He asked me to come, and I wanted to, but after my father's death, there was too much I needed to handle. I simply couldn't."

Nodding, she held his gaze, her dark brown eyes full of emotion that he felt tempted to pull her into his arms. "I'm sorry," she whispered, once more squeezing his hand. "I'm so sorry."

"I know. As am I."

Silence stretched between them as they gazed at one another, remembering the life they had shared and the loss that had torn them apart. In a way, at their core, they were still the same, and yet, time had passed, changing something they could not quite grasp.

Swallowing, she pulled her hand from his…and reluctantly, he released her. "You should go," she said for the second time that day, the hint of a smile coming to her face as her eyes lit up with child-like mischief. "Even if my brother has no sense of propriety, I do. You should not be here when he is not."

Noting the change in the air as though the dark cloud had moved on, revealing the sun, Trent grinned at her. "You seem determined to get rid of me, dear Fred. Are you afraid I have untoward intentions?" Winking at her, he stepped closer.

A deep smile came to her face, relieving the tension that had held her, and she laughed. "Not at all. I am merely concerned for my reputation." She glanced at her half-finished painting. "Still, I could do with a little peace and quiet or my brother will never have a teasing likeness to hang over the mantle."

Chuckling, Trent inclined his head to her. "What a marvellous idea!" Then he stepped back and took his leave, relieved to feel the ease between them returning, knowing that now was not the right time to reveal to her what intentions he had…untoward or otherwise.

7

WALTZING WITH THE ENEMY

Over the course of the next few weeks, Winifred found that choosing a husband was quite time-consuming…at least if one did it right.

As the new season began and London reawakened, Winifred followed her brother from ball to ball, attended performances at Covent Garden and promenaded through Hyde Park. Due to their five-year absence, the ton seemed quite intrigued to have the Earl of Amberly and his sister back in their midst; after all, they both possessed assets that made them quiet desirable on the marriage market.

Dancing with a large number of eligible men—many of which were urged in her direction by overbearing mother's looking for a good match!—Winifred tried her best to discover who would suit her enough to be considered a potential husband. Although her intuition told her quite early whether she liked a gentleman or not, she urged herself not to draw hasty conclusions. After all, getting to know another's character could not be accomplished during one evening, let alone within a few minutes.

Her brother usually stood off to the side, alternately watching her and conversing with the gentlemen he deemed worthy of his sister's hand—quite to the disappointment of London's eligible ladies!

As Lord Haverton guided her across the dance floor, Winifred once more glanced over his shoulder and spotted her brother, politely but insistently extracting himself from a young lady's grasp. Smiling, Winifred sighed. He truly was most diligent in keeping his promise! She never would have expected him to do so, but it did warm her heart and reminded her of how much she meant to him!

"You seem amused," Lord Haverton observed, his kind green eyes gliding over her face. "It suits you."

Inclining her head at the compliment, Winifred considered how to reply. "My brother seems very…watchful this evening."

Lord Haverton smiled, and as they turned he glanced in Griffin's direction. "He does indeed." His green eyes returned to her. "He seems very protective of you, Lady Winifred. That speaks highly of him and you."

"Thank you, my lord." Smiling back at him, Winifred realised that she was enjoying his company quite a lot. He was a decent man, kind and considerate. He always spoke truthfully as his eyes never seemed to disagree with his words, and his smile betrayed a caring heart and respectful demeanour. Her brother had indeed done well when he had encouraged her to get better acquainted with Lord Haverton.

When the music stopped, her dance partner inclined his head to her. "Thank you for this dance, my lady." His green eyes held hers, and he seemed reluctant to take his leave. "I was wondering if—"

"May I have the next dance?"

Goose bumps raced down Winifred's spine at the sound of Trent's voice, and she turned to him wishing her face held more annoyance than she knew it did. Out of the corner of her eye, she noticed a touch of disappointment come to Lord Haverton's face. However, her attention instantly focused on the mirth twinkling in Trent's dark green gaze as he held out his hand to her.

"Or are you otherwise engaged?" he asked, the look in his eyes growing darker as though he dared her to refuse him.

"Not at present," Winifred heard herself say before turning back to Lord Haverton, thanking him for their dance. When he took his leave, Trent instantly drew her into his arms as the first notes of a waltz began to play.

Reminding herself to be annoyed with his overbearing attitude, Winifred stepped on his foot as hard as she dared without it being obvious to those around her.

Sucking in a sharp breath, Trent turned wide eyes to her. For a moment, he seemed taken aback. However, that moment was short-lived. His lips curled up in a smile, and his hand tightened on her back. "You did that on purpose," he accused, seemingly delighted with her actions.

"I did," Winifred admitted freely, trying to straighten her back lest she sink into his arms. "As did you."

A frown came to his face. His eyes, however, still held the same satisfied twinkle she had seen there before. "I'm afraid I do not know what you mean."

Winifred scoffed, "Don't play innocent, Trent. Every time a waltz is played, you appear as though out of nowhere." A frown drew down her brows. "How do you know? Do you have an acquaintance among the musicians? Are you clairvoyant?"

Laughing at the teasing note in her voice, Trent lowered his head to her conspiratorially. "I assure you, dear Fred, it is merely a coincidence."

Rolling her eyes at him, Winifred sighed, starting to feel annoyed. "Stop calling me that." She glanced around. "What if someone overhears you? What if others start–"

"Calling you Fred?"

She nodded.

His hands tightened on her, and the air flew from her lungs at the intensity in his gaze as he looked at her. "If they know what's best for them, they won't." He inhaled slowly, his gaze unwavering. "It's mine. Mine alone."

Staring up at him, Winifred could not help but think that he was saying a lot more than claiming her *nickname* as his. It was as though he was…claiming *her*…as his. Swallowing, Winifred averted her gaze, focusing her thoughts on the steps. Steps she knew in her sleep. Steps that provided little distraction from the man holding her in his arms.

"You seem quiet suddenly," he observed, a touch of concern in his dark green eyes. "Is something wrong?"

Winifred sighed, groping for something to say. "I am…merely concerned about Lord Haverton." Trent rolled his eyes. "The way you claimed this dance was quite rude as you did interrupt him. I don't even know what he wanted to say. I must go and apologise." Craning her neck, Winifred tried to spot the young lord among the sea of guests, glad to have somewhere to look but into Trent's disconcerting eyes.

"Is he the one?" he asked unexpectedly, his voice strained as though her answer would determine the course of his own life. "Have you made your choice?"

Winifred swallowed, carefully raising her eyes to his. What she saw there confused her as she could have sworn that–

"Have you?" Trent prompted impatiently, his jaw tense and his voice almost a growl.

Winifred swallowed. "What is it to you?"

His lips pressed into a thin line, and his gaze was hard as it held hers. "Answer me."

Winifred shrugged. "I have not." All the tension seemed to leave Trent's body. "However, I think we would suit each other. Still, it is too soon to tell."

Trent drew in a slow breath. "Good," was all he said, and when the music ended, he squeezed her hand one last time and then took his leave.

Still swaying from the effects of their dance, Winifred turned to her next dance partner, momentarily at a loss as to who he was.

Never would he have seen this coming!

8

A SENSIBLE MATCH

A few days later, Winifred found herself bundled up in her warmest winter clothes sitting next to Lord Haverton in his open chaise as they took a turn through Hyde Park. After apologising to him for Trent's rude behaviour, he had enquired if she would allow him to call on her. As Winifred had no reason to object, he had stopped by the following morning, accompanied by his mother, a woman who portrayed the evil witch with every fibre of her being.

Winifred had been more than relieved when they had left. Although she did come to care for the young lord, his mother was the making of nightmares. Ought she exclude him from consideration based on his family's attributes? It was a new thought that hadn't occurred to her before. However, if she were to marry Lord Haverton, his mother would become an important part of her life as well. Could she live with that?

"Do you prefer watercolours?" Lord Haverton asked, guiding the two horses pulling their chaise around a bend. "Or oil?"

"Watercolours."

"May I ask why?"

Winifred shrugged, wiggling her chilled fingers inside her muff. "I dislike the smell of oil colours."

Lord Haverton nodded. "I agree. Painting is a very sensory activity. One ought to reduce negative influences as much as possible." Glancing at her, he smiled. "Would you allow me to see your paintings?"

"Certainly, my lord. I've never thought to hide them. You're welcome to visit and take a look."

"I shall."

As they came around a small grove, the Serpentine appeared before them, its waters glistening in the brilliant sun as it gave a magical glow to everything it touched. "What a magnificent sight!" Lord Haverton exclaimed. "I admit I am fascinated by the influence of light on everyday objects. It often seems to change how things appear. The lake, for instance, seems almost mystical in the sunlight. However, in its absence, the waters often appear murky as though danger awaited."

"I agree." Feeling eagerness course through her veins, Winifred gazed at the lake, remembering the orchid she had painted a few weeks ago. "When I paint in the conservatory, I can paint the same objects, but always have it appear differently depending on the time of day. It is truly fascinating."

Again, Lord Haverton smiled at her, and Winifred could see that he was as pleased with their conversation as she was. Indeed, they had a lot in common and his disposition suited her. He never riled her, but instead was always attentive, always considerate. His smile was warm and affecting, and his green eyes held warmth and kindness.

Still, sometimes when she looked at them, Winifred could not help but see another pair of green eyes in her mind. Dark green to be exact, with a wicked gleam in them.

"Good afternoon, Lady Wini*fred*, Lord Haverton."

At the sound of his voice, Winifred closed her eyes for the barest of seconds, wondering if her thoughts had called him here. Why was it that he always knew where she was? Why did he always follow? It was quite aggravating, and from the way Lord Haverton's lips thinned, he did not care for the interruption, either.

Turning toward approaching hoof beats, Winifred balled her hands inside her muff into fists, willing Trent to simply greet them and leave. However, judging from the look on his face, he seemed disinclined to be agreeable.

"Good day, Lord Chadwick," Lord Haverton greeted their unwelcome acquaintance. "It is a beautiful day, is it not?"

"It is indeed." Sitting atop his black gelding, Trent barely looked at Winifred's companion as his dark gaze seemed focused on her. Still, he spoke politely as though their meeting had come about entirely by chance. Knowing Trent, Winifred was certain that chance had had no hand in this.

"What brings you here?" she enquired as uncomfortable silence began to linger in the air.

Trent merely shrugged. His shoulders, however, seemed tense, and he gripped the reins rather tightly. Did something bother him? "After last night's festivities, I had merely hoped for some fresh air." He swallowed, and his gaze met hers once again. "To clear my head."

After a little more uncomfortable and rather meaningless chitchat, Trent took his leave and they went their separate ways. Relieved, Winifred allowed Lord Haverton to take her home, accepting his invitation to have tea with him and his mother sometime soon.

Strangely exhausted, Winifred went up to her room and rested for an hour or two before heading back downstairs to the conservatory. If there were ever a place that had the power to soothe her raging emotions, it was the small glass pavilion. Although it was late afternoon, the sun streamed in, setting everything aglow, and the myriad of flowers beckoned her forward, their scents, sweet and engaging, promising better days. Easier days.

Putting the final touches on her brother's portrait, Winifred felt her muscles relax and before long a smile drew up the corners of her mouth. Despite Trent's interruption, it had been a pleasant day. After all, it had allowed her a deeper glimpse at Lord Haverton's character. He was indeed the kind of man she had been looking for. He would make her a good husband, would he not? Would she make him a good wife? Ought she to make her choice? Or was that premature?

As footsteps echoed closer, Winifred stepped back from the easel. "Griffin, what do you think? Would you say this is a fitting likeness?"

"I would indeed," Trent spoke from behind her, and she whirled around.

"What are you doing here?" Winifred demanded as the cloud of peaceful tranquility that had engulfed her only a moment ago slowly evaporated. "My brother is not here."

Grinning from ear to ear, Trent stopped in front of her. "I

know. I came to enquire after your morning with Lord Haverton."

At his frank admission, Winifred's mouth fell slightly open. "You have no right to ask such a question."

"I know. I'll ask it nonetheless." His gaze held hers, daring her to answer.

Winifred swallowed before stepping sideways to set down her paintbrush, thus giving her a reason to avert her eyes. "However, I will not answer." Lifting her gaze to his, she squared her shoulders. "I need to ask you to leave. It is not proper for you to be here when my brother is not."

A challenging gleam came to his eyes as he stepped closer. "You were out alone with Lord Haverton," he observed, a touch of an accusation in his voice.

"Yes, we were out in the open," Winifred retorted, annoyed with his overbearing attitude. Who did he think he was? Her brother? "For everyone to see. We, however," she gestured to the two of them, "are alone."

At her last word, a spark seemed to light up his eyes, and Winifred felt her courage falter. Swallowing, she took a step back before glancing over Trent's shoulder, wishing her brother were here. How dare he leave them alone together?

As though he had read her thoughts, Trent took a step closer, unwilling to allow her to escape. A wicked smile curled up his lips, and his eyes teased her. "Are you afraid I have untoward intentions?" he asked as he had before.

Winifred rolled her eyes, knowing that the best way to deal with Trent's affinity for mockery was to not take him seriously.

His eyes searched her face, and an amused smile came to his own. "You do not believe it possible, do you?" he asked, then shook his head. "Perhaps you're right. Perhaps I should go. Perhaps it is not safe for you to be alone with me."

Unable to hide her surprise at his admission, Winifred frowned, trying to make sense of this change in attitude. Deep down, there was a part of her that doubted that he was merely teasing her.

Holding her gaze, Trent leaned his head down to her. "I don't mean to frighten you, dear Fred, but I thought you should know."

Winifred swallowed. "Know what?"

A teasing grin came to Trent's face. Still, his gaze remained serious. "That I have untoward intentions."

9

UNTOWARD INTENTIONS

Seeing the understanding on her face, Trent fought to resist the urge to pull her into his arms and show her that she was his and would never be Haverton's. When he had heard about their outing from Griffin, his insides had twisted painfully, and he had not been able to keep himself from going to find them. As predicted, it had taken all his willpower to not throttle Haverton, but instead allow Winifred to leave with him.

Never in his life had he found himself in a more trying situation.

Now, finding the woman he loved only an arm's length away from him, her wide eyes fixed on his, her chest rising and falling with each rapid breath, Trent wondered what she would say if he were to kiss her. Would she reject him?

His teeth clenched. Would she reject Haverton?

Feeling his own nerves flutter, Trent glimpsed the paintbrush she had set down a few minutes ago. Instantly, it brought back the memory of a few weeks ago when she had accidentally gotten paint on his cheek. He remembered her closeness, her touch, her warmth, and a deep longing rose inside him.

Flashing a teasing grin at her, he leaned forward, noting the way she in turn leaned back and drew in a sharp breath, before he reached for the abandoned paintbrush. Straightening, he held her gaze, then quickly brought up the brush and in one fluid motion drew it across her cheek, leaving a trail of black paint. "Quite untoward, I assure you," he laughed, delighted when her eyes widened in outrage.

Shrieking, she slapped his hand away, her own touching her cheek. Then she brought it before her eyes, which widened even more when she saw the black smudge on her fingertips. "How dare you?" she demanded, her eyes ablaze with sudden fury.

Smiling, Trent could not bring himself to feel remorse. After all, it was that fire in her that he loved most. He could never live a life without teasing her. Could she?

Before he knew what was happening, she threw herself at him like a wild fury, snatching the brush from his grasp and attacking him with equal measure. The brush still moist with paint surged toward him, and only in the last instant did he manage to sidestep her attack.

Turning on her heel, she came after him again. "You'll regret this!" she snarled, once more raising her arm, once more aiming the brush at his face.

Laughing, Trent turned, then to his surprise managed to grasp her wrist, the tip of the brush only a hair's breadth from his skin. "Dear Fred, be *sensible*," he teased, delighting in the way her jaw clenched and she growled at him.

As they struggled, he managed to twist the brush from her grip and tossed it across the floor where it came to rest next to a large flowerpot at a safe distance. With the weapon disposed of, he slipped an arm around her waist and pulled her against him, noting with satisfaction the widening of her eyes as her hands stilled. "I never knew you had such passion within you," he whispered. "Or perhaps I did know." Then he grasped her chin—the way she had grasped his—and tilted her head upward, her lips only a hair's breadth away from his own. "Did you kiss Haverton?"

Her eyes grew round—whether at his question or their closeness he did not know—before she pressed her lips into a thin line, glaring at him. Still, she did not try to free herself from his grasp. "That would have been highly improper," she spat as though her words were an insult to him.

Quite on the contrary. Trent felt his muscles relax, finally free to enjoy holding her in his arms…and away from prying eyes no less. Whenever he had swept her into a waltz over the past few weeks—vowing to never allow another man to hold her in his arms—he had been tempted to kiss her more than once. However, with the ton watching that had never been an option.

Now, however, things were different.

"Did you want to?" he pressed, noting the way her long lashes fluttered up and down.

Opening her mouth to reply, she stopped, staring at him for a long moment. Then she straightened her spine, trying to free herself from his grip.

"Answer me," Trent demanded, tightening his hold on her.

A slight blush crept into her cheeks, and Trent felt his insides burn with jealousy. "I can't say," she finally whispered, her gaze lifted defiantly. "I hadn't thought about it."

Once more, Trent felt himself relax with relief. "Then you didn't," he concluded, elaborating when he saw the soft frown on her face. "If you had, nothing could have stopped you from thinking about it."

For a moment her gaze remained on his before she abruptly dropped it, a deep flush coming to her face, and tried to free herself from his grasp once more.

Trent felt his breath get stuck in his throat as hope surged through him. "Are you thinking about kissing me?" he asked boldly, and her head snapped up as though he had struck her.

10

BEING NONSENSICAL

As her cheeks burnt with embarrassment, Winifred stared up into Trent's face, his gaze searching hers. Could he read her thoughts in her eyes? Did he know? Suspect?

Cursing herself, Winifred did not know what had brought on these sudden desires. Why was it that he was the one person who made her feel this way? The one person that made her act and feel like a silly girl? Uncertain? Not in control?

Steeling herself against the tantalising touch of his fingers on her skin, the way his strong arm held her pressed to his body, Winifred lifted her hands and in one fluid motion pushed him away. "Don't be ridiculous," she snapped—or tried to—as she turned back to the painting behind her, hoping to hide the uncertainty and temptation that all too likely showed on her face.

"I don't believe I am," he replied, the tone in his voice daring her to turn and face him. "I believe you're afraid."

Whirling around, determined to put him in his place once and for all, Winifred opened her mouth in outrage. "Afraid of wh—?"

Suddenly, he was there, right in front of her, barely a hair's breadth away. Pulling her back into his arms, he brushed his knuckles along the line of her jaw before his hand came to rest on the back of her neck. "Of being nonsensical," he answered her outburst before his mouth closed over hers.

In an instant, logic and reason and sense went out the window as emotions long held in check surged to the forefront. Although shock froze her limbs for a few moments, Winifred could not deny the all-consuming warmth that swept through her.

As he held her in his arms, his lips teasing her to follow him down this path, Winifred felt herself respond without thought. Something other than her rational mind urged her on, and she did not have the strength to resist.

Returning his kiss with equal measure, Winifred wondered at her own boldness. Still, when his tongue met hers, even that last thought disappeared into thin air as though it had never been.

After wrenching his lips from hers, Trent whispered, "I've been wanting to do that for a long time, Fred. A very long time."

Staring up at him, Winifred tried to sort through the tumult in her heart. His gaze held hers, and his eyes shone with such intensity as she had never seen them. Deep emotions rested in them, and from one moment to the next, Winifred understood…everything.

Why he had demanded every waltz.

Why he had glared at Haverton.

Why he called her Fred.

And yet, it could not be. It simply could not.

Panic began to well up in her chest as her heart and mind locked in battle. What was she to do? What was the right course of action?

Oh, how she wished her mother were here!

Instead, it was Griffin who suddenly stood in the doorway, clearing his throat.

Startled, they both flinched, whirling around to face the unexpected interruption.

With the touch of a smirk on his face, her brother looked from her to Trent. "Care to explain what is going on here?"

Meeting her eyes, Trent nodded. Then his hand grasped hers, and he took a step forward. "Griffin, I apologise," he began, and in that moment, Winifred knew exactly what he would say. "However, I–"

"You need to go," she interrupted, pulling her hand from his. "I need to speak to my brother."

Turning to look at her, his eyes narrowed, and she could see his confusion only too plainly on his face. "But I—"

"No!" Shaking her head, she looked at him, hoping he could forgive her. But she was not ready for this. She simply was not.

Within a matter of minutes, her entire world had shifted, turned upside down, and she was in no state of mind to make a life-altering decision here and now.

Her heart ached as she saw pain and disappointment well up in his eyes. Still, he nodded. "If this is what you want, I will go," he forced out. Then, however, he took a step closer and whispered, "But I will not walk away." His gaze burnt into hers. "You belong with me as I belong with you. No amount of sensible reasoning can change that." Then he turned, nodded at Griffin and disappeared.

As though she had held her breath, her lungs began to burn, and she gulped down a few deep breaths, trying to steady her trembling hands.

"Are you all right?" Griffin asked, a bit of a smirk on his face. When she nodded, his smile grew wider. "And are you aware that he was just about to ask for your hand?"

"I'm not an idiot!" Winifred snapped, taken aback by the harshness in her voice.

Griffin laughed, "Well, to tell you the truth, dear Sister, you've been acting like one."

Instantly, her head jerked around, and she stared at her brother. "This is all your fault!" she hissed as sudden light-headedness engulfed her. "You shouldn't have left us alone. You should've been here. If you had, he would never have…"

"Kissed you?" Griffin prompted, his face suddenly serious. "Whether you want to believe it or not, whether you like it or not doesn't matter, but he has been in love with you for a very long time." Gently, he took her hand. "Only today he finally had the courage to express how he felt."

Gritting her teeth, Winifred shook her head. "It doesn't matter. I know what I want. I told you, and I thought you were willing to take this seriously, to help me." Searching his gaze, she swallowed. "And you did, didn't you? You suggested Lord Haverton, and you were right. He suits me. He does."

A deep frown came to Griffin's face. "I do not deny that. But…" Squeezing her hands, he held her gaze. "Do you truly not care about love? You may be suited to Haverton, but do you love him?"

Bowing her head, Winifred stepped back, pulling her hands out of her brother's grasp. Her heart ached, and her mind buzzed like a beehive. She could not think, and she had no clue how she felt.

Inhaling a deep breath, Griffin took a step back, giving her space. "I apologise for upsetting you. It was never my intention. However, I do hope that you think long and hard about what you truly want. Nevertheless, it is your decision." He turned to go, but then stopped in the doorway. "I actually came to tell you that Eleanor is here. We ran into each other on the front stoop upon my return from White's. She's waiting in the drawing room." A moment of silence hung in the air. "Perhaps you should speak to her." Then he turned and walked away.

Gritting her teeth against the shivers that wrecked her body, Winifred tried her best to gain control of her fluttering nerves. Never in her life had she felt as much at the mercy of her treacherous heart as now. Well, maybe when her parents had died.

Still, who would ever choose to feel like this? And if she chose Trent, if she trusted his words, then he would have the power to make her feel like this whenever he chose.

No. The more sensible course of action was to forget today had ever happened and go back to the way things were.

Inhaling a deep breath, Winifred wiped the paint smudge from her cheek, brushed her hands over her dress, tugged away a stray curl and forced a pleasant smile on her face. Then she left the conservatory and headed to the drawing room to greet Eleanor, determined to pass a pleasant afternoon chatting with her friend.

However, the moment she entered the drawing room, Eleanor's eyes narrowed. Her joyous smile momentarily froze on her lips before she stepped forward, her gaze searching Winifred's face. "What happened?"

Winifred swallowed, willing the corners of her mouth to remain where they were. "Nothing," she lied, stepping around her friend and gesturing for her to take a seat, all the while keeping her eyes firmly fixed on anything but the woman eyeing her with unconcealed concern. "Merely an argument with my brother. He can be quite tiresome at times. Would you care for some tea?"

Eleanor drew in a deep breath, her gaze shifting sideways as though she were contemplating what to say. "My dear Winifred," she began, and even then, Winifred knew that she had lost. "You're one of my oldest and most trusted friends. I admit we haven't seen each other for quite some time and I'm certain I know you less now than I did then. However, even a fool could see that your heart is aching most acutely." A gentle smile came to her lips. Her eyes, however, still held the same determination. "Tell me what happened. Is it Lord Chadwick?"

Winifred froze, her eyes wide, staring at her friend. "How do you…?"

Eleanor chuckled, "Because you love him, and because he loves you." Reaching out, she grasped Winifred's hand. "What happened?"

Winifred swallowed. Perhaps her brother was right. Perhaps she ought to tell Eleanor. After all, she was a woman and perhaps she could advise her in a way her brother simply could not. "He kissed me," she finally admitted, noticing the delight in her friend's gaze. "And I believe he…was about to ask for my hand."

"Was about to?" Eleanor frowned. "What stopped him?"

"I did." Pulling her hand from Eleanor's grasp, Winifred rose to her feet, suddenly unable to remain still. "I could see it on his face, and…and I panicked." Turning to look at Eleanor, she shook her head. "I started to feel light-headed. I…"

"The thought of him proposing frightened you?" Eleanor asked, stepping toward her, her kind eyes suggesting that she tried to understand. "Why?"

"Because we are not suited to one another!" Winifred huffed, feeling overwhelmed by the constant need to explain herself.

"How do you know?" Eleanor demanded before a teasing twinkle came to her eyes. "Did you not enjoy his kiss?"

For a long moment, Winifred stared at her friend, not knowing what to say.

"Why can you not admit that you care about him?" Eleanor asked, a frown coming to her face. "I can see that you do. He means a lot to you. He always has."

Winifred shrugged, trying her best to understand and in turn explain it to Eleanor. "We grew up together. He's like a brother to me."

Eleanor laughed, "He most certainly is not. I've told you before that he does not look at you as a brother does and neither do you look at him as you do Griffin. What you feel for him is different, believe me."

"Even if it is," Winifred conceded. "It is only a momentary infatuation. It will not last, and when it ends, I'll be stuck with a man whose favourite pastime it is to tease me, to mock me, to call me names. How is that a good foundation for a marriage?"

Stepping forward, Eleanor once more drew Winifred's hands into her own, her kind eyes meeting her friend's. "Look at me, Winifred. Do you truly dislike his teasing? Ask yourself honestly if you would wish for him to stop. How would you feel if he were to never again call you Fred? Do you truly believe it to be an insult?"

Remembering the many times Trent had called her Fred, Winifred knew that it was not. For whenever he had, his eyes had shone brightly with affection, with fondness, with tenderness. When they had danced, he had told her that his nickname for her was his…his alone, and no one else was to use it. He would see to that. "I do not," she finally admitted, feeling as though Eleanor had just robbed her of her one good reason not to give in, not to be swayed from her chosen path.

Squeezing Winifred's hands gently, Eleanor smiled at her. "I always thought it sounded like a term of endearment, and he's used it for years, has he not?" Winifred nodded. "To me, that means that you've been in his heart for a very long time. There is nothing momentary about how he feels about you."

Winifred sighed, remembering Trent's intense gaze as he had told her that he's been wanting to kiss her for a very long time. Had he been truthful? Never had he lied to her. There was no good reason not to believe him.

Still, now that her mother was dead, Winifred could not bring herself to sway from the path she knew her mother would have approved of. Would it not be a betrayal? Would she feel as though she'd lost her mother all over again? As strange as it was, following in her mother's footsteps had made her feel closer to the woman who had walked by her side all her life. And although she was not a little girl any longer, Winifred was not certain if she was ready to face life alone.

On her own.

What ought she to do?

11

A HAPPY COUPLE

A mere two days later, Trent found himself at yet another ball, his hands painfully wrapped around a glass as he stared across the dance floor, watching the woman he loved dance with the man she wished to marry. How had they reached this point?

Only two days ago, he had been on the verge of asking for her hand…and then she had stopped him, her eyes wide with panic. Why did she not want to marry him? Did she not care for him? However, the way she had responded to his kiss had suggested otherwise. In the moment her lips had melted against his own, he had felt certain of her affections, of her acceptance of his proposal, of a shared future.

Now, it seemed as far-fetched as snow in July.

Watching as the *happy couple* strolled off the dance floor, Trent gritted his teeth against the bile rising in his throat. How could he simply stand here and allow Lord Haverton to court *his* Fred? Still, he had to admit that it was her choice. As much as he wanted to rush over and pound the other man into the ground, it would not change that it was her choice. Quite on the contrary, such a reaction would probably convince her that he was not the right man for her for good. But what else could he do? Was he simply to stand here and watch?

"How are you doing?" Griffin asked, stepping up next to him, his gaze shifting from Trent's face to the *happy couple* down by the refreshment table. "You seem rather ill at ease, my friend."

Trent scoffed. What an understatement! "Did you come here to mock me?"

"Not at all." Grinning from ear to ear, Griffin asked, "Do you have a plan? I mean besides sulking in the corner and glaring at the man who will steal the woman you love from under your nose if you're not careful?"

Exhaling loudly, Trent turned his dark stare on his friend. "What do you suggest I do? Your sister has made it very clear that she does not wish to marry me."

Shaking his head, Griffin sighed.

In that moment, Trent could have settled for pounding his friend into the ground. Why was he making this even harder than it already was?

"You know," Griffin began, his voice suddenly casual, "given the circumstances I found the two of you in a few days ago, my sister might be persuaded to marry you to avoid a scandal."

Trent snorted, "You know very well that I would never force myself on your sister. In addition, she would never bend her will to anyone," he sighed, "which is one of the reasons I love her."

Griffin grinned, deep pleasure in his eyes. "That's all I wanted to hear, my friend." Jovially, he clapped Trent on the shoulder. "However, you're wrong in one regard."

"And what is that?"

"She is currently bending her will to the ludicrous notion that love and compatibility are mutually exclusive." He shrugged. "Don't ask me how she came to that conclusion. I believe it has something to do with how our parents came to be married. Still, it's a twisted reason for choosing a husband, and I fear that one day she will wake up and realise that she sacrificed her own happiness for the approval of a ghost."

Griffin's words brought back the memory of a cold December afternoon over a decade ago when a young Winifred, barely thirteen years old at the time, had spoken to him quite vehemently of the merits of matching dispositions. That day, her example had been her brother's rather wild and carefree character in contrast to her own more sensible and considerate disposition. She had pointed out how—due to their differences—they would never get along and that she would eternally be burdened with a brother whom she could not understand, leaving them forever in a state of constant aggravation.

Still, was there anyone closer to her today than her brother? Had they not bonded over their shared loss? Was there anyone else she trusted more? After all, she had asked him to choose her future husband. Did that not speak of unwavering trust?

"Have you told her how you feel?" Griffin asked, watchful eyes focused on Trent's face.

"Certainly, I hav—" Breaking off mid-sentence, Trent realised that although he had finally admitted his feelings for Winifred to himself, he had never spoken the very words out loud. Not to her. Not to the one person who needed to know. "I did not," he mumbled, wondering how he could have overlooked such an important detail. "I thought I had made it clear, but I've never actually told her that I love her."

"Don't you think you should," Griffin asked, a touch of amusement in his voice, "before you admit defeat? Even if for an objective observer there is no mistaking your feelings for her, hearing it out loud might help her realise what she is about to give up. Perhaps she simply needs to hear it."

Watching Winifred walk away on Haverton's arm, Trent drew in a deep breath. "What if I'm fooling myself?" He turned to look at his friend. "What if she simply doesn't care for me?"

Griffin frowned. "Then why doesn't she simply tell you? I bet to this day she's never said anything like that to you, has she?"

Trent shook his head. "Perhaps she is only trying to spare my feelings."

Laughing, Griffin stepped closer, placing an encouraging hand on Trent's shoulder. "Listen, from where I stand it seems that she is doing her utmost to keep herself distracted, and there's only one reason a woman would do so."

Feeling his hands tremble, Trent looked at his friend, eagerly awaiting his answer. "Which is?"

Griffin sighed as though all of this was obvious and Trent a fool for not realising it on his own. "Because she's afraid of what she truly wants."

Trent swallowed as treacherous hope swelled in his chest. Lifting his gaze, he looked around. However, the spot by the refreshment table was now occupied by another couple. Where had they gone? What if Haverton proposed to Winifred in this very moment? What if she accepted him? "I need to find her," Trent declared as his heart thudded wildly in his chest, terrified at the thought that he had lost his chance.

A satisfied smile on his face, Griffin nodded. "I'll help you."

12

NO REASONABLE OBJECTION

"These orchids are beautiful," Winifred exclaimed as they strolled through the conservatory, its glass walls making them visible to the attending guests in the ballroom. Engrossed, her gaze shifted from one flower to the next. "I would love to see them during the day with the sun shining in."

Lord Haverton nodded. "I would certainly love to see you paint them. I so admire your ability to capture their beauty. I myself am doomed to admire as I cannot create myself." Despite his words, a delighted smile rested on his face and he looked at her with the greatest admiration shining in his kind green eyes.

Eyes that—unfortunately—reminded her of another man!

Chiding herself for the direction of her thoughts, Winifred lifted her gaze and smiled at the man who had been attentive to her all throughout the evening. She could not deny that he was a kind and decent man and that their conversation was quite stimulating, bringing her great joy as well as peace of mind. On top of that, he was a handsome man with chestnut brown hair and startling green eyes that never failed to light up whenever he saw her.

Did you want to kiss him? Unbidden, Trent's question echoed in her mind, and Winifred could not deny that…she did not. Or did she? How was she to know? Perhaps she had to kiss him before knowing that she wanted more kisses? Perhaps she was simply confused.

Still, in the back of her mind, Winifred detected the nagging realisation that although she cared for Lord Haverton, she did not wish to kiss him. In fact, her heart steered her in another direction, and she could not keep herself from remembering the way Trent had kissed her a mere two days ago.

What she had felt then was still indescribable to her, and for that very reason it had terrified her more than anything else she had ever experienced. How could she feel something she did not understand? After all, there was not a single, logical reason why he should be able to make her feel thus? Constantly, he aggravated her, called her names…

Fred.

A shiver went down Winifred's spine at the memory of his nickname for her on his lips.

"Are you cold?" Lord Haverton asked, his green eyes full of concern.

Shaking off the memory that had claimed her, Winifred forced a reassuring smile onto her face. "Not at all. I was merely…lost in thought."

He chuckled, "It happens to me, too, at times. My father always called me a dreamer." A wistful smile tugged on his lips. "But he was like that himself."

"Has he passed on?" Winifred asked, seeing the sorrow that still rested in Lord Haverton's gaze.

He nodded. "Not two years ago." He swallowed. "I have very fond memories of him. However, I am sad to say that my parents never shared the kind of union that would inspire affection." Inhaling deeply, he remained quiet for a long moment, his gaze holding hers, before he seemed to have come to a conclusion.

Stepping forward, he swallowed, the trace of a nervous smile on his face. "Title notwithstanding, I'm a simple man with simple hopes for the future. I wish for nothing more but a loving wife and a happy family."

Staring at Lord Haverton, Winifred drew in a shaky breath, knowing full well what he was about to say…to ask. She also knew that there was no sensible reason to refuse him.

"My dearest Lady Winifred," Lord Haverton began, tentatively reaching for her hand, "allow me to say that in the short time we've known each other, I've come to admire you greatly."

Winifred swallowed, unable to dislodge the lump in her throat, as panic began to rise in her heart. In a moment, he would ask her to marry him, and she would need to give him an answer. But which one? Was she to accept or refuse?

What was she to do?

"I've thought this through quite thoroughly," Lord Haverton continued, "and I've concluded that–"

"Excuse the interruption," came Griffin's voice from the shadow of the doorway. "However, I'm afraid I must." Stepping into the room, his eyes sought hers, and Winifred could not deny that her heart rejoiced at the reprieve he granted her.

Releasing her hand, Lord Haverton took a step back. "Amberly, I assure you my intentions toward your sister are completely honourable."

Griffin nodded his head in acknowledgement. "Of that I'm certain, Haverton. However, I need to speak to my sister on a matter of urgency. Would you excuse us for a moment?"

"Certainly." Lord Haverton nodded eagerly and left without a moment's hesitation.

Once she was alone with her brother, Winifred felt the air rush from her lungs, and for a short moment, she closed her eyes, her thoughts a chaotic mess.

"Come with me," Griffin said, holding out his hand to her, before he glanced behind her at the tall windows opening the conservatory and those in it to the prying eyes of other attending guests.

With her hand firmly tucked into the crook of her brother's arm, Winifred found herself walking down a long corridor before Griffin opened a large door and ushered her inside. Judging from the rows upon rows of ceiling-high shelves filled with countless books, they had retreated into the library.

"Are you all right?" Griffin asked as his gaze swept over her. "You seem flustered, to say the least."

Swallowing, Winifred nodded. "I'm quite all right." Whatever did that mean? She wondered, realising that her problem had merely been postponed but not solved. At some point, Lord Haverton would ask for her hand, and then she would have to give him an answer.

Winifred knew that he was exactly the kind of man she ought to marry, and yet…

Turning to her brother, Winifred found him looking at her with serious eyes, a warning resting in their dark brown depths. "Tonight, will decide your future," he finally said. "I hope you know that. You need to make a choice and ask yourself if you truly wish to marry Lord Haverton."

Staring at her brother, Winifred noticed her mouth opening and closing a few times. "Did you…did you know he was going to propose?"

Griffin scoffed. "A blind man could have seen that coming. That man is smitten with you, and you're not being fair to him."

Again, Winifred opened her mouth, only this time to protest her brother's accusation. However, he cut her off with a wave of his hand.

"Be that as it may," he continued, his gaze hard as it held hers, "I'm not the only one who noticed Haverton's intentions. I thought you ought to know that before you make any rash decisions."

This time, Winifred's mouth fell wide open and her eyes bulged. "Trent?" she whispered as another rush of dizziness engulfed her.

Grasping her by the arm, Griffin held her tight, waiting until she stopped swaying. "When we found you and Haverton alone, I had to hold him back." He chuckled, "Otherwise, he would have stormed in, swung you over his shoulder and carried you off like a caveman."

Glaring at her brother, Winifred hissed, "What on earth is so amusing?" In that moment, she could have strangled her brother! What was he thinking making fun of her misery!

"You, my dear Sister," Griffin said without preamble. Then he drew her hands into his and met her eyes, his own suddenly free of all humour. "Listen to me. I know that you're the kind of person who makes a careful plan and then follows it to the smallest detail, afraid that if you venture from your carefully laid-out path, disaster will strike." At this point, he waited, holding her gaze, needing to know if she would contradict him.

However, she did not. After all, he was right. There was no denying that.

"But despite everything you thought you wanted," Griffin continued, "now is the moment when you need to be absolutely certain of what you want…before you make the wrong choice."

With a frown drawing down her brows, Winifred stared up at her brother, willing herself to ignore the growing panic that took hold in her heart. "But you chose Lord Haverton for me? Why would you now object?"

Shaking his head, Griffin looked at her as one would a foolish child. "I chose a man who suited you according to your wishes, yes. However, as good a man as Haverton is—and believe me, I have no reasonable objections," Winifred groaned at his words, "he is not the man I would have chosen for you on my own."

As bright spots began to dance before her eyes, Winifred tried her best to keep her breathing under control.

"Whether you like it or not, I still believe you need to follow your heart," he told her, his hands gently squeezing hers, "and it does not lie with Lord Haverton, does it?"

Unable not to, Winifred shook her head.

A pleased smile came to her brother's face. "I know that Lord Haverton is a man who suits you. However, I could also point you in the direction of a man who loves you." His gaze held hers. "It's your choice."

In that moment a shadow fell over her, and Winifred turned her head to see Trent standing in the doorway. "Can I speak to you?" he asked as Griffin was already stepping back.

In that moment, Winifred knew she was lost.

13

FAR FROM SENSIBLE

Trent's hands still shook as he approached, and he remembered only too well the shock that had almost knocked him off his feet when he and Griffin had come upon Winifred and Haverton in the conservatory…alone. Trent had been on the verge of tearing into the room and wreaking havoc when Griffin had grabbed him by the shoulders and told him to leave.

To trust him.

As hard as it had been, Trent had left.

Stepping away from his sister and toward the doorway where Trent stood waiting, Griffin nodded to him. "This is it," he said quietly, glancing at Winifred. "Don't make a mess of things…or I swear you'll regret it." He sighed, "As will I." Then he walked away, leaving them alone.

Shifting his eyes to the woman he loved, Trent inhaled a deep breath.

Something had changed.

Usually, Winifred stood tall, her eyes ablaze, her shoulders thrown back in defiance of anyone who would dare interfere with her plans. Her sharp tongue never failed to hit its mark, and yet, a touch of vulnerability rested underneath her brave exterior, softening her appearance and giving her features the look of kindness and compassion.

Now, all Trent saw was a woman lost.

A woman who did not dare meet his gaze.

And his insides turned to ice. Was he too late? Had Haverton asked for her hand? Had she accepted? Was he speaking to a betrothed woman?

The look of confusion on her face laced with guilt suggested that his hopes had been dashed for good. Still, he had to know. He had to be certain.

As Trent took a step toward her, Winifred's gaze fluttered to meet his for the barest of seconds before it dropped to her trembling hands once more. Then she swallowed, and her feet began to carry her backwards before she turned and approached the tall window, her shoulders relaxing a fraction as her eyes found something safe to gaze upon. "What are you doing here?" Her usually strong voice sounded distant as though far away.

Indeed, what was he doing here?

The truth! A sharp voice hissed, and Trent swallowed, knowing that he would have to risk having his heart trampled if he was to have a chance to secure her hand in marriage. Still, he could not help but remember the moment after he had kissed her two days ago when she had turned panicked eyes on him, sending him away. In her gaze, he had seen that she had been very much aware of his intentions, and still, she had sent him away. It had been clear that she had not wanted him to propose. That had been a mere two days ago. Had anything changed since then? Or would he find himself rejected yet again?

Swallowing, he approached her, stopping at a careful distance, not wishing to frighten her. "I came to ask for your hand in marriage," he said without preamble, his heart hammering in his chest as though he were running a marathon.

At his words, Winifred drew in a sharp breath and a slight shiver gripped her shoulders. Still, she remained quiet, her gaze fixed out the window at the starry night. Agonising moments ticked by before her soft voice reached his ears. "I thought about kissing Lord Haverton tonight."

The shock of her words almost sent him tumbling backwards and his heart ached as though she had stabbed a knife into it. As though determined to protect him from what was surely to come, his feet carried him closer to the door and the only way out.

But then she suddenly turned around, and his feet immediately rooted him to the spot. Her gaze found his, and for a moment, he thought to see something there he had not expected. Intrigued, he took a step closer. "You did?" he asked, hoping against hope that he had misunderstood her.

Still, she nodded. "I did, but it made me realise," she inhaled deeply, and he could have slapped her for drawing this out, "that I did not wish to."

Trent's heart skipped a beat. "You did not wish to…what?"

The ghost of a smile tickled the corners of her lips, and her gaze dropped from his as though she were embarrassed. "I did not wish to kiss him."

Instantly, unadulterated hope claimed his heart, and for a moment, Trent felt strangely light–headed before the need to see his hope made real claimed him. Stepping toward her, he found her gaze. "The other day when I kissed you," he began, delighting at the soft flush that came to her cheeks, "you kissed me back."

She nodded.

"Why?"

Her gaze narrowed, and her chin rose by a fraction. "I could ask you the same thing," she remarked, her voice steady once more with a touch of annoyance to it.

Trent rejoiced, and a large smile spread over his face.

Obviously annoyed with the absence of a reply, she crossed her arms before her chest, her gaze questioning as it held his. "Why on earth would you wish to marry me?"

Trent laughed, and her eyes narrowed even farther. "Because I love you, Fred," he finally said, and having those words out in the open between them felt incredibly liberating. "Can you not see that?"

She drew in a slow breath as though his answer had shocked her, and yet, her lips seemed more than willing to curl up into a smile…if only she would let them. "Why must you call me that?" she snapped instead, unwilling to allow him off the hook just yet. "It is a most distasteful name. Surely, you could find something more suitable."

"I don't care about suitable," Trent replied, slowly walking toward her, taking note of the way her eyes followed him. "It's my name for you. Only mine." The left corner of her mouth twitched, and Trent could not help but think that his answer pleased her. "A name I can be certain will not be used by another. Or has anyone ever called you that?"

Winifred shook her head, and some of the tension seemed to fall from her as she released the tight grip she'd kept on her own arms. Gesturing wildly as though lost, she opened and closed her mouth, trying to find the words to express herself.

"You're adorable," Trent whispered, completely taken with the honest confusion playing over her features.

As expected, her eyes narrowed. "I'm not a pet, you know?"

Trent laughed, "I don't care what you are as long as you're mine."

"If I were to marry you," she asked suddenly, "would you continue to tease me? To call me by that…name?"

Grinning, Trent nodded. "Would you truly want me to stop?" Closing the remaining distance between them, Trent reached for her hands, surprised to find them rather chilled. Wrapping them with his own, he held her gaze. "More than anything I love seeing your eyes light up with fire," he whispered. "I like the way you snap at me." She rolled her eyes at him and tried to pull her hands out of his grasp, but he would not let her. "It is open and honest and unrestrained. Don't ever stop." Trent chuckled seeing her frowning expression. "It makes you look alive."

Shaking her head, she stared at him. "You cannot be serious. Would you truly wish for a future where you wife snaps at you all the time?"

"If that wife is you," he grinned, "then, yes." Pulling her into his arms, he held her gaze. "Now, tell me, *Fred*," again, she rolled her eyes, "will you marry me? Or do you truly wish to spend the rest of your days with a man who suits you?"

Her eyes narrowed, but the corners of her mouth twitched teasingly. "At least, he would not tease me."

"I do not doubt it."

"He would not snap at me."

Trent grinned. "Very unlikely."

"He would not cover me in paint."

"Never."

A soft smile began to play on her features as all humour left her face. "He would not call me Fred."

"Not if he values his life," Trent growled, his arms tightening around her.

Holding his gaze, Winifred inhaled deeply. "He would not love me the way you do."

Lowering his head to hers, Trent looked deep into her eyes. "Then what is your answer?"

For a long moment she gazed up at him, and Trent tried his best to remain calm, knowing that decisions did not come easy to her. "I'll be your wife," she finally agreed, but held up a warning finger, "however, I shall warn you that the consequences will be dire should you make me regret my decision. Do be certain you want to risk that."

"I *am* certain," Trent whispered as his gaze dropped to her full lips. "As certain as I've ever been." Then he pulled her closer and dipped his head to kiss her.

However, her hands on his chest stopped him.

Frowning, he met her gaze, praying that he had not misunderstood her. "Is something wrong?"

A teasing twinkle in her eyes, she looked at him rather innocently. "I merely thought you wished to know that I love you as well." The corners of her mouth curled up into a wicked grin. "Although I cannot understand why. After all, it is far from sensible."

"Exactly," Trent exclaimed, then drew her into a passionate kiss before she could stop him once more.

EPILOGUE

A few weeks later

Winifred had to admit that being married had its perks. Not only was she now free to spend as much time alone with Trent as she wanted, but he had every right to claim her waltzes. Each and every one of them.

And although *Fred* was far from a flattering name, Winifred had come to realise that deep down she had never truly objected to it. It had been more of an obligation, a duty to refuse to be called by such a name. However, in truth, she had always delighted in the knowledge that she was the one and only Trent had thought up a nickname for.

The one and only he had ever loved.

"What do you have against Chad?" she asked as they twirled around the dance floor to yet another waltz. "I cannot call you Wick. That sounds ridiculous."

Now, it was Trent who rolled his eyes. "I don't see why you need to come up with a nickname for me anyways. Trent is already quite short. It's only one syllable whereas Winifred has three."

Winifred snorted, "Don't tell me you only came up with that

unflattering nickname because it was too time-consuming to call me by my given name!"

He grinned. "Fine, perhaps it wasn't the only reason. Still, that doesn't mean you have the right to–"

"That's precisely what it means!" Winifred interrupted, delighting in the way his eyes rolled in annoyance. "After all, I'm your wife, and you are mine to call as I wish."

A large smile spread over his face. "Is that so?"

Winifred laughed at the mischievous twinkle in his eyes, reminding herself how fortunate she was to be married to a man she truly loved. Although she had once thought differently, the past few weeks had proved to Winifred that the two of them were more suited to one another than she had initially thought. Certainly, they still bickered and snapped at one another, called each other names and outright delighted in teasing the other when it was least expected.

Still, Winifred had come to realise that Trent knew her as only her brother did. With one look, he could tell when she was saddened or upset or out of sorts. Although he had no affinity for art, he never tired of discussing her own paintings, offering his opinions and urging her to try something new. He loved to dance, and they spent many nights at home after supper, dancing from room to room. At first, their servants had seemed mildly startled. However, by now, they had accepted their master and mistress's quirks and indulged them with a kind smile.

Life was good. Better than Winifred had ever hoped it would be.

And she had no doubt her mother would have been happy for her. They might have gone down different paths, but was happiness not something everyone hoped for?

When the music came to an end, Trent escorted her to a small group of friends and acquaintances standing off to the side, her brother among them.

A young man with bushy eyebrows inclined his head to them. He was an old friend of Griffin's, only just returned from the continent; however, Winifred could not quite recall his name. "My congratulations on your wedding. From what Amberly told me, he is quite relieved to have his sister well married." He grinned at her brother, a mischievous twinkle in his eyes that reminded her of her husband. "I cannot understand why you had trouble marrying her off. A beauty like her."

Smiling, Winifred felt the muscles in Trent's arm tense as he forced a good-natured grin on his face. "He's a sweet man," she whispered teasingly.

Looking down at her, he rolled his eyes. "You'll be the death of me, woman."

"Only living up to my word," Winifred chuckled, wondering if they would ever tire of these little games. She could only hope that that would never happen.

"Mind you, she had no lack of suitors," Griffin indulged his friend, casting her a wicked grin. "However, I'm afraid my sister was quite particular about the kind of husband she had in mind. I tell you it caused me many sleepless nights."

Everyone laughed at Griffin's played exhaustion, patting him on the shoulder.

Meeting her brother's gaze, Winifred could not keep the words from tumbling out of her mouth. "I suppose that it is now my turn to find my brother a suitable bride."

Roaring laughter echoed around them. Only Griffin suddenly looked at bit ill at ease.

"You're at her mercy now, Amberly!" the man with the bushy eyebrows announced with delight. Then his smiling blue eyes turned to her. "My lady, if you require any assistance, do not hesitate to call on me. I'm quite familiar with a number of eligible ladies and could point you in the right direction."

"How kind of you, my lord." Smiling, Winifred glanced at her brother, who seemed a bit pale suddenly.

"In fact, there are many eligible ladies here tonight," Griffin's old friend continued, unable to drop the subject despite her brother's threatening glares. "However, I would advise against Miss Abbott." He leaned closer into the group and whispered, "She's rumoured to be the most awful woman in all of England."

Intrigued, Winifred nodded, seeing with delight the way her brother's eyes fell open as he realised the danger that lurked in his future. "Oh, no, you wouldn't," he stammered, shaking his head as though that would be able to dissuade her.

Winifred grinned, glimpsing a similarly entertained look on her husband's face. "You gave me your word, dear brother, and besides what's fair is fair." Then she turned to the man with the bushy eyebrows who had followed their exchange with rapt attention. "Would you be so kind as to point out Miss Abbott to me?"

A wide grin spread over his face. "I most certainly would," he replied, winking at Griffin, who groaned in agony.

This season would no doubt prove to be quite entertaining.
Perhaps not for her brother.
Still, one could not hope to please everyone, could one?

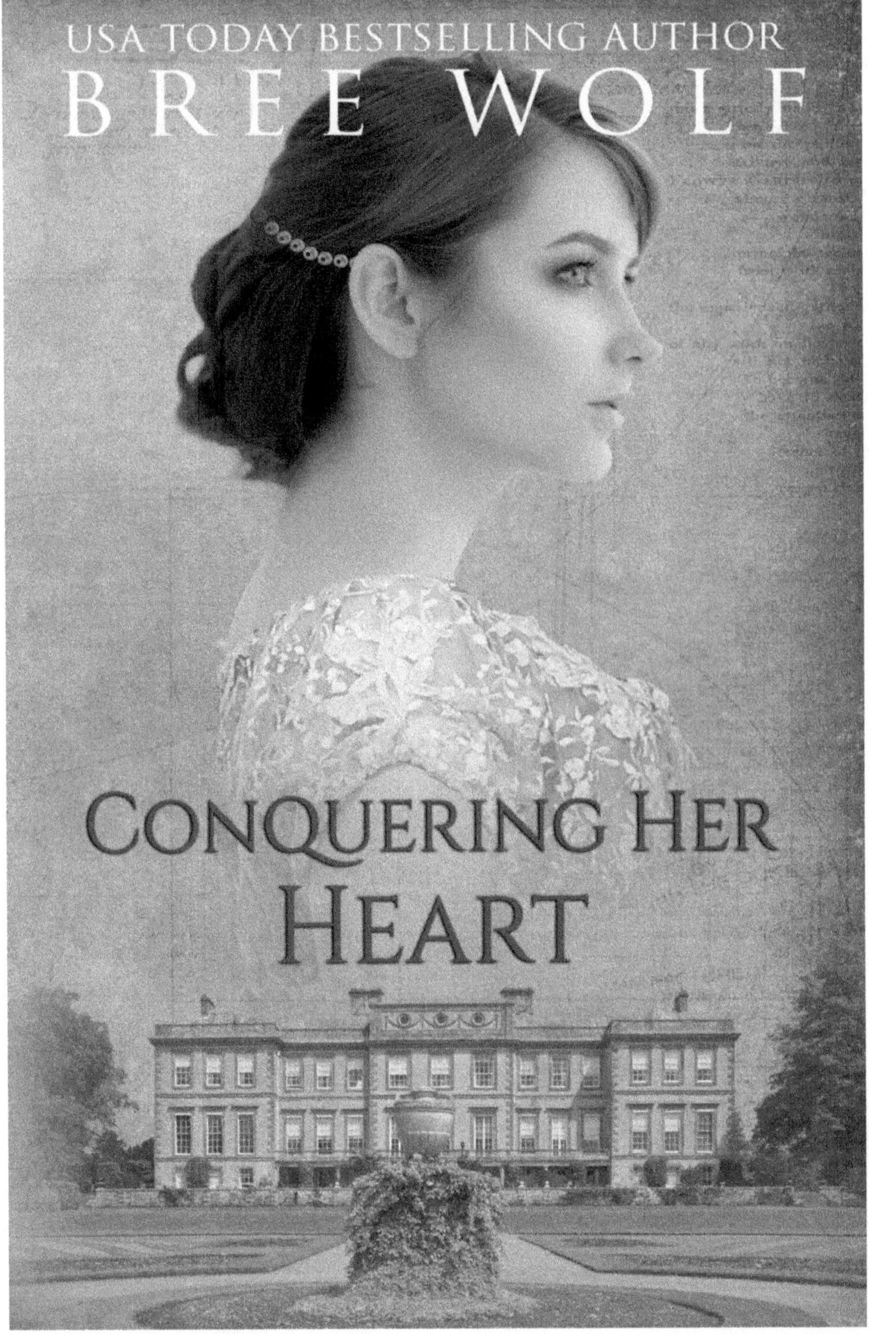
USA TODAY BESTSELLING AUTHOR
BREE WOLF
CONQUERING HER HEART

PROLOGUE

On the road to London, spring 1820 (or a variation thereof)

The world looked different through a curtain of tears.

Gritting her jaw, Abigail Abbott—recently orphaned at the ripe age of nineteen—kept her gaze fixed out the window of the moving carriage, blinking her eyes fiercely to dispel the tears that seemed to fall of their own accord at any time of the day.

Would they ever stop?

Silence hung in the air—uncomfortable silence—and Abigail risked a glance at her aunt Mara, the Dowager Marchioness of Bradish, who sat with her head bowed, her hands linked in her lap, on the other side of the carriage. Not a single word had left her lips since they had set off, and Abigail wondered at the timid-looking woman she had never met before.

Instantly, Abigail's thoughts drifted to the man who had sent Mara—his son's widow—to fetch her to London: Abigail's grandfather, the Duke of Ashold.

Only when asked—begged!—had Abigail's father spoken of the man who had refused his consent, forcing his only daughter to steal away in the night to marry the man she loved. Cold and distant, he had not cared about his daughter's love, her happiness, her wishes. No, among the ton, marriages were forged, based on different aspects, and Abigail's father had been a mere solicitor with hardly a penny to his name.

To this day—even now that he was dead—Abigail could hear the regret and pain over what had happened before her birth in her father's voice, for it had been swiftly followed by an even greater tragedy. Only days after giving birth to their beloved daughter, her mother succumbed to childbed fever. Not even then had her father received word—any word!—from the man who had forced them into hiding. Had he not cared? If so, then why would he send for her—his granddaughter!—now?

Only a week after her father's passing, Abigail had found herself sitting in the small parlour of their home, her gaze drifting over her father's books, neatly sorted and lovingly cared for, a representation of the man himself.

Hours had passed as Abigail had stared into nothing, feeling strangely numb and, yet restless. Sitting idly in a chair was not something she had been accustomed to. After falling ill about two years before, her father had slowly grown worse. No remedy had been able to improve his health, let alone cure him, and as a dutiful and devoted daughter, Abigail had waited on him hand and foot, taking care of their household as before while also seeing to her father as well as his few clients. She had helped him draw up documents, delivered messages and prepared the few consultations with paying clients.

Despite the looming sadness, Abigail's life had been busy from sunup to sundown.

Now, that was over.

For a week she had mostly sat in her father's armchair, not lifting a finger, her eyes red-rimmed from the constant flow of tears. Grief and loss had squeezed her heart, and still, she had noticed the small stabs of fear that assaulted her whenever she dared to think of the future.

What was to happen to her now?

With both her parents gone and no family to speak of, Abigail had been near yielding to despair when a soft knock had sounded on her door.

There, on their front stoop, had stood a finely, though inconspicuously dressed woman, her gaze soft and fleeting, her hands afflicted by a slight tremble. When she had opened her mouth to introduce herself, her voice had come out as a mere whisper.

Abigail's head had started to spin when she had realised what was happening. Bidding her aunt inside, she had listened silently as the dowager marchioness had extended her grandfather's condolences. "His grace was saddened to hear of your father's passing and bade me come here post-haste to extend an invitation to join him in London."

Swallowing, Abigail had accepted her grandfather's invitation. However, she did not doubt that her aunt's words had been far from the ones the duke had uttered. From what she had learnt of his character from her father, Abigail doubted that the man would ever *ask*. No, he was a duke. He would not ask. He would simply order and expect everyone to do as he bid.

Judging from the apprehensive look in her aunt's eyes, Abigail thought that the duke had never seen one of his *requests* refused.

For that reason alone, Abigail had felt tempted to do just that. However, her current situation did not allow her to choose without regard. No, if she did not wish to end up on the streets, she needed to accept her grandfather's *hospitality*. Perhaps, this would be a chance to learn more of the mother she had never met.

Once more glancing across the carriage at her aunt, Abigail heard her father's words echo in her ears: *Use your head wisely, Child, for it is your greatest ally. One who will never abandon you.*

"Aunt Mara," Abigail began, cringing slightly at the croak in her voice, "may I ask you a question?"

Her aunt's gaze rose from the floor of the carriage, her eyes widening as though she had just received a small shock. "Certainly, my dear."

Abigail frowned. Was she not supposed to address her aunt like that? Would it have been more appropriate to call her *my lady*?

After growing up far from any kind of upper society, Abigail could not recall the correct form of address, and quite frankly after what she had been through, it seemed a silly thing to focus on. After all, this was her family—however, strained their relationship might be—and she would address them in the same respectful but personal way she had always addressed her beloved father.

"Do you know why Grandfather suddenly sent for me?" she asked, welcoming the chance to speak to someone after a week of mourning her father's passing in solitude. "I've never even received a letter from him. I admit this is all very strange."

Aunt Mara swallowed, her pale eyes gentle as they looked at

Abigail. "I cannot say what his grace's motivations might have been," she said in a quiet voice. "I am certain you will receive your answers once we arrive in London." A slight shiver shook her frame as though the thought of arriving back at her father-in-law's house terrified her beyond imagining.

Abigail frowned. "I assume grandfather is not a kind man, is he?"

Instantly, her aunt's eyes flew open, and her cheeks turned as white as a sheet. "I would never say such a thing, my dear. He is…he is…He likes everything a certain way. He is fond of order and structure and routine. Nothing is left to chance." Swallowing, her aunt seemed to be groping for words. "To some, his ways might appear cold-h…hearted, but I can assure you he is a most respectful gentleman."

Seeing the signs of terror in her aunt's eyes, Abigail liked her grandfather even less. "I see," was all she said, knowing that her aunt would only grow more agitated if she were to argue the point. "And you were married to his son?"

Her aunt nodded.

"He has passed on?"

Her aunt nodded again.

"I'm sorry," Abigail said as fresh tears shot to her eyes. "You must have been heart-broken."

Her aunt sighed, "He was a good man."

Watching the woman across from her, Abigail realised that no love had been lost between her aunt and uncle. Although she mourned his death as was expected, she had not loved him. Like so many others, she had married for other reasons.

"Did you have children?" Abigail asked, trying to find a more cheerful subject.

Instantly, her aunt's gaze brightened. "We had a son, who is now married with two children of his own."

"That sounds wonderful. You must be very fond of your grandchildren."

Although a smile came to her lips and she nodded her head, there was a sadness in her aunt's gaze that spoke loud and clear of pain and regret. Something was not as it ought to be in this family. Her family!

Once they arrived at her grandfather's townhouse, a tall and imposing structure, towering over its neighbours, Aunt Mara led her inside. They stopped in the great hall to hand their coats and hats to a footman.

"Welcome back, my lady," an impeccably clad older man with a serious frown addressed them. He was dressed in butler's robes and possessed that air of self-importance only a high-ranking servant did.

"Thank you, Orwel," Aunt Mara replied, her shoulders tense and her voice sounding a tad strained. Apparently, she was not so happy to have returned!

"His grace requests to see Miss Abbott immediately," Orwel continued, "alone."

Aunt Mara swallowed, then forced a smile onto her pale face. "I shall see you at supper," she said to Abigail, gesturing for her to follow in Orwel's wake who had already taken off toward the eastern wing. Quite obviously, her grandfather did not hold her in high regard or his most trusted servant would not have treated her with such open disrespect.

Smiling at her aunt, Abigail hurried after the butler, disliking her grandfather a tad more. Where was this to end?

After walking down a wide hallway, Orwel knocked on a large door, waited for the sign to enter and then stepped forward, not even casting a glance over his shoulder to ensure if his master's granddaughter would follow.

"Your grace, may I present Miss Abbott."

Stepping over the threshold, Abigail was not at all surprised to see that her grandfather's study reminded her of a lion charging a gazelle. Everything in it appeared cold and hostile. Dark curtains hung on the windows, half-drawn even though the day was barely at an end. The wood paneling was dark, matching the floors as well as the enormous desk, separating the duke from the visitors he clearly disliked receiving. On top of everything, the two chairs on the opposite side of the desk looked terribly uncomfortable as though her grandfather had chosen them with great care to discourage people to linger.

With everything Abigail saw, she liked her grandfather a bit less.

"Good day, Miss Abbott," a hoarse voice spoke from the dimness behind the desk. "Welcome to London."

Lifting her gaze, Abigail found her grandfather nod at Orwel, who quit the room immediately. Seated in his large armchair—the only comfortable chair in the room—he merely beckoned her forward, not bothering to rise. His grey eyes slid over her with frank perusal, narrowing slightly as though he disapproved of what he saw.

Abigail suspected few people received his approval.

Determined not to allow him to intimidate her, Abigail squared her shoulders and met his gaze unflinchingly. "Good day, Grandfather. It is so nice to finally meet you."

At her informal address, her grandfather's eyes narrowed, and his lips thinned. Then he inhaled deeply. "You are to address me as *your grace*, do you understand?"

"I shall do my best to remember that, Grandfather." Smiling sweetly, Abigail held his gaze, wondering at the slight twitch in the right corner of his mouth. However, it was gone before she could be certain if it had even been there.

"Do try," he stressed, "for impeccable manners will no doubt aid you in procuring a most suitable match. In addition, I am certain that my name and fortune will assist you in that endeavour."

"A suitable match?" Frowning, Abigail stared at her grandfather.

"Yes, a husband," he clarified, a touch of amusement in his tone. "The season has only just begun, which will give you ample opportunity to get acquainted with suitable gentlemen. I have no doubt that your aunt will be happy to make introductions."

At the self-assured tone in her grandfather's voice, Abigail chuckled, "I can assure you, Grandfather, I am not looking for a husband at present. I…" Swallowing, she forced back tears. "I only just lost my father. I am in no state of mind to—"

"Nonsense!" the duke exclaimed. "You're my granddaughter and you will marry a man of high standing. I shall see to it." He held her gaze, a challenge lighting up his own. "And do try harder." Then he waved his hand in dismissal, and as though he had been eavesdropping on the other side of the door, Orwel stepped in and ushered her outside. "I shall see you to your rooms, Miss."

Somewhat annoyed with her grandfather's commanding demeanour, Abigail followed the old butler. Still, she could not deny that there was something about the duke that spoke to her. At the very least, she felt certain that her stay in London would be far from boring.

And that was exactly what she needed.

Not a husband, to be certain!

But something to take her mind off her father's death and circumventing her grandfather's orders would certainly prove to be most eventful indeed!

1

THE COLOURS OF A FLOWER

A fortnight later, Abigail had to admit that her grandfather *might possibly* have been correct.

She had indeed found suitors.

A whole flock of them!

And without even trying!

This was worse than she had expected as they seemed determined to pursue her…no matter what she said to discourage them.

While London was a breath-taking city and Abigail enjoyed nothing more but to wander the many streets with her aunt by her side, allowing her eyes to take in all the many wonderful sights, the society she was forced into due to her station was less desirable. And she had to admit she felt a bit disheartened.

"I've already received a marriage proposal!" Abigail exclaimed as she stood on a small pedestal in the modiste's shop, being measured for yet another armada of gowns. "I've only been in town a fortnight, and I've already received a marriage proposal!" Shaking her head, she stared at her aunt.

"Congratulations!" the modiste beamed, clearly missing the touch of panic in Abigail's voice.

Frowning at the dressmaker, Abigail shook her head, then turned her gaze back to her aunt. "Aunt Mara, you need to help me. What do I do? When I refused him, he looked at me as though I had sprouted another head." She inhaled deeply. "And Grandfather was less than amused…although I did get the impression that he wasn't all that fond of Lord What-was-his-name, either."

Aunt Mara sighed, her mouth opening and closing as she considered what to say. Although her aunt was no one to express her thoughts freely, she had come a long way in the past fortnight, obliging her niece wherever she could. It was also possible that Abigail's way of including her aunt in everything she did, sharing her thoughts and asking for advice was slowly wearing the older woman down. However, Abigail could not help but feel that her aunt led a lonely life and that deep down she wished for nothing more than to be needed, included…loved.

"What kind of gentleman are you looking for, my dear?" Aunt Mara tried, knowing full well that Abigail had no intention of accepting any kind of gentleman.

"It's my dowry!" Abigail exclaimed, ignoring her aunt's question. Settling her hands on her hips, she glared at…nothing, but would have if her grandfather had been there. "He did this on purpose to get his way!"

Aunt Mara frowned. "Would you not say it was kind of him to bestow such a large dowry on you? After all, you're a duke's granddaughter, and you deserve no less."

Smiling sweetly at her aunt, Abigail shook her head. "He didn't do it for me…or perhaps only to upset me." A frown drew down her brows as she remembered the sparkle of delight in her grandfather's eyes when she had come home after refusing her first—and luckily, so far her only—marriage proposal, lashing out at him in her dismay, basically ordering him to withdraw her dowry.

All he had done was shaken his head, once again reminding her to address him as *your grace*.

As Abigail had no intention of ever doing so, she had stormed off, not in the least affected by the dark scowl that usually hung on his face. It had only taken a few days for her to realise that her grandfather loved nothing more than to make others tremble in fear. It was his favourite pastime, which he went to great length for.

Oh, she would not tremble! Abigail vowed. At least not with fear! With indignation, most likely! Annoyance, definitely!

Still, the question remained: what was she to do? If this was a game, then her grandfather was winning. And that upset her even more than she liked to admit.

"All right, let's think this over again." Rubbing her temples, Abigail closed her eyes for a moment, forcing all thoughts to focus on the task at hand. "They pursue me because of grandfather's dowry, and he is most unwilling to do anything about that, which means I need to give them another reason to…come to their senses and leave me alone. But how?"

Aunt Mara sighed, a somewhat amused smile on her face. "Oh, dear, there is nothing you could do to discourage them. I assure you it is not merely the dowry his grace bestowed upon you, but your own charms, your kindness and beauty."

"That's it!" Abigail exclaimed, clapping her hands together, before meeting her aunt's rather widened eyes. "My dowry might be a great incentive; however, I doubt London's gentlemen would overlook a potential bride's enormous deficiencies to obtain it."

Aunt Mara frowned, a worried tone in her voice. "What on earth do you mean, Child?"

Laughing, Abigail brushed a curl of her dark hair behind her ear as relief flooded her being. "It's rather simple, I should say. All I have to do is turn myself into an extreme of the worst kind, and they will have no choice but to reconsider sharing their life with a woman as unsuitable as me."

"But you're not unsuitable, my dear. Why would you think that?" Aunt Mara objected. "You're such a beau–"

"Not yet!" Abigail interrupted. "But that can be helped." Then she turned to the modiste, who had been listening to their exchange with rapt attention. "Do you have anything in orange?"

"Orange?" The woman squeaked, casting a careful glance at Aunt Mara. "I beg your pardon, miss, but it…it clashes with your skin tone. A warm r–"

"Exactly!" Abigail said triumphantly, allowing her gaze to sweep across the many accessories displayed in the shop. "Wouldn't an orange gown look lovely with that turquoise shawl over there?"

The looks on the modiste's and her aunt's faces said quite impressively that it would not…which was exactly why Abigail insisted on purchasing it.

Oh, this was only the beginning! And her grandfather would come to regret the day he had chosen to cross swords with her!

As temperatures began to climb, London's flowers started to awaken from their long sleep, finally able to bask in the warm sun once more and showing off their beautiful colours. As did the ladies of the ton. However, one lady had chosen rather unflattering colours.

Walking into the ballroom with her loyal aunt by her side, Abigail forced herself to suppress the grin that so desperately wanted to show itself to the world. As before, all eyes—or at least most eyes!—turned to her. However, the look in them had changed considerably, and that pleased Abigail greatly as she silently congratulated herself on her ingenious plan. After all, it was working perfectly!

Brushing her hands down her bright yellow gown, a black sash running from one shoulder across her middle to lay gently at her hip, Abigail smiled her brightest smile as though she believed that the crowd that could not help but stare at her thought her the most beautiful creature to ever walk the earth. In truth, Abigail was certain that she resembled a bumble bee!

The only thing that dulled her feelings of euphoria was the rather strained look on her aunt's face. As most people tended to simply overlook her, she had grown accustomed to their inattention and found being in the spotlight a rather uncomfortable experience. Still, she did not abandon her niece, and Abigail was truly grateful to her.

Strolling over to the refreshment table, Abigail helped herself to a glass of lemonade, handing another one to her aunt. Then they strolled through Lord Passmore's large townhouse, nodding their heads at acquaintances left and right. Although people returned their greeting, few dared approach, and when one gentleman with a rather glassy look to his eyes finally did, he was rewarded with a glass of lemonade spilled down his front.

"Oh, my lord, look what you did!" Abigail exclaimed in a rather high-pitched voice, loud enough for all to hear, pretending she had had no hand in the poor man's-soaked shirt. "You ought to watch your step and perhaps try to refrain from indulging in Lord Passmore's spirits." Gasps echoed to her ears at her frank reprimand of an earl of the ton. Still, Abigail could not deny that she delighted in these little games!

Mumbling an apology, Aunt Mara drew her aside. "Please, think this through, Child. If you continue to antagonise these people, you will be left all alone. Is that what you want?"

Abigail sighed, knowing that her aunt meant well. "What I want is not to be married off to a man who could not care less about who I am."

"But this is not who you are!" her aunt insisted.

Abigail shrugged. "Maybe a little. Still, no gentleman has ever tried to find out more about me besides the amount of my dowry."

Aunt Mara shook her head. "Would you if it were reversed? Would you wish to get to know a gentleman who spilled his drink on you? Who stepped on your toes while dancing and then accused you of stepping on his? Who knocks down a priceless antique without even apologising and then blames you for placing it in an inconvenient spot?" Again, she shook her head at Abigail. "I should think not."

Abigail laughed, "You know me too well, dear Aunt. However, at present, I have no wish to get better acquainted with the gentlemen of the ton." She swallowed, and her voice sobered as grief fought its way out into the open. "I've only just lost my father, and I cannot see myself opening my heart to anyone right now." Looking at her aunt with pleading eyes, Abigail grasped the older woman's hands. "But these little games take my mind off the sadness and loss, and for a short while, they make me smile. Is that truly so bad?"

Aunt Mara sighed, then gently patted Abigail's hand. "Of course not, Dear. You have a kind heart, and you do deserve true happiness. All I am worried about is that you might one day find yourself wishing for a husband, only to find that your reputation is standing in the way of a happy union. After all, people are already calling y—" Clasping her mouth shut, Aunt Mara averted her gaze, a tinge of red coming to her pale cheeks.

Abigail chuckled, "You need not worry, Aunt. I am aware what people call me." She smiled at the shocked expression on her aunt's face and squared her shoulders to pronounce proudly, "The most awful woman in all of England!"

"You know this?" Aunt Mara gasped, wringing her hands nervously. "I'm sorry. I—"

"Don't be," Abigail interrupted. "After all, I've worked hard for my reputation. Do you think it's easy to speak with this shrill tone in my voice? Or to step on my dance partner's toes? Not at all. It requires great precision. Not everyone could do it." Smiling encouragingly, Abigail drew one of her aunt's hands into hers. "Do not worry, Aunt Mara. I know what I'm doing, and I want you to know that I'm enjoying myself quite profusely. The added side effect is that I haven't received a single marriage proposal in over a fortnight." Drawing her aunt's arm through the crook of her own, she pulled her toward the refreshment table. "Come, let's drink to this." A chuckle rose from her throat. "I promise I shall do my utmost not to spill my drink on you."

Aunt Mara rolled her eyes at her niece. However, Abigail delighted in the soft smile that came to the older woman's lips. "You'll be the death of me, my dear."

"Oh, I love you, too, Aunt Mara," Abigail trilled, knowing how fortunate she was that her grandfather had sent for her. Otherwise, she would have been all alone in the world. And it felt so good to be loved.

2

THE MOST AWFUL WOMAN IN ALL OF ENGLAND

With his sister happily married to his oldest friend, Griffin Radley, Earl of Amberly, had begun to feel like a third wheel. Although he considered both his closest confidantes, the dynamic in their relationship had changed. Now, Winifred and Trent only had eyes for each other, and although Griffin was happy to see them so...well, happy, he could not help but envy the bond between them. Was it time for him to find a wife?

The thought had occurred to him ever since his little sister had decided she was getting old and would need to find a husband fast if she wanted to be a mother. Fortunately, he had been able to sway her from her path of obtaining a husband through her rather practical approach and lead her into the arms of the man she had loved all her life. Still, their happily-ever-after had come at a price...for Griffin!

To have a say in her choice, Griffin had to enter into a pact with his rational-minded sister, giving her an equal say when it came to finding the right woman for him. And now that Winifred was happily married, she loved nothing better than to remind him of that fact and tease him endlessly. He would have thought she'd be grateful for his interference as it had led to a most fortunate outcome of this whole husband-hunting nonsense. Still, Winifred had a bit of a wicked side to her, and he did not think she would stop teasing him any time soon.

While chatting with a couple of friends, Griffin glanced across the room at the dance floor where his sister and her new husband twirled around to the notes of yet another waltz. Although they seemed to be arguing about…something—as they commonly did—their eyes glowed with devotion, and Griffin could not deny a deep sense of satisfaction at having been instrumental in seeing his sister happily married.

"They look happy," his friend Lord Berenton commented, his bushy eyebrows going up and down like a caterpillar crawling over his face. "Still," he chuckled, a teasing gleam in his eyes, "I cannot help but be cross with you for giving them your blessing. Have I not told you time and time again that she was the one for me?"

Griffin laughed, "I assure you I only gave them my blessing to protect you. My sister has a way of pushing people over the edge, and I'm afraid to say this, but you are no match for her."

Berenton's bushy eyebrows drew down. "Do you think so poorly of me?"

"Not at all, old friend. But I know my sister too well. Believe me, the day they got married was your lucky day."

"You sound a tad relieved." Squinting his eyes, Berenton watched him. "Do you not miss her company?"

Griffin sighed. *Terribly.*

However, before he could answer, the happy couple came walking toward them, joining their little circle. Instantly, Berenton turned to Winifred, and Griffin tried to roll his eyes at him quietly. "My congratulations on your wedding. From what Amberly told me he is quite relieved to have his sister well married." Turning to Griffin, Berenton grinned at him. "I cannot understand why you had trouble marrying her off. A beauty like her."

Griffin sighed. *If only you knew!* Remembering the many sleepless nights and stressful days when he had tried his best to prove to his sister that love was the best reason to choose a husband, only to have her *rational* mind thwart him time and time again, Griffin still could not help but feel exhausted. Maybe he should repay the favour and tease her as much as she always delighted in teasing him.

Grinning at her, Griffin told his friend, "Mind you, she had no lack of suitors. However, I'm afraid my sister was quite particular about the kind of husband she had in mind. I tell you it caused me many sleepless nights."

Everyone laughed, and more than one friend patted him on the shoulder as though he had just crossed the African desert and made it through alive.

As expected, payback was not far off.

Turning to her brother, Winifred smiled at him sweetly. Still, having known her all his life, Griffin had no trouble detecting the touch of mischief that had come to her eyes. "I suppose that it is now my turn to find my brother a suitable bride."

Unable to keep his stomach from twisting into knots, Griffin took a deep breath as laughter echoed around him. Deep down, he had to admit he was waiting for the day she would finally make good on her threat! Would today be the day?

Perhaps it was the suspense that was killing him.

Although he had no doubt that his sister loved him, he also knew her tendency to rationalise emotions. What if she found him a bride she truly believed to be his perfect match? And what if said bride did not appeal to him at all? Would his sister insist, thinking she knew better? Thinking he would eventually come around? Or would she show mercy?

As though he had read Griffin's thoughts, Berenton declared with utter delight. "You're at her mercy now, Amberly!" Then he turned smiling eyes to Winifred, and Griffin felt as though he was going to be sick. "My lady, if you require any assistance, do not hesitate to call on me. I'm quite familiar with a number of eligible ladies and could point you in the right direction."

"How kind of you, my lord," Winifred trilled in that voice that meant she was up to no good.

"In fact, there are many eligible ladies here tonight," Berenton continued, completely unimpressed by the threatening glares Griffin shot him. "However, I would advise against Miss Abbott." He leaned closer into the group and whispered, "She's rumoured to be the most awful woman in all of England."

Griffin almost groaned at the intrigued look that came to his sister's gaze, and he knew that he was doomed. Still, shock had his eyes popping open and his jaw dropping down. "Oh, no, you wouldn't," he stammered, aware that no matter what he did his sister's mind was already made up.

Smiling sweetly, Winifred met his gaze. "You gave me your word, dear brother, and besides what's fair is fair." Then she turned to Berenton. "Would you be so kind as to point out Miss Abbott to me?"

Berenton's face lit up with delight, and he winked at Griffin. "I most certainly would."

Groaning, Griffin forced a deep breath into his lungs, glaring at Berenton as he escorted Winifred across the room. *Very well! This was a friend he could certainly do without!*

"Do you know who this Miss Abbott is?" Trent asked beside him as everyone's gaze remained fixed on Berenton and Winifred, trying to catch a glimpse of London's most eligible shrew!

"I do not," Griffin forced out through gritted teeth, feeling his pulse hammering in his neck. Suddenly, his collar seemed much too tight for comfort, reminding him of a hangman's noose!

With many couples occupying the dance floor and blocking their view, Griffin had to crane his neck. His gaze swept over several good-looking young ladies before he saw Berenton stop to introduce Winifred to…

Griffin's mouth fell open. "She cannot be serious?"

Trent cleared his throat, the expression on his face speaking of a similar disbelief. "One should think so. However, knowing your sister, I'm afraid you're out of luck, my friend."

Feeling the blood in his veins turn to ice, Griffin stared as his sister smiled friendly at a young woman in a painfully bright pink gown with orange blossoms, her dark hair pulled back into a tight bun, making her face appear as though it was stretched to its limits. Even from across the room, he could hear her shrill laugh as she returned his sister's greeting, her hands gesturing wildly and—inevitably—smacking Lord Stockdale on the side of the face.

Surprised, the young gentleman held a hand to his cheek, looking rather taken aback at the young woman beside him. Miss Abbott, however, did not seem to see any fault in her actions for the look on her face did not speak of an offered apology, but a reprimand instead.

"She can't be serious," Griffin whispered, all air leaving his body as his future loomed threateningly on the horizon. "She wouldn't be that cruel, would she?" Forcing his gaze away, Griffin stared at Trent. "Did I do anything to make her angry? Is she mad at me? I mean, did I not do everything in my power to see her happy? I found her perfect match after all."

Trent smiled at the compliment. "Don't take this too seriously.

You know your sister. You know how she loves to tease. Simply play along…and this'll all go away…eventually."

Griffin drew in a deep breath, squaring his shoulders as he watched his sister speak to Miss Abbott. This woman was impossible, and yet, Winifred acted as though she had met an old friend, leaning in conspiratorially and whispering something Griffin did not doubt would lead to his doom.

After a small eternity, Winifred finally took her leave and made her way back across the large room, stopping here and there to exchange a quick word with one of their host's guests. "She is doing this solely to torture me," Griffin growled, willing himself to hate his sister with every fibre of his being…and still failing miserably.

Trent laughed, "I suppose that's fairly obvious."

When Winifred and Berenton finally reached them, Griffin was close to exploding. "You cannot be serious," he snapped for what seemed like the millionth time that night, his disbelief stretched too thin.

Winifred frowned in confusion. Still, the soft twitch of her upper lip did not escape Griffin's attention. "What do you mean? She's such a lovely lady, but gravely misunderstood." She sighed, glancing over her shoulder at Miss Abbott, who in that very moment spilled her drink on yet another unfortunate gentleman who had dared to come near her. "What do you have against her?" Winifred enquired innocently, batting her eyelashes.

In that moment, Griffin wanted to strangle her. Still, all he could do was open and close his mouth a couple of times before his mind was back in order and supplied him with what to say. "I don't even know where to begin," he stammered, his pulse hitching higher with each moment. "That woman is impossible. Look at her! You cannot be serious." Shaking his head, he frowned at the sister he had known all his life. "What do you have against me? I'm your brother, remember? I thought you cared about me."

Laughing softly, Winifred placed a gentle hand on his arm. "Do not worry, dear brother. Yes, I do love you, and I would never do anything to make you miserable. Trust me. I know what I'm doing."

Griffin could only hope so.

Sighing, Winifred turned to her husband. "Poor Miss Abbott is still fairly new in town. I believe I shall call on her and see that she is settled in and not lacking company." Out of the corner of her eye, she glanced at Griffin. "Who knows, soon we might be the best of friends!"

As Trent led his wife back to the dance floor, casting an apologetic glance over his shoulder at his old friend, Griffin gritted his teeth to the point that he thought they would splinter in his mouth.

"Not having a good day, are we?" Berenton observed beside him, a touch of suppressed humour in his voice, and clasped a hand on Griffin's shoulder. "Should we get drunk?"

Griffin sighed. That sounded like as good a plan as any.

After all, he had learnt long ago that he was no match for his sister's devious mind. All he could do was hope that she hadn't forgotten that she loved him.

She would not truly suggest he marry Miss Abbot, would she?

3

SOMETHING RATHER UNEXPECTED

"Grandfather, I need to speak with you!" Not bothering to knock, Abigail burst into the duke's study, pleased to see his head jerk up and his eyes settle on her with a hint of annoyance.

Merely a hint? That was progress! Abigail thought.

"Your grace," her grandfather reminded her, leaning back in his leather armchair, the scowl on his face daring her to ignore him.

Which, of course, was a challenge Abigail could not help but accept. "Certainly, Grandfather."

Rolling his eyes at her, he gestured to the chair opposite his large desk. "What can I do for you this morning?"

Settling onto the chair, Abigail frowned as she scooted left and right, trying to get comfortable. When all her attempts failed, she looked up at her grandfather, a hint of annoyance in her eyes. "You don't want people to stay long," she accused, her lips curling up in amusement. "These chairs are uncomfortable for a reason, are they not?"

The hint of a smile flashed over her grandfather's weathered face, and she thought to detect an almost imperceptible nod of his head. "Is this all you came to say?"

Abigail sighed, "Not at all." Meeting her grandfather's gaze openly, she leaned forward in confidence. "Before I can say anything at all, I need your word that what I'm about to tell you will remain between the two of us. Do you promise?"

A deep frown drew down her grandfather's brows. "I will do no such thing."

"Grandfather!" Abigail chided. "This is important. It's about Aunt Mara."

A scoff escaped his lips, "Then it's not important at all."

Shocked by his cold words, Abigail rose to her feet, her gaze not wavering from his. Then she stepped toward his massive desk and leaned down, resting her hands on the smooth surface. "She respects you greatly. She does whatever you ask of her without ever–"

"She's my son's widow," her grandfather snapped. "It's her duty to–"

"You owe her–"

"I owe her nothing!" he retorted, a touch of red crawling up his neck as he stared at his granddaughter, indignation at her forward behaviour all too visible in his grey eyes. "She knows her place, as should you."

Inhaling a deep breath, Abigail knew what was expected of her, and yet, she could not back down and bow her head.

Raised far away from London society and its rules, Abigail had never been taught to be subservient to titled families, to see them as her betters, to believe that they deserved more than she did. No, indeed, her father had taught her that people were born equals and that one could only set oneself apart by doing what was right and fair and just…not by what was easy.

After everything Aunt Mara had done for her, she deserved Abigail's loyalty, her support, her strength. She had welcomed her into the family and–more importantly–into her heart, easing the pain of her father's passing with her kind words and gentle reminders that he would have wanted her to be happy.

"I know very well where my place is, *Grandfather*," Abigail said, her own grey eyes resting on his, her voice not disrespectful but determined nonetheless. "Do you?"

His jaw tensed as he stared at her, momentarily taken aback, and she could see that he was at a loss. Never in his life had people dared to speak to him thus.

"I came here," Abigail began as she straightened, lifting her hands off the desk, "to ask about her son, her grandchildren. She seems to miss them terribly, but she never sees them. Never even speaks of them." Shaking her head to emphasise her confusion, Abigail sank back into her chair, wincing slightly when the hard wood cut into her back. "What happened? She always looks so miserable."

For a long moment, her grandfather's gaze remained on her before he drew in a slow breath, his eyes moving with the indecision she knew he felt. Did people in his family never speak of how they felt? What they loved? Feared? Hoped for? "My son died almost a decade ago," he finally said, his voice low, quiet, almost imperceptible. "However, I do not believe it affected her much." A grim tone had come to his voice.

Abigail frowned. "They did not love each other."

The duke shook his head. "I suppose not." He swallowed. "She did as any widow is expected to, but I never saw deep sorrow in her."

"Can you blame her?" At her words, her grandfather's head snapped up, and he stared at her with shock. "I don't mean to speak ill of your son, but from what I've learnt of marriages among the upper class, there is very little emotion involved. How do you expect her to mourn someone she never cared for?"

Her grandfather's lips thinned, but he did not question her reasoning.

"What about her son? Your grandson? Are they not close?"

"They were. Once." Meeting her gaze, the duke crossed his arms in front of his chest, and Abigail could see the reluctance to speak about such personal matters in the way he held himself rigid as though he was the one sitting in the tortuously uncomfortable chair. "When Everett made his intention known of proposing to Lord Simwell's daughter, his mother counselled him to reconsider. Apparently, she did not believe they were a good match."

"And she was right, wasn't she?"

Her grandfather nodded. "Theirs was never a happy marriage. At least not after the first year. I suppose my grandson's wife found out about his mother's objections. Ever since, they've become estranged and she's been doing her utmost to keep the children away from their grandmother."

Abigail sighed, finally understanding the loneliness and regret that filled Aunt Mara's life. "Have you never tried to help her? To smooth things between her and her son as well as her daughter-in-law?"

"It was not my place," her grandfather bit out.

"Not your place?" Abigail echoed. "You're a family. He's your grandson. They're your great-grandchildren. It most certainly is your place." Inhaling deeply, Abigail tried to calm her rattled nerves. Never in her life had she heard such nonsense. "What do we do?"

"What do you mean?"

Rolling her eyes, Abigail once more stepped toward his desk. "Grandfather, I can see that all of you have been a little out of practice but let me tell you how family works." A teasing curl came to her lips as she looked at him, trying to break the ice that had frosted over her family's hearts for too long. "When one of us is miserable, so are the others because we care about each other. And even though you will probably never admit to it, you know that I'm right. We need to help her. Any suggestions?"

As her grandfather stared at her a bit open-mouthed, a sharp knock came on the door. "Enter," the duke croaked, then cleared his throat as he forced the mask of detachedness back on his face before Orwel entered.

"I apologise for the intrusion, your grace," he said, giving a slight bow before his gaze momentarily shifted to Abigail, "but there's a Lady Chadwick here to see Miss Abbott."

Taken aback, Abigail blinked. Lady Chadwick? Was that the young woman who had spoken to her the other day at the ball? She had certainly been kind, surprised Abigail by even addressing her, but Abigail would never have thought that she truly meant to call on her. Few people meant what they said.

"Do you intend to let her wait all day?" her grandfather asked, a teasing tone in his voice now that the focus had shifted back to her. "The ton might not look on that with kind eyes."

Abigail snorted, "Quite frankly, I couldn't care less about what the ton does or doesn't do." Then she turned on her heel and headed for the door. However, with her hand on the handle she stopped and turned back to look at her grandfather. "Perhaps you should speak with your grandson. He might be able to find a way to smooth things between his wife and his mother."

Her grandfather scoffed, "At this point, I do not believe he cares."

Fed up with her family, Abigail heaved a deep sigh. "Then make him care," she snapped, then rushed out the door before her grandfather could object.

Trying to put her family's issues out of her mind, Abigail wondered what had brought Lady Chadwick over that morning. After all, never had any lady sought Abigail's company for her devious plan to drive away all eligible bachelors had also succeeded nicely in convincing the ladies of the ton that she was not good company and they did not wish to be seen with her.

Her reputation had indeed suffered. Unfortunately, a few gentlemen still insisted on pursuing her. Only friends she had none.

As Abigail walked by the large mirror in the front hall on her way to the drawing room, she caught sight of her reflection and realised with a start that she had not bothered to dress in her usual hideous fashion that morning.

But why would she have? After all, she had not expected any visitors today. Her hair was gathered in the back and pinned up gently while some tendrils danced down from her temples, and she wore a simple pale-yellow dress, quite unlike the one that made her look like a bumblebee.

Well, it could not be helped, and besides, she was not receiving an eligible bachelor bent on procuring her hand, now was she?

Drawing in a deep breath, Abigail had to admit she was a tad nervous. Never had she found herself craving the good opinion of a lady of the ton, and she realised how much she wished for a friend.

Stepping into the room, Abigail found the young woman admiring a watercolour hanging on the wall by the pianoforte. "Good morning, Lady Chadwick," she greeted her, trying to still her trembling hands. "How nice of you to call on me."

"The pleasure is all mine," Lady Chadwick replied, her eyes aglow and a genuine smile decorating her lovely features. Instantly, Abigail felt herself relax.

"Would you care for some tea?" she asked, already ringing the bell.

"That sounds wonderful," her visitor replied. "It's still a bit chilly outside."

Gesturing for Lady Chadwick to take a seat, Abigail chose a spot across from her. Deciding there was no use in dancing around the bush, she asked, "What brings you here?"

An amused smile spread over her guest's face as she leaned forward as though wishing to share a secret. "I've come to be your friend."

Abigail could not keep her jaw from dropping just a tad. "My friend?" she echoed, wondering if the young lady across from her had the ability to read minds. "Quite frankly, I've rarely had someone speak to me so…"

"Bluntly?" Lady Chadwick offered. "Well, I find being honest about one's intentions saves time."

Abigail laughed, "I suppose it does. May I then ask what made you want to be my friend? I admit I'm rather surprised."

Lady Chadwick shrugged. "For one, I know you to be new in town and as I find myself in a similar position, I thought we might be a good fit."

"You're new in town?"

Lady Chadwick nodded. "My brother and I only returned from the continent a few months ago. We'd been away from England for about five years, and we're only just getting reacquainted with society."

Abigail nodded, feeling excitement rise in her chest. Would she truly have a friend by the end of the day? "May I enquire if there were other reasons?"

A slight blush came to Lady Chadwick's face as she tried to control the large smile that threatened to draw up the corners of her mouth. "Well, quite frankly, my brother has always accused me of being too rational-minded, and I admit lately I've come to realise that he might not have been…completely wrong."

Abigail laughed.

"Well, to make it short, when I saw you at the ball, I was intrigued and decided to follow an impulse. I don't try to make a habit out of it, but I suppose there is no harm in doing it occasionally."

Again, Abigail laughed, realising that she liked Lady Chadwick quite a bit. The young woman had a refreshingly open way of speaking her mind as well as a sense of humour that spoke to Abigail. "You were intrigued?"

Lady Chadwick nodded. "I mean no offence, but you looked quite…odd that night." Her gaze held Abigail's for a moment before she continued. "That hideous dress and your hair pulled back so tightly I swear I felt my own scalp tingle. I couldn't help but wonder why a young woman would do such a thing and thought to myself that a remarkable mind and fascinating character were most likely at its root." She shrugged, a questioning smile curling up her lips.

Not having expected such a compliment as well as the depth of her guest's observation, Abigail could not deny that it pleased her nonetheless. After all, despite the open disapproval she saw at every ball when people regarded her appearance, they never dared say so to her face. Instead, they tried to find one way or other to give her a compliment whenever they found themselves put on the spot. "You're here to enquire about my reason for dressing so…oddly?"

Lady Chadwick laughed, her gaze gliding over Abigail's appearance. "Well, quite frankly, today you do look a lot more like yourself. So, there must be a reason? Isn't there always?"

Abigail inhaled a deep breath. Although she wished to share her motivation with Lady Chadwick, she knew she ought to be cautions. After all, what did she truly know about her? "You're quite right, my lady. I certainly do have a reason, however, I find that—"

"You're not quite ready to share it with a stranger?" Lady Chadwick chuckled good-naturedly. "That's quite all right. Well, then tell me what has brought you to town. I was told that you're his grace's granddaughter."

Abigail swallowed, not fond to retell the story of her father's passing. However, to her great relief, she soon saw honest sympathy in Lady Chadwick's gaze, who reciprocated by telling her of losing her own parents in a carriage accident five years ago. Their loss had upended her life as much as losing her father had changed Abigail's. While she had come to London to stay with her grandfather, Lady Chadwick and her brother had travelled the world, trying their best to find a way to cope with the loss while remembering that life continued and that feeling happy was no reason for feeling guilty as well.

Over the course of the next fortnight, Abigail spent many wonderful days in Lady Chadwick's company, delighting in their new-found friendship. They had a lot in common and discovered more every day. Most days Abigail walked around with a deep smile on her face, noticing that Aunt Mara delighted in seeing her so happy. In consequence, Abigail continued to prod her grandfather, urging him to speak to his grandson.

So far, he was resisting, but Abigail had no doubt that he would eventually admit defeat. Perhaps not as straightforward as saying it out loud. He would most likely conjure ridiculous excuse; however, the result would be the same.

"And she never sees them?" Winifred asked one afternoon as they walked around the new conservatory her husband had added to their townhouse. "How sad!"

Abigail nodded. "She tries not to show it, but whenever we go through the park and she sees children their age, her eyes tear up." Sighing, Abigail shook her head. "I wish I could help her, but my grandfather is currently less than willing."

Winifred laughed, "I'm certain you will convince him before too long."

"I do hope so," Abigail exclaimed, wondering if she ought to speak to her cousin herself.

"Ah, there you are!"

Turning toward the voice, Abigail found two men walking into the conservatory, their faces cheerful as they seemed to be in conversation with one another. One of the two men was Winifred's husband, Lord Chadwick, whom Abigail had met once or twice while visiting her friend. The other, however, she could not recall ever having met.

Strangely enough though, when his gaze came to rest on her, the smile slid off his face as though she had just insulted him, and his eyes took on a hard expression as he turned to his sister, open accusation in the way he looked at her.

At a loss, Abigail turned to her friend, who ignored the young man's glare and gestured for the two of them to enter. "Abigail," she began, smiling at her with a strange new glow in her eyes, "you remember my husband, Lord Chadwick. And this is my brother Lord Amberly. Brother, may I introduce you to Miss Abbott."

Abigail swallowed as the young man stepped forward and then inclined his head to her, the look on his face one of utter displeasure—quite in contrast to the words that followed. "Miss Abbott, it is a pleasure to make your acquaintance."

"It is indeed, my lord," Abigail replied without thinking, still trying to understand what was happening. Quite obviously, something was very much amiss! She could have sworn if it had not been for her presence, Lord Amberly would have lashed out at his sister for…something.

Winifred in turn raised her eyebrows at him…almost triumphantly while her husband tried his best to suppress a smile.

As though lighting struck her in that moment, Abigail suddenly understood with perfect clarity what was going on! Her new friend, whom she had come to trust, whom she had almost shared her secret with, had lied to her for Winifred's own motivation for seeking her out now seemed quite clear.

To introduce Abigail to her brother. To persuade her to accept his proposal when it came. To forward her own agenda of seeing her brother well settled.

Lord Amberly, on the other hand, seemed more than a bit reluctant to pursue her. Indeed, he kept a safe distance, barely even looking at her, as though she had the plague.

Quite obviously, brother and sister were of opposite minds regarding whom he ought to marry.

"I'm afraid I must take my leave," Abigail said, lifting her chin defiantly, unwilling to reveal how much Winifred's—Lady Chadwick's!—betrayal hurt her. "My aunt is expecting me." Then, without another word and ignoring her hostess's pleas for her to stay, Abigail rushed from the room, gathered her coat, shawl and hat from the footman in the foyer and left without a look back.

Stepping out onto the street, she sighed, her heart aching with the loss of a friend she had come to care for.

Alone once more.

4

TRUST GIVEN & RECEIVED

The moment he heard the front door close, Griffin felt himself explode.

"How dare you!" he growled, glaring at his sister with never felt outrage. "Have I not made it clear that I have no interest in Miss Abbott whatsoever? She is not the kind of woman I wish to marry, and I demand that you respect that!" Gritting his teeth against the string of words that threatened to spill from his mouth—words he had never thought he would say in his sister's presence, let alone *to* her!—Griffin silently counted to ten, clenching and unclenching his fists, hoping to relieve some of the anger that surged through his veins.

"You demand?" Gawking at him, Winifred shook her head, clearly oblivious to the rage that held him in its clutches. "Do you remember what you promised me, dear brother? Or shall I help you refresh your memory?"

"I know very well what I promised you!" Griffin hissed, casting a glance at his friend, who stood silent as a pillar of salt, observing the siblings' exchange with rapt attention. "However, I doubt that *you* do. *I* never forced you to socialise with a man you disliked. Why would you force Miss Abbott on me when I've made it unmistakably clear that—no matter what!—I will not marry her?"

Chuckling as though all of this was terribly amusing misunderstanding, Winifred stepped forward, her gaze focusing on his, and he got the distinct feeling that she was about to catch him in a lie. "Are you certain?" she asked, a clear challenge in her dark brown eyes.

Griffin swallowed, wrecking his brain. Was he? "Of course, I am."

Shaking her head in what he assumed to be disbelief, Winifred laughed. "Your memory is faulty indeed, dear brother. Well, then allow me to enlighten you because you did force on me the company of a man I disliked. Not even you can deny that?"

Frowning, Griffin stared at her, unable to make sense of what she was saying. "How can you say that? Lord Haverton was a perfect gentleman in every regard, and you cannot deny that you liked him."

Winifred shrugged. "I do not deny it."

A low growl rose from Trent's throat, and Winifred glanced at him, a teasing smile coming to her lips.

"Then who do you speak of?" Griffin demanded, feeling his pulse speed up once more. "After all, he's the only gentleman you spent a considerable amount of time with. Yes, I made other suggestions here and there, but they never led anywhere, and I never forced you to pursue them, did I?"

"You did not. At least not with these gentlemen."

"Then who?" Griffin snapped, raking his fingers through his hair. "Who on earth do you speak of?"

Her brows drew down into a frown as a soft chuckle escaped her. "You really don't understand, do you?" Then she glanced at her husband, whose gaze grew dark as though promising retribution. But for what?

"I'm talking about my husband," Winifred finally said, a touch of annoyance in her voice.

Griffin's eyes bulged. "What? You cannot be serious? I never—"

"Yes, you did," she insisted, her hands on her hips and her eyes narrowed into slits. "I told you that I disliked his company—"

"But—"

"No! I did, didn't I?" Winifred demanded.

Gritting his teeth, Griffin nodded.

"And still, you kept forcing him on me—"

Trent chuckled, but a dark glare from his wife shut him up instantly.

"Don't even for a moment believe that I didn't see what you were doing, leaving us alone together, always coming up with these last-minute excuses for why you couldn't stay." Her lips twisted into an angry snarl. "Do you have any idea how angry I was with you for that? Did you even notice?"

"But you liked him!" Griffin insisted, unable to understand what his sister was saying. "You even loved him." Shaking his head, he pointed at his best friend. "You married him! How can you say–?"

"I told you I did not want to see him, didn't I?" his sister demanded, growing more annoyed when he stared at her blankly. "Didn't I?"

"Yes, you did, but–"

"No but!" Winifred snapped before she drew in a slow breath and her features began to soften, her voice calm again. "I told you then just as you are telling me now. And just like you, I feel as though I see something you don't seem to be aware of." She nodded. "Yes, you were right. I loved Trent, and I'm glad you did what you did." Stepping forward, she took his hand in hers, her soft eyes looking into his, asking him to trust her. "Now, let me do the same for you."

"But I don't love her," Griffin objected, wondering what his sister had seen that had eluded him.

Winifred scoffed, "Of course not, how could you? You've barely spoken a word to her." Sighing, she squeezed his hand. "I'm not asking you to go and ask for her hand right now. All I'm saying is that I want you to give her a chance. She is not the woman you think she is, and I truly believe that you would be a good match for each other." A soft smile curled up the corners of her mouth. "As much as I love teasing you, I would never jeopardise your happiness. I can only hope you know that."

Griffin nodded, remembering when their roles had been reversed, when he had asked her to trust him, promising that he would do what he could to ensure that she would not end up with the wrong man. Fortunately, she had not. But what about him? Could his sister be right? What had she seen in Miss Abbott that would make her believe that they would be a good match?

"I admit that night at the ball," Winifred continued, "when I asked to be introduced to Miss Abbott, I wanted to see you squirm." The left corner of her mouth twitched. "But that is all. I would never make you unhappy. I would never want you to be with someone who would make you unhappy."

"I know," Griffin whispered, pulling his sister into a warm embrace. "I know you wouldn't." Stepping back, he looked into her eyes, drawing a slow and somewhat agonising breath into his lungs. "Fine. I trust you. I will give her a chance."

"That's all I ask."

Griffin nodded, hoping that that was true.

5

HONEST WORDS

Alone, Abigail stood in the corner of the room, gazing at the dancing couples.

Well, not alone. Aunt Mara was with her.

Still, Abigail had hoped to spend some of her time with her new friend. Someone her own age. Someone who would understand in ways Aunt Mara could not. Someone she could confide in.

Well, that someone had not been Winif—Lady Chadwick.

Swallowing, Abigail brushed her hands over her dark purple gown, laced with brown ornaments, giving it a mud brown impression. Again, the modiste had flinched at her choice, and again, Abigail had insisted. After all, her plan seemed to be working more perfectly every day.

Where her dance card had been bursting full in the beginning, it now had gaping holes, forcing on her many moments of inactivity. Moments in which Abigail wished she had a friend to talk to and laugh with.

Well, that seemed to be a hollow dream.

At least, at present.

"Smile, my dear," Aunt Mara encouraged, a gentle smile on her kind features. "You're far too young for worry lines. Look, there's Lady Chadwick with her husband. That ought to put a smile on your face."

Abigail swallowed as her gaze involuntarily shifted to the beautiful young woman in a stunning dress, walking into the ballroom on her husband's arm. She looked happy. Truly happy!

Abigail sighed, realising that despite her own insistence to the contrary, she envied Winif–Lady Chadwick. What would it feel like to–?

Lady Chadwick's gaze met hers, and her warm brown eyes seemed to light up. A soft smile drew up the corners of her mouth, and after leaning closer to her husband to whisper something to him, she released his arm and hastened toward Abigail.

Swallowing a lump in her throat, Abigail wished she could simply run from the room.

"Good evening, Abigail," Lady Chadwick greeted her, a warm smile on her face as her gaze shifted from her to her aunt. "Good evening, Lady Bradish. It is truly wonderful to see you here."

As Aunt Mara returned the kind greeting, casting a questioning gaze at her niece, Abigail took the moment to square her shoulders and lift her chin a fraction. No matter what, she would not beg for Lady Chadwick's friendship…even if she began to feel the loneliness that threatened her heart.

"May I speak to you for a moment?" Lady Chadwick asked, her eyes pleading, and Abigail felt herself nod in agreement before she had even made up her mind.

"I shall see if they have any lemonade," Aunt Mara mumbled, squeezing Abigail's hand before she walked away.

"I feel the need to apologise," Lady Chadwick began once they were alone, "although I have to admit I do not know why."

As her head whipped around, Abigail stared at the other woman. "You cannot mean that."

Lady Chadwick shrugged, an apologetic smile on her face. "I saw how upset you were the day you met my brother–I can only assume it was him because you'd met my husband before–however, I do not know why. From what he said, I do not believe the two of you are acquainted so I cannot understand how meeting him could have upset you thus."

Abigail stared at her former friend, wondering if the honest confusion she saw on Lady Chadwick's face was genuine. Or was she simply a good actress? "Why did you introduce me to him?" Abigail asked, her voice faint as though a part of her was afraid of the answer.

Lady Chadwick shrugged as though that ought to be obvious. "Because I thought you would suit each other. Because you are both important to me, and I wanted you to get to know one another."

Abigail could not deny the surge of joy that swept through her body. Still, could she trust it? Could she trust Lady Chadwick's words? "Why did you speak to me that night at the ball? Why did you ask to be introduced?"

Lady Chadwick frowned. "I already told you that."

"But was it the truth?"

Lady Chadwick's frown deepened, a touch of concern in her warm eyes. "Of course, it was. Do you have any reason not to believe me?" Her gaze searched Abigail's face. "Why do *you* think I spoke to you? Why do *you* think I introduced you to my brother?"

Abigail swallowed, then opened her mouth before she had even made up her mind how to reply. However, that was as far as she got for Lady Chadwick's mouth suddenly fell open and her eyes widened as sudden realisation showed on her face. "That's why you dress like this!" she exclaimed, quickly lowering her voice as a head or two turned in their direction.

Abigail froze, unable to resist as her friend pulled her aside.

"This is an act, is it not?" Lady Chadwick asked, her gaze seeking Abigail's. "You hope to drive away your suitors, but why? Do you not wish to marry?"

Abigail drew in a deep breath as the need to share her worries grew in her chest. "I do. Perhaps not so soon after my father's death when I hardly know my own heart. But in general, yes, I do."

"Then why–?"

"Because I do not want a man who merely seeks my dowry," Abigail hissed under her breath. "The moment the size of my dowry became known, men flocked to me as though I were a siren." She scoffed, shaking her head. "I wager my grandfather only did this to rid himself of me. He doesn't care about me. Why would he? He never even cared about my mother." Feeling tears sting behind her eyes, Abigail turned her head away, blinking her lashes rapidly to dispel them.

Following, Lady Chadwick sighed, "I admit the ton is mostly persuaded into marriage by superficial attributes," she said, a hint of bitterness in her tone as though she despised that truth as much as Abigail did. "However," she grasped Abigail's hand, "I did not single you out because of your dowry. You have my word on that, and I hope that you can believe it."

Abigail swallowed. "Then why?"

Lady Chadwick smiled. "Did I not tell you already?"

"You did. Still, I–"

"It's the truth," Lady Chadwick insisted. "Although I admit that my brother is currently unable to see past your masquerade," a soft chuckle escaped her, "I do believe that once he does, he will care for you."

Abigail's eyes opened wide as panic spread through her. "You will not tell him, will you? Please, I–"

"I won't say a word," Lady Chadwick promised solemnly, "if that is what you wish." Again, she chuckled. "Perhaps it would do him some good to have to chase after a woman instead of having them always swoon at his feet."

Abigail frowned. "Why would he chase me if he dislikes me?"

Lady Chadwick wiggled her eyebrows, amusement colouring her cheeks. "Oh, that I cannot say for I gave my word. However, be assured that he will seek you out. All I ask is that you give him a chance. Nothing more. Will you do that?"

Completely overwhelmed, Abigail nodded, her gaze suddenly drawn to the tall dark-haired man entering the ballroom.

As though the two of them were magnets, as though he knew exactly where she was, his gaze found hers and Abigail's breath caught in her throat.

Never had she truly looked at the many gentlemen vying for her hand. Never once had she asked herself whether she could like them. Always had her mind been made up by their interest in her dowry alone.

Could Winif–Lady Chadwick…oh, blast it! Could Winifred be right? Would they suit each other? And even if, did she even want a husband here and now? Or was it too soon? Too soon to know who she was and what she wanted? After all, grief had a way of clouding one's heart and mind. What if she decided now, only to realise down the road that she had been wrong? What would she do then?

No, it would be safer to continue her masquerade as Winifred had called it. If her brother would truly seek her out, she would not make it easy for him.

Perhaps that was wise. If he truly cared, he would have to fight for her.

A soft smile came to Abigail's face.

No one had ever fought for her. Not the way her parents had fought for each other.

But did she want him to?

6

A BROTHER'S SUFFERING

Hideous.

There was no other word for it. The woman looked hideous. As though a bucket of mud had been dumped over her. No, not a bucket. A cart-load.

Although Griffin had to admit he knew very little about women's fashion, he could not fathom why anyone would voluntarily choose such a hideous gown. Or such a coiffure. It looked like a bird had made its nest on top of her head, feathers sticking out every which way.

Shaking off a sense of dread, Griffin turned his gaze away, his eyes beholding a more favourable young lady.

Dressed in a dark green gown that shimmered in the light from the chandeliers, her golden hair framing her soft face in smooth waves and dancing curls, Lady Adeline, daughter of the Earl of Kingston, danced past him in the arms of a gentleman. The moment her gaze caught his, she smiled, and Griffin only too well remembered the night of the New Year's ball at Stanhope Grove.

Then, he had been taken with her ethereal beauty, almost forgetting his promise to his sister of scouting the ballroom for eligible bachelors. Instead, he had asked Lady Adeline to dance, and it had felt heavenly.

"Not her," his sister spoke from behind him, the touch of a warning in her voice.

Inhaling a slow breath, Griffin faced her. "Why not?"

Winifred's gaze narrowed as she turned scrutinising eyes to the young woman in the dark green dress. "I admit she's beautiful," she finally said, now turning those scrutinising eyes on her brother. "But that's as much as you know about her, isn't it?"

Griffin shrugged. "Perhaps. But that can easily be changed."

"How often have you danced with her?" Winifred questioned, her gaze calculating as she watched him. "I know you met her at the New Year's ball. However, I've seen you with her several times since then. Can you tell me who she is?"

Griffin frowned. "Lady Adeline. She's Lord Kingston's daugh–"

"I know," Winifred interrupted.

"Then why do you ask?"

"I didn't ask you for her name," his sister huffed as though he was the greatest idiot to ever walk the earth. "I wanted to know what kind of a person she is." When Griffin hesitated, she prompted, a self-satisfied twinkle in her eyes, "Well?"

Annoyed with his sister's overbearing attitude as though there was nothing she did not know, Griffin straightened. "There have not been that many opportunit–"

"So, you don't know? Nothing?"

Gritting his teeth, Griffin glared at his sister. "Have you always been this irritating? If so, I cannot recall. Perhaps being married does not become you."

Winifred laughed, slipping her hand through the crook of his arm, turning his attention away from the dance floor. "Oh, don't grumble, dear brother. All I'm trying to do is point you in the right direction."

"I doubt that very much," he growled, finding himself looking at Miss Abbott yet again. "Why?" was all he asked as he looked down at his sister. "Why her?"

"That is for you to find out," Winifred said mysteriously. "She's a lovely, young woman, and I assure you that the two of you have a lot in common."

"Seriously?" Griffin demanded, remembering the many mishaps that seemed to befall Miss Abbott.

"Seriously," his sister confirmed, the tone in her voice not allowing for an argument. "Now, go ask her to dance. And wipe that scowl off your face."

Reminding himself that he had promised Winifred to give Miss Abbott a chance, Griffin squared his shoulders and commanded his feet to carry him in the direction of the young woman with the hideous dress. They complied, however, reluctantly.

As he drew near, Miss Abbott's head swiveled around, and for a short moment, Griffin thought to see a hint of nerves fluttering over her face. However, within the blink of an eye, it was replaced by a look of haughty superiority he had seen on her face before. He could not fathom how she had ever come to possess such a high opinion of herself. Was she not aware of the mayhem she caused?

Relieved to see her hands empty—no glass that could be conveniently dumped down the front of his shirt—Griffin stopped in front of her, inclining his head and smiling at her with what he hoped was an amiable sort of grimace. "Good evening, Miss Abbott. May I have the next dance?"

For a second, she seemed to glance over his shoulder at someone or something and the left side of her mouth curled up into the barest suggestion of a smile he had ever seen. Then, though, it was as though a veil fell over her grey eyes because they lost their humorous gleam and became sharp…and yet unseeing in a way. "How kind of you to ask, my lord." Her gaze narrowed. "Allow me to ask. Have we met before?"

Griffin tensed, displeasure pulsing through his veins. "Indeed. I had the…pleasure of making your acquaintance a few days ago at my sister's home. Lady Chadwick."

"Oh, yes, I remember now." Nodding, she gestured wildly, her left hand flying by the tip of his nose, missing it not by much. "You were the man with the serious scowl. Griffin, isn't that right?"

Griffin's muscles tensed to the point of breaking. Not only did she dare to address him so informally, but she also had the nerve to suggest that he was easy to forget. Did she truly only remember the way he had frowned that day? Was that all she remembered? For some reason, it bothered him to be thought of so lowly. Did he generally make a bad first impression? If so, he had yet to notice.

Forcing the corners of his mouth to stay up, Griffin instead clenched his hands, hoping to relieve some of the tension. "That is correct, *Miss Abbott*," he stressed, hoping to remind her that they were not on such intimate terms as to address each other by their given names.

The young woman, however, seemed quite oblivious as she suddenly grabbed his arm and all but dragged him onto the dance floor. "I do love to dance," she chatted happily, her voice a bit too shrill to be considered pleasant. "And if I dare say so myself, I'm quite the proficient. Unfortunately, I often find myself surrounded by less skillful dancers, which often robs me of the joy it usually brings." As though to disprove her own point, she moved contrary to the rhythm of the music, her steps too slow, and a moment later, her foot came down on his hard.

Griffin suppressed a groan. If he did not know any better, he would have thought she had done so on purpose, her heel digging into his flesh, almost crushing his toes.

In consequence, the inconvenience of stepping on his foot threw her off balance, and she tumbled sideways. If he had not been a gentleman, Griffin would have let her fall. However, he dared not, instead he caught her swiftly, releasing her the moment she had both feet back under her.

"My goodness," she exclaimed, drawing in a sharp breath. "I believe you would benefit from some dance lessons, my lord. Have you ever learnt? I can only recommend it as it would improve your enjoyment—as well as your partners—considerably."

"I shall keep that in mind," Griffin forced out through gritted teeth, silently counting the seconds until the dance was over. What was his sister thinking? Had she lost her mind? Ought he to have her committed to an asylum?

Quickly taking his leave of Miss Abbott as soon as he dared, Griffin crossed the ballroom in large strides, his gaze locked on his sister's, his blood boiling hot as he saw the amused gleam in her eyes. "I'm glad you find my misery entertaining," he hissed into her ear as he came to stand beside her.

Winifred laughed. She laughed! "Oh, dear brother, you suffer more than you need to!"

"That's what I've been saying," he agreed, trying to force calming breaths down his throat. "Then let us agree that Miss Abbott is not the right woman for me and move on, shall we?"

Grinning, Winifred shook her head. "That is not at all what I meant to say."

"What then?" Griffin growled, glimpsing Trent heading their way, a glass of wine in each hand.

"You are intent on disliking her," Winifred accused, "and therefore, you are miserable because that is what you expect."

"I doubt there is anyone on this planet who would enjoy her company."

"I do," Winifred objected as Trent held out a glass to her, his gaze narrowed as he looked back and forth between them. "Miss Abbott, is it?" he asked, a slight chuckle in his voice as he spoke.

Griffin could have throttled him. "As I've already said to my sister: I'm glad my misery entertains you."

Trent laughed, shaking his head. "Oh no, as tempted as I am, I will not get in the middle of this."

Exhaling a deep breath, Griffin took a step back. "If you'll excuse me, I'll find some more pleasurable company." And with that, he turned on his heel and marched off. Perhaps Miss Adeline would fancy a dance!

7

PERSEVERANCE

Lying awake, Abigail remembered the moment Lord Amberly had asked her to dance. Indeed, he had looked like all the others, determined to pursue her despite their own inclination not to. However, the look in his eyes had been…amusing. He had seemed on the brink of throttling her, and on some level, Abigail had to admit that she had enjoyed seeing such unrestrained emotion.

At least, it had been honest.

Even if his words had not been.

Still, the emphasis in his tone had not been lost on her. He had greatly disapproved of her calling him by his given name. As did her grandfather. Still, there was very little they could do to sway her. After all, it was quite an effective tool in angering those one wished to anger.

Three days later, Abigail found herself seated in the breakfast parlour, staring across the table at her aunt as she picked at her food, her kind eyes dull and distant. "Is something wrong?" Abigail asked, deep concern in her heart for the only family member who had come to care for her.

Blinking, Aunt Mara looked up. "I'm sorry, dear. I did not mean to be so taciturn."

"I'm not complaining, Aunt Mara," Abigail stated. "I'm worried. Tell me what has you looking so forlorn."

"It is nothing," her aunt replied, waving her hand in dismissal.

Crossing her arms in front of her chest, Abigail glared at her aunt. "Whenever people say it's nothing, it's always something."

Looking up, Aunt Mara held her gaze.

"Tell me."

"I was simply…" She licked her lips, her fingers playing with her teaspoon. "I was merely thinking of my son, my grandchildren."

"You miss them."

Aunt Mara nodded.

"Why don't you call on them?"

Her aunt's eyes widened, and she instantly shook her head. "I could not. My son is…rarely home these days, and…I would not wish to disturb his wife."

Abigail's gaze narrowed. "She does not want you to see your grandchildren, does she? She's still angry with you for the counsel you provided your son."

With wide eyes, Aunt Mara looked at her. "How do you know this?"

Abigail shrugged. "Grandfather told me." Chiding herself for not pursuing this further, Abigail leaned forward. "We should go see them."

Again, Aunt Mara shook her head. "I don't want to cause any trouble. I—"

The door opened, admitting the duke inside and cutting their conversation short.

With barely a nod to them, he took his seat at the head of the table. By now, Abigail knew that her grandfather liked to do things a certain way. Namely, his way. And upon enquiry, he had informed her that he took his meals whenever he chose. *No one tells me what to do or when to do it!*

As though to prove himself true to his word, he always appeared at different times.

"How was last night's ball?" he enquired, watchful eyes on Abigail as he reached for his teacup. "Have you received any more proposals?"

Looking at her grandfather, Abigail could have sworn that there had been a touch of humour—sarcasm even—in his voice, and she tried to recall if her grandfather had ever seen her dressed to her *dis*advantage when heading out into society. Since he rarely attended any events held throughout the season—*why would he object himself to such torture?*—Abigail was certain that he had not. Then how had he learnt of her strategy? Because judging from the slight twitch in his upper lip, he had!

Feigning nonchalance, Abigail shrugged. "It was an evening like any other, Grandfather." Smiling at him, she noticed with delight the slight narrowing of his eyes when she did not address him as *your grace.* "Quite uneventful."

"Then why do you attend?" the duke asked unexpectedly. "If you despise these events, simply stay home."

Taken aback, Abigail tried to determine her grandfather's reasons for uttering such a suggestion. Did he not want her to mingle? How else was she supposed to secure a husband? Was not that what he wanted? "I admit that these events are somewhat tiresome," she finally said, deciding that the truth would be a refreshing choice. "However, sitting at home every night with no one to speak to would also not be my idea of an enjoyable night. In general, I like being around people. However, whether or not I enjoy their company is a matter of quality."

With an unintelligible grumble, her grandfather nodded his head. Had they just agreed on something?

Abigail shook her head. Apparently, strange things did happen after all…at least on occasion.

"Did you not enjoy dancing with Lord Amberly?" Aunt Mara asked, her gaze as watchful as ever. "I must say you looked quite pleased when he asked you to dance."

"Lord Amberly?" her grandfather enquired, his sharp eyes once more shifting to her face. "I knew his father," he continued in a grumble, his gaze turning back to the teacup in his hand. "The men in his family possess reason and a sense of honour." He inhaled deeply as the strong aroma of the warm liquid wafted upward. "I would not refuse my consent if he were to ask for your hand."

Momentarily too stunned to reply, Abigail found herself staring at her grandfather, unable to avert her eyes. What had happened in the last few seconds? Only a moment ago, she had thought her grandfather had taken a step back from his marriage plans for her. However, now, he had taken a leap forward. That man continued to confuse her!

Swallowing the lump in her throat, Abigail reached for her own teacup, doing her best to sound unimpressed. "It was…diverting," she admitted, a bored tone in her voice. "However, I received the distinct impression that his attentions were already otherwise engaged." Only too well did Abigail remember the golden-haired beauty in the emerald gown Lord Amberly had swept onto the dance floor after fleeing her company. She had to admit her strategy had worked a little too well that night! With envious eyes, Abigail had watched the couple share a beautiful dance, their eyes glowing and their lips curved upward into amiable smiles. Would she ever experience anything like it? Or was she doomed to chase away any man who dared approach her?

For a short moment that night, Abigail had not been able to remember why she did so. Perhaps her heart was beginning to heal. After all, she could not continue her life mourning her father's passing, could she? No, that would not be right. He would never have wanted that for her. After all, he had recovered—at least as far as possible—after her mother's untimely death, had he not?

Suddenly taking note of two sets of eyes on her, Abigail set down her teacup and lifted her chin. "I doubt he will call on me, so there is truly no point in discussing him."

A slight chuckle escaped her grandfather's lips, and even Aunt Mara turned to him with a confused frown on her face. "Have you already made plans for this afternoon?"

A moment later, there came a knock on the door and Orwel strode into the room, bowing to her grandfather and then addressing her. "This was delivered for you earlier this morning, miss."

Abigail glanced from Orwel to her grandfather, noting that there was not a hint of surprise on the old man's face.

Earlier this morning?

How long ago had the letter arrived? Had her grandfather held it back to be delivered at the perfect moment? Looking at him through narrowed eyes, Abigail thought to detect a touch of amusement in his eyes. Did he have a strategy of his own? One that factored hers in? Was he trying to undo her attempts at driving away her suitors? So far at least, she had not noticed anything.

Taking a deep breath, Abigail unfolded the sheet of paper for that's what it was. A simple sheet of paper. On its own. Not in an envelope. But surely, it had arrived in one, had it not?

Dear Miss Abbott,

I would be honoured if you'd allow me to take you for a drive through Hyde

Park later this afternoon. I shall come by to collect you at four.

Yours sincerely,

Lord Amberly

"As I said," her grandfather broke into her stunned silence, "I do believe him to be a fine young man, and, therefore, I heartily give my permission. Do have fun."

Out of her grandfather's mouth, these words seemed like a joke, and Abigail looked up, wondering if her ears had deceived her. Judging from the triumphant gleam in the old man's eyes, they had not.

"What if I do not wish to go?" Abigail demanded, annoyed with the way people tended to force their decisions on her. Was she not to have a say in the matter?

"I do believe it would do you good to get out of the house for a little while, my dear," her aunt interjected at the most inconvenient of times.

"I do get out of the house," Abigail objected, casting a warning glance at Aunt Mara, which the older woman chose to ignore.

"Nonsense," her grandfather decided. "You cannot refuse him." Then he rose from his chair—apparently tea was enough that morning—and left the room, effectively ending the discussion.

Sighing, Abigail stared at the small note in her hands. Naturally, it did not contain a compliment of any kind or a small declaration of his affections. After all, he did not care about her, about who she was. All he saw was her dowry and the connection to her grandfather's name and family.

Nothing more.

Abigail could not deny that she was somewhat disappointed by that realisation.

Because I thought you would suit each other. Had Winifred been truthful? But how could she know if Abigail herself could not see it? Still, she had to admit she knew nothing of Lord Amberly. As little as he knew about her. Perhaps she truly ought to keep an open mind.

Perhaps.

8

AN AFTERNOON AT HYDE PARK

With a block of ice firmly settled in his stomach, Griffin arrived at Lord Ashold's imposing townhouse, questioning his sanity at going along with his sister's demands. Was he being a fool? Most likely. Still, he could not refuse her.

He was honour-bound.

Bloody hell.

As he stepped into the entrance hall, a shrill voice drifted down the winding staircase from the upper floor, and Griffin cringed, feeling the desperate need to turn around and flee the premises.

However, he did not. He could not go back on his word.

Bloody hell.

Footsteps approached, and he reluctantly lifted his head to spot Miss Abbott descending the stairs in large strides before the butler could even show him to the drawing room. Dressed in a pale aqua green gown, the sleeves and hem set off in a brilliant red, she rushed toward him as though the devil was behind her. "Oh, Lord Amberly, how good of you to come," she exclaimed in that high-pitched voice that seemed to drill small holes into his brain with every word she spoke. "It was so lovely of you to invite me out on such a brilliant day. You don't mind if my aunt comes along, do you?"

Taken aback by the speed with which the words flew out of her mouth, Griffin had no time to answer before she prattled on, not waiting for a reply. Glancing up the stairs, he took note of the dowager marchioness, dressed in mute colours. Unlike her niece, she moved with grace and elegance, two attributes entirely lost on the young woman pulling on an orange coat and donning a dark blue bonnet. Was this woman colour blind?

Still stunned, Griffin could hardly get a word out before Miss Abbott rushed out the front door, her face lifted to the sky and her eyes closed momentarily as she smiled at the sun. "It truly is a beautiful day for walk, do you not agree?"

A walk? Glancing at his chaise parked at the kerb, Griffin walked down the front stoop as though in a trance. No, he had not intended to walk through Hyde Park. Still, as the dowager marchioness was to accompany them, there was no other choice.

As though he was not there, Miss Abbott continued down the street, pulling her aunt along. Following them like a dog, Griffin cursed his sister. After all, she could not possible have been serious? In fact, by now, Griffin was entirely convinced that Miss Abbott was widely referred to as the most awful woman in England with very good reason.

She was in a word -- awful.

As they proceeded toward Hyde Park, Griffin noticed how the dowager began to drift sideways, increasing the space between her and her niece. In addition, her steps grew smaller so if her niece did not wish to outrun her, she would have to pace herself. Step by step, she maneuvered Griffin to Miss Abbott's side and before he knew it, the young woman had her arm through the crook of his with her aunt trailing along behind them.

Although Griffin had no desire to get any closer to the young woman than necessary, he had to admit that he was truly impressed with the dowager's subtlety. After all, judging from the endless stream of words out of Miss Abbott's mouth, she did not even seem to have noticed.

"Oh, what a beautiful day!" she exclaimed for the tenth time that day, her right arm gesturing wildly at the scenery around them. "I cannot wait for spring. I simply adore flowers. All those colours, bright and brilliant. Oh, they so lift my spirits! I truly miss them in winter. I mean, I try my best to dress colourful, but there is only so much one can do. I must say I'm truly disappointed that not more young women dare to display such vibrant colours. It's such a shame."

Griffin swallowed, praying for the opposite. He could only hope that her tendency to mismatch colours would not turn into a trend. He doubted it very much, but one could never be certain.

"I love sunflowers. They're so cheerful," she continued as they proceeded down the path toward the Serpentine. "What about you, my lord? What is your favourite flower?"

At a loss, Griffin swallowed. Did he have a favourite flower? Not that he could recall.

Luckily, Miss Abbott was not in need of a reply to keep their *conversation* going. "But roses smell so wonderful and violets…" For the next minutes, she prattled on about every flower she had ever seen: their colours, their scents, the softness of their petals…

Griffin groaned inwardly, certain he had found his way down into hell. If this was not torture, he did not know what was!

Blowing out a breath, Miss Abbott shook herself, her nose scrunched up. "It's quite chilly after all," she said as they came to stand beside the glistening waters of the Serpentine. "Perhaps it was a bit premature of you to suggest a stroll through the park after all, my lord."

Griffin frowned. Had *he* truly suggested a stroll? He could not recall that he had. Still, he did not argue, but grasped the opportunity she was offering him with both hands. "Then allow me to see you back home," he said, turning on his heel and back up the way they had come.

Unfortunately, Miss Abbott took that moment to stomp on his foot with such vehemence that he could not believe it had been an accident. Suppressing a groan, Griffin gritted his teeth lest the less than flattering words he had been wanting to say to Miss Abbott all afternoon flew out of his mouth.

"You truly ought to look where you step, my lord," Miss Abbott chided him. "You almost tripped me. My beautiful dress could have been ruined."

Pressing his lips even tighter together, Griffin had never been so close to losing his temper. One by one, he forced a deep breath into his lungs, doing his best to close his ears to the young woman's incessant chattering. Instead, he turned halfway back to the lake and let his eyes travel over two young children playing on its banks. The boy tossed pebbles into the water while the girl was picking daisies growing near the bank, handing a small bouquet to her governess.

"Aunt Mara, are you all right?"

Blinking, Griffin turned back to Miss Abbott as he felt her hand slip from his arm.

With a slight crease in her forehead, she started toward her aunt, who stood in the middle of the path, her pale eyes fixed on the children playing near the water. "Aunt Mara?" Miss Abbott called, her voice suddenly softer, gentler as she tried to get her aunt's attention.

The dowager inhaled a sudden sharp breath, blinked a couple of times and then turned to look at her niece. "I'm sorry, my dear. I simply…" Her voice trailed off as her gaze travelled back to the children still playing by the water.

Miss Abbott turned her head, her gaze following her aunt's. Then a soft smile came to her lips as she looked back at the older woman. "It's them, isn't it?"

Swallowing, the dowager nodded, her eyes filling with tears which she quickly tried to blink away.

Stunned, Griffin watched as Miss Abbott gently took her aunt's hand and tried to draw her forward. "Let's meet them."

The dowager's eyes widened, and she dug her heels into the ground. "Oh, no, I cannot. She wouldn't like–"

"You're their grandmother," Miss Abbott stated sharply, a hint of annoyance in her voice. "You have a right to see them." And with that, she marched toward the two children, pulling the dowager after her.

Realising that she had all but forgotten about him, Griffin watched with great interest as the two women approached the lake. As soon as the children's eyes fell on the dowager, they raced toward her, hugging her tightly, bringing fresh tears to their grandmother's eyes.

With a look of concern, the governess stepped forward, determined to interfere. However, she was no match for Miss Abbott. With a stern look in her eyes, she glared the woman into submission, words flying out of her mouth without a moment's pause.

Griffin could not help but smile as he stared at her almost transfixed.

Gone was the shrill, loud woman with nothing to say but nonsense. Gone was the self-involved expression in her eyes as well as the odd grimace that could hardly be called a smile. Gone was the clumsy woman who had stomped on his toes more than once.

In her stead, Griffin saw a young lady, her eyes aglow as she now gazed at the scene before her, the soft smile on her face speaking of honest delight at seeing her aunt so happy. She moved slowly, gracefully as she retreated, giving them a moment alone. Her cheeks shone in a rosy red, and her teeth toyed with her lower lip as she forgot the world around her, her only focus the woman she clearly adored.

Drawing in a slow breath, Griffin took a careful step forward, coming to stand next to her. With watchful eyes on her, he said, "They seem very happy to see each other."

Miss Abbott sighed, her gaze still transfixed. "They do, don't they?" she whispered as though to herself, as though unaware who she was speaking to. "Oh, look how happy she is. She's missed them. I could tell. But she never speaks about them. She's so afraid to–" Turning to look at him, Miss Abbott froze, and he could see in the way her eyes widened that she had just realised what she had done.

The moment she had seen the shock on her aunt's face, Miss Abbot's act had slipped from her grasp.

And an act it was, to be sure.

There could be no doubt about it at this point. The only question was: why?

Grinning at her, Griffin watched with delight as her cheeks turned an even darker shade of red. "You seem quite changed, Miss Abbott."

For a moment her lips pressed together, and she closed her eyes. Then he saw the corners of her mouth twitch before her lips spread into a smile and her grey eyes found his once more. "I suppose you're right, my lord," she said, a teasing tone in her voice that Griffin found quite intriguing. "Is there any chance we could forget this ever happened?" she asked bluntly, a graceful sweep of her arm encompassing the scene at the lake.

Laughing, Griffin shook his head. "None at all."

Miss Abbott drew in a deep breath, a hint of disappointment in her calculating eyes. Still, Griffin could not help but think that she was pleased with the opportunity to be herself. Her true self.

Knowing she would never tell him if he were to ask why she felt the need to put on this act, Griffin chose a different approach. "Are you aware that people refer to you as the most awful woman in all of England?"

He felt blunt to ask such a question. However, his instinct told him she would not be offended.

The smile that came to her face told him that he was right. "I am," she confirmed, a touch of pride in her voice as though it had been a great accomplishment on her part to be rewarded such a title. "Why do you ask?"

Griffin shrugged. "I was simply curious."

"And would you agree?" she asked rather unexpectedly, a newfound vulnerability in her eyes as though his opinion mattered to her.

Holding her gaze, Griffin drew in a slow breath. "I did agree," he admitted, "up until five minutes ago." A soft smile came to her lips, and she glanced at the ground for a split second as though bashful. "Now, I'm not so sure."

Delighted with the deep smile that came to her face, Griffin shook his head. How could he not have seen this? Did his sister know? Was that why she had insisted he give Miss Abbott a chance? For clearly there was more to this woman than met the eye.

A lot more.

And suddenly, he was determined to learn who she truly was.

9

AN ACT OBSERVED

Dressed in a bright red gown decorated with large black buttons—turning her effectively into a ladybird—Abigail sat in her grandfather's carriage, watching her aunt twist and turn a handkerchief in the seat across from her. "You'll rip it in two," she warned, her voice teasing, hoping to distract Aunt Mara from the one thought that had occupied her mind since their afternoon stroll through Hyde Park.

Blinking, her aunt met her gaze. "I'm sorry, dear. I've been awfully distracted lately. I—"

"I'm not complaining," Abigail reminded her. "I'm worried. I want you to talk to me. Tell me what is on your mind, and I promise we shall do what we can to put you at ease." Inhaling a deep breath, she watched her aunt for another minute. "It is your grandchildren, isn't it?"

Swallowing, Aunt Mara nodded.

"Are you afraid it will be a long time before you see them again?"

Tears appeared in the older woman's eyes, but she quickly

blinked them away. "I know it will. She does not want me to see them."

"Your son's wife?"

Again, Aunt Mara merely nodded.

"Why do you let her?"

Wide eyes met hers.

Abigail sighed, knowing by now that it was not in her aunt's nature to seek confrontation to achieve her goals. No, she cherished peace above anything else. Still, the situation within their family could hardly be called peaceful. At best, it was a truce everyone had agreed upon, but none was quite happy.

As they walked into Lord Blamson's ballroom, Abigail vowed that she would speak to her grandfather as soon as possible and once more urge him to seek out his grandson. There had to be a way that Aunt Mara could see her grandchildren more regularly than occasionally happening upon them in the park. That was ludicrous.

After spending considerable time standing by the dance floor, exchanging the occasional observation with her aunt, Abigail found a young man striding toward her. Although she could see his displeasure at her appearance in the way his gaze slid over her, he still asked her to dance…only to regret his decision minutes later.

In turn, watching one of their own limp off the dance floor dissuaded the young gentlemen present there that night from venturing anywhere near her. Although relieved, Abigail could not deny that she was bored. What was the point of attending these events if one could not dance? Or at least socialise?

However, she was the most awful woman in all of England, was she not?

To move her feet, Abigail began to venture from room to room, her thoughts drawn back to Lord Amberly as he had grinned at her, utter delight in his eyes, asking her if she knew about the less than flattering name the ton had bestowed on her.

For a moment that afternoon, Abigail had enjoyed herself.

Allowing her gaze to sweep over the dancing couples, Abigail felt her lips press into a tight line as annoyance rose to the forefront. Why was it not possible for her to dance without appearing as though she was looking for a husband? Why did everyone assume a young woman's life revolved around finding a suitable match? Was there nothing more to life than marriage?

Oh, to hell with them all if they even thought for a moment she would live by their rules!

Spotting a young gentleman by the side of the room, unoccupied at present, Abigail marched toward him, her mind made up.

A hint of the fierce determination that burnt in her chest must have shown on her face, for the young gentleman blanched visibly when he saw her coming, his gaze shifting left and right as though looking for someone who would come to his rescue.

However, fortune did not smile on him that night, and so he found himself put on the spot as the most awful woman in all of England asked him for the next dance. What was he to say?

Seeing him hesitate, Abigail grasped his arm and dragged him onto the dance floor before he had a chance to decline by offering up an excuse to not appear impolite.

Although Abigail enjoyed the chance to move her limbs, dancing with an unwilling partner was far from enjoyable, and so her gaze continued to venture around the room, hoping to spot something—anything!—to distract her from the sheer boredom that had become her life.

Her gaze fell on a well-groomed lady perhaps ten years her senior. The woman's eyes had narrowed into slits, and her lips looked more like the snarl of a charging cat. Then she did in fact charge forward, her feet carrying her toward…Aunt Mara.

Abigail froze as she saw her aunt's face turn white as a sheet, her hands twisting into the handkerchief with an almost desperate need to hold on to something.

Outrage rose within Abigail at seeing her gentle, sweet-tempered aunt thus attacked, and without further thought, she abandoned her dance partner in the middle of a cotillion and rushed across the room to her aunt's side.

In the very moment that the woman opened her mouth—no doubt to spew her venom—Abigail stepped into her path. "Lady Bradish, isn't it?" she said sweetly, her eyes sharp as they held the woman's angry stare, certain that she was none other than her aunt's daughter-in-law. "It's so nice to make your acquaintance. My aunt has told me so much about you." After glancing at Aunt Mara and seeing a touch of relief on the old woman's face, Abigail turned back to her opponent, noting the initial confusion turn to comprehension.

"Miss Abbott, is it?" the marchioness asked, a hint of distaste in her tone. "I had heard you were in town. You seem to be quite the talk of the season."

Holding on to her feigned smile, Abigail ignored the hidden insult. "Oh, that is so kind of you to say. Yes, I've made wonderful friends already. One nicer than the other. I hardly know where to spend my time, but I promise I shall call on you as soon as possible. My aunt often tells me how fond she is of your two beautiful children." She clasped her hands together as though surprised by a sudden idea. "We should take them out on a picnic. Aunt Mara, what do you think?"

Taken aback, her aunt did not reply.

"Yes, that's a marvellous thought," Abigail continued, cutting off the marchioness as she opened her mouth to object. "I will send word." Beaming at the marchioness, Abigail then drew her aunt's arm through hers. "It was truly wonderful to meet you." And with that she marched off, all but dragging her aunt behind her.

Stunned speechless, Griffin watched as Miss Abbott guided her aunt away from the sour-looking woman, who he presumed to be the children's mother they happened upon at the Serpentine.

As he had been unable to get Miss Abbott out of his head, Griffin had spent the past two hours since his arrival at the ball observing the young woman, trying to make sense of her strange behaviour.

Indeed, throughout the evening she had acted as she always had, dressed to her disadvantage, oblivious to society's code of conduct and all but blind to the reaction of others. Still, now that Griffin knew it was an act, he could not help but notice the small signs of her true self lurking under the finely crafted mask she had chosen to wear.

And then she had rushed off the dance floor in the middle of a cotillion, leaving behind a rather stunned looking gentleman, and hurried to her aunt's side.

In that moment, Griffin had seen the young woman, full of compassion and loyalty, he had met that day at Hyde Park.

And his heart had overflown with pride.

Following the two women to the refreshment table, he watched as Miss Abbott put a glass of lemonade in her aunt's hand, urging her to drink it. "You look pale, Aunt Mara. Perhaps you need some air."

"Don't worry yourself, Child," her aunt replied, carefully sipping her drink. "I was merely…surprised at your sudden appearance."

Miss Abbott smiled, then shook her head at her aunt's understatement. "You're right. Lady Bradish is not very fond of you, which is odd, because no one in their right mind could ever dislike you, Aunt Mara."

Miss Abbot's aunt smiled, and Griffin thought to see a touch of red rising to the older woman's cheeks. Realising that the dowager marchioness was probably quite used to being overlooked and taken for granted, Griffin could only imagine what her niece's words, her utter devotion and loyalty, meant to her.

"Still, you should not have spoken to her as you did," the dowager marchioness counselled in a rather apologetic voice. "She might–"

"I was polite, wasn't I?" Miss Abbott interrupted, daring eyes meeting her aunt's while the twitch that came to her lips spoke of suppress humour. "You cannot deny that I said nothing offending."

"Of course not, Dear," her aunt agreed, her fingers clenching and unclenching around the glass in her hands. "Still, you ought not to have suggested a picnic, knowing that it would upset her."

Miss Abbott snorted, "I do not care whether that woman is upset. All I want is to not see you so miserable any longer." Nodding her head with determination, she grasped her aunt's hand. "I shall speak to grandfather again. I'm certain he will find a way to fix this."

The dowager's eyes widened. "I'm afraid he will not be pleased if you bother him with this trifle. I've never known him to meddle in family affairs."

"Meddle?" Miss Abbott gawked before she shook her head in disbelief. "I have to say you all have a strange way to look at family. It's not called meddling if you protect the people you love." The dowager was about to open her mouth, but Miss Abbott cut her off. "He cares for you," she said, causing her aunt's eyes to widen even further. "He will do this."

The dowager swallowed. "No one has ever been able to make him do something he does not wish to do."

Sighing, Miss Abbott laughed, "Yes, I've noticed he likes to appear like a cold-hearted monster. It seems to amuse him greatly. But mark my words, it is only an act."

Watching Miss Abbott and her aunt head out to their carriage, Griffin found himself quite intrigued with the young woman he had loathed to meet before. Her compassionate and loyal side appealed to him greatly, and he could not deny that she was fascinating when she did not pretend to be the most awful woman in England.

Descending the front stoop down to the pavement, Griffin kept his gaze firmly attached to the duke's carriage until it turned at the next street and was lost from sight. "I could like her," Griffin whispered to the dark night, keeping his thoughts firmly away from the realisation that he already did.

10

PAST PAIN

"Grandfather, I need to speak with you!"

Looking up at his granddaughter, the duke rolled his eyes as he set down the paper he had been studying. "Did your father not teach you any manners at all?" he grumbled, gesturing at the door to his study she had pushed wide open without bothering to knock. "This is a ducal household, and we have certain rules here."

Abigail smiled, closing the door and approaching the desk. "Oh, don't pretend you don't like me barging in here, Grandfather." She lifted her eyebrows in challenge and delighted in detecting a telling quiver in her grandfather's upper lip. If she was not at all mistaken, she would think he liked her.

A lot.

Clearing her throat, she reminded herself why she had come. "It's about Aunt Mara." Again, her grandfather rolled his eyes. "We met her grandchildren the other day at the park, and last night at the ball, the marchioness stormed toward her with a dark scowl on her face."

Her grandfather's gaze narrowed, and she thought to detect a hint of concern in his grey eyes. "What did she say to her?"

Abigail blinked her lashes, smiling sweetly. "Nothing."

Her grandfather's frown deepened. "Nothing?"

"Well, I happened to notice—"

"Ah!" her grandfather exclaimed, understanding lighting up his face. "I should have guessed. Then what do you need my help for?"

Leaning her hands on the top of his desk, Abigail met his gaze, hoping that she was not wrong, hoping that he could be swayed into helping his daughter-in-law. "Well, I—"

"Why don't you sit down? I cannot say I'm overly fond of having to crane my neck to look up at you."

Abigail snorted, "In the chair of torture?" Chuckling, she shook her head. "No, thank you. In this regard, your choices are fairly simple: either get a more comfortable chair or stand up."

Her grandfather's brows rose in surprise; yet, there was a touch of pride in the way he looked at her, a strange sense of recognition.

"But let's not lose focus," Abigail reminded herself as well as him. "About Aunt Mara. You need to speak to your grandson and fix this."

"How I am suppo—?"

"I'm sure you can think of something."

Holding her gaze, her grandfather leaned back in his chair. "This has been going on for years." He sighed, and a sudden sadness came to his eyes. "Sometimes it is too late to change things no matter how much you wish you could."

Straightening, Abigail swallowed. "Are you talking about my mother?"

Drawing in a slow breath, her grandfather nodded. "I made a mistake to let her go, to not go after her. I thought…" He shook his head. "I should have told her that…And then she died, and it was too late."

Feeling tears sting the back of her eyes, Abigail stepped around the desk, her eyes intent on the old man sinking into the large chair. His eyes held such sadness, such regret, as she had never seen them before. "She died so long ago, and you never sent word," she said, remembering a life wondering about the family she could have had. "Then why now? Why did you sent Aunt Mara to bring me to London?"

"After I learnt of your mother's death, I was…angry." He shook his head as though to dispel the memory. "Then her loss sank in, and for a long time, I…"

Abigail nodded, feeling tears run down her face. "I know," she whispered, remembering the sudden blow of losing her father, of having him torn out of her life, of being left utterly alone.

Looking up at her tear-streaked face, her grandfather rose to his feet. "After your father's death, I received a letter through a Mr. Melton."

Abigail frowned. Mr. Melton? He had been an old friend of her father's. One he had not seen in years. How would he—?

"In it, your father…he begged me to look after you."

Abigail sucked in a sharp breath, her eyes going wide as her heart hammered in her chest. "He did?" she gasped, her hands shaking as she lifted them to brush the tears from her face.

Her grandfather nodded. Then his hand reached out for hers, slowly, tentatively, before it gently closed around her chilled fingers.

A sob tore from Abigail's throat, and before she knew it her grandfather swept her into his arms, holding her tightly as she cried painful tears for the father she had lost too soon.

"I should have written," he mumbled into her hair. "I'm sorry. At first, I could not and then…time passed, and at some point, I felt it was too late. I know I failed her as I failed you, but there is no changing the past. All I can do is give you all I have now."

Pulling back, Abigail looked into her grandfather's weathered face, his grey eyes full of regret. "But you haven't," she whispered. "You gave me a dowry, nothing more. But what I want…what I need is you…and Aunt Mara. We're a family, and we can help each other through this."

Blinking back tears of his own, her grandfather nodded. "You're right. You're right. I'm sorry."

"Don't be sorry. Help me."

Nodding his head, her grandfather squeezed her hands. "I will. Don't worry. I will take care of everything."

"Thank you," Abigail sighed, impulsively hugging her grandfather to her chest before stepping back, her eyes holding his with a new sense of closeness. "And if you don't mind," she added, a teasing chuckle back in her voice, "withdraw my dowry so I can dress like a normal woman again and not like an insect."

Her grandfather chuckled, "Oh, I don't know. I liked the ladybird. The bumblebee, too, looked quite spectacular."

Abigail's eyes widened. "How do you know what I wore? You never—"

"Don't allow yourself to be fooled by an old man," he chuckled. "I know everything that goes on in my house and beyond." He grinned at her. "How is Lord Amberly by the way?"

Abigail's eyes narrowed. "Are you still trying to find me a husband? Didn't I just say that—"

"I know," he interrupted her, his eyes urging her to listen, "and I'm not saying you need to choose a husband this season. However, I urge you not to discount all your suitors. There might be one among them who—"

"They want my dowry!" Abigail snapped. "Your dowry! They don't care who I am."

Her grandfather laughed indulgently, "Well, you're not making it easy for them to get to know you, or are you?"

Abigail rolled her eyes. "I had to find some way to discourage them. They were swarming around me like moths to a flame. It was unbearable. You cannot fault me for thinking of a solution."

"I'm not. I applaud you."

Abigail frowned. "Excuse me?"

"You're an intelligent, beautiful and—despite popular opinions—amiable young woman," he said, his eyes shining as he looked at her. "And I think it is not a bad idea to make them work for you. *You,* not your dowry," he stressed. "Still, at some point, you need to give them a chance to see you for who you are. How else will they ever have a chance to like you? The real you?"

"Well, it would seem they're not interested in that at all," Abigail huffed, getting slightly annoyed with her grandfather's overbearing attitude.

A knock sounded on the door, and upon her grandfather's call, Orwel entered. "Lord Amberly is in the drawing room awaiting Miss Abbott."

As her mouth dropped open, Abigail noticed a knowing grin spread over her grandfather's face that seemed to scream, *I told you so, didn't I?*

Swallowing, Abigail tried to find her voice. "I'll be right out," she told the butler, wondering what on earth Lord Amberly was doing calling on her again. Had that moment at the lake been enough to convince him that marrying her might not be as awful as she had had him believe before?

Well, there was only one way to find out.

11

A NEW PACT

Standing in the drawing room of the duke's townhouse, Griffin wondered which of the two women would meet him. Would it be the hideously dressed, shrill woman who had squashed his toes on more than one occasion? Or rather the compassionate, fiercely loyal young lady whose smile he had seen in his dreams last night?

Quite honestly, Griffin preferred the latter.

Who wouldn't?

Still, there was no way to know, and so when he heard approaching footsteps, Griffin drew in a slow breath, every muscle in his body tense with anticipation.

Then the door opened, and in its frame appeared a young woman dressed in a simple, yet elegant gown, its subtle yellow fabric shining against the dark of her flowing hair, here and there pinned up, with loose tendrils dancing down to her shoulders.

Griffin breathed a sigh of relief…until his gaze fell on the dark scowl on her face. Swallowing, he greeted her. "Good day, Miss Abbott. It is truly a pleasure to see you again."

"The pleasure is all mine," Miss Abbott said as though in trance, her eyes narrowed as she watched him with no small amount of suspicion. "Please, do sit." Striding into the room, her long legs carrying her gracefully across the Persian rug, she kept her gaze fixed on his face as though hoping to unravel the mystery of his visit.

And surely it must be a mystery to her for as far as Griffin knew she had not received any gentleman callers in the past few weeks. Her act had driven them all away. Certainly, she had to be wondering what he was doing here, especially after her rather memorable performance at Hyde Park. Judging from the look on her face, she had thought herself successful in driving him away as well.

Then she cleared her throat, and a new determination flashed over her face. "May I ask what brings you here, my lord?" she asked, a sudden edge to her voice that had not been there before.

Griffin frowned, aware that she was displeased with his presence in her home. Had she decided to return to her act to rid herself of him?

An amused grin came to his face as he leaned back. "Do you care for an honest answer?"

His question seemed to surprise her for her eyes narrowed, and her voice returned to a normal pitch as though she had forgotten the role she had forced on herself. "Does your question imply that you generally do not speak honestly, my lord?"

Griffin laughed, "Do you?"

The muscles in her jaw tensed. "Well, I suppose honesty rests in the eye of the observer. I, for one, have observed that few people openly reveal their true opinions. Most hide behind civility, manners, social etiquette and, of course, their own ambitions." Her brows rose in challenge as though she dared him to contradict her.

Holding her gaze, Griffin leaned forward, resting his elbows on his knees. "Do you care to know what *I* have observed?"

For a moment, she hesitated, drawing in a slow breath. "Do tell."

"Well, I have to admit it took me a good while to make sense of you," he said, encouraged to forge ahead at her sharp intake of breath. "At first, your behaviour downright puzzled me. Why on earth would anyone act the way you did?" He shook his head, his lips twitching with amusement. "I wondered if there truly were people on this earth completely oblivious to how they are perceived by others. I could not fathom it to be true, and yet, you appeared to be one such unique individual." He chuckled, "But you're not, are you?"

Miss Abbott inhaled a deep breath, her hands curled into the fabric of her skirt. "What is your reasoning?"

"Everything changed that afternoon at the park," he continued, watching her face intently. "Your concern for your aunt overruled your *act*, and from one second to the next, you were a completely different person." He shook his head, laughing. "I admit I could not believe my eyes. For a moment, I thought I'd lost my mind."

Miss Abbott swallowed, her chest rising and falling with each breath as she held his gaze, waiting. "Do you plan on…sharing your opinion with–?"

"No!" he answered her question before it had even left her lips. His gaze held hers, and he could see a touch of anxiety in her grey eyes. Did she wonder about his intentions?

"Then why are you telling me this?" she asked abruptly, annoyance chasing away all concern she had felt before. "Why are you here? If your intention is to…secure my dowry, I might as well tell you now that my grandfather would never force my hand, and I would never accept a man who–"

"That is not why I'm here," Griffin hastened to reply as he saw the slight tremble in her hands. Did she truly think he would go over her head to enrich himself? "I do not want your dowry," he stressed, holding her gaze, willing her to believe him. "Nor do I *need* it."

Miss Abbott exhaled a slow breath, and some of the tension fell from her face. "So, you're not here to propose?"

Griffin shook his head. "Not at present," he said, surprising himself. Did he truly care for this woman? Or was it merely idle curiosity?

In answer, her eyes narrowed. "Then why *are* you here?"

"To get to know you," Griffin said. "I admit I'm fairly intrigued by your charade. It speaks of a strong will, tremendous creativity and no small ability to act. For the woman you portray to the world is nothing like you, is she? You invented her to protect yourself, to rid yourself of your suitors, men who wished to marry you to secure your dowry, is that not so?"

Swallowing, she stared at him, shock clearly written all over her face. And still, Griffin thought to see a touch of pleasure in her grey eyes as though a part of her revelled in the fact that he had seen behind her mask and noticed the real person underneath. "Is that all you've come for," she asked then, "to confirm you suspicion?"

Griffin chuckled, "Partly, I came because…I have no choice."

Her gaze widened, and he noticed a touch of curiosity. "Why is that?"

"A little while ago, I made a promise to my sister," he admitted freely, realising that he owed her honesty in return for stripping her of her mask, "and now she is holding me to it."

Miss Abbott swallowed. "What kind of promise?"

Watching Lord Amberly, Abigail noticed the amusement that never seemed to leave his eyes, and she felt herself relax when she failed to detect any kind of malintent. He wasn't laughing about her. Not at all. He seemed merely entertained by the situation they found themselves in. A man who would see the humour in the world. "So, are you bound to secrecy? Or can you reveal said promise?"

For a moment, he seemed to think her question over before his gaze intensified on hers. "Only if you promise not to reveal it to another? Let this stay between us, and no one else."

Intrigued, Abigail nodded. "From the way you speak, my lord, I must assume the worst."

"Oh, it is quite dreadful, I assure you." Still, there was a touch of mischief in his eyes that led her to believe he was teasing her.

"Well then?" she pressed, realising that she truly wanted to know.

Watching her intently, no doubt looking for her reaction, Lord Amberly took a deep breath. "Well, last fall, my sister suddenly decided that it was time she found herself a husband. However, she went about it in a most ridiculous way." He shook himself as though trying to dispel the dreadful memory. "She started to make lists of her attributes and intended to match them to those she could discover in London's eligible bachelors."

Abigail felt her eyes widening until she was outright staring at him.

Lord Amberly nodded vigorously. "That's exactly what I thought," he answered her silent reaction. "I thought it was a ludicrous plan, especially since she'd already lost her heart to an old friend of mine but refused to acknowledge it because—as she put it—they would not suit each other."

"You're referring to Lord Chadwick, are you not?" Abigail

asked, feeling herself caught up in the story.

Lord Amberly nodded.

"So, you were able to dissuade her from her plan," she concluded, relieved for Winifred's sake. "They truly are a good match. I cannot imagine her with anyone else."

"Neither could I."

"Then how did you manage?" Abigail asked, somewhat surprised that he had a similarly calculating mind. "How did you sway her?"

Lord Amberly chuckled, "In order for me to have a say in her choice, I had to promise her a say in mine."

Again, Abigail's eyes widened until she stared at him, a deep smile on her face as she realised his predicament.

"Not my finest moment," he assured her. "Still, what was I to do? I could not in good conscience allow her to marry one of those mind-numbingly boring *gentlemen* because she could not admit to herself that she was in love."

Abigail felt her heart warm. "You love her very much."

"I do." A soft smile came to Lord Amberly's face. "She's my sister. As much as I want to throttle her sometimes, my happiness is irrevocably tied to hers."

Seeing the devotion in his dark brown eyes, Abigail sighed. Never had she known the love of a brother or sister. After losing her mother before ever having a chance to know her, her father had been her whole world. Until, he, too, had been taken from her.

"Are you all right?" Lord Amberly asked, the smile gone from his face, replaced by honest concern.

Abigail nodded, doing her utmost to blink back the tears that threatened.

"Do you…have any siblings?" he asked carefully, possibly suspecting a recent loss in her family. Had Winifred not told him?

Abigail shook her head. "My mother died in childbirth, and my father…a few weeks past."

At her revelation, Lord Amberly's eyes widened before utter sadness overtook his face. "That's why you came here? To stay with your grandfather?"

Abigail nodded, not knowing what to say. How had they gotten to this sorrowful topic? Would he leave now? Uncomfortable with a weeping female?

Closing her eyes for a moment, Abigail realised that she did not want him to go. Strangely enough, she found herself enjoying his company. Like his sister, he was one of only a few rare individuals who had managed to see *her.* Her true self. And as hard as she had worked to perfect her act, Abigail did not wish to live in the shadows any longer, hiding who she truly was.

"Our parents passed on about five years ago," Lord Amberly said into the silence. "Did my sister tell you that?"

Abigail nodded, relieved when he did not rise to leave. "She did. She said you left England after it happened, travelling the world."

Lord Amberly nodded. "We needed to get away. Everything around us only reminded us of our parents, of a past we had shared and a future that would forever be different." He sighed, "We needed a distraction, something to focus on." His gaze sought hers. "But we still had each other."

Abigail swallowed, "I have my aunt. She's wonderful."

"You care for her greatly."

Abigail nodded. "And my grandfather. He likes to make people think he is cold-hearted, but…he has suffered his share of losses as well. I suppose if there is no one else to live for, it hardens your heart."

Lord Amberly nodded. "Opening your heart to someone means the possibility of a new loss."

"Perhaps that was part of the reason why Winifred refused to acknowledge her feelings," Abigail suggested. "Perhaps she was simply afraid it would hurt more if she admitted how she felt."

Remembering the last time she had spoken to her friend—was she truly her friend?—Abigail could not help but address her doubts. "She said that…we would suit each other," she admitted, lifting her gaze to meet Lord Amberly's. "She said that was the reason she introduced us. Do you believe that is true?"

Lord Amberly grinned. "That we suit each other?"

"No, that that was her reason for introducing us."

Lord Amberly's gaze narrowed, a calculating look coming to his eyes. "You think she introduced us because she wanted to see me well settled? Because of your dowry? Your grandfather's name and title?"

Abigail drew in a deep breath. "She was the only one who tried to be my friend, and the moment I trusted her…"

"You felt betrayed."

Abigail nodded, her gaze shifting over Lord Amberly's face.

His eyes moved about the room, distant and unseeing, directed inward as though he was searching for the words to express what he wished her to know. Then they settled on hers, and Abigail felt her heart warm and her doubts disappear before he had even uttered a single word.

"Despite her rational mind and the strategic way in which she handles life," Lord Amberly began, shaking his head at the deep difference between him and his sister, "Winifred loves as fiercely as I do, and she is nothing if not honest. I do not for a second doubt that the reason she gave you was her true motivation for introducing us. Whether she is right in her opinion or not, I do not doubt that she believes it." He smiled at her. "I know she sees you as her friend, and as that, she would never betray you. I give you my word on that."

Holding his gaze, Abigail felt a new lightness spread through her body. After weeks of hiding and revealing nothing of herself, it felt utterly liberating to be honest with someone. "Thank you," she whispered, touched when his eyes lit up with relief. "This means a lot to me."

He nodded, a teasing grin on his face. "When you're not hiding behind a mask, your emotions are easy to read."

"Is that so?" Abigail dared him. "If you know so much, my lord, then tell me how I can rid myself of these mind-numbingly boring suitors—as you call them—without dressing up like a bug and squashing their feet every chance I get? Any brilliant thoughts?"

Lord Amberly laughed freely, "If I had any brilliant thoughts, don't you think I would have already found a way to circumvent my sister's meddling? I assure you she is as much a nuisance as your suitors are."

Enjoying herself as she had not in months, Abigail laughed. "Well, if we are indeed in the same boat, then I suppose we ought to work together to rid ourselves of your sister as well as my suitors. Perhaps together we can find a solution."

Lord Amberly nodded eagerly. "That's sounds like a marvellous plan. I—" His face froze in mid-sentence.

"Are you all right?" Abigail asked, frowning at the odd expression on his face.

Then his face split into a smile, and he slapped his hand on his knee in triumph. "I've got it!" he exclaimed, and his eyes settled on hers with a new sense of purpose. "What do you say we enter into a little pact of our own?" Abigail's gaze narrowed. "Now, don't look so suspicious! I assure you my intentions are most honourable…at least as far as our shared goal is concerned."

Suppressing a grin, Abigail said, "I'm not certain I dare ask what this pact encompasses."

"Then I shall tell you nonetheless." Grinning from ear to ear, he leaned forward conspiratorially. "You want to be rid of your suitors, and I want to placate my sister. Well, the solution is quite simple: why not act as though we're on the brink of getting betrothed?"

Abigail's mouth fell open, and yet, she felt her blood bubble with excitement as every fibre in her body urged her to agree. Being betrothed to Lord Amberly promised to be a lot of fun, even if it was only an act.

Frowning, Abigail wondered at her thoughts. She did not truly wish to be betrothed to him, did she?

"Are you all right?" Lord Amberly asked, interrupting her thoughts. "You have an odd look on your face."

Snorting, Abigail shook her head. "If you are to be my betrothed, you ought to work on your compliments. After all, no one will believe us if you speak to me in such a way."

"Granted," Lord Amberly conceded. "But only if you promise to be yourself. After all, if London's gentlemen believe you to be all but betrothed to me, there is no need to walk around looking like a bug, now is there?"

Abigail laughed, "I suppose not. Are you afraid it would ruin your reputation if you were seen with the most awful woman in England?"

"Terrified would be a better word," he teased, then held out his hand to her. "Do we have a deal?"

Holding his gaze, Abigail could not believe what she was about to do. Still, her right hand shot forward and grasped his before she had any chance of stopping it. "We certainly do, my lord."

12

A FALSE TRUTH

"You look different," Winifred observed as she looked him up and down before her gaze came to rest on his face and her nose scrunched up as though she was smelling something rotten. "There is something odd about you tonight. You seem strangely cheerful, which–truthfully–makes we worry. After all, you've been wearing quite the tortured expression for the past few weeks. What are you hiding?"

Forcing an unobtrusive smile on his face, Griffin looked at his sister. "I have no idea what on earth you're talking about?"

At his reply, her eyes narrowed, and her nose scrunched up even more. Still, Griffin continued to smile as though he did not have a care in the world, his eyes gliding around the ballroom, wondering when his betrothed–well, almost!–would make her appearance. Perhaps he ought not to have insisted she come as herself. After all, his sister was already suspicious of his odd behaviour as she called it. Would she figure them out if they suddenly got along well? When she saw Miss Abbott in a normal gown that–?

The moment Griffin's eyes fell on his betrothed as she slowly made her way through the crowd—gaping at her and whispering to one another—he knew that he was doomed.

In more ways than one.

Dressed in a stunning, pale violet dress that made her grey eyes shine silver in the candlelight, she walked beside her aunt, her hair gently swept up onto her head, revealing her graceful neck, simple, yet, elegant silver earrings dangling from her ears.

In short: she was breath-taking!

And everyone saw it, gawking at her open-mouthed.

Not quite unlike him.

Unable to control his own reaction, Griffin knew that his sister was most likely putting two and two together in that very moment. Still, he was unable to tear his gaze from the vision before him to confirm his suspicions.

Her eyes glowed, and he could tell with one look that she enjoyed being herself, letting go of the act she had forced upon herself to defend herself against London's bachelors. Although Griffin detected a slight tremble in the smile that rested on her beautiful face—for once not stretched into a grimace—her movement spoke of relief, and the moment her silver-grey eyes fell on his, that smile grew deeper.

Griffin found himself draw in a slow breath as a slight shiver ran through his body. Ever since that day at Hyde Park, he had been intrigued by her. However, he had to admit that over the course of only a few days his interest had grown beyond mere curiosity and fascination. There was so much warmth and kindness in her eyes, and yet, they could appear as hard as steel whenever her protective instincts took over, defending those she loved.

Loved as fiercely as he did his own.

Had Winifred known? If he could have torn his eyes away, he would have chanced a look at his sister. Still, deep down, there was no doubt. Somehow his sister had seen something that had eluded him. Had he been blind because his own happiness had been on the line? Had his sister been right? Was a certain amount of objectivity useful when judging oneself as well as a potential match?

"If you'll excuse me," Griffin mumbled, finally noticing a bit of a gawking expression on Winifred's face out of the corner of his eye. Still, he kept walking until his feet had crossed the large room and carried him to *her* side.

"Good evening, Miss Abbott," his gaze barely shifted to her aunt, "Lady Bradish."

"Good evening, my lord," Miss Abbott greeted him, a teasing grin on her face as she glanced around the room. "It would seem we have everyone's attention."

Griffin nodded. "So, it would seem indeed." He held out his hand to her. "Now or never."

Chuckling, she glanced at her aunt before sliding her hand through the crook of his arm. "Never is not an option, my lord," she whispered as he drew her toward the dance floor. "After all, I've already revealed my ruse. If you abandon me now, I shall be very cross with you."

When they stood up for a country dance, he held her gaze and as the steps carried them toward one another whispered, "Should I be afraid?"

Laughter seemed to bubble up in her throat, but she forced an expression of feigned seriousness on her face. "My lord, it would indeed be wise to heed my words. After all, you already are aware of the pain my heel can inflict, are you not?"

"Is this a threat?" he chuckled.

Shrugging her shoulders, she let her gaze drift heavenward. "A lady doesn't utter threats." A honey-sweet smile came to her lips as her eyes returned to his. "A lady merely retaliates."

Laughing, Griffin almost lost his step, "I shall consider myself warned."

Aware that all eyes rested on them, they finished their dance before taking a turnabout the room. Griffin offered her a refreshment, and they continued to talk. Mostly in hushed whispers as they did not wish to be overheard, but also because it gave the impression of a more intimate relationship. After all, they had a charade to play.

And to play it believably.

Still, Griffin could not deny that he was enjoying himself. More so than he had in a long time, and for a moment, he wondered if he would truly mind being betrothed to Miss Abbott for real.

Throughout the evening, Abigail was here and there asked to dance by a gentleman other than her fake fiancé. Although she felt no inclination to accept them, she did nonetheless for it was part of their plan.

As she twirled around the room on Lord Carlway's arm, Abigail did her best to portray a soon-to-be betrothed woman. More so, a woman swept off her feet.

"Are you enjoying yourself?" Lord Carlway asked, a luminous smile on his face that she had never seen once before when their paths had crossed.

"Tremendously," Abigail gushed. "It certainly is a beautiful evening, and Lord Amberly was quite the proficient dancer. I've rarely danced with a man who knew how to lead as well as he."

The light in Lord Carlway's eyes dimmed. "You look stunning tonight," he tried to change the subject.

However, Abigail could not allow that to happen. "That is very kind of you, my lord. In fact, Lord Amberly was the one to suggest I purchase a gown of this colour. He said violet would look lovely on me. Do you agree?"

"I certainly do," Lord Carlway bit out through clenched teeth.

Abigail smiled her best and utterly fake smile. "I shall speak to him of your kind words. He is such an attentive gentleman, and his return to London has greatly improved society's charm, would you not agree?"

Lord Carlway mumbled something unintelligible under his breath and when their dance ended took his leave with a few polite words. It would seem he had gotten the message.

"The man looked quite miserable," Lord Amberly observed as she returned to his side. "What on earth did you say to him?"

Abigail shrugged. "I sang your praises, of course. Only if they believe me to be quite thoroughly swept off my feet will they leave me alone, don't you agree?"

For a moment his gaze lingered on hers, and he inhaled an agonisingly slow breath before nodding his head in agreement. "I cannot fault your reasoning," he all but whispered, and Abigail could not help the slight shiver that ran down her spine. It would seem their charade was not leaving her unaffected.

"If you'll excuse me, my lord," Abigail said, unable to bear the weight of his stare a moment longer, "I shall see if my aunt needs anything."

He nodded, his gaze holding hers until she turned away.

Inhaling a deep breath, Abigail rushed away, feeling her cheeks warm with the intensity of the moment they'd shared. A mere few days ago, he had been a stranger, and now, it appears he knew her like no other. How had this happened?

Exchanging a few quick words with her aunt, who unfortunately urged her back to Lord Amberly's side, Abigail breathed a small sigh of relief when Lord Tennington stepped into her way, asking for the next dance.

As he led her onto the dance floor, Abigail noticed her fake fiancé approach from the other side, a golden-haired beauty on his arm. To Abigail's great dismay, her insides tightened and a sudden urge to claim him as hers rushed through her being.

Shaking her head, she swallowed. Where had these thoughts come from? After all, this was only a charade.

Trying to focus her mind, Abigail smiled at Lord Tennington. Still, her thoughts continued to drift back to the man down the line, smiling at the golden-haired beauty.

When Lord Tennington addressed her, Abigail reminded herself of her part of the plan and fell back into her role of the adoring betrothed. As before, her utter admiration of another man did the trick, and as soon as the dance ended, Lord Tennington rushed off the dance floor.

Breathing a sigh of relief, Abigail let her gaze travel over the room, searching for her aunt. Perhaps it was time to head home. After all, her feet were beginning to hurt.

"May I have this dance?" an all too familiar voice asked from behind her, sending an equally familiar shiver down her back. Abigail drew in a steadying breath before she turned and met his dark brown eyes.

Lord Amberly's gaze held her in place as he offered her his hand.

Slipping her own into his, Abigail almost flinched as the first notes of a waltz began to play and Lord Amberly stepped toward her, his dark gaze still holding her immobile, and slid his hand onto her back.

Then they began to move to the music, and the rest of the world disappeared.

"I will never understand," Lord Amberly whispered, the words falling from his lips, "how these men can allow themselves to be discouraged so easily." A soft grin tugged at his mouth. "Still, I am not complaining."

Abigail smiled, enjoying the soft pressure of his hand on her back. "Well, I suppose they know when a war is lost. After all, the way I have spoken of you would suggest that…"

"That what?" he pressed, his gaze almost drilling into hers as though his very life depended on her answer.

Abigail swallowed, her mouth feeling suddenly dry. "That I am spoken for." She drew in a trembling breath. "Is that not what we wanted them to believe, my lord?"

Although smiling, Lord Amberly's brows drew down into a frown. "I remember that you called me by my given name once or twice." A question rested in his eyes as he held her gaze.

"Few people appreciate having a stranger call them by their given name."

"You're not a stranger," he whispered, and the hand on her back drew her closer against him.

Abigail smiled, knowing only too well of what he spoke. "Am I not?" she teased. "Does this mean you want me to call you…Griffin?"

"Only if you give me leave to call you Abigail," he answered her tease, his voice light before he paused, his eyes drifting upward as though a new thought had suddenly occurred to him. Then his dark gaze returned to hers. "Or how about Abby?"

Abigail frowned. Still, she could not deny that his desire to address her thus pleased her. "That feels fairly intimate."

He nodded. "It does, doesn't it?" For a moment, he held her gaze. "Do you object?"

Abigail smiled. "I probably should," she finally said.

"Is that a *no*?"

Abigail nodded. "It is."

"May I call on you tomorrow?"

Despite digging her teeth into her lower lip, Abigail could not keep at bay the deep smile that came to her face. "You may," she whispered, seeing the same delight she felt reflected back at her in his eyes.

It would seem their charade was losing more and more of its most essential component.

The portrayal of a false truth.

13

A FAVOUR TO ASK

The next morning, Abigail woke with a smile on her face. For although she knew very well that they had agreed to merely assist each other with their respective dilemmas, she could no longer pretend that she was immune to Lord Amb…Griffin's charms. There was something about him that spoke to her. Not only was he kind and attentive, respectful and honest, but he seemed to respond to her in a way as though he had known her for years.

Had Winifred been right? Were they truly suited to one another?

Later that afternoon, Abigail watched her heart most carefully as Griffin picked her up with his open chaise and they took a turn around Hyde Park. "Is there a particular reason you chose to come here today?" Abigail asked laughing as her eyes drifted down the path they had walked together not too long ago.

Beside her, Griffin grinned, a teasing gleam in his eyes. "To be honest, I thought it would present the perfect opportunity to discuss your *methods of torture*."

Laughing, Abigail felt her eyes widen. "Excuse me? My what?"

"Your methods of torture," Griffin repeated, bringing the horses to a slow trot. "I must say your act was quite refined and judging from the utterly shocked looks on people's faces last night, no one saw your…transformation coming." A slight frown drew down his brows as he looked at her. "How did you invent this person you pretended to be? All these details?" He shook his head as though truly impressed by such an accomplishment.

Abigail shrugged, unable to deny that she enjoyed his admiration. Never would she have thought it possible that someone would see her act as an accomplishment. "It was actually quite simple. I merely did what was considered in bad taste," she said shrugging. "We all have our little faults and imperfections no matter how hard we strive to be…well, perfect. All I did was pool them all into one being." Satisfied, she grinned. "Me."

Griffin laughed. "I admit you did well. That afternoon at the lake," he said, drawing the horses to a halt as they approached the Serpentine, glistening in the late afternoon sun, "I couldn't believe my eyes when the real you suddenly came through. I must have stood there for a small eternity gaping at you like a fool." He laughed, shaking his head as though he could not believe how blind he had been. "Still, I am grateful that I was here to see it." His gaze held hers as he swallowed, a touch of fear in his eyes. "I might never have realised who you truly were if I hadn't been here that day, if I hadn't seen you…change."

Abigail drew in a deep breath, realising how close they had come to simply parting ways without even realising what they would have lost. "Well, I suppose at least your toes must regret coming here that afternoon," she laughed, trying to lighten the mood. After all, he *had* been here that day, and everything had turned out the way it should have.

Had it been fate? What had been the odds of *him* being here with her and not another?

Griffin laughed, "I admit my toes were terrified of seeing you that day." Then his face sobered, and his gaze locked on hers. "I used to dread your company, but not anymore."

Abigail smiled. "Truly?"

Griffin nodded. "Now, I look forward to it. More than I ever thought possible." His hand gently came to rest on hers. "Knowing the real you was worth the pain. Any pain. I would not trade it for the world."

At his words, Abigail felt her heart dance with joy for she had to admit that deep down she had not been pretending from the moment they had agreed to help each other out. Even then her heart had recognised him as someone she could love.

But did she?

Quick footsteps echoed to Griffin's ears from the other side of the door, and without waiting for it to open, he knew it to be his sister. More so, he knew she was on a mission.

As expected, the door to his study flew open a moment later, and Winifred marched in, yanking her bonnet off her head and flinging it aside. "I demand to know what's going on here," she snapped, her eyes narrowed as she fixed him with a scrutinising stare. "You all but sneaked away at the ball the other night, and then I hear from Lady Hamilton that you were seen out in Hyde Park in the company of Miss Abbott."

Looking up, Griffin smiled. "Yes, I was."

Her eyes bulged. "Is that all you have to say?"

"I thought you wanted me to give Miss Abbott a chance," Griffin said, ignoring his sister's riled emotions. "I thought you'd be pleased."

"I am!" she huffed, the look in her eyes quite clearly stating that she was on the brink of throttling him. "But–"

"You wanted to be kept in the loop?" Griffin asked as he rose from his chair and stepped around the desk. "You wanted me to keep you informed?"

"Certainly!" Winifred snapped, her eyes widening in a way intended to make him feel like a fool for thinking otherwise. "Tell me what is going on."

Griffin shrugged, enjoying the aggravated look on his sister's face. "Nothing. I'm merely doing what you asked of me."

An annoyed chuckle rose from Winifred's throat, and she shook her head in disbelief. "Don't try to play me for a fool, dear Brother. I've told you so the night at the ball, and I will tell you so again. There's something odd about you, and I demand to know what it is."

"It's nothing." Griffin said, then walked past her to stand in front of the bookshelf, letting his eyes drift over the spines as he did his best to suppress a grin.

"Nothing? Don't you dare lie to me!" Although a tad shrill, his sister's voice held a clear warning as she stomped after him. "Abigail looked quite changed that night and you…you looked like a besotted fool even before she walked in…" Her voice trailed off, and she sucked in a sharp breath as though suddenly realising something that had been right in front of her all along.

Then he felt her hand curl around his arm a bit painfully—quite obviously she was agitated!—and jerk him around, her eyes wide as they searched his face. "What happened between you two?" she asked. "Were you the reason for the sudden change in her appearance? Are you—?"

A knock on the door interrupted his sister's questioning.

Annoyed, Winifred tried to compose herself as Griffin's butler entered, announcing the arrival of Miss Abbott as well as her aunt.

As a result, Griffin received one of the most glowering looks he had ever seen on his sister's face before he hastened out the door, hearing her footsteps on the floor behind him in fast pursuit.

Ignoring his sister's whispered questions, Griffin pushed open the door to the drawing room and felt his heart almost jump from his chest when his eyes came to rest on…Abby.

Ever since that night at the ball, he had thought of her as Abby. *His* Abby. That oddly reminded him of the way his oldest friend had always referred to his sister as Fred. A name that was only his. A name no one else was permitted to utter.

And in that moment when he walked in the door and their eyes met, Griffin knew that he never wanted Abby to leave. She belonged here. With him. And he would rather concede that his sister had been right than ever allow Abby—his Abby!—to walk away.

"Shall we take a stroll around the garden?" he suggested in a voice much calmer than he would have thought possible.

When everyone nodded their agreement, he escorted Abby out the door, followed closely behind by his sister and her aunt, both of which whispering to one another in hushed voices.

After donning their jackets, Griffin led her down the small steps leading down from the terrace into the garden, quickening his step to put some distance between them and their watchful pursuers. "I'm afraid my sister has become rather suspicious," he whispered next to her ear. "I doubt she will leave before she knows all there is to know."

Abby chuckled, her hand tightening on his arm. "She's your sister, and she has a way of seeing the truth, does she not?"

Griffin nodded, enjoying the weight of her hand. "She does. At least where others are concerned. Perhaps we should have made the change a bit more gradually. She already suspects that your transformation has something to do with me."

Abby shrugged. "Well, she would be right, wouldn't she?"

Her grey eyes held his, and Griffin noted with pleasure that there was not a hint of concern or disappointment in them. Did she not mind that his sister was on to them? That she would most likely expect them to become betrothed for real?

Continuing down the path, they turned the corner and vanished behind a tall hedge, cutting across the garden. When they were no longer visible to their pursuers, Abby's hand slipped from his arm.

Disheartened by their loss of contact, Griffin stopped and watched her walk on a few steps as though she had not even noticed that he was no longer beside her.

Then her feet stilled, and he saw her shoulders rise and fall as she drew in a deep breath before turning to face him. Her eyes held his, and yet, she swallowed as though a lump had lodged in her throat. "I have a favour to ask you," she finally said, her hands wrapped around one another for support.

Frowning, Griffin stepped toward her, his heart hammering in his chest. Did she intend to end their charade? Had she noticed that for him it had ended long ago? Did she not feel as he felt? "Anything," he promised, hoping she would not ask him to let her go.

A soft smile drew up the corners of her lips, and yet, there was a touch of nervousness in her eyes. "I have a theory to test, and the way I see it, you're the only one who can help me prove or disprove it."

Not having expected that, Griffin found himself staring down at her. "A theory? What theory?"

"I shall tell you once I know the results," she promised, a hint of a teasing grin lighting up her face. "Will you help me?"

Aware that there was something he was missing, Griffin nodded nonetheless. "All right. What do you need me to do?"

For a moment, her teeth sank into her lower lip as she tried to dissuade the self-conscious smile that took control of her lips. "I need you to kiss me."

14

A THEORY CONFIRMED

Abigail felt herself tremble as shivers shot up and down her body. Still, she held Griffin's gaze, seeing his utter surprise at her request, which then quickly turned into something more.

Something deeper.

Desire lit up his eyes, and they drifted down to touch her lips. Taking a step closer, he sought her gaze. "I assure you I'm most happy to oblige you," he whispered, a teasing smile lighting up his face, slowly putting her rattled nerves at ease, "if you are certain." The look on his face sobered, and she could see how much he cared for her. How had she not seen this before?

"I am," Abigail answered him, nodding her head up and down like a fool.

He held her gaze for another moment, seemingly indecisive, before she suddenly found herself swept into his arms. His right arm came around her waist while his left hand slid into her hair at the base of her neck. Then his lips touched hers in a soft, rather chaste kiss.

Welcoming his warmth, the touch of his lips, the feel of his embrace, Abigail found herself a bit frustrated with his restraint. Her fingers trailed down the side of his face and found the hammering pulse at the base of his neck. Why was he holding back?

When Griffin lifted his head, his eyes fluttering open, Abigail slung her arms around his neck and pulled him back down to her. Although her theory had been more than confirmed, she was quite unwilling to cease her explorations. After all, one could never be too certain, could one?

At her reaction, Griffin's hold on her tightened and he finally kissed her with all the passion she had hoped for. The world around her began to blur, and she would have sunken to the ground into a puddle of trembling flesh if his strong arms had not held her closer to his body.

Still, after a small eternity, he did pull away, chuckling at her small noise of protest. "What is your verdict?" he asked, his gaze holding hers as his lungs held his breath.

Abigail smiled, feeling her body hum with the knowledge she had gained. Then she swallowed and cleared her throat, trying to focus her thoughts. "Well, the results quite confirm my suspicions," she said teasingly, enjoying the smile that lit up his face.

"What suspicions?"

"That I lost my heart to you," she said without hesitation, her grin widening when she saw his mouth fall open at her boldness. "I keep wondering how it happened and when. I woke up one morning, and it was simply gone."

Holding her in his arms, Griffin sighed. "Did you find mine in its stead? I'm afraid I seem to have lost mine as well. Quite unexpectedly, I assure you."

As the world around her began to sing, Abigail closed her eyes, her teeth once more sinking into her lower lip, unable to contain the happiness that flooded her being.

"Would you in turn help me answer a question?" Griffin asked, the look in his eyes one of calm apprehension. When she nodded, he drew in a deep breath. "You must promise to answer honestly."

Again, Abigail nodded.

Again, he drew in a deep breath. "Do you want to marry me?"

Judging from the look on his face, Abigail had in fact expected a proposal. Still, what she had not expected was for him to ask what she wanted. Not if she would marry him, but if she wanted to marry him. "Why do you ask?"

A nervous chuckle escaped him, "Isn't it obvious?"

Laughing, Abigail sighed, "Appearances can be deceiving as you well know."

"That is true," he admitted, his gaze not wavering from hers. "I ask because…I love you. Is that not what it means to lose one's heart to another? Is that not what you meant?"

Abigail nodded. "It is. And I love you, too."

"I knew it!" Winifred's voice cut through the peaceful moment before she came rushing around the hedge, her eyes sparkling with triumph as she looked from her brother to Abigail. Next to her, Aunt Mara appeared, looking a bit ill at ease.

"See?" Winifred exclaimed, stepping toward them. "I knew you'd like her. Why didn't you trust me? I would never have steered you wrong."

Laughing, Griffin shook his head at his sister. "Would you get lost? In case you haven't noticed, you've just ruined a most wonderful moment."

Winifred's face turned a darker shade of red, and her hand flew to her mouth. Still, there was little to no regret in her eyes as she cast one last look at her brother and marched off, Aunt Mara in tow.

"Now, where were we?" Griffin mumbled, turning back to her, a light-hearted smile on his face. "Ah, yes, you haven't answered my question yet. And please, don't be discouraged by my nosey sister. If you want, we can move, leave the country, go somewhere where she'll never find us."

Her heart filled with delight at the close family Abigail could see in their future, and she looked up at Griffin and knew with perfect clarity what she wanted. "Don't you dare," she teased. "She belongs with us."

"Us?"

Abigail nodded. "Yes, us," she confirmed, feeling her heart beat faster at the utter joy that shone through his eyes. "As do Aunt Mara and my grandfather. They might drive us crazy at times, but they're a part of us. They're family, and we would never be the same without them. They shape who we are, and we do the same for them." A sigh escaped her lips as she sank a little deeper into Griffin's arms. "Grandfather told me this morning that he spoke to his grandson, Aunt Mara's son. He agreed to speak to his wife and ensure that his mother could see her grandchildren on a regular basis. You should have seen her." Closing her eyes for a moment, Abigail smiled. "I've never seen her so happy."

Tightening his hold on her, Griffin sighed. "Let's agree to always be honest with each other and fight openly…and not secretly behind each other's back. Secrets destroy trust, and once that is lost, there is no going back. Not completely. There'll always be doubts."

Abigail nodded, touched by the depth of his thoughts.

"How would you feel about a June wedding?" Griffin asked suddenly, the seriousness in his eyes replaced by a youthful eagerness that suited him well.

"That's in two months!" Abigail exclaimed, knowing without a doubt that she had no objections. "Aunt Mara would be happy to help us plan. It would make her happy to be included."

"But first," Griffin began as his eyes narrowed, a touch of apprehension coming to his face, "I need to speak to your grandfather and ask for your hand in marriage."

Abigail laughed, "He will not be surprised by your visit," she assured him, remembering how her grandfather had winked at her earlier that day when she had left the house with her aunt to go call on Griffin. "If I'm not mistaken, he knew well ahead of us that we would end up together." A snort escaped her. "Kind of like Winifred. Perhaps not only we are suited to one another, but also our families."

Griffin chuckled, "Perhaps you're right. Perhaps we've always been meant for each other."

Whether or not it was fate or coincidence, Abigail did not care. All that mattered was that they had found each other. How often did people who would fit perfectly into each other's lives meet but not realise it? How often did fate go unanswered because people were too busy, too distracted or too stubborn to see what was right in front of them?

Abigail could not deny that she had been one of them, and so had her betrothed. Still, they had been able to wrench their eyes open just in time before they would have walked out of each other's lives without a look back.

Never in a position to regret what could have been.

Because they would have never known.

Abigail whispered a silent thank-you to her father, whose letter had sent her to London in the first place.

To London.

And to Griffin.

EPILOGUE

About Two Months Later

On her new husband's arm, Abigail walked into his—their!—townhouse, greeting family and friends as they welcomed them to their home. Smiling, she saw Winifred and her husband Trent, her friend's eyes aglow with delight to see her brother happily married. Aunt Mara seemed quite changed as well. Although she still stood back, far from the spotlight, her eyes no longer shone with sadness, but with joy, with hope, as she bent down to whisper something into her granddaughter's ear. And then there was Abigail's grandfather.

After their talk about past mistakes and the burden of time passing, there had been a silent understanding between them. Although he still appeared the cold, distant duke—and very much enjoyed the effect he had on others!—Abigail knew that he loved her. He had never said it. Not with words. His love for her was in the little things he did. The way he noticed her, saw her joy and all but pushed her toward it, afraid she would miss out and live a life of regret.

A life he knew only too well.

"Are you happy?" her husband asked, his voice low so only she would hear.

Abigail sighed, "I am."

For a moment, his gaze lingered on hers, taking in the small creases on her forehead, the downcast lids and bent of her head. "You wish your father were here, do you not?"

Abigail smiled. "As do you."

Griffin nodded, the same touch of sadness and regret in his gaze that Abigail felt in her own heart. "I do," he confirmed, "and I'll never not regret that they are not. Still, I cannot help but wonder if we would even have met, had they not been taken from us."

Taking her seat at the large breakfast table, surrounded by the people she loved the most, Abigail knew that he was right. Would she ever have come to London if her father had not died?

Abigail was certain that the answer was, *no*. She would never have gotten to know her grandfather and her aunt. She would never have met Griffin. She would never have fallen for him.

Good and bad did walk hand in hand, it would seem. No one could help that. Tears and smiles could never be without the other for how would we know the meaning of a smile if we had never learnt that of a tear?

Smiling at her husband, Abigail knew that she did not regret her past for it had led her here. Still, she could regret her father's passing without guilt over the happiness she had found in life. After all, he would have wanted this for her.

Not all regrets were dangerous.

Only those that were self-inflicted.

Others were merely memories.

Memories Abigail would cherish for the rest of her life.

ABOUT BREE

USA Today bestselling author, Bree Wolf has always been a language enthusiast (though not a grammarian!) and is rarely found without a book in her hand or her fingers glued to a keyboard. Trying to find her way, she has taught English as a second language, traveled abroad and worked at a translation agency as well as a law firm in Ireland. She also spent loooong years obtaining a BA in English and Education and an MA in Specialized Translation while wishing she could simply be a writer. Although there is nothing simple about being a writer, her dreams have finally come true.

"A big thanks to my fairy godmother!"

Currently, Bree has found her new home in the historical romance genre, writing Regency novels and novellas. Enjoying the mix of fact and fiction, she occasionally feels like a puppet master (or mistress? Although that sounds weird!), forcing her characters into ever-new situations that will put their strength, their beliefs, their love to the test, hoping that in the end they will triumph and get the happily-ever-after we are all looking for.

If you're an avid reader, sign up for Bree's newsletter at www.breewolf.com as she has the tendency to simply give books away. Find out about freebies, giveaways as well as occasional advance reader copies and read before the book is even on the shelves!

Thank you very much for reading!

Bree

FORBIDDEN LOVE NOVELLA SERIES

LOVE'S SECOND CHANCE SERIES

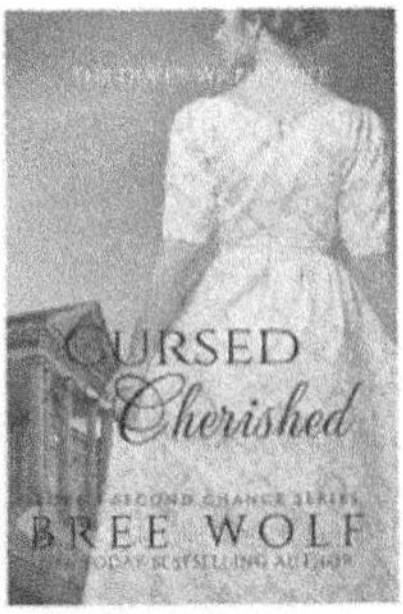

For more information, visit

www.breewolf.com

CPSIA information can be obtained
at www.ICGtesting.com
Printed in the USA
LVHW042250120623
749606LV00003B/15

9 783964 820457